Perfecting

a novel

Kathryn Kuitenbrouwer

Edited by Bethany Gibson.
Cover photograph: "His Hands" © 2004 by Polly Chandler,
www.pollychandler.com.
Cover and interior page design by Julie Scriver.
Printed in Canada on 100% PCW paper.
10 9 8 7 6 5 4 3 2 1

Library and Archives Canada Cataloguing in Publication

Kuitenbrouwer, Kathryn, 1965-
Perfecting / Kathryn Kuitenbrouwer.

ISBN 978-0-86492-515-2

I. Title.
PS8571.U4P47 2009   C813'.6   C2008-907191-3

Goose Lane Editions acknowledges the financial support of the Canada Council for the Arts, the Government of Canada through the Book Publishing Industry Development Program (BPIDP), and the New Brunswick Department of Wellness, Culture, and Sport for its publishing activities.

Goose Lane Editions
Suite 330, 500 Beaverbrook Court
Fredericton, New Brunswick
CANADA E3B 5X4
www.gooselane.com

To all my boys

One

NEW MEXICO, USA, 2004. Martha walked the Pecos River determined, skirting the prickly pear, grabbing weeping willow boughs here and there for stability. Thirty years had passed by and the last six were droughted. The river was but a thin, wet meander cleaving desiccated banks. The land around was a red-skinned beauty with hips to make a man cry or dare to touch.

Martha was a beauty, had on handmade ropers people in these parts could not afford: black horse-leather boots that would make anyone look cowboy. She had sweet hips too, hair cut straight, a bob, no bangs, and dyed black. Hips to dare touch. Black jeans, black eyelet shirt. The river was down to a trickle in most places, and where it ran strong, it still couldn't be called a river much. But they called it that, holding on to hope, while north and south, good neighbours squabbled over who got what water.

There was chatter in Martha's mind that wouldn't shut up — the last weeks coming back at her — but she was quiet, watching for snakes. She thought of Curtis. What would Curtis do? What had Curtis done? And tried to stop herself from such thoughts. She bent down, dipped her hand in that cleave, and it came out silted red and mud-stained; she touched the banks, ran her fingers through the scrubgrass and the deadweed that was waiting for fire to scourge it. It was hot out.

The sky was clear, just wispy rose clouds coming in, light was pale blue going to grey; the scrub cut its shape from the sky. Martha was heading roughly south, deep down to the river's edge, then shallow out of it, so that she could see, now and again, the arroyos angling farther up, wind-cut clay sculptures showing dried-out runnels. The sun was low, day ending. Martha would have to surface soon and look for lodging, and few around here would put her up; few had that kind of trust or space or interest.

She looked like she had walked the whole way from home, from Ontario, Canada, following some map she'd memorized, some hell map of bad places; she was bushed. It was dry hot, she thought. She sweated under her arms, and the cloth of her shirt was damp in a lozenge along her spine. The ridges of her vertebrae undulated as she moved, right down to where the cotton tucked into her jeans. She wasn't young any more. She was nearly through her forties.

The river was drying, farmers and hydro sucking back the water like cold beer and gossip together. Mesquite and grease-wood had taken root in the riverbed, and there were snakes in little holes, rattlers; the poison moved along and blackened the skin. Martha had seen a rattler skin mounted in a museum, and the sight never left her. She'd also seen a movie once, a long time before, with a swollen leg in it, and the poison seeping in slow, faster, and she got the boots as a precaution.

She bought the most expensive boots she could against death. She bought them because they were beautiful, like her, and beauty protects. She looked up. Her eyes were green against the sky, and her eyelashes were thick, and it was very hard not to fall in love with her. Her lips were wide and smiling, her body thin. She had good cheekbones, like a movie star, and she meant well. Oh, God yes, how she meant well. She looked up and she smiled nervously. She was alone. She thought, Nobody goes down here.

Martha was clutching a coarse brown leather bag — there was a handgun in there, and she was not used to handguns. The bag was tooled all over with acanthus leaf designs, hippie-style. She wore silver jewellery, bangles, earrings, and two rings — one with amber, which is from pine trees, and one with turquoise, which grew in the ground, she knew, everywhere along the Pecos. She was walking, and there was chatter in her mind, some of it direct and angry, some of it scared and prayerful, some of it just wanting the chatter to go away. But it wouldn't; their flow established, the words moved along.

She'd left Curtis in eastern Ontario, she did not know how many days ago, left the utopia he'd named Soltane, and the only real family she'd known, left disillusioned, after thirty years or so of faith, love having brought her there in the first instance. She had been thinking these days how love did cling to a person, even when it didn't make sense any more. Soltane was a commune of sorts, and a religious association of sorts, and now, looking at it from this distance, it seemed to her a sad and grasping experiment at perfection. It might have worked. It might have. If her prayers had taken, or if she could have tried harder. Was there no respite from this line of thought?

The mesquite and the wayside plants bent under her boots, the clay dusted the boot polish and settled on it. There were rattlers in their little holes. Nobody would find her if she died, she thought. The red clay would cradle her body, fingers trailing the water prettily, skin falling away, the flies and vultures reclaiming that energy. Bones. Bones, and mesquite and the rattler. *What happened here, what brutal end? A body was found down by the Pecos. This is bad. Bones. And it'd been there a helluva long time.* The earth seemed to whisper. She quickened her pace.

Walking north was Hattie McCann, hacking at the scrub-grass with her cane. Every day, she walked that riverbed for pastime. She was old, a thick woman, wearing calico-print dresses — that she sewed herself — stretching over her backside and rising up at her knees. A solid woman, Hattie McCann. Lived along the Pecos since she was young, heading back sixty years, a mistress she was and always had been. She was down there searching out long-lost fishing lures, the minnow lures that were flung off decades ago by fishers casting out, tugging hard, getting the little silver baits caught in debris or river plants. The river stole them, and the trout stole them, too, sometimes, when there was trout, where there was river. She thought how the years of drying did take a lot of water with it.

Hattie had found one lure that day caught in the mouth of a fish skeleton, the bones of which were tangled in a thicket creeper. It was a big one, a decoy more, hollowed out and filled with pebbles like a rattle, must have been a hundred years old; there hadn't been any decoy fishing in living memory. She held the lure up to the sun, shook it, and smiled, pleased with the soft whirr the stones made inside it. Then she tucked it in the pocket of her apron. Sure had a lovely heft.

Hattie poked at the mesquite with her walking stick looking for reminders of the river, reminders of something. She put the lures up in her kitchen on a display board Aubie'd made for her out of bottle corks and hooks, painted white. There were photographs there too, of Colm and poor Edgar, of Hollis when he wasn't yet fully bad, and of Aubie looking like he owned the whole world and like the world was loving it.

Hattie's calico dress didn't protect her much from the weed and shrub, nor the snakes, but she didn't worry. Nobody went down there. Bones? Not finding anything was evidence of nothing, and this most pleased her. Well, it *had* been a long time since she'd seen her boy Edgar; but thirty years don't mean dead.

It was so hot. Hattie swung her stick over some prickly pear and she'd just about given up finding anything more and the sun was ready to set when she looked up sharp, north along the slowly winding Pecos. *Whosoever seeks shall find*, so it is written. Surprised the bejesus out of Hattie to find someone down there.

The younger woman's hair was clipped up and tinted, and she had slender, fragile bones, a small bird in the hand — skinny. Silver hung off her wrists, long earrings glinting in the sun. Hattie called out, 'Lord, you surprised me. Who are you? What are you doing here?' Hattie had not wanted to be disturbed, the gauze-pink clouds drifting above her, just like that, for her. There were a hundred yards between them, and they were walking closer to each other.

'Oh!' Martha stammered. 'I'm just —' She'd been walking so long, hadn't talked to another soul in days. She carried that big, floppy leather purse. Martha smiled at the stout old lady; she thought she already knew who she was. She wanted to sit down, lie down, but thought it might make a bad impression. She was so tired. She needed a place to sleep, and this woman might... The old lady was pulling something out of her apron. She was rattling something. It had been days and days since Martha'd slept properly.

'Howdy,' the woman said.

'Hello.'

'Fishing lure,' the woman said, shaking the thing. Its snake sound crawled along Martha's skin. 'I collect them from the river; ain't much water no more.' There was a shadow over the two women then. A burr oak on the western bank was casting darkness over them, and it brought a strange chill after the heat, and blurred the view. The darkness was watching them.

Martha smiled, said, 'You must be Hattie.' Curtis's father's mistress. Hollis's woman. She'd heard a few stories over the years.

Hattie offered the lure and the younger woman took it. Woman had a nose that arched down and Hattie thought she might be a mixed breed: Indian and what else? Green eyes to sink into, but God, that void there. Hattie was trying to learn this woman. She could feel the past already getting stirred up. 'Now, who are you and how in God's good glory do you know my name?'

'I'm sorry. . . . My name is Martha Moore.'

Hattie was at a loss. 'You from Mexico?' she said. 'You Pueblo? Or . . . ?'

'I'm nothing.' Martha felt the truth of that in her gut, like sick, like dying. Nothing, was there such a thing? She had lived for thirty years up there at Soltane, her whole adult life, with Curtis, with Benjamin, with Ida and the others, the couples, the singles, the children. Thirty years, and she was part of the centre of the thing, she knew. The first Family member held in Curtis's orbit; there had been such lightness to it, the glow of him shining on her, shining on them all. 'I mean, I'm just Martha Moore, down from up north.'

She could be back there in the softening cold, living with the Family, where everything was set out for a person, and therefore simpler. She could be cradled in belief. This chatter. She would like to box it up. She said, 'Curtis told me about you, told me if I was ever down this way I might look you up, maybe. Curtis Woolf. You know him.' But he hadn't told her this; he had told her about his growing up, the gas station, about his mother, about Hattie, his half-brothers, the Pecos. Had he constructed these stories too? Martha pulled the purse onto her hip, folded it down, and held it close. She had the lure in her other hand. 'I felt I might find you if I followed the Pecos. I caught it east of Albuquerque, and I've been walking down.' She saw the pain suddenly etch along Hattie's eyes. Martha looked down at her own boots.

Martha'd come skewed, down through Ontario, New York, and across and down through Old Nauvoo, Illinois, to see what a Mormon was, knowing this was a clue into Curtis. There wasn't much there for her, though, and she had had to come deeper south. 'I should have never come,' she blurted. It would have all been easier if she could have ignored the gun when she'd first found it. She had thought she might heal Soltane where it needed healing if she took that weapon off the farm, and she wanted to solve Curtis too. Once she'd found the gun, she realized she didn't know him much at all.

'Well, you came.'

Martha shook the lure and smiled at it, her wide, pretty smile, and Hattie thought of her son Aubie and shivered at that, and at the day, which was fast cooling. Martha said, 'It's a lovely thing' and handed it back to Hattie. It was too. It was wooden, had a line of silver paint along it, red chipping under that, and glaring black bead eyes. It went back into Hattie's apron.

Albuquerque was miles and miles, and no wonder the woman was tired. 'Curtis Woolf?' Hattie said, then thought, Hell, thought how Curtis's pa, Hollis, was some clay lodestone, drawing out power even still, that old buzzard. Hattie thought then that Maeve's boy — Curtis Woolf — must have inherited the power from Hollis, that particular power to poison someone without their knowing it. Suck up their energy, accumulate treasure for the sake of just that — the singular, purifying act of possession. Hattie didn't like to give thought to that boy, Curtis, much. Hattie squinted, relieved almost to discover

Martha had a connection to Hollis. She knew what to do with that. 'Curtis Woolf. He run off to Canada, last I heard.' Well, Hollis would need to know Curtis's woman was around.

Run off? thought Martha. She did so want to know what happened. She saw Hattie was old as anything; the years were drawn around her eyes. Where happiness had tried to compensate sorrow. She recognized the old woman, recognized herself there too.

Martha crouched, and Hattie thought the woman would faint. Hattie watched Martha scan the river north. It occurred to Hattie that Martha might be looking for something down in the Pecos. What might Curtis have lost in the riverbed excepting his honour, and any self-respect he ever had? Martha wasn't going to find either of those, not if she looked a lifetime. There wasn't anything much down here now. Hattie had the feeling she was being led along a path she didn't wish to go on. She wished for calm but surmised it would not come. She said, 'What do you want?'

'I've walked for a long time,' Martha said. 'I need a place to stay. I can pay for food.' Really, she had no money to speak of.

Hattie just stared at her, and Martha went back in her mind to Canada, to Soltane, to the forest, the gun, the chatter. She was sitting in the eastern forest, praying badly with a back-and-forth *I will shatter, Lord. I will shatter unto you*, praying if this, then that, if I, then you, with a sense that if only she could get it right, this praying — and she never could seem to — she might change the course of things. She hadn't yet found the gun, but she was slowly coming toward it, as if the Browning pistol that was now tugging her purse down was an idea she had yet to apprehend.

Martha had breathed in spring air, breathed out to her limbs, stretched her feet inside her rubber boots, and stood. Her dress, wicking up moisture from the damp earth, was darker along the hem; she felt it dragging a bit as she folded the chair. She heard the gravel trucks being loaded; the wind was from the south. There was the smell of rain, and she knew she should be getting to the mill-house to kindle the oven for the week's bread.

There were bread and later candles to be made, and she must open the library. Yes, she should hurry back. Only she didn't. Martha's legs would not move quickly through the wet forest; her dress dragged, the chair pulled against the ice and mud, her boots were over-large, and she had persistent memories that slowed everything she did. She had never had much of a birth family, and the cliché of the broken home never really summed up how empty she felt until she met Curtis. He had taught her what that emptiness was for.

Once inside the mill-house, she watched Ida move heavily. Ida was pregnant, and close to her time. She had become more and more insular, and Martha had lost a confidante in her; Ida was protecting this thing, this baby, her place at Soltane, and even her idea about safety. There were all these things in the look she gave Martha, and by this look Martha was again made aware of that which she did not want to be made aware of, the sudden wrongness of herself in this place. They both knew Martha would endure criticism at the next evening meeting. There had been complaints, and consensus, and she would have to listen and nod and reconcile to self-improvement, to reflect upon her behaviour.

Ida tilted her head toward the window, the dust motes hanging there in the slanting sunlight. She was lovely, lovelier pregnant than not, and her child would surely be radiant. Steam rose up from Martha's legs where the cloth of her dress was warm against the brick oven; she felt damp on the skin of her legs. There had been no children between her and Curtis, though there had been sex, unprotected, free, devotional sex, and then desperate sex, and then increasingly depraved sex, until her barrenness became apparent.

'Where were you?' Ida asked. Her belly held the shape of God, thought Martha, still believing that.

'In the woods, praying.'

'Was it good?'

'No.' She wished immediately she hadn't said this, so added, 'It was okay,' in the hope of heading off comments.

'Curtis was looking for you.'

Ida ought to have mentioned this right off. Martha wondered what Curtis might want, and how she should respond, whether she should respond to him. She felt so clumsy lately, as if she had arrived after thirty years from the sky on the earth and hadn't learned how to walk. Something was coming toward her, and she would soon find out. He was asking after her.

She'd slept without him, banished to the sleep-house, where many of the singles dwelled, for a fortnight; he wanted to be alone, so he said. There had been a severing between them over the winter; all these complaints she would endure from the Family had a source, but she couldn't explain that to anyone. Ida's belly pushed out her blouse and Martha knew it to be Benjamin's child. This child was part of the argument that had formed between her and Curtis, between her and the Family, and her obligation to them.

'Does he want me to go to him?'

'Yes, I think that's what he wants, though he wouldn't say it, you know. He wouldn't say anything like that.'

'Can you cover here then?'

'So long as you help with the wax later, yes, I will.'

'Thanks, Ida. He's happy for you, you know that. We are happy.'

'Yes, I do know it.' Martha couldn't tell whether the look on Ida's face was apologetic.

The gate-house was Curtis's sanctuary, a hand-hewn log house outside, inside a temple of sorts; walking towards it, she could hear him chanting.

Martha wished she didn't still yearn for Curtis so. She looked up at this old woman along the Pecos. Hattie was swaying and Martha could hear the faint rattle coming from her apron, and she shivered from her fear, and the lessening sun, and the chattering.

'Curtis —,' Martha said. 'I suppose he might have lied about a lot.' It wasn't easy coming out of her, and she shook from saying it.

'I don't know what he did,' Hattie answered. 'I don't think on him. We all got worries.' Hattie's head had begun to swivel slightly; she didn't want these thoughts. She said, 'Come. You need feeding.' She set Martha's hand on her arm and shuffled down the riverbed to her house, dust kicking up, the lure rattling softly as her legs shifted. Hattie best keep a hold of this lady. Hollis ought to hear about this. There was something here.

Martha said, 'Is it always so dry?'

'Yes,' Hattie said, pleased the subject was changing. 'For years it has been hot and dry and no rain, and the river dying. I buy drinking water in plastic jugs. I've even been obliged to have a deep well drilled and to ration water to my garden.' She stopped now and again through her speech and gesticulated. 'Before I was born, I hear tell, there was water spurting out of the ground, water like waterfalls going upwards, geysers, water looking like huge bridal veils from a distance. I seen a postcard of that once. But they sucked it dry, sucked it right out from the middle of the earth, some say. I blame it on the greed.'

Hattie had heard there might one day be wars over this lack. She was aware that from its head in the mountain country, the Pecos was stoppered by hydroelectric dams, monsters these, twice or three times along the way. Then the farmers drew their water share off too, and there wasn't much left after that. 'What we need is a good rain,' Hattie said, and Martha only nodded as they came upon Hattie's house. The badly made adobe just about vanished into the rest of the red earth. Martha's jewellery reflected the last sun up into Hattie's eyes, and Hattie began to laugh. 'I guess you're the most interesting lure I ever did find.'

'I hope I don't catch anything,' Martha said, a strange smile edging her eyes. Hattie got Aubie back in her head, and tried to shake that.

'Let me show you my collection,' she said and stopped at the display on the white wall of her kitchen. 'You know, I have never been upriver much. I don't fish neither. Still, I like finding them. I guess it gives me something to do with myself.'

'They're beautiful,' said Martha, and drew her finger over a pink-painted plastic lure with a red gill stripe. She looked at Hattie and nodded.

'I found them over the years in the riverbed.' Hattie said, then, out of the blue, 'You running away from him?' and Martha missed a beat and Hattie knew. She thought how not good that could be and said, 'He hit you?' thinking more about how long it would take Curtis to find her back again, drag her home, and why in God's good name had Martha come here?

Martha shook her head. 'No.'

She had walked into the gate-house expecting to find Curtis waiting for her. He was chanting upstairs, low; she heard *love* and *taste* and *save* in little peaks before whatever else he said curled back at him. There was a stack of letters on the table in the kitchen, and she rifled through them: an old one from his mother, a recent postcard from his father that said simply *Come*, and one more, a postcard, stamped *Islamabad 2003*, a year old. *Wish you were here.* It showed four minarets, a geometric dome. She read the caption on the flip side; it was the Shah Faisal mosque lit up at night. No sender. She looked closely at the handwriting, but no. She didn't know. *Wish you were here.* She hadn't known Curtis's father had the address, that he'd maintained any contact at all. And then there he was — Curtis — standing at the landing, and he had left the letters there on purpose. She could see this. She held up the mosque one like a question mark.

'I don't know,' Curtis said. He shut his eyes, said again how he didn't know. 'Ex-Family, is my guess.' He shrugged, not wanting to think about ex-Family, how that tinged things. 'I've missed you.' This was an apology. She knew to take it so, and let him have it.

Martha went upstairs with him, and the room was desert hot. He walked around her. He was wearing linen, a linen suit, and he had a bit of beard and his hair was slowly, in the right places, going grey. He stopped, took an item of her clothing off, a scarf, and then an earring, and then walked some more. It was an old game of theirs, like peacocks flaunting themselves. He wore only white nowadays, and he waited until she was naked, standing there, before he undressed himself. 'I love you, darling.'

Could she ever really leave the farm in her heart? Martha closed her eyes tight and held her hand up to Hattie. 'No. He never hit me. I just ... it just got so closed in there. He would save me, not hit me.'

'Save you?'

'Yes, I suppose so.' Other people could not be expected to understand, Martha thought, and she was not able to explain. Soltane was as much a feeling as it was a place.

Hot vapour shed off the single-pane window in the gate-house. It was hotter inside than out, and the air condensed from the heat of the oil stove. They were fucking, there was roughness, roughness toward opening, and it was — her eyes were pressing against her eyelids, she could feel herself, that her body mattered, manifested. *Wish you were here.* And she turned toward him and opened her eyes and saw he was scared, that he was scared of her, maybe, or something. It felt good, this sex.

The bedclothes were strangled; he had been sitting meditating on this bed earlier, and now it stank of body, the residue of just flesh, or the evidence of it, she did not know. And then afterwards he was sleeping and she was lying on her stomach with her face on his chest. She could hear his heart shushing, his heart that did not know how to beat a proper rhythm. The carpet in the corner was oddly buckled. She thought how his heart rattled, thought of snakes, and she got up. And that is how she found the gun under the floor, under the buckled carpet, how this idea, 'gun,' solidified. Had she created it? she later wondered.

The gun was wood and engraved steel, and heavy. It had an oily smell, and she could see the handle was nicely worn. It wasn't right to find it pretty, but she couldn't help it; it was a well-built thing. Martha twisted it around and looked at it from various angles. She had never seen a handgun before, had never held any sort of firearm. It was prohibited. It was prohibited to take the life of another creature. It was prohibited to have a gun at Soltane. It was in the code that Curtis had himself written down. The Family walked through nature harming only when it was necessary to sustain themselves. This gun insisted on something foreign to Soltane. The smell of steel and oil suggested evil; she held her palm up to her nose and breathed it in. She cradled the gun in her hands and held it out toward him, saying really quietly and then louder and louder, 'Curtis?'

'Huhn?' To be fair, he was sleeping.

Hattie led Martha into the living room and set her down like a dead thing, the woman was that tired. Set her down in the old pressback rocker Hattie usually took for her own cup of tea. There wasn't another object one could reasonably call a chair; the rest was mends and will holding it together. Hattie would visit Hollis later, when the Canadian slept. Martha slid her leather bag from her shoulder, and it thudded heavy to the floor beside the chair. 'You can sleep in the spare room,' said Hattie.

'I do wonder what really happened with Curtis. I do have questions.' Martha would have liked to sort out what was, and what wasn't, true. She wondered why Curtis had run off from this Pecos, and what he could have done here. The gun changed every piece of his story. She knew by now he was not as he had once claimed, not a pacifist.

'I'll make you tea,' Hattie said, and she did. The radio had been playing music but went to news: a former soldier living in Los Angeles charged with homicide had toured in Afghanistan, *the theatre of Afghanistan*, it said; Hattie turned it off and watched the chipped teacup hang loosely from Martha's fingers. What really happened? Nothing happened. Edgar was long missing. And there was Colm and Aubie and Hollis, Hattie was fast in that current. And it was a long long time ago and she preferred not to recall it. She said, 'It is all so long ago. It would be best —'

Martha looked at her so hard, and sad, Hattie looked right

back. Martha was wearing tight black jeans and an Indian-cotton shirt, black eyelet, seamed high in the waist, her nipples showing through; she wasn't wearing a brassiere. Her boots were newer than any Hattie had seen in years, but the rest — the face, the hands — reminded her of the Depression days, and all those hungry-eyed nomads passing through.

'Well,' said Martha. She wanted to put her hands over her face, wanted to go back to Canada. She could go back and stay on the farm, she could atone her own running off. She would pay, and then it would be fine, paid. She continued, 'Something must have happened.' She was beside herself with exhaustion.

'My boy Edgar,' said Hattie. 'He ain't been seen in thirty years. Curtis neither. That seem strange to you? It sure does to me. You see how it would be best.' It would be best not to pick at that scab, she thought; it had just about closed over.

Martha tried to keep her eyes calm. She recalled watching Curtis wake up. The sex always led him deep. He had been chanting earlier, and he was sleeping far in himself. 'Where'd you find that?' he said when he woke, but he meant, 'Why? Why'd you find that?' She clasped the gun and let her arm drop, the gun hanging there by her leg; it had a heft. She was naked. He was watching her skin and she could see him doing that. He liked the skin, the smell, the gun hanging there; what old habits died hard? 'I love you,' he said. 'The gun. It's nothing, Martha, forget it. I had that thing since I came up here.' He was whispering, smiling. 'Come here, girl. I want you.'

'What about love and peace?'

'It isn't loaded.'

'But you kept it. How does this fit in?' she said, but she knew that it did, she knew that suddenly. She watched his face scurry away from some recollection, and she knew.

'I kept it,' he said. He was up, then, coming toward her; her back was against the large plate-glass window overlooking the valley, and the apiaries. He was coming for the gun, and he had his arm stretched out for it. 'I kept that — ,' he said.

'No.'

'I kept that to remind myself of who I was,' he said, 'is all.'

'No.' Soltane had all been a lie. She had lived here and it had been entirely wrong. Curtis was not a conscientious objector, not a pacifist, not pure, nor perfect. 'No!' she shrieked. He was coming toward her and he was already upon her; his skin was on her skin and it was hot in the room, and everything, everything for years and years, since the beginning, was shifting under her. Martha turned and shoved him. She didn't know she had this power, nor did he struggle. The window was behind her and she heaved him at it.

And from across the farm, Ida and Benjamin and the others heard Curtis scream, but they didn't hear the shattering glass; they stayed away, and then later Martha picked the shards out of him. She pressed the tweezers into Curtis's scalp, working at a chip of glass. There was glass wedged into him everywhere, along his torso, little glinting shards down his legs.

No, she thought, but she stopped saying it. He was inside, lying on the ottoman with the carpet upholstery, the paisleys and the reds, and she was digging triangles of glass out of the shaft of his penis. There was blood.

'Where did you get that gun?'

'My father gave it to me when I turned eighteen.'

'Why did you keep it?'

'I don't know,' he said, but she saw him shudder saying it.

'Tell me,' she said. He had lied to her and to the others. God had not summoned him; Soltane was harbouring some secret, possibly something awful. 'Soltane is a lie,' she said when he failed to answer. He looked away.

He swung on her meanly and said, 'It isn't a lie. I never lied. It's you who can't see it. Or won't.'

And when she cried, he coddled her and they kissed again, and the kiss was anxious. It was the kind of kiss that meant she was leaving.

'He wouldn't tell me what happened to make him leave. I only know he can't have been a proper pacifist.' Martha preferred not to mention the gun, so she added, 'I have some evidence.' She was so sure.

'Pacifist?' Hattie scowled, then said, 'Curtis killed my son Edgar, that's what they all say happened.'

. Martha picked her teacup up by the little handle and sipped. It was going to fall. She sensed it falling. Her fingers slipped and released the tiny arm, flicked the edge of the china trying to right it. Hattie sucked in breath, thinking whether that was an accident, and thinking whether anything ever really was accidental, then held her surprise in check, watched the cup fall and listened to the end notes of the crash, the smallest tinkle. 'Oh!' said Martha. 'Oh.'

The tea formed a little tannic pool, then sucked into the tile grout. Hattie concentrated on the spill as it followed down the slant of the floor, detouring a fault in the tile and sinking into the space between Martha's feet and the large purse. It was not a favourite cup, but the loss of it made its worth grow in Hattie's estimation. What had Hattie just unearthed in the Pecos, after all this time? Oh, Lord.

Martha bent for the shards, wondered if she would always just break things.

'It used to be common,' Hattie said — she wanted so to change the subject — 'to see Hollis's children — Maeve's, that is, and mine — down by the Pecos minnow fishing; just a line of kids, jostling, sun freckles crossing the noses. A brood of children, there were twelve — girls and boys. They sold their catch as bait over by Hollis's gas station. Twenty-five cents a bucketful, dumped into washed-out oil pans and handed over to all those necessary fishers, hungry folk. The silvery minnow it was, a small bottom-feeder, good eating for trout. A bitty creature. They say now the fish is at risk from upstream sludge, and from disregard, and from what them experts call dewatering. There just isn't much water, at all. But then, all of life is going. Hollis's brood is all grown up, and my boys — Edgar, Aubie, and Colm — are mostly gone. Edgar went missing more than thirty years ago; then the other two packed up and left home too. Like the river, like time, all things come to an end. Oh, Aubie and Colm come back around when they smell some drama cooking. They say Curtis killed Edgar, and sure he did shoot him to die.'

I kept that to remind myself of who I was. 'He told me something,' Martha said. 'I didn't want to believe it. He just could not do that. I didn't think he could. If you'd meet him —' He must have been scared. Martha heard the shift of the lure in Hattie's apron, a susurrus. 'It must have been an accident —' She turned her face to look sidelong at Hattie, straight on being too intimate.

'In cold blood, they say, and they were friends, brothers, of a sort. He shot Edgar while Edgar was fishing the Pecos, where he knew to find him.' Hattie wagged her head slightly and pulled back from crying. She said, 'I don't know I'd recognize Edgar; my eyes are not too good any more, and I have tried to forget him. Maybe I have forgotten him. Time is a salve.' Hattie leaned over to a small table in the corner, opened the single drawer, and took out a stack of Kodaks. She gazed at the shiny, white, rippled edge of the photographic paper and then over to the unnatural cerulean of the 1970s desert sky and back again, her eye flitting over the line. She said, 'They never did find his body.'

The figure in the picture — her own flesh and blood — was foreign to her and presented as a negative space, as if he had been cut out. 'No, I can't concentrate on this face.' Hattie peered at that picture of Edgar, at the sparse facial hair of the man-boy and the openness of the smile, and she thought how he looked so like Hollis that, Lord, it was no wonder people talked, but talk never did bother her. She loved that boy so much she didn't think she really knew what he looked like; he looked like the shape of her affection, the texture of her hands holding him that last time she remembered. Sometimes she wondered if she loved him more now that he was gone than she had when he was home. It pained her how this might be true.

'He was handsome,' said Martha. She did not know what else to say.

Hattie was bone tired. All this business wasn't good for a person; it was better to sleep and get on with things, but Hattie felt her body winding up, thinking about Edgar. In the picture, Edgar wore a belt, the strapping thick on his boyish hips, a buckle of blue-green stone drawing the focus to where he wanted it drawn. He went from being a child to a needy man in the time it took her to blink. Seemed like it.

'Yes, he was,' Hattie said. She had heard pity in Martha's comment, accepted it; it was a pitiable situation. She recalled Aubie and Colm and said, 'They searched high and low for him. Sent out missing person reports, tried to mobilize the police, the community — and did manage to do this for a time.' They were vigilant, Aubie and Colm were. Then they went peculiar with missing him and searching for him and they changed. And then they left for a time. 'The river is going. It's all past. Ain't no sense in dredging that,' she said. 'Oh, that damned river. The bed is mud and then hard-cracked clay and then the mesquite begins. You see a roadway of brush. And I find you down there in that dead river.'

The teacup was a delicate little pile now, an offering in Martha's hand. Hattie chose what felt safe and talked. 'All up and down the Pecos, committees is bickering, trying to cancel old deals and let the river run its natural course.' The river would die. Hattie did not look forward to that time but saw it was fated. How the tiredness was on her. She just needed to put her feet up. 'I suspect they will argue too long,' she said. 'When my mother was alive, she told of great spouts of water burbling up out of the earth. Then it was oil. When I was a kid, there wasn't a month went by we didn't hear about some new oilfield blowing wide. Now, they're talking about reclamation, and thirty more years and she's all done.'

Martha couldn't really listen. She pictured that belt leather rotting in the sweet water, and all at once, impossibly, Curtis standing over Edgar's body, the Browning a glinting curl in the scrubgrass beside him. What had he finally said when she had persisted in her questioning? He'd squealed, 'Let me amend, please.' And she had merely snorted derisively. She had thought he meant amend for concealing a weapon on Soltane. This news now about Edgar confused her. It wouldn't line up.

'That's down Artesia,' Hattie was saying. 'Where my boys still live.' She was talking about the oilfields, but it didn't matter. She just needed to spout herself. Hattie hadn't talked to another about her missing boy in some years. She suddenly thought how lonely she'd been, even though she hadn't really even noticed it before, all by herself like that. The night was on them. The house was dark, and Hattie turned on a table lamp behind them. Martha's shadow edged along the floor, shifting with her, long and thin. 'My boy Aubie, he went to jail on account of Curtis. Curtis don't even know that, I guess.'

That hit Martha in the eyes, her chest. She did not know

what to make of it, so she decided none of it could be true. 'I'm sorry,' she said. She leaned over and set the shards of china on the table. 'I forgot I was...I forgot I was holding it,' she said. Martha pulled her boots off. 'I'm so sorry. Curtis is too. I know he is. We believe —,' she said.

Hattie interrupted. 'You're in a bind, ain't you?' How a person could lie, and to herself, and how that lie could turn and turn around until it resembled truth so you couldn't tell one apart from the other. Curtis trying to save this woman. Martha's feet were bare, no socks, and creased from the boot leather and as thin and rough as she'd seen. The woman truly did look as if she might need saving.

He didn't do it, Martha thought. He didn't do it. Please. The gun was a Browning, a working reproduction of an older gun, etched with decorative lines and sporting a well-worn handle. Martha didn't know how to apologize to Hattie. She nodded earnestly and said, 'We believe in Jesus Christ. We believe in perfecting ourselves, in our offerings —' It had never seemed so precious and false before.

Hattie said, 'Amen, I guess.' She didn't totally trust Jesus, not for some time. She loved Him, she supposed, but there was a wariness she could not deny.

The last of the spilled tea pooled between Martha's feet and the purse.

Two

The gravel pit trucks sent tremors through the earth. The growing pit was on the farthest edge of land, south, and there had been arguments against it, but in the end the income compensated. The Family simply needed the money. The clang of stone against metal made the Family stop what they were doing and recall to breathe. Some were turning the garden, some were in the barn melting wax for candles. They stopped and looked up and listened, then went back to work. If they offered it all up — their work, their pure thought — they would be rewarded, even on this earth. Belief made the very work ecstatic. Anyone would have noted they were radiant as they worked. This in itself was a sign.

In the barn, the forms were ready for pouring, the two halves of Jesus Christ pinned together in small, medium, and large sizes. There was an upcoming craft fair, and these candles sold well. They ranged in size from two to four inches. Curtis Woolf had dreamed them and Benjamin — a first-generation elder and now Ida's husband — had formed the moulds that brought them into being.

They all adored Curtis, turning toward him when he wandered in looking for Martha, knowing she would not be there. He was weak; he had a weak heart, they all knew, and must be protected. Ida pressed her hand to his arm. Benjamin, with scraggly beard and soft, boyish eyes, came and spoke to Curtis quietly and he nodded. Martha had left, and everyone needed reassurance. The news had travelled, as these things do, quickly, with little mercy. Amid the faithful, especially amid the faithful, the faithless deserved no mercy, but Martha was different. No one ever thought she might leave; she wasn't a leaver. There had been a critical meeting at which she was to have been the subject. It was routine, especially in light of the miscarriage, but she had not shown up. This sort of thing rarely happened, especially with the first generation. The Family was steadfast. It was certain she would return. The miscarriage and her advancing age had led to this vanity. Surely she would return soon, atone appropriately.

Ida was sitting, her belly pushed out, and she reached up and touched Curtis and said something the others did not hear. One of the children began pouring molten beeswax slowly into a small mould; another waited, watching, every so often touching the metal mould, testing its coolness. They giggled between them. Benjamin said, 'Where has she gone?' and Curtis raised his shoulders slightly and could only shake his head, as if he did not know. He was scared. 'She'll be back,' Benjamin said.

But Curtis knew she had taken the gun and he knew how her mind went. He thought he knew. He had checked to make sure it was secure, under a floorboard, under a factory-made, fake-Persian rug Benjamin'd picked from the trash years ago. What had he told her? *I kept that to remind me of who I was.* It wasn't true. He'd kept the Browning replica, with its softly worn handle, its etched metal, to protect himself from who he was, and because Hollis had given him that gun, and he couldn't let it go.

One of the little girls, Lea, was snapping the clasp of the mould open and easing out the beeswax Jesus. The pong of the beeswax was all through the barn. Lea was edging the Jesus with a paring knife and letting the scrap fall back into the pot beside her. Jesus had his palms open, hands out. Lea held the candle up for Curtis to smell, and her smile opened his heart. There were twenty-one people on the farm. How the hand of God had intervened here, and made this land feed them. The candles gave some kind of unearthly energy back unto the earth; what they did not sell, he decided, they would give away to fulfill this ministry. Curtis took that first candle and walked back to the gate-house. He would sit; he would wait for Martha to return. She would return. She could not leave the farm, she was central to it; he loved her, and she had the gun.

He thought, How long have I got to pay for this? Wondered, too, if he'd been paying the wrong currency to the wrong debt. Soltane had been his salvation; he'd crossed the Canada–US border so long ago, playing at change, thinking that the imaginary limit could transform a bad man into a peaceful, kind man. He'd taken what he had, the legacy of his Mormon grandfather, his RC mother, Hollis, and the oil he'd known growing up, and he'd teased it into something better in this new, vast land; it was alchemy if it was anything. And thirty years God had seemed to go along with this, so that Curtis'd begun to believe it wholesale. Soltane was God-given, a restoration of Eden, and they must be custodial. Why had Martha not simply endured the criticism and stayed? He feared she would pull away from this perfect thing he had made and it might unravel to nothing.

Curtis placed the candle on the table, struck a match to it, picked up the stack of letters lying there, and sat down, holding them, watching the glow as Jesus's head cast its truth around. The letters from his mother he'd read time and again. They were dog-eared now, each one reminding him how he couldn't ever go home and see her, take the burden from her. And now she was dead and it was too late. He'd have to live with it.

It was the postcards, from Hollis, *Come*, and from Islamabad, with the undermining *Wish you were here*, that he struggled against. If he came home he'd be arrested or killed, and who knew his whereabouts over in Pakistan? Ex-Family. Some old friend, maybe. Some mean old friend. Robert Wilson would sign off, so it couldn't be him. Or maybe it was. There was another letter he hadn't left lying around. He'd kept it tucked in his linen jacket, thumbed it, and worried: *Due to unpaid taxes, we regret.*

The candle began to hollow out at Jesus's head and send a thin trail of wax floating along His hair and down His shoulder toward the table. The wax would need to be rendered better next time, there was too much splutter and it shouldn't trail down so; Curtis would have to talk to Ida about that. Martha should be home. She knew how to do this right. Curtis thought suddenly how a person could not ever pay for what he'd done. You did it and it owned you; you did it and you were created by it. You could run, you could hide, but you could not expect to be free.

The darkness blurred at the edges of the candlelight like a halo. It'd been years of his inside scratching at him, debasing him, while his outside drew the people in. He'd showed love, he'd showed peace. He'd showed them how. They could fish love and they could catch God's love. Now Martha was gone, and the space she left was a keyhole through which it all looked corrupted. What had he done? He had followed orders; he had merely followed orders. And it was still so clear, what a damned bad thing he'd done all those years back.

The darkened room absorbed the light right out of a person. Curtis could just make out his pa lifting a cold pack at regular intervals to his shining forehead. Hollis had on a ratty, baby-blue terry-cloth housecoat; the pocket was ripped where one of the little ones had pulled down on it. He sat like a great, demented Buddha, cross-legged and swaying slightly.

'I have something to tell you, Curtis.'

He had seen his father like this many times before, but there was a difference here now. Curtis sensed something grinding out toward him, a task he would have to bear that would seal him off from further choices, a task that just might fuck him over for life. He was just a kid, for crying out loud. Hollis had tied one on the night before and Curtis had heard him in the yard around the gas pumps but had not bothered to look out the window. It was nothing he hadn't seen before.

The crackling of ignition, flashes of spraying firelight — Hollis's own private, drunken prayer — woke Curtis and he lay there listening. Curtis gauged how drunk, how big the hangover, how high the payment, and judged how contained he'd be able to keep himself. He reckoned on a great deal on all accounts and sank back into the blank that was his dream world.

'Set you down, Curtis. I have something to tell you.' There wasn't any place to sit, so Curtis crouched to make himself eye level with the old man. Hollis was getting on sixty by this time. It was 1972, July, and hot like stink. It was three months since Curtis had broken eighteen, and three months since he had been deemed unfit to serve his country. He had stood there naked while the doctor ranged over his chest with that cold stethoscope and located his weakness. All the while he was feeling the buzz of his heart valves, willing it to be someone else's problem, and waiting for the doctor to react, giving in to it as if he knew nothing, as if it were a test. Curtis tried to hood his eyes and look menacing, but it wasn't any good. The doctor had a hand on his shoulder.

'You want a specialist for this, boy.'

'Nothing special about me, sir.'

'You have some irregularities in your heart pump.'

'That don't make me special.'

'Maybe.'

Curtis's best friend, Robert Wilson, had already gone off to military training, saying, 'Chump,' and Curtis had thought that if he wasn't a chump, he was a pawn in some game he didn't exactly know how to play. The tears that had pressed against the back of his eyes when he said goodbye to Robert were frustration and jealousy, nothing more. And Hollis gave him such a look when he found out, said something about the Woolf boys being kings at avoiding active duty and that it was a gift from God to have a heart that shut down on you, but his eyes said otherwise. His eyes said how he owned Curtis now, and how Curtis would be part of something bigger, a family that became more powerful with Curtis beholden.

'Set you down, boy.'

'I'm good, Pa.'

There had been three robberies in the last month, the last one a convenience store that hadn't learned yet to keep a safe — not that it would have stopped Curtis and Aubie much. Curtis had patience where safes were concerned. He would just pull up a stool and wait, humming to his new pistol. Curtis wasn't high; the pot he'd smoked was to slow himself down, slow his heart down too. The humming got everyone off-kilter long enough for him and Aubie to get what they needed. This last jackass had kept the entire day's takings in his till. All Curtis did was point the Browning and smile while Aubie reached around the poor bastard from behind, humping at his rear end just to scare the living shit out of him, some wiseacre joke, and grabbed more than nine hundred greenbacks.

'Talk about convenience.'

'From the look on your face, Aub, I'd say you liked that old fella.'

'I liked what he had in the till.' Aubie wasn't even sixteen. He was slapping the stack of bills against the dashboard of Hollis's Dodge. This had transpired two nights before, and Curtis, for his part, was still charged up. They'd twirled the store owner, got his arms out of his sleeves, and tied him up straitjacket-style. Aubie had taken his one-third cut, and Curtis had dropped him off home, upriver. The rest had gone to Hollis, who had only nodded and slipped it away somewhere, a magician's trick it always seemed to Curtis. Now Hollis looked like he was breathing through his eyeballs. The flash of his wet eyes was all Curtis could see in the room, the green-and-yellow-flecked irises as they forced him to a sober thought: We've been caught.

'Now, don't begin to worry, son.'

'What's going on?'

'It's Aubie, is all. Why you let that boy into this business is beyond a mortal soul's understanding.'

'You, Pa. You told me to get him in on it. For Hattie's sake, so there'd be something left over for them boys.'

Hollis wouldn't take guff. 'Don't twist things on me. It won't do twisting things now, at this time. The thing is done. That mindless, stupid, clerking twat-sniffer at the convenience store got too good a look, see? And the county is lining up every single robbery and matching your name and Aubie's name to what's been done since the time of Moses's birth on. There ain't a crime committed and unsolved in Guadalupe County for the last ten years and maybe even in the entire state they won't try to pin to you two. I don't trust it. No, I don't.'

'Where'd you hear of this?'

'I got my source.'

'Well, that just ain't right.'

'Neither is nine hundred dollars outta that man's cash register. This isn't about right. This is about what you can get away with, boy. I tell you. There's a direct line from Aubie and you, and that line is tugging at my heart, just as sure as shit. It's Edgar, and don't you know, he yanks the line and we all topple, cardhouse-style. That boy won't let his brother go down, and sure as shit, your old pa will get the blame. You do what's right, here, Curtis, and the house will shake but she won't collapse. You do what's right.' Hollis was rocking.

'What's Edgar got to do with it?'

'He holds the key. I feel it. He has his mother's face and his mother's hold on justice. There ain't no whichway for people like that. He's going to bring me down. I can feel that. And, son, he don't know what he's doing, because if I go down, then the whole thing comes down.' Hollis's voice went up an octave. Curtis never liked to see his daddy cry, nor did he wish to now. He thought how there wasn't anything he wouldn't do for this man, how there wasn't ever a time in his short life he'd known his father to be wrong.

'I don't understand, Pa.'

Hollis leaned in until his lips were brushing against Curtis's hair. His voice normally came out deep and resonant, a low boom. It was the kind of voice that could be all clarity but through a wall would muffle and sink into the plaster, come across like the sweep of wind down a stream. It went back to deep as he spoke. Maeve, Curtis's ma, who was in the kitchen on the other side of the wall, she must have heard it as a warning, like a beast's growl, and she cut the stew meat faster. Tomorrow's dinner already halfway made. That rumbling voice of Hollis's always put her on edge. What was he up to? Heck, she could easier hear the other boys racking up sales outside on the gas pumps, the satisfying clunk of the nozzles fitting into a truck tank or the pump holder and the soft, boyish Thank you, sir, Thank you, sir. What was Hollis on about in there? Well, she half knew.

Hollis's voice went shrill and wheezy again and Curtis wondered if he was taking ill, but he was not. 'You want your pa in jail? I say, there ain't no whichway for such people, or there oughtn't be no whichway, and what I say goes. That boy Edgar, they don't call him The Judge for nothing. You think he's going to let Aubie take this from us; we're all going to pay — you, and me, boy. And then who do you think is going to take care of things here at home? Edgar hears of this, and he will if he ain't already, the cards will fall. Hell, I don't like this no more than you. But all you got to do is act, son.'

'What about Aubie?'

'Aubie's solid as they come.' And then with an edge that made Curtis freeze up and down his backbone, Hollis said, 'Boy, you need to stop questioning. The cards will fall while time ticks out.'

And with his father's wheezy voice still speaking to him, and with his father's eyes staring into him, he walked out past his brothers, whom he loved, where they stood looking worried by the pumps, until they couldn't bear it and they stopped looking at him go. And he walked also by his sisters, who were playing out behind the station, playing trikes and snakes, how you zigzagged across as many sidewinders as you could find and the one with the most dead ones won. 'S'long.' Curtis stood and watched them for too long, but they did not look up from their game and so his lasting image of them was of their dresses and their pudgy legs running on the pedals.

Curtis followed through the back way to the water and took the river's edge up Hattie McCann's way; the Browning warmed the flesh on his hip. His heart was racing and thumping and skipping and he was thinking how his best friend, Robert, would be killing Chinks in six months but that he'd be in jail by then, likely, having killed his own half-brother. He walked a quickened pace then that got his heart singing, and found he could achieve something, achieve a drifting off that went past revelation to leaving; he left his body and watched it march on to do its duty.

He found Edgar fishing on the bank and he sat with him for some time and tried to gain courage to do what he would do. They did not speak much. It was damned hot. The air shimmered with humidity around Edgar even though about a foot or so over his head and up, the air was cracking dry. When Curtis walked back home, his own skin was hot to touch, the sun beating at him like that. But sitting there with Edgar in the condensation from the river, it was cool, or felt cool relatively, and he hunkered down, let the moisture along the bank wick up his jeans, and he was relieved by it, calmed.

Curtis had not known for all that long that Edgar was Hollis's son by Hattie McCann. No one had ever told him; it was the small inferences that finally after eighteen years connected up. That Hattie was held in some esteem by Hollis but never quite knowing why, these rules Hollis had around the McCanns, that he and his brothers had to be friendly toward her children, which hadn't anyway been a struggle (well, they were good people), plus obscure comments made by this or that adult, church gossip, all this had lined up into a solved riddle, the impact of which was inconceivably far-reaching. Curtis could not seem to lock it all onto Hollis; the picture would not attach itself in any meaningful way to the truth. What about his ma, her recessed wide eyes even wider it seemed as he had just passed her elbow deep in beef; how did his mother fit into this puzzle? And did Aubie know or did he not know? It was unsettling to have a secret. Something to be so sure of he'd wager his life and, yet, never to have been told it. Curtis picked himself up. 'Well,' he said suddenly, as if to no one, 'if I have to, I might as well.' It was a bravado born of fear.

Edgar half turned, a silver flicker of fish swaying from his line. 'What?' And he was up, the gun's sights beetling, Curtis trying to follow the motion of his head. The rod dropped away, twanged when it hit a stone.

'Hold still.'

'Why the fuck would I?'

'Well, for one thing the store owner identified Aubie.'

Edgar considered what Curtis might mean by this. He considered up and down until he realized what Curtis was telling him. 'Aubie ain't going down alone,' he said. He was trying to cap the pressure that was hurtling up his throat. 'Aubie is not taking this from you people. Hollis has got to pay. You know he does.' His cheeks were all twitchy.

Curtis's lip curled into a grimace. 'Shit, brother. I was afraid you would say something along those lines. Pa was afraid of that.' There was an awful noise, then, that smelled of acridity and metal and blood, and then there was falling and then nothing. Curtis had pulled the trigger and the gun worked.

That's what Curtis thought too, as it happened. The gun worked. It killed. A bullet entered the body of this boy, and it was a shock even to Curtis. There was movement that reflected impact and then the hole where the bullet entered seemed to fray and become viscous and red and then it was blood everywhere. Curtis thought, 'It worked,' and a trauma overcame him and also a realization that he really did love Edgar, whom he had just now killed. He dropped the gun and went to cradle the boy's head into his lap. He keened without any tears, just sobbed and apologized to God for his stupidity. The bullet wound was through Edgar's chest and there was an enormous amount of blood loss. It was lifeblood, Curtis was certain, and he stared.

The Apache cod on the end of Edgar's line had fallen back into the Pecos when the rod was dropped. Curtis watched it hold still for a great long time, only opening and closing its gills to keep calm. Now, it seemed to feel a strength and began to fight the lead and the hook that cut into its jaw. There was a ripping to be sure. The line strained, the rod having caught along a stump. The fish was pulling with the stream to gain momentum. It would not give in. There were other, smaller fishes gathering, not to witness the struggle but to pick at strands of flesh that ripped from this bigger fish's mouth. The skin was ragged; there was a minnow attaching itself to the cod's mouth and nibbling at it.

The lure Edgar had used was handmade, a chiselled alloy of tin and something else, and it flickered, its lifeless eye taunting the cod, and slammed into the cod's nose as it strove. The lure would be the reason the cod would prevail. It became furious with the hard, flicking menace and yanked and yanked with a strength it did not recognize in itself and that it would immediately afterwards forget it possessed. The hook sliced through the cod's flesh and snapped the bone at its mouth. Curtis imagined this would heal later into a gaping monstrosity. He watched the fish swim away, all torn up. After a time, he saw how useless it was to be there, and the smell of blood began to unnerve him. Curtis wedged himself out from under the heavy body and crawled over to the gun and then ran scared home.

There had been that last time with Hollis then. That was bad. Hollis called him into the half-lit sepulchre of his room. The old man was so fat, Curtis could smell the richness of his body. It had been only hours ago he had last seen him. There had been a severing, Curtis could feel that. Time had danced away. 'Where've you been, boy?'

'The river with Edgar.' Hollis's fury was palpable and so to placate, Curtis added, 'I did what you said.'

'I heard already what's been done. It's all over town by now. You misunderstood, son. You misunderstood.' And Curtis

Woolf was backing away, the metallic scent of blood suddenly hitting him, and he looked down and his shirt was soaked with it. He had walked through the centre of town not wet from the river water but soaked in the deep, clotting blood of Edgar McCann.

'I did what you said, Pa. I only ever did —'

And all Hollis said was, 'You best be going, son. If they ask me, I swear I never saw you.'

'But —'

'You're on your own.' And that last was like a gavel rapping.

'You're a liar.' Curtis said this without conviction; the more profound knowledge was that Curtis believed Hollis already knew this — and that until then, *he* hadn't.

The Jesus candle flickered and poured down itself. Curtis cried. Cold tears went down his face, and he didn't bother stopping them for more would come. Let them flow. Where was Martha? She had the gun. She had pointed it at him and it was not loaded, and she had said, 'Why?' and he had not told her how he had shot a man and left him to die.

'I paid for it; let me continue to amend,' he had said. He was so scared of Hollis back then. He had misunderstood. And he had killed Edgar. And he would not like to misunderstand again. There was a rattle in his chest because of the stress of crying and he wished he would die. He looked through that memory keyhole and all he saw was wasteland, and twenty-one people, and what had he been building here against the inevitable? *Due to unpaid taxes, we regret.* Tax people didn't know about regret.

There had been a woman in a suit knocking at the gatehouse door. Unpaid taxes, missed mortgage payments; Soltane was being foreclosed. The letter and the visit made Curtis nervous, made him irrational, he saw now, made him send Martha away for those weeks to the barn. Shouldn't have done that, he saw now. The woman in the suit had said, 'There may be some way you can still keep the farm,' and he tried to explain how it was not a farm, how it was a sacred, energetic tribute, and she only nodded, then shook her head. 'There may be some way.' The Jesus candle smothered itself and went out. He would sleep and it would be okay in the morning. Martha would be back. He felt sure.

Three

Michael. Corporal Michael Dama. There was a helicopter hovering far off toward the hills, and the men in the market looked up anxiously. Michael knew what it looked like from up there. The land was a carpet, ochre, teal, and browns, lacking symmetry to be sure, but both dealing in symbols. All that history. He thought of Baku. A thousand years ago there was a fire raging in one spot. Oil was alight, crude spraying fire, people gathered there to pray. It wasn't funny, but he laughed anyway. People praying that gave way to oil rigs, and derricks debauching that same earth: the old in-out. He liked the irony. From a helicopter, a Hind, say, the landscape was still after all that history a carpet — small, patterned. Here was a paisley, a border of paisley shapes. Symbol of flame, eternal life, but the shapes were changing, shifting.

Michael looked back down, pulled his hand over the pile of the rug, testing its integrity; he flipped the rug's edge to check the weave, and back again to the symbols. The weaver had created an explosion and a line of burqas; there was only war left, and who would win, and the carpets were as much stock-piling blind faith as they were talismanic. It was a crappy carpet, and he was in a crappy border town market and didn't expect more. He was waiting, felt his scars stretching deep toward his ribs, pulling at him. He was dark. Where the fuck was the boy, Omar?

'You buy?'

Michael mustered a look of disgust, of insult. Soon, with Omar, he would enter a tent city outside Dera Ismail Khan packing a small arsenal of weaponry. This did not make him feel safe, but it did not make him feel not-safe either. The guns he carried shifted against his skin and chafed him; he would have a rash the shape of a pistol on his outer shin. Pain, progress, and it might form into a tattoolike bruise. Neither life nor death touched him much; he had scars from both. He had always walked in between, all his life; his father used to say how Michael was neither on the road nor in the ditch but watching from the slim shoulder of gravel between. And still he was just the same, buying back guns while ostensibly just buying carpets with this translator he'd picked up in Peshawar. Omar, a university kid, languages and history, someone's nephew; the kid wore a Mujahedeen camel wool hat, one of those rolled-brim affairs that looked old-timey and crazy all at once. Kid was a cover. Fucking kid. Where was he?

Michael had drunk way too much the night before, had taken this boy to the Pearl Continental and watched the kid's eyes bug out of his face at the hotel's mock opulence, watched him try to keep his eyes from bugging out. Wealth always impressed poor people. But the boy was sharp; yes, he was that. 'Tell me, sir, I couldn't help but notice, sir.'

'What's that?'

'You are a brown man. Your skin is dark.' It was brandy Michael was drinking. Omar drank Coke, and did not look him in the eye but stared down his nose at the tumbler. It was cultural, this lack of eye contact. Michael had been, long ago, briefed on this, but it never seemed right no matter how often he encountered it. He wished he could assimilate better; wished he could disappear within this land too. He would never be dark-skinned enough, or dark-skinned in the right way. He would always be hated here, or tolerated in a hateful way. 'Well, my mother is hereditary Black Irish. They're dark.'

'Yes, yes.' Omar's face had opened — his teeth had gaps, his thin, desperate, peach-fuzz moustache curled with his wide smile. 'The Moors. You are my brother then. A lost tribesman.' Omar took Michael's hand in both of his and held it for longer than Michael would have liked. It was awkward, the Arab camaraderie, the intimacy of men toward men, and he didn't know what to do with it. And he was tired of all this bullshit. This making nice to people so they wouldn't want to kill him.

Moorish blood, though. Michael had never considered this, that there might be an Arab gene buried in his family history. He paused to think about it, mentally scanned both sides of his family tree, thought about his brother's darkness, the build of the man, and his dad's calculated cruelty, and he imagined the Spanish roaring through the desert on their small horses and considered Genghis Khan and the Mongols and the wild Moors rising up. Hadn't they conquered everything, the whole known world? He about laughed thinking it'd break the old man's heart if he ever found out he was a Muslim. 'A lost tribesman, huh? I hadn't ever thought of things like that. It does make sense, though, Omar, and cheers to that.'

'Cheers, sir.'

'Hadn't we better quit this drinking and pray or something, in that case?'

'That's very funny, sir.' But Omar wasn't laughing. He set his cola down and stared at it as if the drink itself had forced him into some sort of betrayal. He was getting up to leave.

'Sit. Sit. How much will you charge for a day's work? I want war rugs. Bring me to a good place, that camp southeast of Dera Ismail Khan. Name your price.'

DIK was on the old spice- and carpet-trading route, the Gomal Pass, but no one of any importance for hundreds of years had passed through; it was all grey mud buildings and open sewers, Afghan refugees and destitution, and damn was it ever hot. In the shade, something like a hundred and twenty degrees. Omar pulled the jeep alongside him, bringing the children out, their hands begging, their eyes shifting into that look: You owe me. And Omar ignored them and brought him to the seething tent city on the edge of this Podunk town just like he wanted him to, to the camp where Michael was to make his connection; there was a gun there he'd been tracking for months.

What he didn't like about Omar's translating was the way the kid would compress a paragraph of his carefully worked-out charm into a grunt. Or the other way round. Omar would expand on a simple *no*, filigree it to the point where Michael wondered what the hell he was really saying, wishing he spoke Pashto himself, but he'd never mastered it. Michael wore greens so he wouldn't smell too much like money, but still the scabby kids begged candy, begged water, for Christ's sake.

He walked through them, Omar shushing them and scattering them with broad sweeps of his arms; they moved off into cliques and pressed in upon him again and again until Omar barked at them. The whole place stank of spent uranium, stank like death and dust. Michael could practically feel himself growing cancer. Fuck. A man came out of a tent and was waiting for them.

'Aksi.' Omar whispered this as if it was a code.

'Aksi, aksi.' The place was suddenly like a paper wasp nest in August, a fucking sudden vespiary. It was all the same, all over, all the time, and Michael just stood there and waited for it to die down, waited for the desperation to filter down into something more manageable, to fear, to twenty dollars, to ten dollars. He did not want to be ripped off by these people; he wanted his gun, his gun rug, and he did not want to be ripped off. He would see one, two, a hundred carpets by the end of the day and drink enough tea to water a herd of Saharan camels for a year and he'd hold it. A man is a man who can hold on to his tea piss. He looked out at the camp. There were tents and then more tents and more still, and Michael felt a slight shift in his emotions that he did not consider useful. There was a box for this remnant, this frayed, useless swatch of guilt, and he put it away and continued to stare out at the endless, perfect array of brown canvas tents, each upon each. Some fucking circus this was; hell, how did people live like this?

Eighty per cent of the people in this place wouldn't be able to provide one gun icon, one interesting poppy, or even a slight variation on the wheat sheaf, and then it would emerge like a glass slipper. *The* carpet. One perfect carpet that he had to have. Years ago, he hadn't cared much about the carpets, but since the weapons started cropping up on them, it was almost all he cared about. It would take all morning, part of the afternoon, the heat seeming to affect only him, though he had ways with the heat, ways of containing his discomfort and keeping focus. He wanted to meet his connection, yes, but what he really wanted? He wanted a goddamn gun rug. Tree of life. Fuck tree of life. Surely someone in this camp was weaving military devices?

And then. And then a young man passed a very sick-looking child to a woman. She looked about thirteen, the woman did, and eyes like tunnels going nowhere; he could see her hips jutting under her skirts. She stared at the rolled-up carpet her husband was unsheathing. It was a Baghlani, a runner, with repeating medallions, blood red, and he saw nothing at first, nothing until he inspected the pile, the knot count, abrash, the border. Michael glanced up to see if the owner even knew what he had. He looked at the woman and the kid, and tried, he could be a bastard, to make eye contact; the woman roved her eyes skyward, to Allah, to that safety, and Michael smiled. He looked back at the man, thought, He's hungry, he's the one, he'll bite. 'How much for this one?'

Omar barked something at the man. Sounded like an insult the way only a foreign language could. 'He wants fifty American.'

Michael snorted. It was nothing. The border was so gorgeous he thought he'd go crazy. Instead of poppies or roses lining up around the medallions, there were ochre burqas alternating with baby-blue bullets, and it just about took his breath away. The rug was almost ten feet long, about two and a half wide, wool on wool, with some of the best material he'd seen in years, good knots.

'Fifty?'

'Fifty. It is old.'

'It ain't old. Don't lie. Tell the young fella not to lie.' The imagery was recent, Michael knew, and there wasn't a sheep left in Afghanistan. He hated the constant lying over here. 'The wool's too good. It's Paki wool.'

Omar let fly at the man then, and they salaamed back and forth and, in between the niceties, insulted each other heartily until the price went down twenty dollars. 'His wife wove it from wool they carted, from before the sheep died. This is sheep's wool from their own authentic sheep. So not old but still old, sir.'

'Do they have any more? Come on. I'm in a hurry.'

The Afghan brought out a smaller rug with a wheat sheaf ballista, in browns, and Michael sent Omar for a walk. 'Get the fuck out of here and take this man's wife and kid with you. I want to talk to him alone.' Before they left, the woman genuflected, and he saw her face again peeking out of her chador. She gave him an ugly look. It wasn't anything new, this reciprocal disgust, but he knew he'd think about her later. Now he and the man were alone and staring at each other. The man could barely grow a beard, he was that young, but around the eyes he looked like a grandfather. This was his man, the carpet fragment told it. In Urdu, Michael asked, 'Where is it?'

'Your Jeep. The back of your Jeep.'

'Good then.'

It was easy, after that. He walked out to the vehicle, found the carrying case, opened it, closed it, and went back to the wild-eyed Muj waiting for him there. 'I'll take both rugs,' he said and handed him a bag.

The man looked in the bag, then said, 'Excuse me, I will count.' He pulled several bound stacks of cash out of the bag and slowly counted it. He then smiled, said, 'Praise be to God,' and salaamed Michael. Michael rolled the runner and the little carpet together, tucked them under his arm, and nodded. He was almost out the tent flap door when the man began screaming in accented Urdu at him, shrieking like he'd been physically hurt. He was saying 'thief' and 'dog' and 'money' and Michael realized he'd forgotten to pay for the carpets. He pulled three twenties and a ten from his wallet and crushed this into the man's open palm, muttering, 'Shut the fuck up.'

'What else did you buy?' Omar was more than halfway back to Peshawar, flicking the headlights on whenever he noticed oncoming traffic, to save on gas, but otherwise moving steadily along the pocked road through the dark. Michael looked hard at Omar.

'I could tell you the answer to your question, but then I'd have to kill you.' And then he laughed. Omar did not laugh, so Michael said, 'Shit, man, it's a joke,' but that changed nothing. Omar remained quiet.

Michael waited until he'd been dropped at the hotel to pay Omar his rupees, tipping him handsomely in dollars; he threw the carpets over his left shoulder, let them balance there, and slid the carrying case off the back of the jeep. Thirty-five-pound load; he thanked Christ he wasn't the sucker hauling it through the hills. Last, he made sure to get the boy's whereabouts should he need him again.

He dropped the gun inside the door, unfurled the pieces in the hotel room, and, while he smoked, noted the condition of the rugs, their exact measurements, their qualities, knots per inch, type of knot. They had surely not been knotted by that woman nor anyone in that camp; they'd likely been looted somewhere along the journey. Circa 1987. Worth nothing much unless you could find the right completist — a carpet nut wanting a full set of the ongoing war rug narrative. He knew someone. Michael considered keeping the runner. He liked the idea of people he knew standing on it, him being the only one to know there was ammunition underfoot. He kept only very few pieces for himself. At the end of the day, as Omar had made a hard right into the hotel driveway and inertia pressed him to the door, Omar had asked him what he did. And he said import-export, which, strictly speaking, was true.

'What was in the metal carrying case?'

'Nothing. Something I was owed.'

'Nothing, and then something?' The Pakistani boy had looked in his eyes then. A young man's soft eyes grown suddenly cold. 'It's a myth,' Omar had sneered. 'The myth of the Black Irish. We are not brothers.'

'What?'

'There is evening call to prayer.' And it was. The loud-speaker's piercing feedback and the muezzin's wail like a vapour then, ululating across the rooftops. 'I will go now. Thank you, sir.' They had both exited the vehicle; the hotel staff would park it.

'Relax, Omar. We are on the same team, my friend. We are all fighting for justice.'

'Yes,' said Omar, 'but I am not fighting.' He raised his hand as if waving and left, walking hunched over. Strange boy, thought Michael. And then, the thought: How could anybody be anything but strange, here in this strange, brooding country?

The wheat sheaf carpet had a small tear in the lower left border that had been repaired, darned badly. It was signed, a knotted Dari signature. Probably it was a woman weaver following a cartoon. Hell, it didn't matter. It was fucking beautiful. The traditional wheat pattern had been developed into a pointy, otherworldly ballista, a ballista as only a person who has heard about ballistas but never seen one could render one. And when he looked closer he saw something even better. There was a Zoroastrian paisley, nothing new there, a flame symbol; Michael liked that he knew that the ancients had worshipped the combusted crude wells in oil-rich Russia. Michael stood back from the carpet to see that the paisley had morphed with his perspective change; the thing was a fucking hand grenade.

'Beautiful,' he said.

It was a small carpet, not three feet by four, but it was special. It wasn't the workmanship. It was this: someone had expressed herself, and the thing was, it sent shivers up Michael's spine, the vibrancy of it. The hand grenade had replaced the paisley as a symbol of power, of rebirth. The leaf motifs, the wheat, the roses were gone from the iconography or quickly being altered. This was the story. Even the carpet weavers strove for equality. They were crafting this and selling it back to Americans — a gun for a gun. Anybody should see this, but nobody was looking.

Michael leaned back on the bed and shut his eyes, held on to his cock, and thought about that Afghan woman. He would sleep with her hatred until the concierge buzzed him, until the purchaser made his way up the elevator and down the hall, slipped him the payout he felt he had now earned, and was handed the portable missile. Easy. Where was Omar praying? He imagined him entering a dismal apartment he shared with his family and the son of a friend he had mentioned — Khaleed — who went to the university with him. Khaleed would look at him from under his lovely hooded eyelids and ask what the American imported and what he exported.

'Misery. He is a misery importer-exporter.' That's what Omar had said later, and he was just about right, wasn't he? Looking back, Michael knew the boy was trouble; nobody deserved to die an ugly death, one that nobody would want to look upon. But was there a dying that wasn't embarrassing? Michael Dama lay on the hotel bed looking down at the fragment, jerking off. He would sleep and the concierge would call up, and men would arrive and they would make a trade, and he would take his cut. He pulled the rug scrap up on to the bed, and drew over the ballista, let the pull of his scars ease him to sleep.

Four

Martha and Hattie stood outside the adobe. They had not yet gone in, the cup was not yet broken. Land around Santa Rosa wasn't tillable, nor much good for cloven creatures; south there was beef and field on field of oil derrick, metal beasts going down-up-down, benignly draining the middle of the earth. North was forest, and mountain, but where the Rita and the Pecos flowed alongside each other there was nothing but poverty. The land looked like a great monster had once raked its fingernails along it, left it to scar over for a million years, and still there was beauty in that ugliness.

'Pecos used to flood,' said Hattie, her arm hovering, hand caressing air. 'The water moved fast by my place; I had a picnic table went off down it once.' Hattie laughed then, a sweet, low murmur of a laugh that got her head down into her neck and gave off a shyness and a hint of youth, like her body hadn't forgotten yet what being young was. They went inside and Hattie began making tea, plugging in the kettle, fishing leaf into her teapot. She handed Martha a cup, and they sat down. 'Do you keep huskies?' Hattie said, thinking huskies were, at least, something to talk about.

Martha smiled over her tea. It was tannic and bitter; she picked up the sugar pot and spooned once, twice into her cup. Martha was not smiling at the cliché, but because for a time they had kept huskies. In the mid-1980s, Benjamin had bought a pack and two sleds and tried to make money bringing people for tours along the snowmobile trails that ran through the municipality. It was the barking that had settled it; the way the animals howled whenever a car drove by. Keeping the dogs cost them more than they had earned. 'We keep bees, a few cows, and grow vegetables. We live within a community.' That they did prayer healings and body fished, she did not mention. The bulk of the farm's earnings came from the quarry, from donation and prayer tithe, Jesus candles, and pots of Curtis's honey.

'A commune.'

'We prefer community.' And then, because she felt nervous, she added, 'I've known Curtis thirty years. I remember first meeting him at the bus depot.'

'Bus depot?'

'Yes.' He had just arrived, and he was sitting there on his army bag, looking more prepossessed than anyone she'd ever known. She had thought he knew himself. 'He was dodging the draft. There was something about him.'

Hattie knew Curtis hadn't made it to the army, too weak a constitution, and she suspected suddenly that Martha was lying about being Canadian. The woman just didn't present hardy at all, and somehow Hattie'd this idea of Canadians being strong; hell, she'd seen Canada on the RCA television in the corner of her own kitchen. People throwing eggs and rocks at the police from outside a chain-link fence. A tough-looking people. But Martha tilted slightly in the chair, and Hattie thought she might topple over onto the floor. She offered one of the cakes she'd made that morning, a baking soda biscuit with some butter and jam.

And then the talk of Edgar came and Martha had looked at a photograph and declared Edgar handsome and there were shards of china on the floor, tea seeping down grout, and Hattie wondered why God had sent her this woman and what would become of her. It wasn't worth bringing up all this past. There wasn't no need for it. No good need for it. 'You tired?' she said.

'I am.' So Hattie brought her to the spare room. 'It's good of you to keep me,' Martha said, placing her hand on Hattie's forearm, and Hattie thought on Hollis again and nodded.

Hattie left her there to sleep, went and turned on the TV in the far side of the kitchen — had to grip good as the knob was broke. She searched out the channels hoping to find something to let her mind rest. She sat in the chair with her feet up on the bench for a bit, watching, but the six o'clock news unsettled, a jail on the other side of the world, and prisoner abuse from American soldiers. How do you like that? she thought and turned it off. She answered the phone when it rang.

It was a short call, but then after that she knew she wouldn't sleep, so she got up, held her cane, and took the opportunity to walk to the Allsup for small supplies: onions, sugar, then over to Hollis; he might as well know right off about this Martha. The woman'd said how Curtis had something special. My.

The skin under Hattie's triceps was a sluggish pendulum; long goodbye, she called it. Her back ached so that she no longer thought of it as separate or curable, damn knees and elbows clicked as she walked. Her hair was thin and white and pressed to her skull. From across the interstate, against the burnt-out remains of a motel, a young boy called out to her: 'Hag.' She just kept walking. There was something calming about this boy and his comment, though she could not say why.

The Allsup was a store had come in years ago and looked its age too; something broody and tired about the place, but it was well supplied and easy reaching. For larger and heavy items, Hattie counted on Colm to bring her cut-rates from the Wal-Mart where he worked, down Roswell way. They called her granny at the Allsup checkout, the Hispanic cashiers did, in a way that assumed she appreciated it. Again, she did not resent it. Life was too short.

The cashier now was a woman named Valerie, with long hair and piercings along her cheek and through the hair on her eyebrow. She was chunky in a way that was not unpleasant. The metal thing in Valerie's eyebrow seemed to be nailed straight in; Hattie wondered whether it was just lodged there in the girl's skull. It was hanging out a piece and looked dull, as if it had rusted, and Hattie was put in mind of sweet Santa Librada on the cross at the RC church. Santa Librada, the crucified woman. She shuddered a little at that. Valerie cracked a paper tube of coins open into the register, money crashing against money like water, only hard. Valerie then reached over and let her hand linger on Hattie's arm. It was warm. Hattie thought, How nice, and then Valerie said, 'How is Auberon?'

Hattie wondered whether her son Aubie had already slept with this woman or if he was just about to. She wondered if there was a woman in Guadalupe County under the age of sixty who didn't know her son's name. 'Thank you. Aubie is fine. I don't see him much.' She lied; he came by regularly to see her. Valerie came out from behind the counter and handed the bag of food over.

'I'm glad to hear he's fine.'

Wait until I see that boy, Hattie thought. And thinking about Aubie brought her back thinking about Martha. She did not like to wonder how these connected up. So instead she focused on why Martha was there in the first place, and what possible good could come of it.

She marked the walk to Hollis by cane strides. The way was along the new road, crossing over and over the old route where the greasewood and the cacti and the sagebrush had split through and crumbled the bitumen. Eight hundred cane thumps to get to the grocer and it would take more to return, heavy goods in hand, from the care facility later. God brought that woman Martha here, she thought, and it stands to reason He might know what He is doing. She figured on keeping Martha close by her, keep her eye on that.

Hattie walked east, over the highway to where Hollis's old station used to be, long abandoned now. Hattie had once hated the cars sweeping dust into her eyes, making them cry, so she developed strategies, carrying a handkerchief and feeling the vibration of oncoming traffic through her feet before she heard it. Over time, she'd come to enjoy the wind churned up, the earthy breeze of time passing by. The slower she moved, the more she stood in awe of it, the rush of busy folk, the wind of their business cooling her body. There was a time long gone when Hattie never went anywhere without a car wrapped around her. Hollis and her; Richards and her too.

She went in the scrub at the side of the road. The trailer had been hauled off years and years ago to make way for the permanent body shop. That was gone too, or not entirely, but caved in, nothing much for posterity. Busted pumps, the earth a quiet rusting steel container down there, waste, spilled dreams. The red and white and blue paint on the pumps was still fighting against the elements, pigment curling off rust. The chrome had blistered, but here and there the sun still glinted in it. The adobe shop was red clay rubble.

'My God,' she said, marvelling at how it was all gone just as sure as it had all been there. She walked around the first pump, holding on to it for balance. 'It looks to me like the pumps just up and walked away from him, not the other way.' She was muttering to herself, is what old age did. It was hard to believe what nature had done there in Hollis's domain. Hard to believe that they'd got him so he'd stay in that old folks' home, just going downhill, his health was. All that accumulated power just going. Somebody had spray-painted an expletive in the shape of a cosmos flower. Hattie turned toward the care home, and Hollis. She'd passed by the Blue Hole swimming spot, a Casey's, Route 66 plowed over where the scrub wasn't eating it, the interstate bridging the Pecos, an ash ruin, cars driving slow past the restaurants, the hotel chains, the gas stations all east of Hattie's place. Guadalupe County Care. Here she was.

Martha pulled her clothing off in Hattie's little house, sitting with her face to the window, her reflection sharp in the glass. She got her purse up onto the bed, groped around for the gun, and sat there, her ass pressing into the soft coverlet, looking at the gun as if it could tell her anything at all.

There was a bedside lamp shedding little light; the gun was dull and antique-looking, beautiful, she thought, and again did not like the thought. She wondered whether it could even fire any more. Curtis had perhaps shot someone with this gun. She had left the farm. Aubie had gone to jail; she wondered what he looked like. She wondered, too, where you even bought bullets; there must be someplace.

She was so tired, and she couldn't sleep. All she could do was think, and fret. If she wasn't going back, she would have to look for work of some sort; she couldn't beg forever. Back home, there was the manmade forest of red pine, a matrix of trees that smelled of nature, its liveliness, its decadence; she had hid there asking nonsensical questions. She walked in her mind now past the dormant hives, the unpainted outbuildings, and everywhere she had been throughout the farm, and she went over all the thirty years of being there, and it counted; never returning felt like death strafing her insides, made her feel faint. Soltane's landscape was all she knew; that family, the candles, the honey, the doing, and Curtis were everything.

She had been sheltered. And it was pulling away from her,

as if it was not real, as if it had not happened but only been imagined to have happened. Then the gun, this shiny mechanism of truth; she pointed it at the window, at her reflection, and pulled the trigger. It had a pleasing resistance, so she did it again. She was not for guns, but could not deny that the pulling back of the trigger gave a giddy joy; and she was naked on the bed, and this, too, was funny.

She had said to Hattie that she just wanted to know all the lies she'd been told, delineate all the betrayals, uncover all the manipulations, and here she stopped. She was not sure whether she had said any of this to Hattie or only meant to, or had not meant to and didn't want to know any of it. Maybe there just happened to be a gun in the floor, and it signified nothing at all. She pulled the trigger on the gun again, aiming it at the dark window; a thin light came from the bedside lamp, and shadow edged her skin. She still had her body. She had been taken care of, sheltered, and maybe that should count for something. She had heard the phone ring earlier and listened to Hattie's conversation.

'I found a woman from Canada in the Pecos today. No, I ain't crazy. She told me she lived on a farm with Curtis for thirty years. Some kind of Jesus commune. I don't know. Yes, I intend to do that. Yes. I do. She ain't going nowhere fast, I'd say. Don't you worry about that. Lost? Oh, yes.' And the conversation ended, and Hattie had left the house.

If the gun had bullets, the window would have shattered. Martha ran her finger along the shaft of the Browning. She'd walked through Nauvoo, Illinois, with that gun, stood through a lecture on Jonathan Browning in the Mormon pioneer village, and how Browning'd found the faith and gone from black-smithing to gunsmithing as a ministry, and all the while that gun was weighing in her purse. The gun seemed like the only real thing she had to go on.

Standing in the vestibule of the Browning gunsmith shop in Old Nauvoo, pressed in by an eager group of clear-eyed witnesses, she had come to know something new about Curtis; he came from this stock, she recognized him here — a ghost, a holy one, had lingered on him from his childhood. She had been sheltered by him, by her trust of him. She was grateful.

She'd met Curtis at the bus depot; she was there with friends to meet American pacifists as they came in on the bus, and Curtis had a halo around him, and they had laughed and welcomed him. She was netted, caught. It wasn't a year before he had organized them all, got their money pooled, and the farm was theirs. And she saw it now, she thought, how it all lined up. They wore white, the men and the girls. Around town, even farther, they were known as the Family, that they were all strangely beautiful went around.

That they farmed according to biodynamic principles, read the Holy Stories to their children, sold Jesus candles, and sublet to the gravel pit was generally accepted, even condoned. What was less well known by outside people: it was a blessing on the Family to welcome new members, and they sometimes converted new Associates. Potentials the Family committee agreed upon were fished; a member was used as a sensual lure, an extension of God's will. This was how Benjamin had found Ida, and she was clearly a fine conduit.

Martha's hand went instinctively to her belly. Yes, she still had faith in that code. She was aware that the body motivated the soul. Beauty bore Beauty. It was a simple covenant. Martha reached for her purse, plunged the gun deep into it, and felt around for her pot; she'd been rationing it these days as she wouldn't smoke unpure weed. Off-farm weed was not sacred. She rolled a thin joint, watched herself in the window, got calm.

The Family seldom left the farm to go to town. They were

needed; Curtis stayed too, sent Benjamin, or one of the other steadfast men. The news seeped through then, of wars, of debauchery, of danger. They were sheltered. They sheltered themselves purposefully. Who would not want to be sheltered from this? But then, there had been a great deal of blood loss with the last miscarriage, and it had come late, five months, when all expectation of blood loss was past, and Martha was really expecting. There had been matter and blood loss; she had stared at it and tried to identify body parts. A small finger, a nose.

The miscarriage suggested imperfection. As soon as she healed, she would be criticized for it at Meeting, there would be suggestions of how she might improve herself, and mostly there would be an air of defeat; she would not be given the gift of pregnancy again, this much was certain. It was common knowledge that she could not carry. She'd been given more chances than many others, and she had failed. She would be relegated. Already Curtis shunned her. The questions about what she might do hit her like an unavoidable wickedness. She had so wanted that child to radiate her belief to the others; she had so wanted proof.

Proof. Perhaps this was the vanity then for which she was now punished, this was the taint on her, that faith and prayer were not enough. She had failed to carry precisely because she wanted to prove something with it. This was why she was an inept conduit. She wanted the outcome to reflect her, and it never could, and the Family had seen this all along. She had not believed in her own humility enough. She looked down at her purse, thought how the Family had held the gun within its boundaries all this time. This knowledge made her anxious. She did not like what it might mean, did not like where things were leading her.

At Soltane, she had built a collection of books. These were

mostly useful books — manuals on farm equipment, on type-setting, on esoteric farming practices. There were books on various other spiritual practices, and these had been used in the early days to codify the Family, and aid in the education of the Associates in ways that would contrive a harmonious community. They had studied the Oneida, the Mormons, along with various other short-lived messianic communes — these mostly for what not to do. Their central tenet was inner and outer perfection achieved through a system of proper hygiene, sexual practice, prayer, and work ethic. The body, the earth, and the soul were inseparable ideals. They reflected one another directly.

The library housed the printer in its annex, and Martha was part of the team that oversaw editorial on the monthly news-paper. There were also hundreds of pamphlets printed in the library annex over the years, and several short, hand-bound histories archived in the library. There was a novel, entitled *Body Love*, that Martha had always felt overemphasized the erotic. The author had run off in 1985 with an outside person. And now Martha had run off with a gun.

She'd come through Illinois to see where Joseph Smith, the founder of Mormonism, had been shot dead — Carthage — and to see what the Mormons had built long ago in Old Nauvoo out of donations and belief and hope. She wanted to see where Curtis held his spiritual roots to be, his own begats. Curtis used to say that Mormonism was the most proudly American religion there was, born and bred on American soil, for the people, and then he'd rattle off the begats from Curtis Woolf right back to Joseph Smith himself. The lineage made him real to himself, he said that too. Plus, he liked to add, the Mormons were successful, they had persevered. They shone. Ideals *were* achievable.

The tour guide was a high-school missionary dressed like a nineteenth-century gunsmith, plaid shirt and grey pressed slacks, named Brother Dwight. His sleeves were rolled up, and he wore suspenders. He told how Jonathan Browning started out smithing and then, as God entered him, took to locks and guns. Locks and guns that were wrought of persecution and retribution.

The gun shop had a stepped roof. An elderly woman with blue-rinsed hair on the tour said, 'Steps right on up to Heaven, now, doesn't it?' and Martha had nodded. Brother Dwight placed a rifle in her hands, and she looked into the spiral receding down its barrel, and the soft lines of the thing, and how it made her feel responsible to hold it. Near numinous. She looked around at the others there waiting their turns so patiently; there was indeed a sparkle to these people that Martha recognized. The Family, too, sparkled in righteous joy.

'I have to leave, Curtis,' she had said to him the day after finding the gun, and he said he knew she would, he had dreamed her leaving like a prophecy, and then he cried, said to leave it alone, that no good would come there. She had stayed through that next day in the locked library, afraid to do anything, and then had gone to him again and said, 'I'm leaving.' Her resolve was stronger the second time around, and he was not paying so much attention; she had gone into the gate-house, up the stairs, pulled the carpet and the planking aside, and cradled the gun again in her hands. She didn't know what she was doing, only that she had to do it. The gun was drawing her someplace. She had walked out through the forest in the early morning, alongside the quarry, before anyone was awake. She was jubilant, and she just had to hold that long enough to leave.

Martha slipped under the covers of the strange bed where Hattie had left her and felt herself up for comfort, then pleasure, offering even this up and looking at the window, where she could no longer see her reflection but instead the moon, like a fingernail, where it had pulled back the night. She closed her eyes when she climaxed but didn't sleep; she became more awake, turning in the bed until she finally gave up on sleep.

They wore white and they congregated at Meeting once the work was done each day and she had loved them all. She had loved Curtis from the first meeting; she saw he had a story and wasn't some local boy with the same old local past. The halo was a mythology. He had no halo, but there he was, wearing an ill-fitting suit and a cowboy hat, a line of baby hair above his upper lip and clean-shaven otherwise; his hat was tilted back and he was pulling an army bag, and there was something waiting in him, and she'd been reeled before she even knew the body possessed that kind of magnetic glory. It was the first time she'd felt there was something to run to instead of something to run away from. Fifteen years old and she felt holy whenever he was kind to her, and sought that out. Curtis was a murderer. How this jammed up against all the rest. How it unravelled things.

She tried to picture it, the river wild and full, the boy fishing, his line undulating through the air, the lure crabbing down through the water, the boy settling in to wait. Edgar had looked so stalwart in Hattie's photograph. He was standing in front of a baby-blue truck, the sky achingly blue too, and his buckle turquoise, his eyes matching the truck, his skin olive, no trace of beard yet, befreckled, legs far apart and solid, and he would stand like that forever, it seemed.

She would have to look at that picture again. Curtis must have shot him in the back, and he would have slumped forward or to the side, unknowing of his own death as it approached. His body lay there, then slid down the bank and floated, the clothes filled with air behind him, and then wicked water until soaked. Edgar's body had not been found, Hattie had said. No nose, no fingers. They had dredged. And there was Curtis at the bus depot claiming status, peace. Martha thought, if it was all true what Hattie claimed, Curtis must have suffered, must have been already suffering then.

She did not know, of course, how Edgar had died. But she could not imagine Curtis shooting Edgar from the front; she could only imagine Curtis killing in the most scared way possible. She pulled out of bed and turned the lamp back on. Her clothing was folded in a pile on the floor. She shook her pants for spiders and put them on, put on her blouse too, and left the door open for light as she made her way down the short hallway. She turned on a lamp in the kitchen, saw the heap of china shards on the table as she passed by, felt bad about breaking that; she sat down and tugged the little drawer in the side table against the wall open, and there were hundreds of images, some bound in elastic, some stray.

A tiny framed shot of a man, the picture shiny, almost three-dimensional; he was naked from the waist up, his arms bridging two old-fashioned gas pumps. He didn't smile for anyone, she could see, stared out like he would sooner die than have this picture taken, and on the back it said, *Hollis, 1939, Route 666!* So this was him.

'Hi-dee-ho.'

Martha couldn't have whirled around faster. The belt. Its dulled silver buckle scrolling around the centre blue; she'd conjured up Edgar, oh Lord. *I found a woman from Canada in the Pecos today. No, I ain't crazy.* This man smiled hungry at Martha. Martha wished she hadn't shown her weakness.

'Edgar?' she said.

'Hell, no, lady.' He was a big man. He'd bearded over all his facial inconsistencies, hair covered most of him. He wore jeans, leather square-toed boots, black as night and highly polished. A fine, pink-piped, black cowboy shirt, gabardine it looked, that ran a bit hollow over his chest, rings on near every finger except the third of his left hand, and that massive silver buckle, which seemed to be there in order to contain the man, yet there was no containing him. She realized the belt buckle was similar to but not the same as the one in the photograph Hattie had shown her. His hand shot out. 'Aubie McCann. I'm pleased to meet you. And you are...?'

'I'm...' He had been in jail. She thought he might break her hand in his.

'What does Curtis want here?'

'He doesn't know I'm here.' She felt as if she might be hit. Thought how this man had known Curtis. 'I snuck away.' *Snuck* was not the right word. 'He doesn't —'

'The hell he don't.'

'He doesn't.' Curtis cried that first time she said she would leave, but she never said where she was going, hadn't really known herself yet. He had prophesied this leaving, though; he might know everything. She wondered again where you bought bullets; if you could buy bullets for such an old gun; she ought to have bullets in the gun, she thought, otherwise it was just an empty shell. Loaded, it might be a sort of talisman against all bad things, and at least it would be complete unto itself, as all things should be.

Her mind went back to when Curtis had found the land, and Benjamin and her and the early Family had moved there and farmed, and Curtis had built the apiaries, moved them all with his speeches, helped them form committees, and helped them know what they wanted, really know it, and have it set down, and they had been humbled toward him, and their own ideals. A community had to move in one direction. Curtis wore white linen so that he looked a little like Christ. What would he advise in just this situation? Prudence. Love, extending hands. Aubie was not beautiful, but she felt he might be one day and she put her hands out reflexively, toward good, toward that possibility. 'I'm sorry,' she said. She did not really know how to behave down here. Jail. She could be a conduit; she could always show him the way.

'The hell.'

Her palms were open. She could feel heaven like a sheath over them; only look, she thought. She noticed her feet were bare, and by her noticing this, Aubie also looked down to her naked feet. The skin on them was rubbed raw from the boots and there were inky blue-black stains creasing them up. They were filthy and broken from all that walking. She smiled at Aubie, a wide smile, and she nodded.

He said, 'Ma found you in the Pecos. What were you doing down there?'

'I thought if I could find you people, I would find out.'

'What? There ain't nothing worth finding out.'

Bones, she thought now. She imagined a rib cage, a tatter of cloth, bleached structure, a jaw smiling; she'd only been trailing the Pecos as a way to find the house, and because she felt easier away from regular folk, and then being down there with the sway of the land, and the trickle of water, she had seen bones, of fish, of larger creatures drowned there, and she'd got to thinking how she could maybe help Curtis amend, as he called it, make him take responsibility, bury this thing, whatever it might be, and with it...

The man in front of her — Aubie McCann — was staring at her, shaking his head; his eyes were wet, and he was pulling back into himself. She said, 'I misjudged. I shouldn't have come. Hattie told me —'

His eyes narrowed. He said, 'We used to swim in that river. Me, Curtis, his brothers, and Colm, and Edgar. We'd strip down and we didn't care; we came out covered in red silt half a mile down where she bends. I knew Curtis since I was a baby. He's a weak one. Hollis was like a puppeteer handling that boy.

Everyone said it was best that he disappeared. I don't know I agreed.'

'Thirty years is a long time,' she said. 'People change.'

'No, they don't.' The smile on this woman, Aubie sank into it without wanting to. This woman was a trap, but he knew himself well enough to know it was a jail he would get inside the pants of. And from the look of it, she wouldn't care one way or the other. Her hands were outstretched like she'd walked off a Bible, and her feet needed a bath. 'No one changes. When was the last time you changed?'

She just stared at him with her palms up, looking good.

'Okay,' Aubie said. She could have it her way. Aubie never moved slow when he could get what he wanted moving fast. And here he was now; he'd seen his mother was out — she was up with Hollis, surely — and Aubie had spoke with his ma earlier, and had known that a woman was here and he drove up to have a look. He leaned over and kissed Martha and then again, like he meant it, though he wasn't sure whether he ever meant anything, not really. He was always just all show and feeling good and worrying about it later.

He was getting hard for this woman and all she thought she knew and all she didn't know. Well, she didn't seem to know too much. He liked it that she was getting on in years and had her body still. He liked her hairdo that made her look like she was trying. But mostly she could kiss. And she wasn't fat. That counted for something too. He stopped to say, 'I been to jail on account of all this. I guess you don't know much about that.' Some women liked ex-cons, he had found. Some women liked fixing things.

Martha could think of nothing to say. Her eyes grew wide thinking how it must be true, Aubie in jail, and here he was, the product of jail time and whatever else. She recalled driving out of Albuquerque and seeing men dressed in orange coveralls —

the same type of coveralls the Family wore to do heavy chores — but these men were moving slow and steady through the highway median, stabbing pop cans and takeout bags with long thin poles and putting this garbage in sturdy green bags. And then she'd read the huge sign: *Albuquerque State Penitentiary: Do not pick up hitchhikers for the next 5 miles.* There was a loneliness to those men, a dreamy sorrow as they turned now and then toward the traffic and gaped. Who were these men? she had thought at the time, and what had they done, could they be saved? 'For what?' she said.

'Armed robbery.'

'Why did you just kiss me?'

'I wanted to, and because I could.' Aubie sat down on the bench at the table, put a plastic bag down, and tugged the corner; a couple of steaks in a Styrofoam tray, all wrapped up in plastic, slid out, flesh sucked onto the plastic window, and she salivated from hunger.

'You always do just what you want?' That kiss had gone right down her legs, freezed up her cunt; she knew he'd liked it. She smiled at him, she had made an honest step toward him. She knew he'd felt it too. He was as good as caught.

Aubie rustled the plastic, turned on the stove. He plunked a cast-iron pan down and flipped the steaks from the Styrofoam into it. Then meat. The smell. 'Get some iron in you,' he said. The white tray was beside him on the counter, plastic wrap torn, bloodied in a little heap there too. 'Mother been feeding you tea?'

'I don't mind,' Martha said.

'She ain't got any money to speak of.' He stared at Martha's hands, her feet. He pulled a cassette out of his back pocket and then there was music oozing out the Panasonic player bolted at the bottom of Hattie's kitchen cupboard. *In a town this size.* There were two thick rib-eyes in the pan and the butter was on its way to black, no garlic, no pepper, just cow. 'John Prine,' he said, and then, 'No, ma'am. I don't always do whatever I want; I have self-control.' Martha'd never met someone like this.

'Well, I have no self-control,' she said. 'That's what Curtis always says.'

'He know you go around kissing other fellows? He don't mind?'

She shook her head, said the standard: 'He's not here.' He was back at the farm, she thought, crying — no. He was back to normal, the Family was busy making candles, tending the spring hives, turning the garden; the candles were lining up and Benjamin was rubbing Ida's belly. Martha should go back to the farm and forget this. She felt like Curtis was looking in at her, imploring her to come home, and angry too; there would be repercussions. There was a special room in the sleep-house for realignments. Martha cringed when she thought about it.

'I saw that,' Aubie said.

'I'm just cold.' Curtis would approve of her kissing Aubie. Love spreads, he liked to say, so spread it. The cleansing would be self-imposed, to bring herself back rightly. Nothing more. Heaven was right there to look at. Aubie'd gone out the door. She heard a truck door slam and considered he might be leaving, but no, he came back. 'You want beer with your meal?'

Aubie was holding up a six-pack. He had elegant fingers, even if they were etched with grime, and his nails were perfect little rectangles, cut straight but black to the flesh underneath. He was wearing that fine cowboy shirt, gabardine, and she tossed back and forth what it could mean, wearing his best — she tossed whether it was his best — shirt. He handed her a beer and pulled out a pack of cigarillos. There were two short benches at Hattie's kitchen table and they sat there. Aubie pulled a handkerchief from his pocket and worked the dust from the crevice between boot and sole.

'It hasn't rained proper in years.'

And after that a wide silence opened up and Aubie wanted to let it stretch and then he rose and pulled plates off a shelf near the sink and placed a steak, a knife and fork on each, and that was all. Martha put her hands out over the table and Aubie stared down at them, unsure what to do, and she said, 'A blessing on this meal,' and shook her palms so that he'd know to hold her.

There was a kind warmth coming off her hands when he grabbed at them that he put down to body heat, and he could only half listen to her. 'Lord, help us not to fight Your crushing, Your bruising, Your smiting. Help us not to quench that beautiful song, even when it's sad; help us to thank You in spite of the sorrow.' Shit, he thought, oh, shit. This lady was crazy.

They ate. She did not look up but focused on the flavour, the thin sweetness of the blood as it rolled over her tongue; she did not notice he was watching her. Aubie was still eating long after she was done. Then she watched him, amazed at the length of time it could take the man to swallow.

'I cooked mine good and well; I like a strong chew.'

'You were in jail,' she said. It had something to do with Curtis, with the unravelling of this thing. She wanted to know how the one thing, the shooting, meant other things. But it was like scar tissue that built up, and pulled, shifting what happened in all directions. Her mouth gaped a bit and she tried to avoid his eyes but couldn't. He watched her like he had days.

'I was everyone's scapegoat,' he said, then, 'You don't drink?'

Martha shook her head by way of saying sorry, taking a sip anyhow, though it was disallowed and strange to her taste.

'It don't matter, not the drink or the scapegoating. I was happy to do it. It gave me a chance to school some, and mull over the facts as they seemed to lay out in front of me. Five years from my sixteenth to my twenty-first year. Kept me out of trouble.'

She thought about those men collecting garbage. 'You were a baby.'

'No, ma'am, I wasn't. I was a shit-disturber, convicted for this robbery and that and every damn unsolved break-and-enter in the history of the county. Well, I *had* participated in any number of those crimes and a few not listed; retribution is what I heard Hollis called it. "We all make mistakes, but we don't all got to pay." That's what I heard Hollis said. Hollis told me he'd make it up one way or another, though the cards are out on whether he ever really has or will.' Aubie was trying not to smile, and then he did, and he had a deep dimple running down his cheek under his beard. 'And the food? You never tasted anything like that food,' he said.

The steak they were eating had no real flavour other than blood and a tinge of animal rot; it wasn't an animal that'd been cared for in its life. Martha hadn't tasted anything lively about it, no integrity, is what Curtis would have said. No energy. No Scorpio in Venus. She said, 'I've been living on a sort of farm these last thirty years.'

And Aubie about choked to hell on that mouthful he gnawed at. 'Curtis's a farmer?'

'Bees. Honey. Honeycomb.'

'Now that's a good one.'

'Uh-huh. Biodynamic.'

'Never was much one for science —'

'It's more religion than science.' She regretted saying this. Explaining things to outside people never amounted to much, and besides, there were always Curtis's eyes behind the explanation, like he was a custodian of the body earth, of God's grace. And the guilt bloomed like that.

'Never was a churchgoer neither,' Aubie said. 'And I can't see Curtis there.'

'He isn't a churchgoer so much.' Curtis was more of a church than a churchgoer, how the Family came to him, how there had been people desiring him for what he could offer them, for the way he could find the good side of bad, for his sweet looks, his charm, his hope. There was no church at Soltane, of course; every man was his own church. Martha should have stayed put in that beautiful place. She felt suddenly sorry for Aubie. Beyond the fact he'd been in jail, and that his brother was dead, it was that he did not Know. She said, 'Curtis has this Glory to him.'

'God Glory, you mean?' Aubie said. 'Oh, hell.' He knew there were guys in jail that found it, and there were those that lost it, but nothing anyone found or lost changed anything. Aubie popped a large hunk of meat into his mouth, shoved it to his cheek. Nowadays everyone was holding tight like the Apocalypse was upon them. Well, hallelujah. Bring it on. He muttered, 'A bunch of backward brown little fuckers drive some airplanes into a couple of buildings and all of a sudden God has arrived. Big times calls for big measures, I guess. But I don't buy it.'

The news of this world event had filtered through Soltane. She had herself hitchhiked across the border, walked through New York City, seen the glint of the sun and her own reflection on all the buildings left standing. She'd gone down to Ground Zero and gaped at the hole, what looked not unlike the quarry, and had been alarmed by a large black woman at the mouth of the subway screaming that Christ loved her, and that Christ had died for her, that Christ wanted her to repent. Her own God was more sensual — He had His hands on her, loved her so — and Martha had walked on, had meant to walk the whole distance here, but exhaustion intervened and so she had begged, and handed out pamphlets for donations, and taken buses and hitchhiked, and finally bought a wreck for a hundred dollars, driving herself across and through Nauvoo, then Albuquerque, any place Curtis had mentioned that she could remember.

'Two thousand and one was a hallmark year for God,' he said.

'That's a rough thing to say,' she said.

He stopped mid-chew, not expecting the scold. 'Damn straight,' Aubie said. 'Call a spade a spade; someone has to do it.' He looked at her. She was pale and thin. She was older than she looked. She wasn't so much pampered as preserved, he thought. There was something else about her he couldn't put his finger on. 'Resources is what it's all about, darlin'. Oil. Water. You met old Hollis yet?'

'No,' she said, and then in some misguided attempt to placate something in him, 'He's a lapsed Mormon, isn't he?'

'Curtis tell you that?' said Aubie. He was laughing. 'I don't suppose Hollis has had a pure Mormon thought since he was a child. He's a picker and a chooser, that man.' Aubie got water going in a kettle on the back of the stove and soon it was boiling so that the lid bounced. He could feel in his heart he shouldn't have brought up Hollis; his heart felt stiff. That man still owned everyone, whether they liked it or not. Hollis Woolf was the point they rotated around, though Aubie did try hard not to. 'Hollis's daddy was a Mormon, but he quit too.'

Aubie took a scoop of cold water from the bucket on the floor and mixed it with the boiled water in the sink. 'You know,' he said as the soap bubbles were rising up and he began to wash the dishes, 'I suppose there's only one good way to solve international problems. The trigger — truth from a double barrel.' Aubie glanced at her, wondered whether her squirrelly look signified disgust or fear. He said, 'Curtis go back with the Mormons then?'

'No,' Martha said. 'No.' She was thinking about the gunsmith shop in the old pioneer village of Nauvoo, thinking about the Browning too. She wondered if she could ever shoot a gun, if she had the strength, or the weakness, for it. She would look for bullets, at least. It could not be hard to find them.

Curtis wasn't like Aubie. Nor was he like those people in Nauvoo. She'd asked after his lineage in the archive building there. His grandfather had been excommunicated for sexual misconduct; the archivist had turned pink saying it.

Martha turned away from Aubie and said, 'I think Curtis took from it what he could make sense of.' She was thinking that he had taken the idea of communal living, of family, of cleaving to one's people, of knowing where you came from. Curtis charted everything, the cattle they owned, the seeds, the Family already in a third generation; he would chart the bees if he could keep proper track of them. There was consolation in order, he always said. No one of the Family ever dared wonder aloud about his real family before.

'The only God Hollis would ever let him pray to was the God of crude and guns; Curtis did his preaching out of the old man's earshot,' Aubie muttered.

His jeans were tight; he had the John Prine on loop.

'Had some wacky notions back then. Obedience was a big one; I didn't hold much to that. If I didn't hate Curtis, I'd feel sorry for him, I guess.'

She thought about the gun again then, about guns. It had fascinated her to learn about rifling, and to see the simple wooden dowel contraption that rifled the gun barrels. Brother Dwight had asked her whether she was an LDS, and she had said, 'What?' and he had explained, Latter-day Saint, a Mormon. He had seemed so happy about the prospect. She'd said, 'No,' because what the Family did was something higher; she saw that. Brother Dwight looked as if he might cry. Martha stared at Aubie's butt shifting back and forth.

'You like that?'

'Sorry.'

'Don't sorry me, lady.' Aubie had turned around, but he was laughing, still dancing — a two-step solo. 'Tell me. Whyever did you come here, anyway?' She knew by the way he said it, staring at her hard, that he'd been saving that question up for some time. 'You came through Mormon country? What are you searching for? There's nothing to find here.' He stopped dancing then and looked at her, miserably. 'You didn't do the famed Mormon Hope Trail.'

She had walked a piece of it, along the Mississippi, figuring south was south. She hadn't thought too much about how the Mormons had fled down that path when their homes were torched. Fled to sanctity. Martha fiddled with the edge of her blouse. 'I didn't know it was all that famed,' she said and wondered what was in store for her, whether there would ever be an end to her walking other people's paths, hope trails, hope, what have you. She didn't know why she seemed to be disappointing this man; she'd only just met him. She didn't dare apologize, as that had seemed to annoy him. He was grinning at her now.

'What I mean is famed in the family legacy. Oh, how the Mormons suffered — like that. I suppose Curtis went on about old Joe Smith and how the Woolfs are directly related; he used to preach at us when we were kids, down by the river, and we would sit there like dumb cows looking up.'

Martha wondered why this upset him. Curtis was wonderful to listen to. She wished Curtis had told her more about all this, but he had told her so very little that she'd begun to revere what he *had* said. She was uncomfortable talking about what she knew from Curtis. Each bit of information had become a sacred clue to the big picture. Martha said, 'I went to Old Nauvoo, to the pioneer village. That's all. I found it interesting. Curtis talked of lineage sometimes. I thought I would see.' Curtis would be looking for her, she suddenly hoped it.

Aubie was talking. 'You know the Muslims do that. They trace their ancestors back to a prophet. They chart it all going back. It's crap, don't get you any deeper into the story, so forget it.' And he could see all over her face that he'd messed up before he finished talking. 'Forget that, lady. Like I said before, there ain't no story —'

'I don't forget —' And she knew now for certain there was a story, and that Aubie held it.

'Oh, yes, you will. I'll make you.' He was fast. He leaned into her and bent over her and took up her mouth in his again, and took up her tit in the palm of his hand; he swung his leg over the bench, over her, like she was a horse and he was a movie cowboy, and it was so damn funny, it charmed her. The kiss was fine and the hand, this new, blackened hand on her breast, was good. 'Ain't got bees, but I got honey,' Aubie said. And Martha thought she was going to die jubilant, laughing. 'What're you laughing at?'

'Oh, nothing.' It was lovely he believed she would forget. 'Nothing.'

'Nothing is right. Curtis ever talk to you about old Hollis?'

'No.'

'Tell.'

She didn't know what she knew. She could feel Curtis's disappointed eyes, and the expectant faces of the Family at Meeting. She must try harder, she must acquiesce more fully, perfect herself. She would lock the sleep-house room from the inside and sit for hours in the dark praying; she would scratch her skin with a tool they had for that, slowly, and increasingly harder, and bring that toward prayer too. It was like a homeopathic remedy; a pain to remind one to come back unto Him.

The method was rarely used, or needed, but sometimes, when a member fled and wanted to return, it was the only way to ensure renewed fealty. To help forget the outside people. It would likely be necessary in her case, she reasoned.

'What were you doing all this time with the bees and Curtis? What was it you were doing?'

He watched her face retreat; she didn't like these questions, shook her head, then she deflected: 'What do *you* do for work?'

And he held up his oil-creased hands. 'Derricks.' He did not mention his carpet dealings. He made little off it, and it wasn't anybody's business. He said, 'And I'll tell you something. I'll give you some advice. My brother Edgar ain't your concern, so you can quit wasting your time on that bullcrap.' And then Aubie ran his hand down her sternum, along her belly.

Five

The Guadalupe County Long-Term Care Facility was brand new, just south of where the old gas station used to thrive, and Hollis sometimes looked out and watched scrub slowly push through the bitumen. Hollis didn't look out much though. He was waiting. He'd sent his postcard and settled back, waiting for the boy.

He knew Curtis was on the way out, a father knows. Hollis just sat there all day, with extra oxygen by his bed, wheeled himself out for a smoke when he craved one, and drank in private through each day. 'Save me from myself,' he said. Well, it was more a wheeze. He tried not to move. The less he moved, the less it hurt. The eczema was atrocious; his skin was droughted. There were scales on his scales. The whole expanse of Hollis's back and even down the soft folds of his enormous, vulnerable belly, where it joined his pelvis, was afflicted with curls of red, flaking dead cells.

Most of his kin never came to visit. People'd lost what little interest they had for him, he figured. What good was family when you serve and protect them their livelong days and they hate you for it? They did hate him with a kind of fearfulness, he knew that. They'd went off to unthinkable corners of the country, and in their suburban boxes, out in fields better suited to cattle and derricks, they'd hid themselves from him. Maeve's boys, that is, not Hattie's, not Colm and Aubie. They still came by once in a while. Well, Colm came by out of Catholic duty, and Aubie sent regards from time to time. And there was someone else too, some shadow visitor of late — just the other night, some nighttime guest who would not identify himself. But it didn't matter; Hollis would find out sooner or later, and he wasn't scared of no shadow.

Everyone had ran off with their remnants of Hollis, their enragements, their holding and holding until they couldn't no more. None of it newsworthy — just that one hits the wife, the other the children, and for days there would be a softening, a public churchy confession, say, a chastening, the aftershocks. Oh, he heard the gossip one way or another, word came back to him eventually. He could still work up a fury when he heard what some of them were up to. Well, it wasn't like he hadn't tried to help them get strong and able-bodied. It wasn't for lack of trying. And anyway, it was all past and gone. None of them boys figured any more. Well, except Curtis did. He missed that boy: Curtis of the everlasting joy, of the perfect silences, of the boyishness. The chosen one.

And my God, how Curtis had loved him in return, it was a gift. How old would he be now? He liked to think on Curtis. That boy had riled it all up, hadn't he? Hollis was proud of that child if he was proud of anything he'd done in his life. The fourth son of Maeve's, and Hollis already calling him the seventh son, even if he wasn't; cracking jokes at the devil, is what Maeve dared whisper.

The boy was born on the kitchen floor in one or two low, grunting heaves, an event so lacking in drama that people said Maeve had a hard time bonding with the creature when he did emerge. Well, she was so dead tired and malnourished trying to keep the weight down, she might be excused; the child had an aguey pastiness to him, and the summer heat didn't help matters. An honest man had to work hard to make a go of things. Maeve was so run ragged with the diner and the other children that it was Hollis who would come in from the pumps and scrape the frost out of the faulty pop fridge and run ice along the boy's little arms.

'Settles the kid right down.' Hollis watched the cold brand baby Curtis, icy yellow skin against the feverish red. 'Ain't he hot, though; you'd have to say the devil had him in his grips from the minute he was born.' The child roamed with his eyes back and forth in a way that seemed to capture everything that went on. He was eye roving to signal he was listening. God, his eyes followed even the conversation outside, far off by the pumps and also in the little mechanic shop. Kid was memorizing, so it seemed. Hollis took to racing through the customers so he could be with the boy, watch him watch.

'That boy is yours if he's anyone's.' That's the sort of thing the regulars took to saying. 'Yours entirely.' And Hollis half believed it at first, and then with time, he entirely did. He began to keep Curtis by him like he was some charm, handling him with grease-dirty fingers, so the child was swaddled in thickened, oil-salved blankets. Maeve knew she'd lost him one Sunday when she came out with the others, them all dressed in gingham and paisley cotton, the shirts and dresses handmade, the jeans purchased by distance and sent by post, turned up at the ankle, as was the fashion. The children were dour, in a line behind her, and she came forward to the pump with a basket and a layette. Hollis didn't even look up from what he was doing. 'The boy'll stay here with his pa.'

'It's a church-day, Hollis.'

'Not for this one. He'll get all the faith he'll ever need right here in the yard. I can't save everyone, but I can save my own.'

'Hollis.' Maeve's voice was low, but her body showed its resignation; a younger woman would fight for this, a braver woman, some other woman. Maeve was not one hundred pounds. She had no bosom to speak of any more and her feet pressed into her good shoes against the packed dirt of the yard. Someone honked a car horn.

'Hollis, I —'

'He needs to be God-fearing; he don't need to be church-fearing. You go ahead and pray for us, Lady Maeve.' He moved over to her, gruff. 'Come here,' he said and held her so she lifted in the air. The children looked in wonder. They could not see their own mother so wrapped was she in his arms. Hollis squeezed her until there was just the hint of pain, and then a little tighter; the children saw her face draw into itself. Everyone would behave then. There wasn't time nor cause for anything else as far as he was concerned. He placed her back on the earth and she smiled to save face, smiled and called for the children to follow. She was a lady.

There was a line of cars waiting for service, and Hollis ignored them for a bit, watching his brood stride and toddle off down to the prayer house, swinging the basket gently back and forth. Then he turned to the file of automobiles. 'Who's the asshole honked at my family?' he said. A young boy standing out away from his daddy's car stared solemnly at Hollis until he looked like his eyes might bust right open, and then he started and pointed out his own pa.

'Get the hell out of my station,' Hollis said to the man. 'I ain't going to serve you, mister.' And then Hollis got to work, and did not look up to watch the fellow leave, to see the derision on the man's face, nor the tears that coursed down the boy's blistering cheek, where his pa had slapped him hard, nor did he see the gob of spit the man horked at him, until it landed close by his boot.

Hollis glanced over at Curtis to make sure he was safe. There was no reason he wouldn't be safe, but still Hollis checked on him reflexively from time to time. The child's arms had wrestled out from the cotton wrap and were waving in the air, passing through a sunbeam and the shadow of the second pump, as if trying to latch on to something. He was in his portable bassinet; Hollis had made the thing out of a dolly and a washtub and an old wooden wagon pull, so as he could roll Curtis over the yard wherever he was moving to himself. The child was making cooing noises. Curtis was not three months, but it looked as if he was older owing to the sickly thinness of him; his arms were like sticks, the elbow bones pressed out the very skin of him.

'— *and anointed with oil many that were sick, and healed them.*' Hollis murmured this under his breath as the last vehicle drove off — a hodgepodge truck some enterprising easterner had cobbled together from a spent old Model T, some other hunk of metal, and a number of fruit crates he'd now be returning to California. As the owner had said, 'If the wreck makes her there.'

Hollis murmured, '— *and anointed with oil.*' He was stuck on this Bible passage, as it had got him thinking. He went over to the boy, tiny Curtis, whose skin was hot to burn at the touch. Hollis considered going into the Sunday-closed diner, considered opening up the pop refrigerator and rasping off some more of that snow growing inside the lid and rubbing Curtis down with it. But then he reconsidered as the phrase '*anointed with*' and then '*and healed them, and healed them, and healed them*' looped in his brain, like a joyous lasso.

'I know what I'll do for you, this church day.' He pressed his fat scaly finger down on the child's stomach where the ribs met in an upside-down V, pressed and heard the little gasp of air he was pushing out. 'Don't you love your pa?' There was a metal can of spent motor oil in the shop that he was after. The boy weighed nothing as he rolled him in the bassinet. The big eyes shocked when first Hollis began to move but then settled in to the motion, kept as still as you please. Hollis didn't know whether the boy was too scared to move or whether he was enjoying the ride; you didn't always know with the young ones what they were thinking.

Damn, it was hot. Hollis hovered over the oilcan in the cool shadow of the mechanic shop. '*If any of you is sick, they should call out to the elders to come and pray over them and anoint them with oil —*' He stopped because he didn't remember the rest. Had a brief thought he might be quoting the old Book of Mormon from his childhood and not Maeve's Holy Bible. Then he reasoned it didn't much matter. God was God, wasn't he? The baby looked on with solemn eyes. Hollis thought, Sacred is what them eyes are.

He leaned over and scooped a lick of thick grease onto his index finger, pulled the cloth off the boy to reveal his hot, hot skin, and began to work. The black oil went brownish as he swirled it over the baby's skin. There wasn't a patch left on the kid when he was done; he even went carefully under the balls and into the crevices of his body making sure there wasn't any piece he had missed.

Then he held Curtis up all tarred like that, out in the yard; there was no chance of a witness, they were all at church, that false church of tithes and beaten-down priests masquerading as conduits when it should be apparent to anyone that the only conduit was the self. But nobody had much intuition no more. Hell. There was only one way to travel to God, as far as Hollis cared; moving in a car, that was the proper vehicle. Hollis held Curtis up to the sun, by way of the pumps, and sang out his hallelujahs. The baby was looking at him in such a way Hollis began to feel unnerved though, like the baby had some under-standing.

'I done it. I done it.' Hollis shouted in spite of the boy, shouted for a full minute before his own face went red, and then held the boy to his chest and coddled him, wiping what he could of the oil off onto his own shirt, and then hurriedly heating water back in the kitchen sink and lathering castor soap in order to clean him before Maeve should come home. He winked at the baby when he was finished and said, 'It's too late to take it away; we got you good, didn't we?' Curtis was already asleep, a thin curl of oil still smeared into his left nostril; breathing oil that kid was, his whole young life.

The old folks' home was not quiet at night. Hollis couldn't sleep too good. The skin on him ached. He was twitchy. The scabs did seem to shift around his body. They migrated to and away from his genitals. He suffered it under his armpits. Over the years he had grown used to being in a state of heated itchiness and found he could locate certain rhythms in his body that would shift the sensation out his fingers if only he could concentrate.

He swore he could feel his blood circulating through his veins, actually feel the warmth and the flow of it. Hell, by the time he'd turned thirty, he was medically declared lichenous. He resembled a tree that had become a host for small, shelflike fungi. But mercifully, his face was clear. Well, what they said about old people was true, he figured, that they didn't need so much sleep. Anyway, he went in and out of it through the night. People dying made a lot of noise, and he woke easily, his brain negotiating what was going on around him.

It was eleven p.m. Visitors weren't allowed at night unless it was close to the dying end, and he sure wasn't there yet. But he could sense someone again in his room. Hollis could make out, against the curtain, the outline of a body inside his room; there was a shadow over by the window. The security light outside in the parking lot gave the person a glow around the perimeter. It was a big fellow, Hollis saw. 'What do you want?' The form didn't move or speak and Hollis closed his eyes, wondering whether he was really awake, and whether in all his life he had ever really stopped to wonder whether anything ever came back to haunt a person and whether it now might. It wasn't his worst nightmare. He wasn't scared; he said that to himself.

'What do you want? I said.' Hollis found he was whispering and considered that he didn't want the resident nurse to come in, especially if he was imagining this. 'No visitors allowed,' he said. 'Goddamn.' The figure did not move and Hollis felt himself tense. He lay as still as he could and stared at the place against the curtain. 'Who?' But the form did not speak or move. 'Aub?' The form seemed to be larger than Aubie, but it had something of Aubie to it. But Aubie never came around, and why would he?

Hollis pondered this, wondering every now and again whether it had moved or whether he had seen the rise and fall of breath around the form's shoulder area. Did ghosts breathe? He'd never asked himself this sort of question. He thought, What might I be about to pay for? and his mind went back far, really back far. Edgar's face kept popping into the mental viewfinder; he didn't like to think why.

When was that bad time, was that 1970 or so? He didn't know what to do after that. It had been a bad time, sacrificing one child to protect the rest; he was the one responsible for the entire brood, and no mouths were going to be fed if he wasn't around to feed them. Hell, he didn't like it; no one who knew what had happened thought he liked what he'd had to do. First time Hollis had ever been lost, felt like a strayed beast that'd got so nerve-racked it didn't remember home. He blamed the damn road, then the damn government for not respecting a man's right to keep a family, life and limb, together.

Hollis had just painted the front of the diner a rich teal blue, detailed a rookery along the top, like a battlement on a castle. He could already see the future pretty good. 'This road's the lifeline. It's gonna connect up all the money dots. There's no going back on progress.' His was an adobe castle mechanic shop, with an add-on castle diner. Maeve deserved that; he could see her smile still, a wide, pretty smile that made him feel pressed up against goodness.

'Goddamn lifeline, this road.' He said shit like this to anyone accommodating enough to listen. Now it was to a certain Henk Parsens, who'd already inside five minutes told Hollis how he'd lost his farm squat three months earlier and along with that, due to malnutrition and bad luck, a daughter to heaven and then his wife, who decided for better chances with her folks back home, up north. Henk didn't care about anything but just kept on moving so as not to settle, so as not to have time to think much.

'A deathline is more like it,' he said.

'What's that you say?' Hollis was getting gas for the fellow.

'This road's but an artery west or east, with more sadness and false hope than I care to say. If that's what you mean by lifeline, I guess I agree.' The man watched Hollis tap the nozzle and swipe the last drip of gas into the tank, watched Hollis flinch a little at what he just said, and waited for the ricochet. 'I got people — friends and relations — up and down this road, trying to make a living, and that ain't no kind of living.'

'That'll be two dollars and fifty-five cents,' Hollis said. Hollis never gave a deal nor credit on the gasoline. He stood at the pump, his feet just over where the reservoirs were, and he imagined the depletion. It wasn't more than a week since they'd filled them tanks up and Hollis could sense it all running dry; dry worried him. He was never more satisfied than on the day the tanker came and replenished. It was like his skin even flushed out in health. 'I can spot you a coffee, though.'

'Coffee and a slice of pie sounds right.' Henk pulled a thin bill clip out of his sock. His leg was purple veins, patchy black hairs, and filth accumulating above the sock line. Two one-dollar bills ate into the stack considerably. The quarters came out of a jar tucked under the passenger seat. Henk wrapped the bills around the quarters, made it into a box, and tried to hand the money over to Hollis without coming into contact with the man, like there was instinct there he seemed not to fathom yet could not deny. Hollis thanked Henk without looking at him, turned, and nodded to the next in line.

The door to the diner was propped open, and Henk was almost through it to the counter when Hollis called after him in an almost girlish whine, 'Pie's extra. No free pie.' Henk's stomach clenched realigning for the now inevitable wait until its next meal. He drank down a coffee smoother than any he'd had in weeks and thanked the wife of that man outside. Maeve told Hollis all this later, told him everything, always, and he wouldn't have it no other way. Now, she was watching this man like she needed to learn him; she never felt good around the walking poor, like it might rub off.

'Much obliged for the coffee. That's some coffee, missus.'

'It's just what I make,' Maeve said.

'Well, you make the most of it then.'

'Tell your friends.'

Henk was looking out through the aluminum window at Hollis. Maeve could see Hollis's back. His arms were poking out of a shirt that was too small. She wished that he'd wear button-down shirts and dark jackets when he worked, add some class to things, like they did at some of the other gas bar operations, but he wouldn't. His arms were massive flaking things that seemed to squeeze themselves out of the short-sleeved T-shirt; she flinched a bit watching him, out of habit. It looked like a dirty undershirt too, but Hollis did not care. And she knew that. Maeve did make the most of most everything. Hollis sensed them watching and glanced over. He saw Henk looking back up at Maeve and imagined him thinking she looked nothing like his own wife that ran away; here was a staying sort of woman. He was right. Maeve wasn't going nowhere.

There was a boy in front of him, well, a young man. Hollis liked the fresh face and the short hair and the overall eagerness of the blond boy. He had half a mind to offer him a bit of part-time work if the fella cared to, pay was pretty good, and he was just about to ask when the boy started to go on about some road they was going to dig and build, never mind the 66 wasn't even close to being clean and done with.

'What road?'

'North of here, I heard. She's to replace the old road, make transit a bit more central to the state. I might ask for work there. I'm thinking about it. Stands to reason work will fall away down here.'

'I haven't heard of no road, son.'

'Well,' the boy laughed, swung his chin at the diner. 'The husband is always the last to know, I guess.'

Hollis glanced at the diner window and saw Henk Parsens in there with Maeve. That piece of nothing hadn't wanted to touch him, had wrapped his coin up like it was a gift from the gods, had assumed a piece of tart with his free coffee. Henk was leaning over the counter, was breathing into his wife. Didn't matter; Maeve wouldn't sense a man's attention even if he was pawing at her. Hollis ought to know. 'I still haven't heard about no road,' he said, after some thought.

'We'll build her and you come sail on her. Move your business up there. You sure better do.'

Hollis slammed the nozzle into the boy's car and tied the handle with a rope he had rigged, to free him up while the thing filled. There was a bolt stuck good on a car in the shop he felt he had the strength now to loosen. He turned away and then turned back. 'I could always use a hand here, part-time.'

'Thank you, sir. I'll take my chances on the interstate.'

Hollis considered chances. Considered who might have a hand in this new road, and a stake in things going bad for Hollis Woolf. There were too many possibilities. He looked up into the diner as he walked by and saw Henk sipping coffee like a body could skirt starvation with that silt and stave it off. Sipping like a skittish fool. And later Hollis knew why, for God rest her soul, Maeve never could keep a secret from him when he wanted that secret told. Maeve had waited until Hollis had passed from sight and cut a slice of cherry pie for this man. From time to time, she told Hollis, she baked one pie extra and hid it away from Hollis.

She said Hollis didn't need to know he was being saved, so long as he was. When she told him this, he'd slammed her into the table, where her hair caught fire on a candle burning there. She ran screaming, the flame licking the air behind her out into the desert night, and he had watched a while in wonderment, nodding, thinking it beautiful, thinking how much pain she was causing him in her disobedience. And then he'd made his way slowly to the well and got the pump going so she could douse herself, and then he held her like he loved her, and she said, 'Sorry.' He did love her, a possessing kind of love that felt right to him.

But that was later, after Henk left, after the boy left. This is what Maeve had relayed to him. That right at the time that Hollis was learning about the new interstate highway, Curtis came in and stood behind her then, fourteen and tall as he'd ever get, and just stared, mouth open, at Henk eating a thick slice of pie.

'School's done, Curtis?' Maeve knew he was there, even without looking.

'Yeah.'

'Take over from your father then.'

'I could use a piece of pie too, I guess.'

'What did I tell you?'

'Yes.'

Henk ate and thanked again and said she made the most of it again and she ignored him while he left, preferring instead to watch Curtis walk out toward Hollis and witnessing his alikeness to his pa and his not alikeness. 'I do not make the most of it,' Maeve said to the percolator. She sat down and pulled her shoes off, stretched and pointed her feet; the arch was still perfect.

Outside, Henk Parsens was already choking the engine to go and then he was gone, never to be seen around again. There were many a soul dead along the waysides of that road, Maeve thought, and he could end up one. Or else he might meet success or just keep living whether he wanted to or not; that was for the Lord to say. The Lord had the final say in pretty much all cases, hers included. Curtis's too.

Through the diner window, Maeve watched Curtis move around the pumps, lithe and young and still boy-pretty, anticipating anything Hollis might need and doing it before the asking brought up Hollis's malice. She'd watched Curtis hone this over the years until he was the manifestation of Hollis's wishes; it was a joy to watch a boy care so for his father, she'd said to Hollis, but still, watching it gave her misgivings. She had misgivings all the time about those two. Maeve had lifted her feet up, one at a time, and with her hand pressed the toes toward the heels, then released them into her shoes and gone outside.

Her husband and her son were moving around each other in a manly dance; wiping windows, their hands, the nozzle, with the sun, the dirt, the fat and the thin bodies in motion. And when Hollis had questioned this and that, the little holes he found in her telling, later on, she did break down and admit about the pie. Dared admit how if she ever had loved Hollis she could not recall when. And he had thrown her at the wooden table and watched her flame up. Misgivings, crap. It was Maeve needed a realignment. He'd kept her away from church to show her who was boss.

But there they were, he and Curtis moving around the gas pumps in their ungodly dance, and there was Maeve watching, and what was family but this? Hollis could cry thinking about the past at its best, when it was just him, and the older boys and the little ones in the back biking around, and Maeve cooking and the stream of cars, and the earth below him filled with liquid gold, damned fine treasure. And then that ugly Henk shutting down his joy, and that blond boy with that deathline prediction, and that stolen pie, and his damn wife needing a lesson, and quick.

'Can I bring you out some coffee — you're too busy to stop for it?'

'News is what I have.' Hollis was pent up. His shoulders had shifted along his neck and his skin was flaring, beginning to redden. 'What that fella just told me is they're building a new highway, north, bypassing my pumps; the government has new friends and the money flows in that direction, I suppose.' He looked over at Maeve, said, 'What were you doing, anyways, with that a-hole?'

Hollis was slowly wiping his hands on a gasoline-soaked rag. He pressed the rag around each finger and ran it down, rubbing against any grease or crude he'd picked up from the engines. He was fully focused on it, cleaning until the surface skin was rubbed clean and only the cracks held trails of black. His face had grown fatter with the concentration; the red anxiety of his neck accentuated rings of flaking skin, great looping rings that moved up from his collarbone and filigreed his larynx, like the skin of a shedding snake. He was working at a crease of teal paint on his pinky. 'I'm heading out for this evening.'

'I made supper for the crew of you, Hollis.'

'I won't be expected nowhere.'

'It would be nice, is what I meant. Curtis? Wouldn't it be nice?' Maeve looked deep at Curtis's eyes, but he had them turned off. Hollis had taught him good. His eyes were implacable. Curtis stood beside Hollis and for a long time didn't say anything. What could he say? Hollis had extended his plan and it was Curtis's job to help implement it.

'Curtis?'

'Yes, Ma?'

'Wouldn't it be good if your father stayed in this one night?'

'It would be fine, yes.'

But Hollis pushed through the diner door to the backroom. He dropped his trousers in a greasy heap on the office floor and tugged on a clean pair he pulled from the closet. Maeve and Curtis were standing outside when he walked by them, saying, 'I'm gone tonight then; you be the man for this time, Curtis.'

'With no one around to teach him man skills,' is what Maeve muttered, low. Even Curtis did not hear, but Hollis heard. He heard everything, all the time.

'He'll learn by watching, if he didn't already learn.' Hollis took Maeve's arms, one in each big hand, and held her still. 'Honey,' he said, 'I'll deal with you later.'

Then he took the straight route through brush along the river to find Hattie. He did not find her at the adobe so he wandered upstream for a time, not finding her there either. An hour searching passed and he was becoming frustrated, thrashing at trees with a stick he had picked up and roaring at the tumbling river as it sought gravity; there was no one to hear him. He backtracked after a time and found Hattie in the kitchen of her little home, their three boys looking up at him when he walked in.

'Where you been?' And she had just looked sidelong at him and not answered. Wasn't any of his business, now was it.

Hollis turned on Aubie then; at least this one could be counted on to listen. 'What's so interesting?'

'Nothing, sir.' Aubie looked away. Hollis liked that child.

'You going fishing.' Hollis pulled a string of flies out of a handkerchief and laid it on the table. He cocked his head fast by way of telling the boys to scram, and they could take a hint. Then it was just Hollis and Hattie standing in the kitchen. It was smaller with the boys gone. Hattie had on a light blue cotton dress that looked like the sun had been at it. There was a stain from bacon grease. 'You got something on your tittie.' Hollis made like he was going to wipe it off and Hattie slapped his hand away. 'Hell, darling,' he said. 'I need you.'

'Hollis. What are you doing skulking around my house in the middle of the afternoon? You're supposed to be working, aren't you?' She said it mean, but they both knew it was a flirt. Hollis kept coming at her with his hands until he had what he wanted. He was already pulling up the skirt of her dress with his knee. 'Hattie, I miss you.' She wasn't letting him in.

'You miss me or you miss something.'

'Don't mess.' With his mouth biting her neck, his hands on her, and his leg coming around under her skirt, he felt he was showing her how he missed her. He had his hand running down under her bra.

'What are you doing?'

'I would have thought you'd recognize it.'

'Well, you big, fat bastard, Hollis Woolf.' Hattie never would take this from Hollis, no cake and eat it too. 'You want me free and easy, and then when I am, you think you can call me a slut?' She had pushed him away using herself as a wedge between him and the kitchen counter. The aluminum edging pressed lines into her back. Hollis let himself be pushed away. He didn't lose balance but acted like he had and then acted like he had regained it and then sat down in the chair Aubie'd been occupying. He was hanging his head laughing, which only got her going harder and fiercer. 'Mark my words, Hollis. I'm going to open this up in church one Sunday. Open it right up for the whole little world as you know it.'

She was ranting, spluttering mad when Hollis looked up and said, 'So long as you'd only open up, Hattie.' And she picked up a skillet and went for his head like she'd like to see it spilling on her floor. 'Now, now, girl, don't be flirting with the devil.'

'Okay,' she said. 'Say you love me. Say I'm the only one.'

'You love me. I'm the only one.' A tired-out old joke, but still.

'I'm gonna brain you, Hollis. I swear.'

'All right. All right. I love you. Put the pan down. Before the whole little world finds a big, fat bastard on your kitchen floor.'

'I didn't mean that about the big and fat part.' Hattie waited a short time and then asked him if there wasn't anything he wanted to take back, if he'd said anything he wanted to retract. But he only stared at her; he didn't know what she was talking about. So she swung the pan as wide as she dared and slammed it into the side of his head, braking only slightly at impact. Hollis took it.

'Shit. Why the hell did you go and do that?'

'The devil works in mysterious ways, Hollis.'

'Come here, girl.'

'Do you really love me?' she said.

'I come back, don't I?'

Hollis did not tell Hattie about the new highway, or about how the gas station would crumble and all that he had worked so hard for would crumble with it. Moving north would not be an option, is what he primarily thought, what he had come here to examine, whether it would or not, and now he knew it would not. The gas station was his moral centre and that centre stayed damn well where it was set down. Hollis ran his hand over Hattie's breast, over her collarbone, and where, if he wanted to, he could easily kill her — he ran his fingers over her chin, up along her lips. He wouldn't want to do without this woman.

Hollis considered what steps he would have to take to survive this thing. He considered who his enemies were and why they had chosen now to strike. His little world came again into sharp focus; he saw Curtis and all his boys and knew he would need to tighten his grip on family; that's all there was after all. Family. He would find a way to get back what was his; no one was going to take from Hollis Woolf. That was when he'd seen what he had to do; it was always his Hattie who gave him space to think. He would train the boys; if the government was going to spend his tax dollars on a new road, he would find a way to tax the government right back. Curtis would see this his way, Aubie maybe too.

He walked home rejuvenated. He had a woman who understood him, and one who obeyed him. He had fine young boys, a growing army of boys. He would train them, and they would be shining examples of his strength of will. He cornered Maeve in their bedroom. He had drunk several beers at Hattie's place, had swaggered home with a bottle of tequila; everything he did felt true and large. 'Henk, huh? Tell me.' His arms were pressed against the wall behind her; she was the tiniest woman he'd ever known. 'Tell me how your day went.'

'Hollis, where have you been?' Her eyes had so much pity in them, Hollis thought he might hit her, but instead he tried to hold her, throw her down on the bed; she deked and ran, goddamn it all, and he had to scramble after her and watch her hair catch like dead scrubgrass, and the flow of cracking light made him know again how valuable she was, how lovely; enflamed, all things were godly. He listened to her sigh as the cold groundwater whined from the pump, and her sigh was one of forgiveness, he was sure.

'Darling,' he said to her, 'times will get difficult, and you must trust me.' And she had nodded, her hair stinking, and a raw burn travelling along her cheek.

'Yes.'

Many years had passed, and a good deal of history, and still he was paying for that Henk and that pie and that highway; a man had to do what a man had to do. 'If I didn't have trust, I couldn't get along ever.'

Hollis peered at the silhouette in the window frame, thought he heard it clear its throat. Hollis said, 'I think I know who you are.' It wasn't light out yet, but it was coming; he could feel it.

Hollis had armed the boys within the year. He had shown them what to do; it wasn't so hard back then to rob a bank or a grocery store, and Curtis had a talent, even at fifteen. And he had always known Curtis had a talent, and now here he was: that silhouette, that quiet ghost, was the prodigal son.

In his half-dream, Hollis's heart leapt for joy. He woke up some time later and heard himself whispering, 'Curtis? That you?' But there wasn't nobody there any more, and then Hattie had come by and pressed a cold, wet cloth over his forehead, saying, 'Shh,' which made him have to pee. She wasn't supposed to be here outside visiting hours.

Six

The backhoe and the digger were yellow die-cast toys being worked by a remote hand; the claxon was distant, tinny, again like a child's toy playing at real. In the barn, the Family hardly noticed the noise. They were filling an order. Several of them dwelled on Martha, even as one or two were becoming pleased she was not there; there was more space for them in Curtis's heart. He said love spread, now it could spread thicker on them. But there were the unsettled ones too, and that threatened the balance. It was raining, had rained all night, the droplets on the wooden roof of the cabin were like chatter pinning Curtis to his dreams overlong; there was a reason he should wake, but he couldn't locate it and so couldn't wake.

And when Curtis finally did, it was with the good smell of spring dirt in his nose. His first thought went to his apiary; he imagined the thrum of activity in the hives, the pleasure the bees must derive from the first waft of nectar. The bees, the spring, but then Curtis noticed as he surfaced that there was something missing, a tension he had almost bodily grown used to, that had for so long held him intact. That tension was gone. He pulled himself off the floor, already praying, left the featherbed in a sweat-soaked heap, and stumbled half asleep down the stairs and out the cabin door to pee.

He felt heavy with exhaustion. The day did seem to lack urgency, and a fear started to rise in him, which he tried to quell by following routine, by honing the rotational prayer he was pretty well always busy with; years he'd been praying it, it had gone over from words to sound only, holding more energy than words could, that drone. He went back into the cabin, lit the stove, made and drank coffee, lumbered about naked letting the cool air steal the dream warmth from his body, letting that enter prayer too. He was cold, but, he thought, let the body shiver before it sought comfort. Know pain and comfort in equal part. Hollis would be proud.

For the longest time, Curtis had tried to excise his pa from his mind, but the attempt had proved fruitless, and he'd come to reconsider. Hollis loomed at night, when he slept; he took up residence in Curtis's stomach or behind his eyes if he made false statements; and even on lucky days, when Curtis managed to keep the image — pained, cruel-eyed Hollis — at bay, there was still the brooding darkness to contend with, and that was borne in the skin, had become him. So Curtis had given up on the strategy. He'd stopped trying to keep Hollis out of his thoughts years ago.

Instead, he opened his heart, breathed with it, allied himself with whatever fear the darkness brought on, and this seemed to settle him, give him strength, even lightness. He breathed now, slow in and slower out. And so Curtis witnessed and prepared for the day. The Family would come soon for him; they would come flowing up to the door, and he must be calm, and prepared — calm for veracity and authenticity, prepared in order to lead the short prayer before breakfast.

Today, he would impart his lineage from the first Mormons, and then segue that into the Family lineage, going not back but always coming forward toward the great possibility of perfection. He would make comment about Ida, and the forthcoming child; the third generation approached! But it was the Mormon lineage he looked forward to. Reciting it always centred him. It went Curtis to Hollis, Hollis to little orphaned Samson, Samson back to the great convert, Hosea, who knew and fought alongside Joseph Smith in Carthage, Illinois, where poor Joseph was martyred. He must convey this to the Family that they might know and understand his own Divine lineage. It proved him. It proved. He must...Curtis went back into the gate-house and ate honey straight from the pail, digging at it with a wooden spoon, letting the sweet electrify him. He must...What was missing? Why did he not feel strong? What was it? He let the sweet enter his anxiety, travel down his blood and run, brought this into prayer, and that is when he realized. There was a thin whine, and slowly he knew it was he, himself, who cried out, and he remembered. Martha. He had made space for her to leave, and she had.

'She back yet?' Benjamin was standing over him, saying, 'Brother Curtis, it's too hot in here.' Curtis had been laying log after log into the barrel stove; he liked it hot, it gave him back something of home. The panic around Benjamin's eyes mirrored his own. 'We'll lose more if she isn't brought back. It will be a signal to any with doubts.'

Curtis shook his head at Benjamin's comment, which was hanging over him, that sweet honey racing through him. Benjamin shut the door, paced awhile quietly outside the cabin, and then moved off.

Curtis shook his head again, pushing away these truths. He decided to conserve his own energy; he holed up at the kitchen table, lit a joint, got up only when necessary to load the fire barrel, sloughed dead cells and sweat off his chest with the edge of his hand, listened to his heart hiccup, and thought how to protect himself from this. He flipped again through the stack of old mail he'd left out. The ex-Family postcard, the old letter from his ma, and saw that the one from Hollis was missing. What would Martha find out if she did go south?

There was a trickle of misery within him too, he recognized. A line of thought that unwound far away in his mind. A tinny, weepy, imploring wail that went, 'Martha. Martha. Martha.' He needed her. He loved her, had trusted her, had felt her to be a part of him. Benjamin was back outside the door, peering in at him. 'You have to go after her. She's the third one to leave in a month. The farm is falling behind, Curtis. We can't have a first generation walking out.'

'We need to hold a special meeting.'

'It's four days now. She'll be lost among the outside people. She won't come back. She may not fit any more, if she's out too long.'

Curtis waited while Benjamin wandered off again; he wished he could keep his damn thoughts straight. One was that the Family would be there at the gate-house soon, wanting from him. Two was the lineage, which suddenly seemed a thin offering, but it would have to do, as he couldn't think of anything else to give them today. Three was the bees. Four was the gun. Five was Martha. Six was Martha, and on and on. What had he done? Martha was gone, and Curtis knew now where. The knowledge seeped in under his skin like a slow, true river flowing. There was only one place a person like Martha would go, only one place she could go. She'd lived at Soltane so long, she didn't know of many other real places.

Curtis got more coffee going and put more wood in the stove. What was it? May something. Early May, a Friday. The place was heated up; it was like the desert. Hot was an old addiction, from the times he used to find his spot out there, off the 66, away from the shambles called home, and lie as still as a creature, letting the sweat bead and paying it no mind so he might concentrate a bit.

Curtis sat now, this time on the little ottoman Martha had reupholstered with carpeting. The upholstery scratched him. He thought he would have to do something. He ought to go check on the hives and make sure the bees got enough sugar to keep them going until the trees flowered. He should help Benjamin and Ida get in the garden too, and move some dirt, get air in there, dig up last year's offering, rejuvenate the soil. It was nearing the solstice and solstice celebrations, but he could not seem to move. Curtis felt shame coming. He shouldn't have kept the damn gun on the farm.

He sat perfectly still with his legs pulled up and his head stuck between his knees and witnessed the tickle of saltwater moving down his skin and thought about what he ought to do, what line of action was required. He was scared, and there was no knowing how a scared man will react; Curtis was as certain of this as anyone. The rain dulled outside noise and the quiet ran adrenally through him. A revelation approached, one as thick as treacly maple syrup. He dreaded it.

Curtis looked over at the window even though he couldn't see anything from where he sat. Then through the rain chatter, he heard the arrogant repeat of a red-breasted robin that'd been at it every morning for weeks, and the refrain from the white-throated sparrows. There was also the crash of industry far off. The gravel pit. A car went by and still the revelation was slow coming. It would not reach him, and he knew better than to chase it.

After a time, Curtis did not know how long exactly, Benjamin pushed the door open and called. Benjamin tried to look authoritative; he could see Curtis was falling apart. 'Curtis. Get some clothes on.' Curtis, hunched over on the ottoman, was in the process of pulling snags from his toenails. He had no fat to him, just muscle on his heavy bones. He was tall, thin, and strong. And he was alert even if you wouldn't say it looking at him.

Curtis wanted to cry, but that was moving slow toward him

too. Everything seemed to be moving extra slow, like time had altered the speed at which things progressed, and he could now witness life in intricate detail. There was a beauty, for instance, to the triangular lines of the wrinkles on his hand, and he wished not to be interrupted from this witnessing.

'I don't like this.'

'Get up, Curtis.'

'You said that already. There's no need for me to get up.'

'There's a need. She's gone.'

'How many days now?'

'Three. Maybe four. Four. That's too long, and you know it is.' Benjamin had nowhere to go if the Family fell apart. Many of the Associates had no ties to other people at all, and none of them had private money.

Curtis did know four days was too long; would she know already about Edgar? He could not get up, he didn't even look up. His beautiful hands had become itchy, and his heart was getting all slippery, damn it, and Benjamin was making him feel small; he tucked his head between his legs and scanned the floor until he found it. He had a tied handkerchief with about a half joint's worth of weed in it, and he intended to smoke this, slow down his blood, and float. *Woe unto the murderer, woe unto the liar, woe unto the blind, the deaf.* Book of Mormon, he thought, a paraphrasing of Nephi 9:31–35. He considered how redemption visited only the truly damned.

'I love you, Brother,' he said to Benjamin. He did love Benjamin, who had been with him almost as long as Martha, and upon whom the foundation of the Family rested. Four of the Family Associates were Benjamin's children. 'I truly do,' he added. He wondered suddenly whether this would be a good time to mention the tax lady. Or if he could fix that up before it got worse. Curtis's mind threw him back in time: he was sitting on Martha's sofa in her shared home in Toronto that first night he came to Canada; he had spent the night smoking weed and he knew he had a way in. The density of all the experiences that brought him to that sofa, that city, that rough spot, had hit him square and he had cried. Not soft tears, but the kind of racking cry that breaks up chest muscle. He was sore for days. All the heat left him and he shivered to the point of convulsion. That kind of cry. And Martha had been kind to him. Kind.

And now recalling himself shaking with the restraint of trying not to cry like this brought on the thing, the revelation he'd been expecting. It came at him like a wall, him driving toward it. He saw himself lying in the desert sand and, like the thousand times he'd gone through this before and shook it loose and convinced himself he had forgotten it, resolved it, prayed it to abeyance, he felt himself begin to decay. First the sun changed the colour of his skin until the baked red took over the dead blue-grey.

He could smell himself in his revelation, a putrid, hateful smell. Then patches of his skin began to curl at the edges of small holes he had not previously noticed scattered across his chest. His skin peeled away in small, neat circles. There was no blood seeping out, but pink-red sand blew toward him and away from him as time passed. It hurt. Sand entered the holes in his body and the balance shifted, skin to sand until the skin dried to dust and floated across the way and met with the sand and was succumbed into it. Curtis was shaking, now, shaking hard in spite of the heat, for he had witnessed this reverie many times before with no comprehension of what it might mean, and suddenly, in light of Martha's disappearance, he believed he understood it.

'I best get going and find her back again,' he said. 'I have seen what I must do.'

Benjamin didn't respond at first. 'You have people coming,' he then said.

'Tell them I'll be back soon. And to pray.'

But it was too late. Curtis could see them clearly from the window. The women and children were swaying up to the door; the men followed. Curtis, Hollis, Samson, Hosea; it didn't matter about Samson's excommunication, that the through line was broken, by blood, by belief. The Family gathered in the shadows where the pines met, right at the gate-house. Curtis grabbed a long cotton nightshirt and pulled it on. He went to them, touched them all, one by one. He was gentle, he touched them on their cheeks, foreheads, along the backs of their hands. They were happy to see him, be noticed by him, and they touched him in return.

'We won't be together for some time,' Curtis said.

'Why?' It was Ida. 'What's happening?' She was beautiful and she shone with belief and nodded whenever he said anything meaningful. Her belly reminded him of Martha suddenly. He tried not to look at it.

'I am being called. I am being called to mission and I must answer this call,' he said, and then he quoted, *'Because I said unto them that they were a lost and a fallen people they were angry with me, and sought to lay their hands upon me, that they might cast me into prison.'* He did not know why this passage had come to mind, and wished he had come up with something softer, less direct, especially when one of the little ones suddenly turned away, crying. He tried to compensate, saying, 'We will be again together, and I will hold hands with you all.'

Curtis knew that this sense of grief, of loss and worry, was enough to hold these people to this piece of land and so to sustain him on this journey, to bolster him even in his absence — he was truly already thinking of it as a mission. He would bring Martha back and he would reposition her, and the property would be solid again; everything would be okay. *We regret to inform.* That was bullshit. He needed the strength of these people to hold him. There was Hollis staring in at him, *Come*, and he was weak; his heart was a bugger. Maybe his pa could help him out of this foreclosure. Yes, finally, Hollis could help him. 'I'll be back,' Curtis said. 'I'm bringing you all with me.' And his fingertips shifted along his chest.

He would leave that very day. He dressed carefully, and packed carefully. He was leaving, and leaving meant being careful, and being careful meant at the very least packing with care. He wore a white linen shirt, a jacket, and white linen trousers. The shirt billowed in a way that lent him Holiness, a reason to admire it even more. He felt forgiving in this shirt, of Martha, of everyone who had ever wronged, including himself, and even those he had never met and would never meet.

He thought about the Family and how their ranks over time had dwindled, and how that worried him. There was less energy to support him, he felt, and it made him insecure. It was that there was less inclination for hard spiritual work in these times, he reasoned. At midday, he sat on the ottoman and thumbed through his Book and his Bible looking for something helpful but coming up with little, only this: '*Whatsoever ye ask, believe that ye shall receive it, it shall be given.*' This would bolster him. Curtis rose with the solid thought that something had to shift, and that it would soon do so. He procrastinated, repacking until the sun began to chase the moon across the sky. It was three o'clock.

Dear Benjamin was not around. Curtis did not know where he had got to, only that he hadn't been around most of that whole day. He walked north past the mill-house, where Benjamin and Ida would live until the baby was born, when they would move back to the sleep-house, and east down the hill to the apiary. He felt comfortable around the bees in a way he had never really felt comfortable around any person. They buzzed around him as cosmic breath, and he knew that any apprehension from him would signal some large disruption in their pattern; he did not like change either, and now he was leaving, and the bees deserved more.

'Bees? I'm so sorry.' He was bereft. There was such sorrow all around him, he felt. He opened the hive from the back of the wooden stand. The wooden gum was chopped into the shape of a Confederate soldier. It was a hollow log, paint now faded, and the bees exited and entered through a hole in the belt buckle. He had built this hive and the several around it twenty years earlier to show off to Martha. Martha, who was now gone. He would repaint the hives when he returned, in celebration!

Curtis's chest rattled, and he was scared of what was happening. Why had he obeyed blindly all those years before; why had he not listened to his heart? It still ached to think of what he'd done. He did not want Martha to know all this about him, how weak he had been around his father. He didn't want her to know how cruel Hollis was either, how cruel a person could be. He wished to protect her. Curtis made sure the hatchway was clean and watched a few sluggish bees emerge from the soldier's belt buckle — they were lovely — and fly off toward the maple trees. There was some brood disturbance in the hive, he saw. The drones and workers were agitated by something.

A young Queen had been developed. It was sudden then, what happened. Curtis could name it even as it did: a swarm. The worker bees sensed the intrusion of a young Queen and rejected her. They moved out of the hive, as one, with the old Queen, loyal. It was like an apparition, an alien sighting, he thought, the way the swarm contracted and swung through the air. It was like the swarming bees were a simultaneous singular presence. They were trying to form one entity, something he had read about years ago when he was starting the hives. Also he thought of Ether 2:3: *'and thus they did carry with them swarms of bees.'* Curtis wondered at the magnitude of this sign to him — that Martha should leave, and that he must follow. He saw this sign as a gift in all the confusion he was experiencing.

Something else too. He'd seen it before many times, of course, only never registered it so clearly. The way the bees, so close together, somehow merged as a mass, energized by the whirr of wing and the buzzing, it was like they went from being separate, intricate, dull-yellow singularities to one pulsing, collective blackness. He shifted out of the way. He would not have time to gather them and help them enter a new, clean hive. He nodded and almost put his hand up by way of giving a blessing but stopped himself. They were wild now; they would learn wildness and were already blessed in their perfection.

He reached into the hive and pulled out what honeycomb he thought he'd need, placed this in a lined apple box he'd brought with him for that purpose. He walked back by the farm car; the trunk was open, and he placed the comb in it. He was thinking that the Volvo was safe, even if the gas gauge was recently busted, and that no one, not even a border patrol, would feel a Volvo presented any risk. It was a 1990 rusted wave-rider of a car. He prayed it was safe.

He left a note in the gate-house, *Give me two weeks*, tucked inside the bank foreclosure notice. Curtis lugged his army bag out to the car and put it, too, in the trunk. It was the same green bag he'd arrived lugging. He considered how he had accumulated so little tangible in all these years.

And he left, pulling out of the farm gate; loss, ache, fear, and the feeling he must go, and then he drove, and the driving had its own challenges. It was like a trigger in the brain that he wished would just do its work and annihilate the whole past, but instead relived it for him. The motion of the car disturbed him.

Nineteen seventy-two, he thought. Damn it. Hollis, the

whole bloody thing, coming back at him. What the mind would recall: liar, murderer, petty criminal. He didn't like the terms. Curtis recalled pulling the bloodied T-shirt over his head and using what wasn't stained and wet to rub the blood off his skin. That was ineffective, so he had walked back to the old pump behind the house, where his younger sisters were still triking over sidewinders, and he listened to their shrieks and their 'Curtis, Curtis look at me. Look at me.'

He splashed the cold well water up at his stomach and thin, pink rivulets of blood and water mixed ran down him. He wasn't thinking so much about what he had done, but more how was he going to get away with it? His jeans were soaked down the crotch but he didn't much notice. He stared out at the girls knowing he wouldn't see them again, that they weren't anything to do with him any more.

He walked through the pump yard, past the red, white, and blue federal 900 pumps with the Stn. 666 decal his pa had put there, and smiled at his brothers as if they were strangers — they were about to be — and then he walked into the cash room, popped the till, and took the day's catch. That ought to hold him awhile. His fifteen-year-old sister handed him a button-down cotton shirt, mauve stripes on white, with lapels right down to his nipples, and this army bag, already packed, and then she'd let her arm drop and stared, looking like she already missed Curtis.

'I'll come back,' Curtis promised.

'Don't you dare. This's a gift you better receive, brother.'

'Tell Clarie goodbye if you see her.'

'I will.'

Curtis put the shirt on, fastened it up right to the collar, set his jaw, walked back out through the pump yard to the highway, and proceeded to hitch. His brothers and sisters stood and watched him. Hollis yelled at them to get back to work, and when they didn't, Hollis came barrelling out the front door in his housecoat, barefoot, hollering he was going to wallop someone. They did not care. They stood and waited for twenty minutes until someone — a thin man in a bowler and the saddest-looking Cadillac Curtis'd ever seen — stopped and leaned over and pushed the passenger door open.

'Where you going?'

'As far north as you'll take me.'

'Hop in.'

North. Curtis was careful not to reveal anything personal, not with the bowler man, who said he directed funerals, not with the sassy blonde who drove like she was headed to her own. Curtis said nothing about himself where a wily question or a nod would take its place. Hardest was the trucker. That mother-fucker never shut up and never stopped asking him questions about who and what and where and how. Curtis trailed his finger over the dashboard, through the road dust lying there.

'You draft-dodger or what?' The trucker was a black man with aspirations, a detail that made Curtis uneasy. He was trucking to pay for college. College! Hollis did not believe in paid-for knowledge; the catch was built in, as far as he could tell. So, as far as Curtis could tell too.

'No, they wouldn't take me.' The trucker laughed heartily at this. Curtis planned to head to Nauvoo and Carthage, to check out his Mormon roots, and then, who knew, maybe down to Utah, where he figured someone might help him hide, let him preach some. But draft-dodger; that was an idea that hadn't occurred to him, and he pocketed it, thinking it might come in handy, though it enraged him to think anyone would call him a coward. 'What do you study at that school you go to?'

'Civil rights. African-American history. Whatever I please.'

'Whatever you please of what they have to offer.'

'You could look at it that way.'

'I do.'

'Well.'

Curtis stared out the passenger-side window, saw quick slices of landscape and roadside accidents and fields and little gothic revival houses and porches like snapshots — a slideshow that never added up. He did not want to swerve his head or appear eager in any way about what he was now seeing, so even things that might have interested him remained snippety and nothing. He wanted to seem uninterested to this man; he was not sure why, only that it seemed prudent. The trucker clenched his jaw; Curtis could see him in the window reflection, see him growing tense. He could see the man was pissed at him.

'You ever hear of the Muslim Brotherhood? The Black Panthers?' the trucker asked.

'No, I never did.' He wondered what Muslim might be and thought, Ain't all panthers black?

'This doesn't surprise me in the least.' The man was shaking his head as if he was really sad about something. Only Curtis could see he didn't mean it, that he was more dismayed than sad. The man said, 'I'm going to tell you something.'

'Just let me off here, is good.'

'Now listen to me, would you?' The driver geared down, the brakes hissing and spitting. 'Open up the glove compartment. There's a book in there.'

'Don't mess with me.'

'It's a gift.'

'I don't read much.'

'Take it. Yeah? Take it.'

It was a second edition titled *Manual for Draft-Age Immigrants to Canada*. It had a maple leaf in red on the upper right corner of the front cover and some phone numbers scribbled down under the title. They were outside Chicago. Curtis felt like he had never expected to feel in his life. Alone. He felt he had no father. No mother. No place. He flipped the booklet open and read something about FBI agents, something he did not want to read. *'FBI agents have told parents that their sons can be returned. This is not true.'* Curtis knew he would not be returned.

'Why are you giving me this?' Curtis said. He could feel the blood rage coming up behind his eyes. 'You think I'm a red commie!'

'No.' The man was suppressing a laugh. 'I think you are part of a resistance, even if you don't know it yourself. You're a peaceful man!'

'No, I ain't.' Curtis frowned, folded the manual and shoved it into his waistband, opened the truck door, and eased himself down, pulling his bag after him. Recalling his mother, he said, 'Thank you,' though he was not sure he entirely meant it. He watched the man engage and drive off, watched until the truck was around a curve and out of sight. There was a cornfield beside him, row on row of unripe corn, and falling over by the split-rail fence on the roadway, a hollowed-out log, carved and painted like a rebel soldier with bees coming in and out its belt. Peaceful man, my ass, he thought; he wanted to change the world. Everything had a purpose, and this dismissal by his family was slowly opening a new door, on a new promise.

Curtis watched that industry, the bees' honey sacs bulging at their little legs, never forgot that. He turned and looked at the fields of corn; he'd never seen such a thing before. But hell, there was nothing here for him. He should have just dealt with the driver and got right into Chicago, where he was sure to get a lift west or north, for it was a long walk into Chicago's outskirts, the good part of two hours. He finally found a bus that took him to a hostel, where he lay on a cot and read and reread the book the trucker had given him.

He read with an impatience born of questions around the

rate of decay and whether the body would be immediately found and how much time he had. People had seen him bloodied, but which people, and which side were they on? The book said cut your hair; it said wear a suit, look respectable. On the fourth read, Curtis had it. He lifted himself from the bedclothes he'd wrapped himself in and went in search of a barber who could hear him. Hollis had taught him a few things.

'I want a haircut I can be nervous in without seeming nervous,' he said. The Greek nodded, handed him a little ceramic cup filled with ouzo, and gave him the best haircut he'd ever had and the last he'd have for many years. Curtis then walked into seven banks, sizing up the tellers before he lighted on the perfect composite suit for a man taking a bus into Canada for the express purpose of job hunting; it was a deep blue, just a little too large, off-the-rack affair he then went and bought; he began to sweat as soon as he'd put the thing on.

He bought a briefcase such as he had seen the northern bankers swinging and, looking in the window of the leather goods store, he saw another man, fully presentable, as distant from blood feud and corner-store robbery as a man could be. Curtis held his breath as the bus stopped at the border, as the burly Customs officer swung his head from side to side measuring the worth of this, then that, passenger.

'Shouldn't you be in the army, son? You win that lottery?'

'No, sir. I have a heart condition.'

'Lucky for you. My boy left last week.'

'A patriot.'

'I guess.'

Curtis breathed deep then and fooled the fool. He had a hundred and fifty dollars in his pocket and he was in. He would keep moving on this bus until he reached Toronto; he would not stop travelling until he found the Yonge Street mentioned on the back of the manual. It was a miracle he was not questioned, that his bag was not searched, nor his empty Naugahyde briefcase, that his suit waistband was not patted down, nor his ankle, where the gun was tucked into his sock and rubber-banded to his leg.

He must think for himself, to try not to consider always what Hollis would think at every situation he found himself in, but this was difficult. He couldn't barely light a smoke without wondering whether Hollis would approve. And now he could not help but consider how proud Hollis would be of him, the only draft-dodger too weak of heart to be allowed to sign up, entering Canada armed and fully loaded. 'The northern boundary of the Mason-Dixon Line is your border, son.' Curtis recalled Hollis pointing to a map of the world he had push-pinned to the wall. 'You memorize this boundary and you won't go wrong in your life. This side is family. This other...? There's no accounting for the way these people will behave.'

'Can't that boundary be pushed, Pa?' Curtis was fourteen, eager to appear smart.

'Only of the mind, Curtis. The Mason-Dixon Line of the mind can be pushed, but I'd advise you to be armed and ready.'

Of the mind, Curtis had thought, and he had not really understood what Hollis had meant by that. Curtis was on the bus, and the happiness had caught in him and he was laughing so hard he had to put his face in his hands so nobody would see. This was joy. Oh, Lord, he thought he might never feel this free again, and he thought how he better memorize this. Canada already felt good. Curtis looked down at his suit and considered how easy it all was, and how he was going to make a life up here on his own terms. God-given, it was God-given.

He slowed the Volvo now outside Windsor and pulled in to a doughnut shop. He wasn't for false sweets, but caffeine would sustain him. He ordered a double, thinking how Benjamin and Ida would chastise him for his worldly addictions. The drink went in calm and nice, and within fifteen minutes he was as jumpy as he felt he needed to be to get across the border, to drive through another night.

It was Nauvoo, Illinois, he'd decided. It was there he would go first, just as he figured Martha'd gone there, tracing a line of research she likely believed would lead her somewhere better than where she was already. There was so little he'd ever told any of them about himself, and at the time he had reasoned it was to protect them as much as to protect himself. He was a new man, a new constructed man, made from the remnants he felt were worth saving. He had tried to discard the rest. He had told them about Nauvoo, as a tragic utopian example. Maybe she would be there still; he missed her. At the border, he passed Benjamin's passport to the young patrol guard and waited for the worst. Curtis was a bit twitchy, and he tried to compensate for this bad neural feeling by being friendly. 'Howdy,' he said.

'Can I ask you to pull over, sir, and step out of your car?'

Curtis suddenly thought how he didn't look as much like Benjamin as he'd previously believed, and wondered whether there was any sort of pardon on thirty-year-old crimes; if the premise to a life lived was false, was the life also false? He supposed Martha was asking this same question. It didn't seem real, and also not kind, that he would be captured in this way, so pure of heart as he was, so filled with good intentions, so atoned, so near perfection. He thought that, and also how he wished he wasn't so caffeinated.

Seven

The sun left an ochre line on the horizon. Hattie'd been to see Hollis, and he wasn't doing too good. On and on about Curtis, and nothing made much sense. He'd wet his bed, and she had got the orderly in and helped him change the sheets. Then she walked old Route 66 back of the water hole and up across the new highway homeward; that highway always irked her good. Hadn't it shot down every little business along the old road, hadn't it marked the end of Hollis's gas station, robbed him of a decent, honest living, and hadn't it killed the towns of Cuervo and old Newkirk? She had family that came from that way, not that it told much. They were all dead by now, these people, and those who weren't, they'd moved on years and years ago, she did not know where to.

People didn't keep in touch with people so much any more. That Hollis was dying came to her mind then. He didn't look healthy, was taking oxygen while she visited, and was speaking in riddles — something about Curtis being his prodigal son and 'Quick, Maevie, I have seen him' — and Hattie hoped she wouldn't die first, and thought how she ought to get a prayer in for him at mass. Just in case Someone was listening; for thirty years she'd prayed as a safeguard, out of habit, not sure whether it made a bit of sense.

She did not like the thought of Hollis being alone. He was going peculiar, and also she worried he might try to touch one of the younger nurses; she had seen his eye stray there. This sort of possession was a kind of ghost-limb, she thought, which proved, in any event, that she still did love him, even though sometimes it felt more like disgust and habit, nostalgia and fear of change. How long could that first shock of love survive all the rest? But hell, it lingered, made her dutiful.

Hattie thought back to that first time she had seen Hollis; she was twelve years old, first day of high school. She'd been praying, and she knew when she saw him her prayers were answered. His gangly legs stuck into a cotton football uniform told her so. He was just all knees, and sharp shoulder angles, and even though she hadn't been asking God for anything in particular, she could see Hollis answered the want.

'Lordy.' She'd said it under her breath so that she was the only one who heard. She thought, 'Please God, let this be for me.' The earth sure looked young back then. God seemed to kick around in unlikely places: the sun refracting off the river surface, the golden hairs on Hollis's calves. If Hattie could believe in that, she might believe in anything. It was getting on dark. Hattie must press forward. She didn't much like this turn of events, this girl, how everything was riled up where it had been calm. There was Edgar in her mind, static after all these years, and now it was like he was moving around. Well, it hurt is all, and she was too old for it.

Every story had a beginning, but many never ended, she thought. Hollis had arrived out of nowhere, all those years ago, a perfect stranger come from Ramah; some Godly miracle at work, she believed then. Hollis didn't even return her gaze, but she knew. And she followed him around until he knew; she was tenacious that way. It must have been very embarrassing to him, she considered now, having a little star-struck kid trailing him like that.

'What's this?' he would say if he saw her watching him. And

she ran, then, as fast as she could and as far away. Hattie'd lie in bed and concentrate on him. She wanted something to happen, though truthfully she didn't half know what that something was. She followed him for one full year before he took advantage. It finally happened one hot afternoon, just before Hollis and his buddies went off to their call-up duty. 'Come by me,' he said.

He was sitting on his parents' lawn with Martin Flint and some other boys. East side of Artesia, just a little box house it was, but a paid-for house, at least. His feet were splayed out in huge tennis shoes and his hands were clutching the armrests on the folding wooden lawn chairs. 'Come by me and set you down.'

Hollis was drinking beer straight out of a bottle, wasting the afternoon away, blue sky, speaking of his own grand future. The sun was beading up sweat on his skin. He had a line along his neck where the burnt skin met white. Freckles rose over his nose and he had looked so handsome. She seemed just to be walking by, but she seemed like that all the time, and was sure the boys knew what she was up to. Their laughs were soft, knowing. Hollis caught her arm and swung her down onto his knee.

'This here is Hattie,' he said. The introduction was a joke that she could not penetrate. They all knew Hattie McCann who had a deep crush on Hollis, one that wouldn't be shook. 'She's my best girlfriend. Ain't you, Hattie?'

She batted him across the top of his head. 'You don't know nothing.'

'You're through thick and thin, ain't you now?'

'Hollis, don't say what I am.' She stuck her finger into his chest and said, 'You're nothing but a dog.' The boys laughed.

'She got you marked,' Martin Flint said.

Hattie lifted herself up to leave, but Hollis held her by the waist in the crook of his left arm and pulled her closer. He took a swig of his beer and looked through eye slits up at the sun.

'She's mine. All I got really. My little girl. You gonna wait for Hollis now, ain't you?' He looked right back at her.

'I don't have anywhere else to go, do I?'

Martin gave a big laugh and said, 'Now that's what I call love.'

Hollis laid his big hand-paw on Hattie's skinny little leg. 'Now don't you listen to Martin Flint,' he said, 'because Martin Flint is just jealous.' She laid her head against Hollis's chest then. She could feel his total vitality coming in through that open palm on her leg. Strong Hollis.

If she had known then what she knew through time about Hollis, how many sacrifices would be made in the name of Hollis Woolf, she would not have changed this moment. Something would always fall away, it was natural a person felt pain and sorrow on this earth, else how would she know pleasure?

A clump of primrose opened out of the dirt on the side of the road, streetlight haloing it, and Hattie leaned on her cane and bent to pick one pretty yellow flower. Where that thing got enough moisture to shoot a bloom she didn't know, but it was pretty and she tucked it in her blouse buttonhole, carried on. Back then, her head on Hollis's chest, the boys all swaggering, tilting back on those chairs, swigging beer like they supposed men might, trying to keep off worry, it had felt so free. The next day, Hattie had walked by and the chairs were still there, now empty, of course.

Martin Flint, Hollis Woolf, and the rest had shipped out for army training, to learn the good safe way to hold a grenade. The wooden chairs had fallen over, but from a distance, they still looked nice, painted pink and orange, lying there on the rich green grass, under that sky. Training was all. The one war was just won and the next one not started up.

Hattie smiled that day when she walked by the lawn chairs,

thinking of Hollis giving her that attention she so badly craved. Her stomach shifted around as she recalled how he had later hauled her into his bedroom window, after she'd snuck out of her own and found herself scratching her nails at the glass of his, only that pane between them, and how they had lain next to each other on his cot, his hand pushing up her T-shirt, the rough skin of his palm like a cowlick against her little breasts and how she never knew kisses could come so wet; so wet she just about melted into him, like they were one big liquid heat, and how gently he put his self into her and lying very still whispered, 'Do you like that, Hattie?' And how she was too scared to answer and too scared to know even how to answer and how she began to sway until everything was white and buzzing. What it felt like to be entered by Hollis felt more like God than ever it did at church. 'Your eyes are so big,' he said, brushing the bit of tangled hair off her forehead. 'I'm gonna be thinking about you.'

'Don't go away.' She said this as a dare more than a plea.

'No,' he said, looking somewhere off into the middle distance. 'That ain't noble.' They looked under the covers at the shock of blood and mess, his hair, hers was inconsequential yet, and his organ, its slit eye. 'Spitting cobra.' He laughed.

'What are you going to tell your mama about this disaster?'

'Nosebleed?' Then he laughed again and shoved Hattie back out the window, into his mother's row of petunias, all road-dusted and limp, patted her like she was a horse that'd wandered by, and she went running off, only turning to shout back at him.

'I love you, Hollis.'

No answer. The darkness took it up and held it for a minute or so until it merged up with the cricket song. What became of words once they were spoken, spiralling out into the universe, decaying like vegetable waste? What grew from that? Hattie looked down at the primrose in her buttonhole, thought she might give it to Martha when she got back; she was more than halfway home by now, and so tired.

Hollis wasn't to be army fodder, he was careful. He barely finished basic training when he was back, couldn't have inflicted much of anything. 'I missed you,' he said, his hand taking no time to find its home.

The boys were milling around again on Hollis's front lawn like they never left, except now they were shyly changed, rougher. Hollis pinned Hattie's arms behind her and though she squirmed, she didn't mind. Hollis, even just holding her, warmed her all over like bread baking; she moved as close as she could in public company, edged sidewards up and down his legs until it was all he could do but laugh and fling her away. Hattie was pushed right off by Hollis. 'You're a wily little coon.'

'You oughta know, barkin' up my tree.'

'That girl,' he said. 'That girl's gonna put me in my grave.'

The boys just laughed and twisted their boots over their dropped cigarette butts, already pulling their packs out of their chest pockets and popping fresh smokes between their lips. They stood around all day smoking and laughing. Conserving energy, holding it all in like they were saving up for something really special. But the truth was the parents were at all of them: 'What are you going to do with your life, son? Settling down is what you need.'

There was a bench in the lake park, and Hattie sat down on it. She slumped a bit and almost slept; she would have liked to be able to sleep, but she had to get back. She looked down again at the flower as if to remind herself of the woman, and saw it was wilting in the night heat. She just needed to rest her legs a piece and then get up. The water of the little manmade lake was still, opaque.

Of course, it was Hollis who was the first to expand, get at life. He bought that land up north at Santa Rosa and started out with two lone pumps, wrangled some deal with Conoco whereby he bank-loaned for the deposit and that land, away from his family, and Conoco, they supplied the pumps and the gas on credit. Route 66 was going to be his yellow brick road. He wasn't ever going to drive it, never see where it might or might not lead, but he was damn sure going to profit on all those miserable men who were. His own father was against it on moral grounds, the strict upbringing edging against common sense.

'The road to hell,' Daddy Samson had proclaimed.

Hollis muttered back, 'Ain't no good intentions here' and carried on with his business. Hattie watched the work, the pits being hand dug until Hollis got it in his head to speed up the process; he buried a stick of dynamite in a drill hole and ran the hell out of the way. Supposed to have a permit for that sort of thing and when the county sheriff got wind of it he covered his ass by issuing one as fast as you please. Everybody knew Hollis by then, knew he wasn't going to be swayed by the law. The explosion? Phew. That was something.

'Army taught me good.' Hollis smirked. 'Goddamnit.' The earth just rumbled and burst inward. So he had his hole dug for the gas tank, had his station up and running quick as jack. Hattie thought of him still, off to the side of that hole, wiping his forehead and laughing, his teeth already shit, rotting here and there into sharp little points, but the joy in that smile was good. It was all excitement then, no one knowing where it would all lead.

She wished sometimes she could help but love the man. She was his shadow on the flatland of Route 66, station number twenty-nine on Conoco's chain of ochre liquid gold, always and ever more. Hollis scrimped and saved. He called that gas station 666 on Route 66. That was it, the sense of humour he had. Hattie would skip school some days and hitchhike up there, watch the cars come in slow and leave reinvigorated. She saw the money changing hands, poverty and hope all mixed up.

It was only a trailer he lived in there, but it was his. She watched Hollis growing paunchy, his body filling into manhood, his skin already problematic, and his hand, when he couldn't stop himself, running up into her skirts. It wasn't long before he bought her that old adobe she still lived in, to keep her nearby, thing cost him a song. Hattie never did understand why he didn't really love her, why he couldn't be drawn in to her. Why it wasn't enough for him. And the more it showed, the more she tried; she moved in and he stepped back, like some godawful dance.

It was coming to her in her old age: he couldn't love and not own a thing at the same time. In this way, she reasoned, he came close to giving her something, giving her freedom, though she would have traded it a hundred thousand times over the years. She'd been stupid. 'I don't mind,' she said once to him, 'I don't mind so much that you don't love me so long as you keep touching me like you might one day.' And he seemed to hold on to the value in that. It was in the beginning that she didn't mind, while there was still a chance. And then afterwards, she was past minding. She was locked in the habit of him. Like smoking or drink.

Martin Flint with the greased hair, dust settling into it in little congealed balls if you looked close. He said, 'She's a live wire.'

'I can't shake her.'

'You made her what she is, giving her the wrong impression.'

'You accusing me of using a minor?'

'You use everyone else. Why should this be any different?'

'She's no good for me,' he chuckled. 'She don't give, she only takes.'

'Keep her as a sideline.'

'Half a mind.'

It took Hollis two years to find the right girl.

Hattie heaved herself off the bench and began to walk, poking the cane down, whacking the earth, thinking on Maeve Hardy. That was the girl he loved, and when he found her she wasn't a sideline. He main-lined her, fuel-injected her. She was always small. Beside him she was smaller. A bird, swallowed. She came in on the back of her daddy's truck. He was a photographer come down to document impoverishment for posterity and several newspapers, New Hampshire, New York, Maine. He took a daguerreotype of Hollis.

'A mirror to the soul,' Mr. Hardy said, handing the finished product over. 'That's a dying art right there in that picture. There's not too many can do that any more.' Hollis looked larger than life, even though the picture would fit into a back pocket and wasn't more than two inches by three. He carried it with him and glanced at it from time to time as if to reassure himself of who he was. In the picture he was standing, each arm propped on a gas pump. It was not visible in the picture, but behind him had been a stand with a neck brace, a contraption to hold him steady while the picture was being made. He must have been just twenty-one in that picture, but already he had emerged into his adult self — the belly hung slightly over his belt, the eyes burned, the teeth were like little fangs.

Here was a man who knew his mind, who had gathered energy and had learned how to hold it. Hattie owned that daguerreotype now, found it difficult to look at the picture without seeing her own face reflected just under its surface. She'd taken the daguerreotype when Hollis had been moved into the care facility, kept it now in a drawer in the kitchen. She wondered whether Martha had found it yet. The girl might have touched everything in the house by now — learning it, filing, something. Hattie picked up her pace for a bit, but then slowed right back down — old age.

Maeve Hardy and her father stayed in town for some time and it went around that Maeve stood to become wealthy, that she had a trust fund account coming due, that the family money had skipped a generation when Mr. Hardy had chosen a craft and not a profession. The Hardy people had been doctors and professors from time immemorial. There had been a rancorous argument and Mr. Hardy had been all but flung out of the family. Hollis was sensitive to this.

He deflected his attention from Maeve to the father; they drank together until drunk, and Hollis always paid. For several weeks Hollis kindly set Mr. Hardy up in a booth beside the station, a little makeshift photography stand, which attracted all manner of people, passers-through and local people. Every-one wanted a picture taken. There was even one of Hattie, not a daguerreotype, just a regular black-and-white. She was sixteen, and Hollis paid for it; she had worn a pinafore and was un-comfortable, didn't like all the layers of cloth on her body. This photograph, too, she still had; it hung along the corridor to her bedroom.

Maeve Hardy assisted her father, ran back and forth between the two men with messages. When Hollis and Hardy went taverning, she stayed back and stretched her limbs behind the photo shack using a stick as barre. Hattie caught her once twirl-ing like a crazy Indian. She appeared to weigh nothing, a small insect, and to move to some inner music, a tune Hattie hadn't ever heard, of course. Hattie was uncultivated. She stood off some distance and stared, until Maeve stopped and frowned.

'Can I help you?'

'I'm just looking. What are you dancing for?'

'Dancing for? You don't need a reason. I'm just dancing.'

'There ain't melody, though.'

Then Maeve started humming it out loud. She flung around. Hattie had never heard anything like it and wasn't sure about it anyway. It sounded like show-off music to her and she was also a little afraid of the lack of knowing in herself. She had never noticed how stupid she was, but when Maeve sang, it showed to her how impossible it would be for her to not be stupid. And how stupid she was to not even know the magnitude of her own stupidity. Her ignorance weighed on her for a time.

Meantime, and very slowly, Hollis fixed Mr. Hardy's truck, which had sprung a gas line leak and also had a crack someplace important. Hardy said he didn't know how he would repay Hollis for his work because the newspaper work was on spec. There was a little cash flow from the picture booth, but this was dribs and drabs. Not enough to pay for the repairs, the food, the general hospitality and the lodging of almost three weeks. That's why Mr. Hardy did the daguerreotype, to repay.

But Hollis had some other idea, because he kept on indebting the man to him. Hollis had his ways of always getting what he wanted. He was overly generous, the wealth of good tidings streamed right abundant from him into Mr. Hardy's lap. Hardy began to look at Hollis in a different way, looking not at his face but at his body, sizing him up. 'Goddamn,' he said, 'you are one heckuva man. Look here!' And he took a hold of Hollis's arm, not able to reach around it with his two open hands. 'Look at this, Maeve.'

'Daddy.'

'Bigger than Maeve's waist. I bet.' Hollis watched Maeve, who was casting her eyes only at the one spot where her daddy's hands were holding Hollis's arm. 'I can never repay you,' Mr. Hardy blurted out. He stepped back as if half expecting a blow from Hollis's immense arm. But no.

'I would like to ask for the hand of your daughter in marriage,' Hollis said to Mr. Hardy. Without anyone really seeing it, Hollis had swept Maeve up at the waist and was holding her off the ground in his bear paws. It was like a dream come true.

Hardy was smiling up at her with the smug look of a man who has settled a big debt.

Maeve was coming into her happiness slower. 'Put me down, Mr. Woolf, right now.'

'He won't. Yet.'

'Not until you say yes.'

'Yes to what?'

'That you'll marry him.'

'Put me down first.'

'You're something, Maevie.' No one had ever called her Maevie before Hollis. And Mr. Hardy didn't seem to notice.

The wedding truck gleamed where Hattie could see it, where it wasn't festooned in puffy cotton carnations. Hollis had polished it with petroleum, had taken a clean chamois and rubbed little circles of iridescent gasoline all over the black paint. Martin Flint, in a tuxedo, fastened little white paper carnations all over the bumpers, back and front. There would be a wedding. Hattie fantasized herself in the wedding dress, in that festooned automobile, but the image was too ridiculous even for her to be convinced.

And still, there was no wavering between Hollis and Hattie. He was steadfast. They met often in unexpected places late at night, locations where the ground was dry and the cover was sufficient. The moon could bathe her skin if it liked, she was blue in the midnight light, Hollis over her so that she could only be seen in patches. She felt nothing but him and sank into that. What did the reality of Maeve have to do with this? Hattie was sure nothing at all. This thing would not be tainted. Hattie's belief was so strong, not even the marriage affected it. Not even that she was a bridesmaid. No one, not even the most foolish fool, expected change from Hollis. Maeve was a fairy in her silken dress, she couldn't be seen beneath the gossamer, she was gone in all that cloth.

''Til death do we part.' Hollis kissed her and Maeve submitted to this. 'You are mine now, Maeve, as God is my witness.' She smiled at him, but there was a twinkle of fear in her eyes. Hollis lifted her into him as he kissed her and she was nothing, hollow in his arms. Hattie never thought what all this would come to. It wasn't like a real story; this one just went on and on and on.

Hattie clunked her cane down on a spot in the sidewalk, where they'd come through and stamped the pavement with a sign saying *Historic Route 66*. Stamping it didn't make it any more than it was already, she thought. She had a mission now, heading home, what Hollis had said to her right before she left.

'Bring that girl to me. That girl of Curtis's. She's wanting to meet me, ain't she?'

'Yes, she is.'

'Well. You send her over with Colm. I can't wait to see her, and hear about my boy.'

Hattie dipped down off the roadway and into the valley of the Pecos. Didn't like to be on the road past dark. She could no longer see where the ground gave way to the riverbed and felt her right foot slide down a couple of times before making out her house. The lights were out, so that she was certain the woman slept on. She let herself into the hall and moved about in the dark, turning lights on here and there. The place looked different at different times of the day — now it seemed closed, the lights giving off an orange glow in pockets. She went into the bedroom and saw the bed had been remade — clipped hospital-bed corners — and Martha was gone.

Well, hell. Hattie sat on the edge of the bed and wondered for a bit. She was bent over herself, folds ribbed her stomach and how like velvet they were to the touch. She noticed there was a certain odour in the house. Spice, sweet, and bitter. Perfume, maybe, or candle. Hattie's body was spent. Her skin tingled up and down her legs. She would find that woman in the morning. She pulled her feet up to rest them and fell asleep, laid out on the guest bed without any covers.

Eight

Martha practised a walking prayer up and down the dirt road along the Pecos, walking like a beetle until it hits a wall and tries the other way until it hits another wall and back again, never mind. The streetlight extended, then contracted, her shadow, so that now and again it was just her, now and again the dark suggestion of her loomed huge along the grit. She prayed, altering the wording so as not to bore God, to ask with gratitude, to seek guidance in this calling she'd been given. *Dear Heavenly Father...* There was just one streetlight, the glow going from white to orange. She stopped and stared into it, and it exalted her, that light. She was scared walking up and back, but the prayer took over sooner or later and then it was nothing but that, and she was one with it.

I will hold this in the palm of my hand and cradle it until I understand, looking at it. This was the communion they must seek; she had lost her way, and God had helped her to locate it. Perhaps it was a God-given mission she was on, and she must see it through. Aubie had left back to his home, she did not know just where, but she heard his truck bumping along the pocked road, and she knew he thought he had taken something from her in that kiss, and what followed, some promise. She knew this in her heart.

He was used to taking, she saw, but it wasn't true here. She had given him something, some Godly insight, and that was the difference. It would come into him slow, and faster, and he'd recognize it after it caught him up in it. This was the difference between the Family and the old Mormons, she thought, that the Family understood how love extended physically, that the body was a conduit to His Bounty; outside people didn't understand this.

She had reached out to the young man in the rifle shop and he had recoiled, gun-shy of her hand on his sleeve, and she'd felt an uncanny thing in herself, a shame, and had blushed. She had not blushed in years. She hummed as she stepped slowly along the road, kicking a small stone up and up and down. She was at it hours. She watched Hattie slink tired into the house, and she raised her hand in greeting but did not speak. Curtis had killed. She marvelled at this possibility.

It was the inexplicable ending to a vivid waking dream. Martha's arrogance had been revealed through His Hand. And it had traced her in its glory and made her realize her own shape in this big world. Soltane called her, and she had been wrong, she'd been arrogant to leave. This story about Curtis was too big for her. Too worldly. Her taint could be amended. She could go back. She could go back and tell Curtis, and he would help her to forget.

She must convey to Hattie somehow that she had solved this, that Curtis was free, that he'd atoned for this debauch. He must have been in such pain over the years to hold this on his own. The paddle, its thin nails, the length of it strafing her skin; how pain went over into meditation if you trained it to, and then a kind of joy, that bare separation between oneself and not one-self. It was an entry point into the divine, to feel the limit of the body, and push through. *I will serve you. I will shatter.* She would seek punishment, to show her remorse for leaving; the paddle would tear along her belly.

Aubie had leaned over, the trail of his maleness, body stink, and then his black hand over her beating heart, her nipple pressed between his fingers, and they kissed. She had concentrated on all of it, on everything she knew, a fireball of God's love, and given it to him. He would begin to feel part of something bigger than himself. He would begin to feel it first as happiness and then as something less speakable, but she would see it, and that witnessing was all that mattered for now. There was a line of light on the horizon, growing, must be four a.m., shush of creatures in the wayside.

Martha kept to the middle of the road for a time, mortal scared, and then the light made her feel watched and she tucked her body into the frame of Hattie's doorstop. How to tell that kind woman how her path would open to only exaltation. And sleep tumbled her to dreams and for some hours she was not noticed. Had she checked the door, she would have found it unlocked, only she never checked.

Hattie pulled the door to. She shrieked at this body pressing in at the door and falling, a corpse, and on Hattie's doorstop; it wasn't right. But then it curled open, a black cutworm, and it was Martha, shocked awake. Martha opened her palm and said, 'Do you know what these are? I've been kicking them up and down the road all night. I couldn't sleep, and I walked the road until I got tired.' She saw she had worried the old woman, so added, 'I'm sorry. I could have left a note.' The stones in her hand were revealed as translucent, red-tinged crystals; quartz, Martha figured.

Hattie peered at them and said, 'You gave me a fright, just now, and last night too. I thought I dreamed you for a second.'

'What are these?' Martha held the stones up for closer inspection.

'But that's only Pecos diamond,' said Hattie. She thought,

Pecos diamonds — what men killed each other over until they found out it wasn't worth a damn thing. But night walking. Nobody walked much any more, and the boys often chastised Hattie for her pedestrian ways, saying it wasn't safe. Colm said it wasn't American, said he'd teach her to drive, and that had ended badly with a dent and cussing, and looking at Martha, Hattie had the urge to tell her not to walk. It wasn't that it was so dangerous, just somehow it seemed like it might be dangerous for this particular person. 'Not the best idea to walk in the dark around these parts,' she ventured.

'I was scared — you're right,' said Martha. 'I prayed through it.' Her eyes had that sheen believers get.

'You sleep at all?'

Martha almost said something about Aubie, caught herself, then said, 'No. Well, a little in the doorway.' Martha was off the floor by then and had wandered into the house a ways, found that old chair, and sat down in it. The purse, which she'd been clutching the whole night through, as if the idea of a gun, loaded or not, could protect her, she let clunk to the floor at her feet. The tea had sunk deep into the grout now.

'It's Sunday,' said Hattie, 'if you want to get to church. You church-going?'

Martha wondered why everyone wanted to know this here. The Family's connection to the Almighty had no construct; it led personally and from nature. Curtis had said the bees were a prayer once. Curtis was watching a laden honeybee wait its turn into the hive, whirring in place, when he said that, and she had felt a surge of adoration for him, the way love can be reinvented when someone says something nice or moves just so. He reverenced all things.

Aubie had said not to mention his visit, not to mention about Edgar, that his ma had enough pain and leave it there. Martha said, 'We don't go to church. I didn't know Curtis ever did.'

'Oh, he did,' said Hattie. 'He went in with the Mormons for a time. Until Hollis caught wind of that and converted him back to nothing. Hollis's pappy, Samson, had broke with that church over any number of things, and Hollis liked it that way; Hollis had his own way with God, still has.' Hattie looked out the kitchen window, peered on an angle as if to see if someone was coming. 'You know, he loved that boy.'

Hattie looked down at the sink, and above, at the plastic card with Jesus's torn white body pinned to the shelf — she'd got that from Hollis — and then at the digital clock. Ten thirteen; good thing the house had cast its shadow over Martha, or she'd be cooked by now. 'Now, nobody much goes to real church no more,' she said. 'They used to. They used to sit catholic on them hard pews and worry their way out of that week's sins. People used to give a care what God thought.' Hattie looked at the cup in her hands, then at Martha, her wondering green eyes. 'Hollis believed in Curtis more than anyone else; he let him preach out front the station...that boy could preach — he was born to, some said. He still hold forth?'

Martha smiled, nodded. She saw how sweetly beautiful Hattie had once been and also, around her mouth, what joy had been withheld from her. What kind of obeisance had been expected and what toll that had taken over the years. Hollis had loved Curtis. Martha would bring that to Curtis. She would give him that. This would soften things between her and him.

Hattie said, 'Nowadays, there are churches along every main street in every town in America, they line up beside and between the hotels — looking not unlike the hotels, neither. People come for a performance, and before each service, they all stand, hands on heart, and sing the National Anthem. Now I believe in God and country, but I do wonder why these churches look so like office buildings.

'Well. The buildings is there,' she continued, 'and people get their voices going and there is a kind of community of voices that if it hits the right pitch can get the spirit moving. You hear them shouting and you see them a-shaking. I don't dismiss that. But for the most, it's yelling and talk of Satan. And I figure, the talk of Satan only makes him more real.' Hattie looked again out the window, then at the lenticular, then the clock. 'I guess scared gets the juice moving.' For good measure, she added, 'I was raised Roman Catholic, and we like a quiet mass. We don't go in for hollering.' She preferred the Catholic mass anyway, as it was easier to hide her thin disbelief there; she'd prayed for Edgar to come back so many times, she figured there was a secretary at the gate intercepting messages.

'Scared makes it real, you think?' Martha said. She was scared herself, and did not think it made her more or less real; only open, which she supposed might amount to the same thing. What would Curtis say? That every crack is a way in for the devil. That every opening is a keyhole to salvation. How to protect and reveal at once? She had to think.

Hattie had not had an audience in some time. She said, 'If you are a good person and you lead a good life, nobody sees you.' It was good to have company, and she would have Colm bring this girl to Hollis; maybe Curtis would be trailing her, tracking her to bring her home, and Hollis would get his last wish to see his boy, after all these years; there would be a salvation to things for Hollis on his dying bed, and that would be something anyone would wish for anyone else. It would be a gift to him. The kind of gift given out of mercy.

'The good are invisible,' she continued. 'It's the bad and the ugly that get attention. Old Satan gets talked about as if he's going to leap out from behind a shrub and attack. Everybody all just says how bad is a disease that made them do it. When do you hear people talking about the disease of good? I tell you, lady, I'm glad for you that you ain't church-going. I'm fed up to here with that.'

'You don't go yourself?' Martha said. She could feel a shiver all up and down her spine. She felt watched; she would go back north, but before she left she would reach out further to Aubie and make him understand how Curtis had recompensed. Curtis was sorry. Curtis as much as glowed with it.

'Oh, yes, I do go,' Hattie was saying. 'I go and I half believe to be on the safe side. But it won't change anything, you see what I mean?'

Martha was thinking about what Aubie had said, wondering if it would fix things for Hattie that Curtis was sorry. And then Martha realized she was thinking about Aubie again. About jail, men in orange worksuits. 'You said about Aubie being in jail —?'

'Aubie?' Hattie was standing with a cup dripping into the sink; she stared, thinking on the space of time he was not around and the space of time it took for him to leave off being a kid and start being a mean son of a bitch. 'Aubie's like no one you will ever meet. There ain't no hope in Aubie. He needs taking care of like his father does. Comes a time when all you can do is stand alongside and look after a man when they get like that. It's a sort of love, I guess.'

'Get like what? What do you mean?'

'There's nothing left to him,' said Hattie, 'not for a long long time now. He doesn't feel or care much for anything.'

'Was that jail?' Martha wanted it not to be Curtis's fault; sometimes it felt like God's hand was squeezing her lungs.

'He came out of there different. You'll meet him yourself tonight if you want. He and Colm are coming by to eat.' Martha felt Aubie's lips soft, then hard, on hers and nodded. She excused herself and went to wash her face; she took her purse, said how she would wander through town, pass time.

The people driving by slowed and turned, and by this she came to know it was not done to walk at all, that she made people nervous by this walking; even smiling at them did not dispel their nerves, but worsened their hard looks of worry. She walked past a church called Santa Librada and then some ways out of the main stretch of town and found a gun shop.

The Browning looked small on the counter, and she was afraid they would ask her for ownership papers, which she did not have, but they did not; the bald, goateed man just fitted the gun with bullets, and so she asked him to take them out and sell her the closed box. 'What's the good of a gun without ammo in it, lady?' But she had insisted. He'd asked her only why she had this old gun that couldn't shoot too straight anyways. And when she told him snakes, he had laughed softly at her and thrown in a poly-canvas concealment holster, which she thanked him for. And then she made her way, feeling at once whole and worried, back to Hattie's; she had a gun. Halfway out the door, she turned and asked if they were hiring. The bald, goateed man smiled and waved her off.

Aubie and Colm came together, like always, and like always Hattie wondered whether there was weakness to them singly, like they were weak to the past that she reminded them of, and then why that might be. But they came and it broke the worry about Martha some and gave her peace to have them there, for a time anyway. Hattie sent Colm around to the hutch for a rabbit. They would feast. Colm did not like the chore, hesitated, and the not-liking passed over his face.

'I'll do it.' Aubie was looking hard and longingly at Martha. 'I'll do it, Colm.'

Colm's shoulders loosened, but Hattie said, 'No, you won't. You take too much pleasure in that sort of thing. It's Colm who'll do it or I'll do it myself. Though why an old lady should have to —'

'Ma.' Colm took a knife and weighed it, glancing over at Martha. 'How do you do,' he said. He looked rabbity himself, like he thought she might lunge at him and wring his neck and skin the skin right off him.

'I'm Martha.'

Colm, like always, wore trousers that creased permanently, a golf tee, blazing white, gold chain holding gold cross, baseball cap. He'd melt in a crowd and nobody would say they saw him. He put the knife down and shook her hand, and from his face she saw he did not like the strength of her grip. 'I'm Colm,' he said, 'and this is my brother, Aubie. Don't you mind him.'

Aubie half rose and already had his hand out to grab at Colm. He said, 'What the hell do you mean, don't mind —,' and Hattie shushed him for language.

'I'll wash out your mouth,' she said.

Martha's eyes floated up and down Aubie. 'It's good to meet you.' She did not see Colm pick up the knife and leave the room. She didn't notice old Hattie wandering out after him for a little talk; she did not hear the sound of the hutch opening. She seemed to give no thought to how Colm hated this, the hand chasing down the caged animal, and she did not know that with his eyes closed, distracted by what his mother was telling him, Colm sliced through that rabbit's neck so it could be served up for dinner, and that with his eyes closed he'd also cut a wound into his palm. She saw the bandage only at mealtime, and when she asked what had happened, even Colm laughed.

'Rabbit bit me good.'

'Really?' Martha was looking at him, wide-eyed.

Aubie smiled hungry at Martha. 'Hell — uh — heck no, lady.' He pulled a shank from the roasted rabbit and bit in, and she stopped him and asked Hattie if she could give a meal blessing and already he saw her lips bearing some gratitude. Her eyes shifted upward.

Aubie wasn't up for talking much. Hattie hadn't heard him this quiet in years. So loud was he in his silence, Martha seemed to get nervous and retell her story to try to cut it. Curtis this and that. That's all Hattie heard. Was no wonder Colm kept glancing at his ma and his brother, was no wonder Hattie had to keep interrupting with Parker House buns and more beer and how about some tomato relish, some prickly pear jelly, it's real good. Aubie just stared and ate and nodded, and when dinner was over, he leaned back into his chair and drew both his hands down and pulled open his belt buckle, leather slipping through silver.

'Well,' he said. 'That was just right.' Aubie was looking everywhere but at Martha, on purpose, for she was staring at him like she was transfixed by the headlights of an oncoming vehicle; she would not look away. He tugged at the edge of his waistband and undid the button for good measure, and leaned farther, tipping his chair back. And then he swung his eyes over to Martha, starting low on her body and sliding them up to her face. She startled pretty good. 'Colm,' Aubie said slowly, 'what time do you have?'

'It's seven thirty.' The clock radio was just behind Aubie, right along his sightline; he could see it fine.

'I guess we should be saying goodbye and getting you off to bed then, Colm.'

When they were outside and leaving, Aubie and Colm, Hattie called from the door. 'Auberon,' she said.

He smiled at her and said, 'Yes, Mother?'

'There's a young lady at the Allsup pining after you.'

Aubie got halfway into the Camaro and hunched over with a smoke, his heels still on the dirt, and said, 'Just one?' staring at Hattie with this wicked grin spreading out over his face. And when she didn't respond in kind, he just said, 'Aw, Ma.'

Hattie'd already turned around and gone back inside the house. The smell of barbecue lingered, even though the meat was cold. Hattie was surprised at the quantity of food Martha put away, the slow burning out of hunger in her face. She gave the woman second helpings, a plate heaped with meat and garden greens, leftover biscuits smeared with drippings. 'You better slow down with that food; rabbit's rich.'

'I'm forgetting to savour it.' She had not had a good meal in some time.

'You are sure hungry.'

Martha wiped the last trace of food from the plate with her biscuit, the edge of her mouth with her shirtsleeve. A healthy pink was on her skin, and she sat back and smiled as if she was suddenly embarrassed at her own appetite. 'I'm never usually so hungry,' she said. 'I'm sorry. I guess I ate all your food.'

The threshold to Hattie's home was framed by boards milled from stolen railway ties and puzzled together. This'd been painted over so many times, it was twice as thick as the original boards. Hattie'd painted it green herself just last year, oil paint, shiny. The walls were light grey to hide grease, but Hattie didn't see too good any more anyways. She stood with one hand on each side, the hem of her skirt brushing up against the jamb on both sides. Hattie felt strong until Martha started in chuckling.

'Aubie and Colm are just like you said,' Martha said.

'You watch my boys. They bite.'

'How often do they come around here?'

'And watch Aubie. He bites hard.'

'Hattie, he just doesn't seem mean.'

'Oh, he's mean. He's had five years' time for thinking. Locked away from home in that federal prison. He's read some, that boy.' Hattie could hear the mingled laughter of Colm and

Aubie and engine noise and car doors closing and she might have crossed herself but instead she let the chill run through her body. Where might all this be heading?

Hattie wished she hadn't told that just now about Aubie; that was long ago, that hell he put her through. Martha's face was all held together, confused, and Hattie changed the topic. 'They come,' she said, 'whenever they smell pie cooking.' She closed the door tight, got Martha to help her shift the ten-gallon jugs of spring water Colm had kindly brought her and that Aubie had set in the kitchen.

Colm touched the crucifix he had hanging off his rear-view mirror and said, 'You hear anything?'

'Nope.' Aubie leaned over and turned down the radio; the army had been taking the crap for days over this Iraq prisoner torture mess, and a few unfortunate photographs. What did it matter so long as they got what they needed out of those people. War was war, and anyway, he didn't want to hear about this, he did not want to think about it.

Aubie turned the radio right off, thought how he wanted to sleep. He just wanted to get back to his place. He thought, too, how he was running low on funds again — the derrick work paid shit and he wasn't good with money — and that he was going to have to cull the collection, sell a few repeats, some of the garish ones, he didn't care for them much anyway. He wondered when he'd get another shipment; Aubie hadn't had one of those strange rug deliveries or a cryptic note in something like a year or more; he didn't like to count, it had been that long. 'I'm going through the rugs, putting them in some kind of order,' he said.

Colm was shaking his head, changing the topic to get away

from this. 'I heard that woman gasp in there, you just about taking off your belt,' he said.

'Nothing's ever over.' Aubie bent his neck, chuckling in the car, windows down looking back at his mother's little house, where they'd all grown up. 'Shit.'

'She did. She actually gasped. She thought you were going to take them pants right off. You're a prick, Aub. That poor missus.' But there was awe in his face. There'd been reverence on Colm's face since the moment he was born and laid eyes on Aubie.

'Your hand okay?'

'Skinned, is all.'

'My, my.'

'Huh?'

'I was thinking how that woman's gonna be up close for me.'

'What girl isn't?' But Colm knew how Aubie'd seen shit, he'd seen the inside of nothing, and how he should get whatever might come his way as recompense. From the time he was sixteen Aubie'd known about parameters and the nothing of nothing. But Colm only said, soft, 'You never will get out, you get in there.'

Aubie had his cigarillo drawing air and that ash-to-ashes taste — damn thing wouldn't stay lit. 'I take my big old motherfucker belt right off for that girl.' The lady was getting on, Aubie thought. The lady was burned and seasoned. Aubie watched Colm glance at the rosary hanging there, praying for his soul, likely. Well, it was too late for that shit. 'She can talk, though,' he muttered. 'The lady can talk a blue streak. I'm going to let her talk and talk until I figure out why she's up here, until Curtis gets here.'

'You think he'll come after her?'

143

'If he does, I'm going to be fighting you over who gets to shoot him first.'

'No, you ain't. But if he does come, I'll stand by and watch while you do what's right.'

'I guess I'm owed that small favour.'

Colm considered what exactly might be owing and what stakes were held and by whom and thought to shut up. He hadn't said nothing when he saw Aubie begin this seducing. And so he did not now mention the look of disgust on their mother's old corn-doll face, and he didn't pass judgment, not out loud.

Aubie would have her clothes off and his cracked work hands across her struggling skin faster'n white bread. Aubie had that knack; he owned them girls. Colm bet he barely took that damn belt lower'n his shins. Shoot. She'd be saying, 'Where you been all my life?' and half meaning it, pulling her boots back on. And it was their mother who'd found her, took her in. Colm thought, What some call destiny, others call misfortune. He said, 'Ma told me to take her over to see Hollis.' He pulled in to a gas store and braked. 'You want some water?'

'Sure.' And when he came back out, Colm tossed the ice-cold spring-water bottle at his brother's crotch. 'Cool you down some,' he said.

'You going to do it?'

'I guess I'm going back tomorrow and bring her to the old man.'

'If you got something for this lady,' Aubie said, 'I'll leave her be.'

'What?' Colm looked out the windshield. 'No. I don't want no trouble. I said I'd bring her by, though, and I guess I will. I have a half-day off tomorrow anyway; I might as well keep busy in it.' He twisted the lid off the water and said, 'You know, this water's costlier than gas. Cost me a dollar a bottle plus tax.'

Aubie smiled; he was fingering Colm's lavender Holy Virgin Mary air freshener, thinking where the hell did a soul get one of those.

Nine

'I'm innocent, I swear,' Curtis said. He meant it as a joke, as a way of breaking the ice with this serious young man. The border patrol guard was more a boy. The boy-man had not responded to the joke well, had only pointed to a small room. Curtis wished he had shaven, and trimmed his hair, worn clothing that was cleaner, more regular, maybe jeans and a plaid shirt, the kind of clothes he hadn't worn in years; he would need to clean himself up before he saw Hollis, anyway. There was Hollis thickly infiltrating him again. Curtis brushed at the musty white linen jacket he had on; it had a horsehair odour he noticed right away, and so he stopped patting himself, as the smell was only made worse.

It had been a routine inspection, in the end. The patrol guard asked him to fill out various forms, stating who he was and what his plans were. He asked him if he was entering the country with any items that were not permitted: firearms, that sort of thing. Curtis read the list and said, 'No.'

'You look a little rough,' the boy-man said. It was an apology, of sorts, for having detained him.

Curtis nodded and said, 'Yes.' And even hours later, now, he was thinking, Damn Windsor coffee. It was sure rattling Curtis's nerves; he felt hollowed out. He stopped at a McDonald's in Detroit for some food to rebalance. In the parking lot, just as he got out of the Volvo, a little boy, maybe twelve years old, came up and said something to him that he did not understand. It was a slang he could not decipher. Curtis gave the kid a Canadian five-dollar bill and when the boy looked at it as if it might be fake, Curtis tried to explain, and then popped the trunk of the car and fished around for a jar of healing honeycomb. He wished he had brought something more obvious, a Jesus candle, maybe, but there had not been time; he had none.

'Here,' Curtis said, 'take this.' He noticed a bee hovering over the trunk, swirling up in circles near his heart. The bee was in behind the right hinge of the trunk door, just above where he'd placed his Bible, and the Book of Mormon he'd owned since he was a boy, and as he looked closer, he saw there was a small hive being formed. He gasped. 'Look!' But the boy had already turned away.

And then when he offered it, the child had taken the small jar, looked at it, then looked back up at him. 'Fuck you. Fuck you very much.' Then he jabbed the air once with a fist, the small honey jar barely visible inside it. Curtis could help this boy somehow. He reached out to touch him, but the boy ran away laughing, pumping his fist into the air. Things here were much worse than Curtis had imagined. This was only a very young child, and already.

Curtis sank into himself, felt light-headed then. Hollis was coming into him as he made his way south and this worried him. He would see him. He would not know what to say. His actions had been so automatic back then. He raised his arm, the bullet came out of his fist, flung into Edgar, and the blood, which both woke him and lulled him to a waking sleep, was all over him. He had dreamed it. He wished he had dreamed it.

He had felt the love of Hollis looming over him, and that love had struck him, transfixed him in its desires. How many times he had gone over this thing. *Come.* No. He was not drawn down here now on account of a postcard; he was only rescuing Martha from her own naivety. Please, let that be true. But still, Hollis would be there, and he would go, and he would ask for money too, whatever was his due and no more. He would say to Hollis how he forgave him after all these years. Curtis was light-headed. He was just hungry, he thought.

He needed a burger, something with protein to get him deep into the night. He figured it would take him until three a.m. or so to get to Chicago. He walked toward the fast-food outlet, turned to wave goodbye to the child. He had packed a quantity of honey, along with the honeycomb, to give out along the way, not a huge amount, just four boxes; the rest he left for Benjamin to sell at the fair along with the candles.

'It's okay,' he said, 'it's just okay.' The boy was again watching him, punching the air, but with less vigour now. The child had been abused, surely, psychologically abused, and maybe physically as well. He recognized himself in the kid. He hoped the boy would eat the honey; it would energize him, trigger his soul to open up. Curtis turned and walked toward the restaurant.

'It's okay?' the boy was saying. 'Who the fuck says so? There ain't nothing okay, old man.' He heard the child shout this as the door to the restaurant, swinging in a wide yawn, closed. Then quiet. The restaurant smelled of grease and humanity; there were line-ups for food. Curtis went into the restroom to wash his hands. He didn't look in the mirror; he knew how he looked like hell, looked rough. His beard was still patchy after all these years, flecked with grey and the morning's porridge and wood chips. The hair on his head was too long, but full and healthy. He was old. But his eyes had a glazed hopefulness, he assured himself they did, a youth to them, a lingering beauty.

It had surely been a kind of pity the border patrol guard had expressed. And the child in the parking lot? That had been concern, worry that he was some sort of wild man, a crazy vagrant. So the child had been afraid. Pity and fear. Curtis hadn't experienced such reactions in years. He cursorily ran his hands under the tap water, and again, hoping the water would warm up. He was shivering and the water was so damn cold. Sink, he thought, and then dumbly, *The righteous are spared and are not sunk.*

He thought of the bees' industry in the trunk of the Volvo. The swarm had followed him, just like in the Book. He nodded happily to himself. He felt so blessed suddenly to be heading home to find Martha. She would buffer him against those negative forces that were waiting on him, and they together would transform the forces toward lightness, the sun, that desire. She would give him strength; he knew her.

Curtis glanced around the shoddy bathroom, the plastic liquid soap dispensers, the dirty floor, and suddenly didn't like this place. There was no attempt, no striving in it. He would skip the burger and just eat some honeycomb in the hope it would revive him. He didn't have all that much money, anyway, only enough for gas and a little food along the way, and the Volvo would need filling soon.

A janitor made a face at him as he left and said, 'This washroom is for paying customers, mister.' Then he pointed up at a camera mounted outside the bathroom. 'We got you recorded, dude, so don't try denying it.'

Curtis nodded and said, 'Sorry, I didn't know.' He held up his open palm and said a silent prayer on behalf of the janitor, who was clearly so held in the sway of life, he could not Live. Curtis then got in the Volvo and backed out of the parking spot, not looking, and almost ran over the angry child. He waved apologetically and continued. He saw the child was trying to say something to him, and so he stopped and was rolling the window down when the boy reeled his arm back and hurled the jar at him. Miraculously, the jar did not break.

'This is good shit,' the boy shouted at him. 'Where'd you get this, motherfucker?' The jar bounced off the Volvo door in a way Curtis thought might have dented it, then bounced once on the pavement before it rolled along the asphalt and under a minivan. Oil had leaked from this van, or a previously parked vehicle, and the jar rolled back and forth a little, becoming coated in the iridescent purple-blue goop. Curtis wanted to retrieve the jar but felt a sudden panic, a feeling that he ought to stay in the car, drive far far away.

'Hey,' Curtis said, 'why are you so angry? You're blocking the good things from coming your way; your life force, child.' He said this out through the merest crack in the window, and the boy started stomping and seemed about to run toward him, so Curtis accelerated out and away, thinking he would stop somewhere else, when he was calmer and the night angst he was experiencing had worn off some. He would check to see whether the car had been harmed. He missed Canada, he thought suddenly, and toyed with the notion of turning around and heading back.

It wasn't really Canada though, it was Martha he missed, and so he drove on. He thought back on Martha, that first Martha in the bus depot, smelling of rosewater and girl. In the beginning it had been hard for him to tell whether any of the Canadian girls were pretty. They didn't look like the girls he had known back home; there was something different about them, and he couldn't decipher their looks, good or bad. And then one of them smiled so wide open he thought he'd about pitch right in.

'Are you a police officer, sweetheart?' It was his hair, he knew, clipped close like that.

'No, ma'am.' Curtis pulled the duffel bag on its end so as to use it as a seat; his heart was crackling and pulsing so fast, he knew he had to take a breather. 'I sure am not a policeman. No.' He could feel the Holiness coming through him in that depot; he was a road for it. And now the girls were giggling and looking at each other.

'I'm Martha Moore,' one of them said. The one with the smile. Smile like an empty vessel, an angel. He'd started in praying for her right away, and God worked with him on that one.

Curtis manoeuvred the car behind a transport truck, hoping the slipstream would save him on gasoline, and considered how pleased — no, proud — he was that he'd left his childhood all behind him, the racism, the father, the past, and how he'd managed to take the good out of all that bad and turn not only himself around but so many others too, and how prayer could make a heavy thing so light it could fly. Then he wondered about steeling himself for the near future. It might be hard, this next bit. Yes.

Martha had smelled of nature overtaking, sweet leaf rot. She pulled a cigarette out of a deck, was fumbling through her pocket for a light. Curtis leaned over and lit it before she even had it to her lips. Martha looked startled, as if she hadn't really considered him yet. 'You must be American,' she said. 'I'm so sorry,' as if being American was a terminal disease. Curtis was out of water, drowning in air, and did not laugh, did not know he was supposed to. She was like velvet.

'I'm only kidding,' she said, then, 'There's a party. You coming?' She had been so simple, so strongly nothing, and she might have reminded him of Clarie, except there was something of him in her too; he could not name this. Martha was familiar. He had fallen so quickly for her, in a time when he should have been wary, and this falling he saw might now undo him. He had thrown his bag over his shoulder and followed. He had needed someone so bad.

And Curtis had never seen anything like the party this

Canadian girl took him to — the house, the level of civic-mindedness, the outrage. He was a hick, he knew this now. He wafted around gauging the limits of his own behaviour, trying to fit in, and then when he became exhausted from the falseness of this, he located Martha and waited until there wasn't anyone else in hearing distance, waited until Martha smoked down her cigarette, waited until he'd caught her eye enough times to alert even a corpse that this might be a come-on, and then he asked her if she wouldn't mind walking with him, checking out the city.

'Tell me.' She stubbed out the cigarette on the bottom of her boot. 'Are you really a draft-dodger?' The girls around her had giggled and moved off, and she had waited for them to move off. She told him later how he just seemed to her so different than the other boys streaming across the border.

It was early in the morning, they were outside, with the rain soaking them, when Curtis first kissed Martha, pressing his lips into hers and his hand into her lower back. His other hand was running along the cotton piping of her waistband, back and forth, wanting, wishing he did not want, for it would only lead to trouble; it was too late. Martha licked his ear, the lobe she took into her mouth, and then swept the tip of her tongue in behind, deep into the fold where his ear met his neck. Still, his fingers scurried along the waistband of her skirt.

She aped his drawl. 'Honey, that ain't no state border.' They were in the back alley of a residential neighbourhood. A feral cat was twining their legs, and when Martha said these words, it brought Curtis around a bit, enough for an unsettling seed of absolute terror to enter him. Even now it sent a shudder along his body, grabbed at his heart. The truck ahead braked hard, and so did Curtis.

The Volvo lurched side to side, screeching past a child — hell, another child, standing brave at the edge of the highway.

He turned to watch as long as he could, wondered what that boy would be doing there, so young, eight maybe, wearing jeans and a denim workshirt, just standing there, on that interstate. He thought to that other boy in the parking lot, who had sworn at him, and wondered whether he was hallucinating things, or whether he was being sent down signs.

'Who are you, Curtis Woolf?' she had asked, and he had held her hands together and had prayed aloud to her in that alleyway: *I am the Way*, he had said, and recited the scripture as he recalled it.

Looking back, he saw how this destiny had always been there, that Martha would always have to leave, that the farm, the Family that checked and balanced — that he'd created to hold himself together, to complete himself, he suddenly thought — would buckle; people were tenuous, and perfection would require some sort of fall-out, he imagined. He had smiled at her, all those years ago, and pulled his shirt up over his torso, stretched his arms out, with the rain runnelling down his skin, thinking about Christ on the cross and wondering whether she would get the allusion. 'I'm a peace lover,' he had called out, though he did not yet know whether this was true.

He wondered whether Martha would sleep with him that night, but she had walked up the stairs when they got back to the house. There was party debris all around, but no sign of people; the party had been abandoned. Curtis pulled the couch bed out. It was quiet in the house, but he could sense her above him, and this aroused him some. He tugged at himself until he got bored with it and then he took a few tokes of a joint he'd rolled earlier.

He was still unsure at that time what to expect from Martha; he painted her in different lights and couldn't quite see whether she believed he was a draft-dodger or whether he just badly wanted her to. Much certainly depended on how you created a person in your mind. 'I'm a pacifist,' he muttered to himself. 'I will work on that.' The truth was that Curtis wasn't against the war per se. Didn't Vietnam give a lot of guys a way to vent their toxic build-up of spleen and a hero's route to redemption? Look at his friend Robert Wilson. And take him. What had been so great about the democracy of a shitty gas station trailer house with Hollis as a father?

But he knew Hollis would kill him if he found out the cat was out of the bag and wandering unchecked, and so he began to create in his mind a Martha who would always help him, and then project that, make it happen. He would exude love. He would gather her unto him. He would work at becoming himself. He caught a phantom whiff of oil, like a ghost amputation, from the petroleum candle lit on the table, and left it lit, slept familiar in it.

And what he remembered first thing upon waking that morning in that new land was not that he'd plunged his hand under Martha's skirt and his fingers into her panties, not that he'd absently nudged the sad tabby cat away as he felt up the soft folds of her labia, not the kisses, though they had been good, but instead this unbeckoned memory of the paralyzing fear he'd experienced at each state border from Texas on up. The fear of reprisal, of capture, of consequence, of whatever was directly opposite to all this Canadian openness and frank anti-war protest, and give peace a chance — the possibility of imprisonment.

Hell, take away his freedom, and there wasn't nothing left for a man. This he knew. Really, if he could have picked himself up back then and walked home to Hollis, he would have. He was scared, caught inside his newfound freedom. He would be a pacifist, now, a draft resister, and the rest would fade into nothing. He hoped so. How the heck did it work up here with girls?

Well, now he had the answer to that. Oh, Martha. Come back.

That passage: *'Lay their hands upon me, that they might cast me in prison.'* He wished he could get that out of his head. Night driving, the lights flicking like a tic, Curtis weighed Martha's knowing now. He had always been scared of her knowledge, of what that burden might do to her. But none of that told now. There was something dreadful about her going down there, about her knowing him through and through, and about him going home, to undo this thing further.

It could be a gift, he decided, a gift of his own making, though in all this time he was as near to forgetting he had made it as a man could be. It was a secret ready to be disclosed. God had plans, as He always did. Martha would be down there, and Curtis would have to respond, take responsibility. It was his to use whatever way he could. Yes, there was pity, and fear and time working against him, but these he would try to reconfigure, just like that, in his mind, and they would be his allies, walking along beside him, helping him. Curtis meditated on the highway lights passing, let the pulsing light into his heartbeat, and was suffused with terror. How kind of the universe, he thought bitterly, how kind.

Tired out from driving, Curtis began to wish he could apologize but didn't know quite what he ought to apologize for, or to whom. He was skirting Chicago; he almost wished he could go back to that hostel he'd stayed in all those years ago, go back to that cornfield, see if anything remained of the rebel apiary. The world had changed though, and no one got to go back, and no, he wouldn't apologize. His whole adult life had been an apology of sorts; why wasn't that good enough?

The highway lights flashed and flashed again; he was a little comforted in the dark, moonless night. Or was it just cloud cover? Curtis hadn't looked at the sky in days, ever since she left the farm, and now he swore to make a better effort. Chicago was a golden glow to his right. He was tired, dog tired. He would have liked to pull over and sleep on the margin, but he didn't feel safe, and so he kept driving. He pulled a jar of honeycomb from the glove compartment instead, spun the lid open with his right hand, and sucked some honey down. That was something, anyway. It'd keep him going. He recalled the hive growing in the trunk, got a glow about that, *'and thus they did carry with them swarms of bees.'* This sure was a migration; the bees knew it.

He stopped for gas and marvelled at the sweet-smelling vapour drifting away from the pumping nozzle; it brought him home, almost right homesick. They surely had space back as kids. Curtis and his siblings and Hattie's boys. The Pecos and the desert was their playground, its dry baked earth, its caverns and cenotes, its lizards and its deadly insects, its bower of sky. They played together, Hattie's boys and Maeve's kids did. Rode their bicycles and tricycles in circles and made a game of severing sidewinders and baby gilas that scuttled over the dryness.

Their childish figures had cut shapes from the blue, blue sky. The still, hot air had a kind of friction; it was like God was present and he had known this. Grown men slept their entire lives away from siesta to night sleep, the images of wakefulness and those of sleep merging into some impenetrable reality. Hollis was one, his energy ebbing and flowing with his eczema and his mood. Man ought to be respected and awed and feared.

'Hollis's wanting you, Curtis. You best get in.'

How could Martha be expected to know this? And if Curtis had told her, really gone into detail about it, then what? He shivered, sloughing off the night chill, rolled the window up and hunched his shoulders, peered ahead. It would not do to talk about it. It wasn't worth opening, so he tucked it deep.

How it had been his ma who always came for him, and how that was a fact that never ceased aching. But Hollis never would get up for anyone, and someone had to keep him happy. He just told Ma to find Curtis or whoever he wanted, and she did. It was her weakness and her power.

Maeve'd rat-scurry looking for him. Curtis went in, the fear and the love catching in his throat, the other children stopping their play just briefly in acknowledgement of the slack he was cutting them. And then they'd return to the game with an air of reluctance or resignation that was really just another type of terror. It took time, he realized now, for them to seal off the complexity of Curtis walking proud toward the trailer back door.

He was hand-picked, and he did not take that lightly. His shoulders slung low, his boy chest puffed out. Hollis sat in darkness, the roll blinds implacable barriers to light of any kind. Hollis had painted them a grey more dark than black. The booze would be eating at his father from the night before, and Curtis knew this, that Hollis would be focusing all his attention on the migraine, as if it was an icon, a bloom of pain, to be meditated upon. 'Get the Doak, son.'

It was a tar product, stinking of fossil fuel, and Curtis would rub it in small, circular movements over his father's back. Hollis was a wonder of parched wounds. In places the skin was so dry it was callused in looping scales. And while Curtis worked, and while Hollis concentrated on the rhythm of aching blood flow, he would guide Curtis, give small advices to which Curtis was to be obedient. Hollis would never praise, but Curtis knew — he was meant to know by the shine in Hollis's eyes as he looked him up and down — that Curtis was fully held.

Approval was everything; Hollis's massive personality could protect Curtis from that sort of neediness and he was safe.

Curtis had freckles sprinkled like small petals over the bridge of his nose and along his cheeks: black eyes, hair, temperament. He rubbed the Doak in circles into the dry areas. He listened to Hollis talk about Hattie McCann and how she was fighting an uphill battle bringing up three wild boys on her own and Curtis could hear his voice rise in pitch and was frightened by what it might mean.

'She's a fine woman, that Hattie, and she don't have a fine man to treat her good. Them little bastards don't have half a chance, but you treat them good, son, and I swear it'll come back on you tenfold. I swear.' Hollis cried out when Curtis worked the oil in and so Curtis stopped and waited for him to relax again. And Hollis said, 'Don't stop, son, a little bitterness never harmed me.' The salve got in under the skin and burned. 'It ain't right for a boy to see his pa crying.' Hollis slumped over with his great hands on his face and he slobbered all over himself. 'Preach me something, boy. Preach me.' And Curtis would sermonize Job or somesuch for his old man, to bring him back to earth.

But tenfold. That word took on weight for Curtis. What was it to have kindness come back tenfold? It made him miserly toward the McCann boys. He needed to protect himself from tenfold as much as he imagined that tenfold might feel like the glory of God raining down on a person; it stood to reason this would be overwhelming. Curtis was not unkind, just one-tenth kind of what he felt he could handle coming back at him. And then there was a hint of sour to his kindness, a touch of superiority that stemmed, though he would be hard pressed to name it, so young was he, from jealousy.

Even back then, Curtis knew there was something about the McCanns, but he didn't know what. Hollis never asked anyone to be kind to Curtis, he was sure of this. There was a debt system to kindness, Curtis knew. You gave and then eventually you received. You received and then you had the heft of owing on you. You could not bank on the return of generosity.

Curtis gave where he didn't want return, in ways that cost him nothing. That is, he gave to the McCann boys in this way. To others he could be talented at kindness, but it was never completely selfless. There was always a carefulness to it. And he gave to Hollis without expectation of return, like prayer. He watched the Doak swirls soak under the scurf. 'Scrape it good, boy.' Curtis took a wooden shim Hollis'd sanded smooth and drew it over his father's back. Dead skin flaked off like old paint and looked mixed with the oil. 'Like the skin of an old dragon, that is,' said Hollis. 'That what the people in town call me now, Curtis?'

'I don't know.' Curtis did, though. They called him the fat dragon of Ramah, after Hollis's own hometown.

'You're lying.'

'I guess.'

Hollis laughed at that and let it go. 'Boy?'

'Yes, Pa.'

'It's time you learned how to shoot.'

'I can already shoot.'

'Son. I'm going to make a promise to you. We're going to stick together, this family. And it's going to be because of you. They're going to try to take this away from us, but you are our hope, you understand?' He didn't, but here Hollis swept his palm around at the room, and the window, which was dark and all shut up, and the door to the hallway and the kitchen. 'The house, the pumps, the shop. We ain't going to let them have it. It's all riding on you, but I will teach you good, and you listen, and it'll be okay. Maevie?' he shouted, though the walls were so thin there was no small reverberation that did not pass through. A clear whisper would have sufficed. 'Maevie, come get the boy.'

And just as immediate as his need to have Curtis, Hollis unchose him.

Maeve drew Curtis out of the room, his eyes blinking to acclimatize to the bright desert day. She dragged him by the elbows over to the sink and ran the tap and soaped him up to the forearms, scrubbed the Doak away, and took a flat piece of metal to his nails. She popped a Life Saver into his mouth, 'To sweeten you up,' she said. 'He don't know what he's doing, Curtis, but he does so love you.'

'Sure he does,' Curtis said. The Life Saver was like a sweet host on his tongue. 'Of course he does.'

'Say a quick Hail Mary, then go run and play.' Maeve held his hands in a dishtowel and indicated with her chin the picture above the sink, a lenticular she'd been sent from Oral Roberts. One way you looked at it the Virgin Mary was holding her shining red heart, the other way showed the Pietà, Jesus' long-dead torso so white and vulnerable it broke his heart to look too long at it. Curtis always tried to keep to the left of the picture so as to avoid that view. He whispered the prayer quickly.

'That's a good boy. You go out now and play until supper is called.'

The others gave Curtis key positions then, let him be the leader, the rule maker, and in this way, Hollis's power did filter down. 'Let's play at the heresy in the temple,' Curtis would say, and his brothers and sisters would run inside to collect things to sell, and lay these out on the desert floor behind the gas station. Their voices would rise up, haggling, calling out prices, and Curtis would descend upon them and scatter the treasures — the little toys, precious quirts, lures and polished stones, Pecos diamonds, and Indian spearheads, rattlesnake skins — and he'd rant. He would bring his face in close to one of his sisters' faces: 'Why have you forsaken me? Why have you betrayed me?' And she would quiver, and press her hands

164

together for forgiveness. He played it up so high they believed it, and that is when Curtis first knew belief was more powerful than God. Chosen and chosen again.

Stars were out, he could see the Dipper through a gap in the cloud, beckoning him along, thought how much of his childhood was him playing at faith — faith in Hollis, in the gas station, in some intangible central figure who could and would hurt him if he missed a beat, if he misplayed. There was a time that he'd been angry about all this, how it hadn't panned out, how his real family had fallen apart in spite of all his sacrifices, and those of Aubie, and of Edgar, but he was through that, he told himself now. The past was not the truth but a narrow tunnel to the truth — and here he was returning to that bosom.

Ten

The car seemed to know its own way. Curtis lulled right into the past, blinking his way awake through that long darkness, the spattering rain, just recalling and recalling. Tired, so tired. Curtis would wake and crawl over the sleeping bodies of his brothers. He'd ease over the bodies, careful not to disturb anybody, careful to maintain this illicit privacy. He would be dreaming so deep he wouldn't recall getting there. And then he'd notice the crackle of fire, even though it had been the smell of fuel that woke him. From the bedroom window, he'd see the swirls of flame first and then he'd stare at the trail of shadow light they'd leave on his brain; he'd turn and see it repeat and repeat on the bare walls of the room.

He didn't remember the first time he'd witnessed it: Hollis swinging like a massive dervish. How Curtis loved and hated it. His father had soaked towel after towel in gasoline pumped from the reservoir beneath the station. He lit them two at a time and danced a vortex. There was something awful about his fat pa fire dancing, moon dancing. Curtis never could bear to laugh; he felt sorry and he felt in awe all at the same time. The incandescence of fire was the only light Hollis could stand. The sun exacerbated his condition, and so he hid from it. People thought him evil, but people will conflate all sorts of circumstances to meet their preconceptions.

It wasn't nothing but pain and drink that made Hollis how he was. He wasn't an evil-doer; he was surely Job. Eventually Hollis would fling the towels away in order that he didn't burn himself. The flinging was a sight to see. Great curls of splintering fire catching pockets of oxygen, dancing their final dance mid-air, fireballs catching their own tails, invisible cheerleaders, their pom-poms ablaze on the wind. His father's face was flushed as he watched the wicks find gravity and wilt and contort and die. Curtis did not yet understand what drink could do to a man's sense of complacency.

Next day, Curtis would search for the burnt debris of Hollis's fire dance, but he never found much evidence. Most times, after these episodes, it was Curtis and his brothers who ran the pumps. They serviced the train of cars heading east and west. They made normal while Hollis hid in the dark. And when they weren't working, taking turns manning the pumps and counting change, they were off, fishing bait — silvery minnow — and pulling riverbed worms up for profit.

They played over near Hattie McCann's place, old Hattie McCann, they called her, though she couldn't have been more than forty years old at that time. They played and fished and swam with her boys, and Curtis couldn't recall better friends than them boys. Edgar, Colm, and Aubie were the kind of kids to be with and not have to explain nothing. They were just there.

Chasing Martha. A van honked at him. Curtis checked the Volvo right, pulling back over the dividing line. Martha. Hollis. Martha. Curtis couldn't expect or even want for Martha to understand all this, so he had kept most of it to himself. She had snippets and fragments, enough to keep her held, but not enough to endanger her. This had been a mistake, he realized. She kept the library, liked to archive things, would want the rest of the puzzle, and he didn't even know himself what it looked like, or whether it would end well. He wondered whether Martha might be getting into any trouble on his behalf — he sensed she might — or if she was keeping apart. He wanted to believe what he taught, that sensual love was God's love, even though, in this case, it picked at a part of him he'd thought fixed.

Curtis looked through the blur of the rain that seemed to follow him. Soon he would be in Nauvoo, his ancestral home, where he would stand a little to the left of the picture and keep his head clear. He would find small strands of evidence that she had been there, and he would praise God that he ever knew her; she was his kin, soul kin, and even as he was concerned about what she might be doing, he was absolving her because she was a product of God's will and was only doing what she was put on this fine earth to do. Mercy, he thought, mercy, pulling his hand off the steering wheel and crossing himself while the car drove wonky, almost off the damn road, almost killing him. Jesus Christ. How he saves. It was raining so hard Curtis could barely see out the windshield.

A sign, then: Nauvoo, Illinois. The Volvo stuttered along under the speed limit, Curtis thinking about turning back, thinking about how turning back wasn't an option and all the while catching sight of the road and then not as the wipers shifted a wave of rain and then another. He drove into town, then from one bed and breakfast to another with no luck, circling the monolithic, lit-up Holy Temple several times counter-clockwise, marvelling at its beauty. Martha had been here, he just knew it. Finally, he found a room at the Family Inn & Suites, an outfit run by Latter-day Saints.

The Saint at the counter of the family fun hotel/motel hadn't batted an eye when he'd asked whether a Martha Moore had stayed there. And the very room she'd stayed in, number fourteen, was vacant and available. Curtis would spend the night in

Nauvoo in a mouldy motel room in the bed Martha had slept in on her way through. Proximity brought on revelation sometimes, he knew, and prepared for that possibility. The house across the street was white clapboard, nothing but poverty, but still the windows were festooned with red, white, and blue bunting, and the mailbox had been painted as a flag. Curtis liked it that these people had tried; there was faith there.

He slept for a short time, thinking he could smell her. When he woke, and dressed, he went over to Uncle Bob's Restaurant for the night buffet, and it was all large-toothed, smiling families and extended families; he was the only single person in the packed house. As he ate, he looked around the room at them all and was glad to be in Nauvoo, in the place of the Mormon pilgrims, and to know his own forefathers had built this. He found himself nodding at everything, even though it was not all as he had imagined it. Instead it was, he supposed, as it should be. The quiet little place, bustling with tour buses of the faithful, roused a joyousness of Truth in the town, and microcosmically in the whole state, country, world. It reminded him of Soltane, only Soltane was free.

There had been a time in the early days when he wished he hadn't strayed from the Mormon tenets, but times had changed, and he felt a responsibility to that. Still, standing there at the Jell-O table, he thought smugly how he was not, in spirit, one of these people, that a person truly could deny his birthright. He spooned some marshmallow pudding onto his plate. He would try everything on the buffet. He was hungry.

Curtis thanked the woman at the counter in the restaurant foyer when he left, and she gave him a beaming smile in return. He worried at how happy she was as he walked back to the motel. He wanted to demonstrate to her how far from whole this vision was, where exactly it had veered away from perfection.

But he recognized the wide gap between them and weighed how little time he had, and only said, 'Thank you.'

It rained still, a fact that only strengthened the mossy smell of the motel room. Curtis liked thinking about his great-grandfather and how he'd fought, actually killed, for his religiosity, as this made his own childish obedience seem less of a mistake. He smoked a joint, lay still, and listened to his heart jump around, thought on those twenty-one people living in absolute integrity at Soltane, and held a moment of calm before his mind went squirrelling around again for the whereabouts of Martha, how the farm wouldn't hold together without her there, an arc of the circle missing. It made him nervous. He tried for meditation, trying to ignore the springy bed, the damp coverlet, and the overall whiff of rot the room gave off. He achieved something, some small, inconsequential interference, but what vision he really wanted never came. He didn't get to Martha, to where she was, what she was doing, whether she was fishing Aubie or Colm — no, it would be Aubie, sure it would. He wished he knew for certain. Instead he got the past coming at him in unhelpful pieces, and he prayed he might control his thoughts better.

There had been a kind of destiny to the way things had gone, hadn't there? Or doggedness. Right from the beginning, from the first kiss, from the time they had later walked on that abandoned Ontario farm. He had felt then he had to connect himself and Martha. And he had, he saw now, done just that. It hadn't taken him long to realize that she needed him too, that they matched up.

He thought about his pa and all that crap, about poor old Hattie McCann and her dead boy. About how God-fearing bad he felt about it all, and he wanted to think about Clarie and his friend Timmy, the one he wished he could have saved, and how he'd run till the breath almost ate him inside out, and about what a colossal loser he was, and how he wanted to feel so close to God with all this hurting.

He had prayed, and his prayers had been answered. And now he knew what he was moving toward. He would approach it with his arms opened wide, imploring: Welcome, he would say, I know you. And he would say this because it would simply be time. God had purified something evil in him, had absolved him. God was ready for him.

Was *evil* the right word for it? No. He hadn't ever been evil.

He pondered Hollis and the mess he'd left behind, and his eyes were barely holding back an intense feeling that might culminate in actual weeping if he wasn't careful. His mind suggested to him Loretta Lynn — a hurting song to act as a refrain to his emotions. But Loretta was long behind him now. There was a cassette tape of music the Family had put together in the car, and he would listen to this on his way out of town in the morning.

Hollis. Hattie. Aubie. He wished they wouldn't keep coming to mind, that something good he'd accomplished might arise unbidden in his thoughts instead, but it never did. He tried to focus on the Family hugging him that last time he'd seen them, and how it was self-evident that he had helped them, that his existence held importance. He thought of the Latter-day hotel manager to whom he'd given honeycomb, and the strange look he'd received. He'd touched the man and said, 'It's going to be all right.'

There were times like that, like the time with that boy in the Detroit parking lot, too, that he realized his gift might take years to filter in to the person he had helped. It did not matter whether he was recognized, though. That was just it. It did not matter in the least. He had slaked a thirst for God, and that was all he cared about. Even this, this business with Martha, was

God's will. From their first meeting, it had been necessary, an important unwinding that would, could only, lead to something Holy. He'd come far, he could see that.

Curtis nodded off happy, and slept thick through the night. And then he was running. In his dream he was running and running and never arriving. He woke up with a hard-on, fully dressed. He found he couldn't shake a strong feeling of uselessness; his mind wouldn't keep still until he had sectioned off a square of honeycomb and sucked it until the wax coated his teeth, palate, and tongue.

He needed her back, before she got too deep in. No one in the Family need know what he had done back home; he couldn't explain all of that. Christ, help. Curtis splashed water over his face, scooped and ate some more honey with a coffee stir stick he'd found in a packet in the mini-bar. The sun was shining low as he drove out Mulholland Street with the intention of going south on the 96 toward St. Louis. Then he caught sight of the Temple again and parked instead.

The begats. Curtis knew the Woolf genealogy from Hollis, Hollis muttering it at him — into him — as far back as he could remember, getting the words into him to the rhythm of Curtis rubbing that oil over his sorry back. And here was the beautiful temple his kin helped build. Well, that wasn't strictly true. The original had burned down to the ground; this one was a replica.

A man, thought Curtis, he added up to the men who came before, and that's all, Amen. That's what Hollis used to say to Curtis, though Hollis didn't hold to what the Mormons preached any more than he held to what anyone preached, unless he was preaching it himself, and then it was as good as Gospel. A man was the culmination of his father and his grandfather, and so on. He could make something of himself only in the next generation; family was the only hope for progression. So the lineage was worth recalling.

How did it go? Curtis to Hollis, Hollis to Samson. Curtis's great-great-grandfather William had been a slave trader back in the days, bringing slaves into Jamaica from blackest Africa and making a fortune at it. Hollis was proud of this. Fortune excited him unduly, Curtis thought, and he made a mental note to bring this up when he saw him. It was a flaw, and as such should be addressed. Curtis looked up along the white stone structure and marvelled at its straightness. Shit. He needed Martha. She could undo everything he had built; the Family *was* him and he was the Family. He should not have waited those four days — that was hubris. If only there had been children to keep her there, but she could not seem to hold his seed. He wondered if the gun and his past had held them back from manifesting their love in a child; it had been the one offering he most wanted to give back. A perfect child. But no, it was some imperfection in her, some imbalance she was unable to shift. If she had prayed just a little harder.

The Temple imposed, that's what it did. Curtis was scared of it, scared of a building. But then he thought again to his rightful attachment to this place, how his own great-grandfather Hosea had reacted against William's lifestyle and joined with the Mormons. How, as the story went, he'd fallen in love with a Canadian Mormon in 1832, converted, and married her. All his inherited wealth went straight to Joseph Smith's coffers, and he was saved.

It was heartening to Curtis that he had just come from amongst the Family. Sure some had fallen away, a few to join a church in the city, a dead church. He had spat when he first heard. The devoted leftovers had done their best to fortify Curtis. He had felt them trying.

It was, and had ever been, difficult to believe something so heartily when the time for sacrifice came. It had not been easy for him to leave Soltane; he could feel it had cost him. Curtis rubbed his hand along the white stone of the Temple. It had already heated in the morning sun. He gasped and pulled his hand away, looked up again at the seemingly endless wall, and felt himself suddenly to be noticed.

'God?' he said and nodded, smiling. The thought of Soltane had pumped him up, and the Temple standing so solemn and gracious before him filled him with love, a love for himself first of all, but that was a bounty he would spread. O Glory.

'The Mormons were abolitionists,' Hollis told him once, 'so Hosea hid the fact that his money had been the legacy of soul trading. He never told the Mormons where he got all that money, and I doubt they would have cared, as money is money.'

Curtis had been focused right then on a small, deep wound in Hollis's back. He had a beeswax ointment Maeve had bought from an itinerant and was dabbing at the edges of the sore with care. Curtis thought *soul trading* was a strange term in light of what the Mormons were after, which was just another kind of soul trade. And Joseph Smith, he had learned already, had always been a gold digger, digging up old burial mounds. There was treasure to be found within the earth, and this treasure could sustain him too.

Hollis grunted. 'There wasn't much peace for the Mormons back then, boy; the Missourians made sure of it. I always conjecture that's just the way old Joseph Smith might have liked it; there hasn't been a religion in time's long history that survived too much good times. God thrives on misery; it binds up his people. Anyway, by the time Hosea was foot-washed and converted, the wealth he entrusted to the Mormon treasury was repossessed by enraged slave-owning farmers; they burned every building right to the ground. Hosea and his people was on the move again. Like I said, the belief got stronger the poorer they got. And that's how it always is, ain't it?'

Hollis winced as Curtis pushed the salve into his sores. 'Hosea and his bride walked in poverty with the multitude of other faithful communists to that beautiful hill nestled up against the great Mississippi River that would soon be named Nauvoo.'

'Communists?' Curtis marvelled at the very name Nauvoo. It was the Eden of his childish imagination; many nights before he fell asleep, he played there in his mind's eye, and he described it in detail to his siblings, and preached it to them as their rightful Zion. He wanted everything to be nice. He had always wanted just that.

Hollis said, 'That just means they wanted to live in peace together, not like them red commies.'

The whiteness of the Temple made Curtis feel queasy in his stomach. There was something about the piety that had built this thing that made him feel like more of a sinner than usual, made him feel small, and he gloried in that, let his sinning self feel that smallness as a connection to the great oneness. He would enter this edifice in honest fear, he would approach his past, he would name himself one no longer like them. Here, where his fleshly history, too, had walked. He suddenly wished some of his brethren, the Family, were with him; why had he not been more generous on this account, let them come with him on this pilgrimage?

He crouched at the foot of the Temple and rummaged in his jacket pocket. Inside the handkerchief was a tinfoil-wrapped piece of hash. He opened this and crumbled a piece off the little brick. He crumbled it further along a strip of rolling paper and added the tiniest amount of tobacco before rolling the joint. He was anticipating the relief it would bring, and chanting on Jesus, on his loving body, he began to smoke; it was a sacred moment. And in it he recalled his aunt Agnes, who had died of Pepsi-

Cola. Curtis hadn't thought of Agnes in way too long. Curtis had seen her drink her fifth bottle one Christmas mealtime, and then he'd seen some evil manifestation circling her, and it caught his breath and stole it for a moment. 'Aunt Agnes will catch her death of Pepsi.' Young Curtis had baffled himself; it was his first prophecy.

Agnes looked over the barrel of the pop bottle, smiled as she watched the cold drink condense in a wisp of sweet. Curtis always would remember her just so. And then later with Hollis, his pa had caught him off focus. 'You paying attention, son?'

'Yes.' Curtis had stopped rubbing ointment into his father's back but briefly; he'd been thinking whether his prophecy might have killed Aunt Agnes. 'Can thoughts kill, Pa?'

'No. Looks can, but not thoughts,' Hollis said, laughing real fast. 'Now, you listen to me.' Hollis looked over his shoulder at Curtis to be sure he was listening. Curtis made like he was, even though he wasn't. He already knew it by heart. 'Hosea and this woman,' Hollis was saying, 'they had one son, who later waddled between the bullets of devils and angels alike to survive one of the bloodiest religious battles ever fought on American soil. Little wee Samson Woolf — your grandfather, my daddy — pulled himself out from under his mother's sagging corpse, nudged his father, and got his hand sullied in the mess of him, and even though he didn't know about death yet, he knew enough to abandon false hopes. That's your legacy, son.'

Hollis kept dead still while Curtis plowed a dry cloth over his back to pick off the scurf. It wasn't pretty. When it was over, Hollis said, 'I never did know my foster grandmother; people said she died of the ague before Daddy was two and a half. But my daddy, he beat me and Agnes for precaution every day of his life.' Hollis's shoulders rocked with something Curtis wished he understood, some hidden humour Curtis almost got but didn't.

'This'll hurt,' Curtis said.

'It already does.'

'Pa?'

'Yeah?'

'I wish Agnes didn't swig it so.'

'Don't you worry now. Nobody dies of the cola. Cancer and bad manners, yes, but cola just cleans up the system.'

Aunt Agnes died within the year. Curtis was twelve by then.

He smoked down the joint and went right to the Temple doors and touched them, thinking how the Mormon connection was just stories Hollis told. Hollis never understood how carefully Curtis listened, how he yearned for a family that prayed for more than just a regular stream of customers.

Curtis recalled how after Agnes's funeral, he'd cried, waking up in the damp sheets, euphoric to find himself finally weeping. And Hollis then had wandered by. 'What the hell is going on here?'

'Nothing.' Curtis shook his head.

Hollis had a little folding knife in his hand, Curtis saw, and he felt fear rise in his legs, his groin; his heart pump sputtered uselessly. Hollis leaned down and gently took his hand. Curtis knew what would happen next; he tried to calm his heart down, to endure this. In the flesh on the inside of his forearm, Hollis scratched a light line, one inch long. Then he wiped the knife on his shirt and inserted it into Curtis's skin. Blood beaded there and began to drip as Hollis pressed an even wound along the template he had made.

'Don't lie to me, son,' he said, and smiled. 'I love you, boy, and so I'm counting on you. You understand?'

'Yes, sir.'

The trail of neurons in Curtis's mind conflated the prophecy, the body, the blood, the pain. He watched his father recede in the distance, this hulk of a man, who meant well, who had himself so much pain, he must transfer it sometimes for relief.

Curtis already understood this. He watched Hollis until he was gone around a corner of the gas station, and he let his breath out.

Curtis thought then on old Joseph Smith, and on aunt Agnes; as he watched the blood sheet out of him and begin to congeal, he prayed clumsily on all this and felt himself rise out of it, rise above the earthly truth of this into something sweet. He was revelating, spiralling out into something Godly. He would make something of this new knowledge, when he could, when the time was right. What brought the Family to him had been more fate than fortune; he had been able to give long before they had found him to take. It had been years of preparation, he knew, years.

Curtis had started reading the Bible and the Book of Mormon and whatever he could find about Joseph Smith. He didn't read anything but God books. It was Smith's gold-digging past that got him, his attraction to shiny things and his charismatic power. The gist of Curtis's interest then went over pretty fast to him believing quietly that he, too, could be a prophet. At first, he felt protected, as if the very wings of an angel enfolded him, but later he felt it wasn't enough. Religiosity must run in families. And did not belief itself beget a kind of spiritual lineage?

Years and more he had been in the making. Curtis wasn't proud of it, but he wasn't ashamed of it neither. Curtis's hand slid off the Temple door and onto the great handle. He was almost surprised to find the door move when he pulled. The building — however deserted it appeared — was open. He entered the grand foyer and wandered through, marvelling at the gleaming cleanness of it all. He came to the end of a hallway and turned left. A man in a suit was standing there, nodding.

'Hello.'

'Hello. I was looking. My ancestors —'

'Yes.'

The man told him he could go no farther. He had a kindly face, Curtis thought, as a reasonable man might, and so he decided to press on. Curtis stepped around the man, but it was useless. The man moved in front of him, as if he had been expecting this.

'Even regular Mormons can go no farther than this, sir. You will have to leave.'

'I'm... I must —'

'No.'

Curtis recalled some tenet about being ritually foot-washed, or, hell, even clean, before one could enter the Temple. His reasons for wanting to enter weren't sanctified, either, so maybe that was partly it. That he was touched by God's right hand wasn't enough, he supposed; he had no proof. Maybe, he thought, maybe. He reached into his jacket then — the linen had become a maze of creases — and pulled out a small jar of comb for the man.

The man stepped back, and so Curtis reached out and offered it up. 'This will help you,' Curtis said. The man nodded for him to place it on one of the foyer tables. But Curtis wished to touch him. It was his duty to do so; his touch would seal something. So he took the man's hand in his own and placed the jar within it and smiled. Then he turned away and walked out of the building.

It had been two days since he'd been held in the grace of the Family, and as he walked down the pathway and back to the Volvo, he felt lonesome. He wondered how his bees were getting along, and then recalled the growing brood in the trunk of the car. He opened the lid and saw the hive had further developed; waxy comb edged the grey polyester carpet, and the bees had even begun to encapsulate the box of honey jars he had brought. The comb was dark yellow and uneven, and the bees hovered about him searching, as if he might be a flower. He smiled, imagining the ancient pilgrims with their swarm. Curtis marvelled at how the bees knew what they must do. God was surely in His heaven and all was right in the world.

It started to rain again. He closed the trunk with care, got back in the Volvo, pulled onto the street, and turned on the radio. *Flooding in the South has been causing community relocations.* Newscasts always made his heart race; Curtis flipped about, heard a sombre voice saying *torture*, before he realized it was Sunday. He kept flipping until he found a church radio. Talk of the devil. He left it on. It soothed him to hear the preacher's mellifluous convictions. He glanced at the old pioneer town on his right and found his eyes drawn the other way, to the great Mississippi. She was a beauty. All that water was a sight. And it was raining in earnest again; the windshield was fogging up. He cracked a window, settled in.

Eleven

Many of the carpets were not intact; they were fragments of larger carpets and not marketable. At some point, in part to insulate the steel interior walls of his shipping container home from both cold and heat and in part for the effect the rugs had on him, Aubie had begun to hang them up. The gun rugs. Some subtle, some garish, some so damaged he had to wonder why he'd purchased them. The ones with massive Kalashnikovs in blood-red wool blazoned across them, these Aubie liked least.

Aubie's place was in a suburban housing park outside an oil town called Artesia, on I-285. He lived in a building that was no more than a couple of shipping containers pinned together. Two metal containers that he'd punched windows and doors into, joined amateurishly at the opened butt ends with bolts, and clad with board-and-batten plywood; these were bought and paid for by a numbered company Aubie had opened long ago.

This company made infrequent sales of carpets and other imported trinkets, but mostly carpets, bought for nothing and sent through a military contact, at some expense, in mass shipments, each carpet rolled and wrapped individually. Aubie had had dealings with a carpet shop in Santa Fe, another in Albuquerque, and one in New York City. Well, the solid truth was, he hadn't had dealings with anybody in a while.

Martha, he thought. The woman's kiss had gone deep. She did not hold God, but her belief that she did was strong enough that it might not matter whether she did or not. She'd let her tongue roam through his mouth, and he'd never had a hard-on that fast or that pressing. He hadn't controlled himself too good, but what was that woman thinking, what kind of a girl jumps the first stranger she meets, her boyfriend's brother, for Christ's sake? He thought, then, that he himself wasn't all right either, hadn't been in some long years.

Then he recalled that at dinner this night, Martha had asked to say the blessing. Ma didn't much hold to prayers neither, but Colm ate it up like an appetizer, like he'd just been sent something that he could understand. They had held hands around the table, but Aubie hadn't listened to the words, just waited on the Amen and got to eating. Then she'd stared at him through the meal so hard that Hattie had made faces. He didn't like it much that Colm was going to be with her. Not that she was going to Hollis neither; he would skip off work early tomorrow, get Miguel to cover his ass, and get up to Santa Rosa first. Old Hollis could wait.

Aubie was sitting in the little room at his place now, where his bed and the sink were. The walls were covered in carpets such that he hardly noticed any more, but there was one that sometimes he couldn't help singling out, a thickly knotted mat with the Twin Towers being driven into by an airplane. When he'd got that one, he'd thought, How the fuck could someone knot that, and then, How the hell could someone not knot that? That was the last carpet he'd received, and he tried to find its story, but there was no way, and besides, he could barely keep his thoughts straight.

He'd just that night picked up Colm from the store and dragged him to Ma's place, not even giving him time to shower. Aubie took a ride with a workmate as far as the Wal-Mart in

Roswell and walked the last leg, passing only a derelict walking the road who had rigged a wagon for his scabied dog. The man stopped and waited for him to go by, not looking, not saying anything; the dog was about halfway dead.

Aubie walked past him and through the parking lot, waved to some people he knew who were eating burgers in the back of a truck — a man he worked with and the man's family. The man wondered aloud why Aubie wasn't driving and Aubie just shrugged his shoulders, like it was no big deal. He strolled the aisles until he found Colm stocking tins of beef gravy in faultless array, labels out just so, and then came up behind him and sank his hand deep into his brother's front pocket and fished out his car keys.

'Hey!'

'I'll punch you out at the time clock, Colm, and you go put some decent clothes on you.'

Colm had on his striped blue workshirt, grey, perma-pressed, fake flannel trousers, and a blue cotton apron. He looked down at this attire and looked back up, hangdog, then shrugged. 'I got ten more minutes yet to go.'

Aubie had already bounded halfway down the aisle to the time clock, but now he spun around on the heel of his boot and said, 'I got you a date, brother. I'll wait for you to change.' On their way out, the air hit them in the face when the door slid open. It was humid. At the front door, they passed the man with his dog. The man was panhandling, wheezing out, 'The meek, the meek,' his grizzled hand cupped for money. The animal lay panting.

Aubie strutted past, set himself in the driver's seat, and shifted forward as he sat down. He grunted and pulled his old Browning out from the back of his jeans, looked at it like you might at a spoiled child that has just insulted you, and shoved it under the seat next to an empty Coca-Cola Classic bottle and three spent chip bags. 'Christ, this thing is uncomfortable. And you ought to clean out your fucking car once in a while.'

'Aubie, I wish you wouldn't carry that darn thing around everywhere with you, and don't swear in my car.'

'It's my lucky rabbit's foot.'

'The swearing or the weapon? Where's your truck? You lose your licence again?'

'No, I didn't. I thought we'd carpool, save on gas.'

Colm looked at him hard and laughed. He said, 'I like that.'

'I had a call from Ma for dinner. We are going to visit a new friend of Ma's, close friend of Curtis Woolf, all the way from Canada.'

Aubie drove. He always said that not driving made him some kind of half-man, incomplete, and then Colm always said, 'What that makes me, I don't want to think about.'

Aubie moved the Camaro — Colm had saved four years and it was practically brand new — pulling out of the parking acreage and onto the main street, past the endless developments, the hotel and motel buildings, and now he was moving farther out, to take the highway up toward their ma's place. They had been mostly quiet on the way there, after Aubie had told Colm about Curtis's woman.

The small carpet on the wall of his bedroom had come in the last package. The piece disgusted Aubie when he unfurled it. Just two feet by four, small stick bodies falling away from the Twin Towers. Four aircraft seemed to be drifting into the buildings at various levels, and an orange missile rose up from a tarmac, a spiral jetstream propelling it toward the misspelled *Terorest*.

It was difficult to tell whether the piece was woven as a lament or a show of might, but either way, it felt cryptic, felt as if it was suggesting something — something Aubie could not penetrate. There had been no note. Not that a note was normal.

In fact, there was seldom a note, and then only: *Don't sell this, M. D.*, that sort of thing. The carpet had been nothing, as far as Aubie could see; a small, misused, rat-and-moth-eaten thing, with several repairs, and colours too loud to be marketable. What Corporal Michael Dama got from these carpets he'd probably never understand. But Aubie did know that he wanted them to keep coming.

Aubie'd taken the *Terorest* piece and nailed it up. Tacked up there with the rest of them, the piece became just part of the catalogue; the impact of the Twin Towers and the already nostalgic revulsion of that history kind of flattened out as it merged with the rest of the armament rugs, just so long as he did not single it out and look straight at it. The overall effect of the room used to overwhelm him, but now Aubie was inured to it. The bombs and burqas, the Stingers and the ballistas and the Kalashnikovs. He knew they had been knotted mostly by women and small children, their fingers nimble and tiny enough to do the fine, tight work required to make the carpet stiff and strong. That small children worked hours on these things should offend him, but it didn't; he didn't think about it. He just received the rugs, sold the odd one to pay the duty and shipping, and nailed the rest up like he was some sort of wack completist.

The weapons crowded in on him around the room. An index, that's how he'd always tried to see it, but with this last piece, and the growing dread — no news and no news and still no news — he had begun to re-evaluate. He worked hard to remember, but failed to recall the order the rugs had been sent, as if that might add up to something — hell, anything. It had been a year or more, he figured, since he'd heard from his fellow over there. Not a shipment, not a letter, not an invoice. Nothing.

'I still got the paper wraps they came in; I kept those, Colm. Few nights ago I sat down with them and tried best I could to trace the postmarks. The last one is from the North-West

Frontier Province, Podunk Pakistan, and as far as I see, that's his final location, the last stop so far.'

'You think something is up?' Colm asked after Aubie'd filled him in on Martha — well, as much as he wanted him to know — and the questions had started to form. He was always slow on the uptake, Colm was. He just prayed and kept out of trouble.

'It's going to rain,' said Aubie.

'That's not what I meant.'

'Hell, I try not to think,' Aubie said, but in fact his thoughts were a jumble. This woman came down from Canada all wrecked and holy, and the only thing as far as he could tell that tied her to Curtis — and that farm, as far as that went — was the yearning of her own body, the conviction that a regular orgasm equalled love, or God, like that little release was enough to enrapture her until the next time, so she might never have to deal with the bondage she seemed to be trying to escape.

She was running away, and her running away had brought her here, but any fool knew how that went. Nothing felt safe about it. Something had broken that conviction of hers, and it was central to the whole business of why she'd come down. And he was after finding out. He was sure it had something to do with Edgar. He thought to himself, We are all dying all the time. But he didn't say this aloud.

Colm was staring out the windshield, beyond the rosary and the new air freshener he had hanging down behind the mirror. 'I guess we're all running around in circles one way or another. You sure as heck are.' And Aubie knew from the way Colm'd said this that he was talking about Martha.

'Shit.'

'If the condom fits —'

'Fuck that noise; you try resisting that. I don't know how I do it.'

'You don't, as far as I know. You never resist. You couldn't resist a crippled grandmother if she flashed her withered tit in your direction. You already slept with that woman, didn't you?' Colm had kept a steady gaze ahead, looking neither here nor there all that time. He didn't want the answer to his question. He said it offhandedly, calmly, like he didn't care to know the answer to it neither or like he didn't want Aubie to think he cared. 'You're asking for it. What does that girl think she's doing here?'

Aubie calmed himself. 'I don't know. I asked her that. "What do you want from me?" I said. I had a hope she would say cock. But she didn't. She said, "Information." "A puzzle piece," is what she said. She said she wanted to figure out what happened. Said she didn't believe Curtis would hurt anyone.'

'She said that?'

'Yup.'

Aubie was driving wild, with a looseness, fast, then slow, steering broadly; it was about space and driving with the shifting gears of possibility, of a fatal car crash, of spilling blood, oil, and fire. Colm looked over at the gas meter.

'Full,' said Aubie. 'Like you don't know what you got in the tank. Don't you worry, brother.' But there was something to worry about; it hung there, always, all the time, waiting to be asked after. This wasn't about anything if it wasn't about Edgar. Edgar's story wafted over and through everything these last days, ever since that woman had shown up. They drove in silence, Aubie thinking about Edgar before this shit took him away, how he was the careful one, how he weighed things. How full his commitment was once he made it. He was the centre of the family, the moral centre. Aubie wished him back, but that wish, he knew, wasn't going to manifest.

⚝

They were parallel to the Pecos by now, taking the road north, and the air coming in the windows was sweet with the scent of grass. There was a coolness to the breeze, like it remembered water, even though there wasn't even so much as marsh in the riverbed but just enough underground water for some dry-looking bulrush. On the other side of the road were spent drill holes and the remnants of industry — rotting cast-iron derricks scattered over a ranch that was finding its way back to nature.

'As far as I can tell the only thing that lady believes is the singing of her own flesh. She thinks she's a conduit to the Lord. She gave me a pamphlet when I left,' Aubie said. 'It said how the sexual body is a vessel to the Lord. Shit, she's as depleted as this old oilfield. Curtis has got some Jesus-freak love-in happening up there. I wouldn't be surprised if he beats her; she flinches at his name.' They stared as they passed by the ranch at the derricks like dinosaur skeletons, some of them corroded through and buckling under their own weight, stared like they half expected the things to creak back to life, the sliding tick-tock-suck was what was missing from the scene. Aubie pulled over and stopped in the grassy verge.

'Why you stopping?' said Colm. He was still thinking about the term *sexual body*.

'Come on.'

'Shoot, Aubie, you're going to get us killed driving like that, and I still got ten payments on the car.'

But Aubie was already out the door. He rapped on the roof. 'Let's go.'

'This is bull.'

'It might be. It might be.' He leaned back into the car and retrieved his gun. He checked the safety and rammed the thing into the back of his pants so the pipe pressed down his crack. His belt held it steady. 'Let's walk.' And he waved in the general direction of the old stream. There was a burled scrub oak to their left, and Aubie walked over to it and circled it, as if appraising it.

'Oh, come on, Aubie, who has time for this? I sure don't.'

'All you got is time. I'll have you back snug real soon. I swear.' Aubie crouched now at the base of the tree and rubbed his fingers over a place where the bark had long ago been scraped away. 'Have you ever seen this?' Aubie shifted his hand out of the way and revealed a heart with the letters *HM* and *HW* carved into it. 'Ma did that, I'd wager, love being stronger than common sense.'

'So our mother loved our father.' What did he care? It didn't change the rest.

'You never think about the circumstances of your beginnings?'

'No.'

'Well, I do. I think about it all the time.'

Colm looked at the heart. It had a jerky line, black and gnarled where the tree had tried to heal what amounted to a wound. 'Our mother is a simpleton, but at least she wasn't married to him. That gives her something.' And Aubie saw that Colm was uncomfortable, that his body twisted in on itself, that his breath shortened, that he had betrayed something deep.

'You got something to say?' Aubie could feel the gun pressing along his spine. He'd brought it out of habit. He always carried some kind of weapon, and when he went into the long grass, which was rarely, he always had a gun. There was no telling when you might meet a snake or a madman, and you might as well be prepared. Colm was twitchy. He had broken into a sweat, and Aubie could already see the wet forming a ring under the arms of his T-shirt.

Colm said, 'She any good?' The derricks rose up behind him, cutting the sky into little triangular frames.

'I ain't had her yet, so I couldn't answer that.' Aubie looked through the legs of a derrick at a wisp of cloud and acted like it held his attention. It was a lie. Martha had straddled him. Her skin wasn't young no more, her breasts had seen better days, but her waist and hips curved in the right places. He liked the hair she left growing under her armpits and in a line up her belly. 'She's not good so much as something else, I think. She's dangerous.' He said that, but what he thought was that she was not dangerous, but powerful, which in the normal scheme of things might amount to the same thing. He tucked this away. The fact of the matter was, she'd possessed him for the five short minutes it had taken him to cum.

'Dangerous?' Colm started laughing. 'Well, let me know what happened then, brother; I might as well live vicariously.' He pulled a package out of his back pocket that he'd grabbed from the open fridge at work as he walked out. It was a bologna he'd grown fond of. Colm stopped laughing and just smiled at his brother, pulled at the plastic where it said *tear here*, took a round of processed meat off the slab, folded it once and in quarters, and then pushed it into his mouth. He waved the package at Aubie. 'You want some?'

'Naw.'

'So she get to you?' Colm kept a hand over his mouth, but it didn't stop his voice from coming out wrong, warbly.

'She didn't get to me. No.' Aubie was a damn fine liar. It was his appraisal now that Colm wouldn't begin to understand what he meant even if he could put it into words, which he couldn't. Colm had sure not been laid in months if not years, and even if he had been laid, which was unlikely, he couldn't have been properly laid if he went around eating bologna like a fucking pasture horse, all teeth. At least he learned himself a few manners in jail, he thought. And no. She hadn't got to him. What was it about that woman? The one weapon she had was the part of her body that was empty, made him feel like he was chasing after lack. She pressed down on him, held him still, and in five minutes had him bought and sold. And then she'd shown him what she wanted. Touch here, touch here, touch here. He'd felt like he was blessing her.

'So how is she dangerous?'

'Well. That woman's gonna bring Curtis to her. If I know anything, then I know that.'

'Let that dog lie, brother.'

Colm was the kind who could pray it away and feel clean in doing that. Aubie shook his head and said, 'Oh, that dog will sure come.' His gun was rubbing a raw strip down his back. Damn wet heat, rain coming.

On the way home he had said, 'So, Ma wants you to take her to Hollis. You going to do that?'

Colm peeled off another slice of the meat and sank it in his mouth. 'I'll take her to the old man.' He offered the packet again. 'Almost don't have to chew. A fellow at work, he calls this the working man's Holy Host.' Colm held up a perfect round. It tasted of petroleum and ketchup.

Aubie stood on his bed now and traced the outline of the plane with his finger, wondering whether any of it meant anything and deciding that even with all the clues in the world he might not catch that meaning. He lay down and pulled the phone over, dialled Ma but didn't get an answer, and he fell asleep thinking about Martha's hands over him. He'd take her out, make her real for him again.

Aubie slept then, dreamed her on his bed, in his office. She hauled a couple of the more violent rugs out of the room, asking first if he minded. He was over minding anything much when it came to her, her body, the way she seemed to offer it up, and make him work for it, against it, whatever she wanted. 'You sure are sexy, lady.' Aubie was just grinning. Martha said, 'No, it's honeykeepers,' and she held up a little bee and let it struggle between her fingers. He woke up to the alarm clock vibrating his leg where he'd slept on it.

Then the day was shit on the oilfield; running in the hole with a submersible pump, he almost sliced himself good strapping banding. Like a machine, he was, like a heartbeat, clamping cable to pipe, feeling it slide down below him, so that it was a wonder he didn't later dream the filthy petroleum pipe slithering down, down, and the mechanical way he became around it, only banding and not thinking. The floor hand had passed him a length of banding, and he'd reached over with his ungloved hand. It was the Mexican who'd pushed his hand away gently, else he'd have been cut, maybe handless. That shit happened, and he'd seen it. He laughed it off at break, saying, 'Chick is breaking my heart, Miguel. You know how it is.'

But Miguel hadn't even smiled. He was a man who didn't want to be held responsible for nothing. 'Keep your mind on the job,' he'd said. But what had Aubie been thinking about except her. The way she'd taken his one hand and put it there and the other and put it there, hadn't said a damn thing, and hadn't needed to. It was like magic running through his body; and he was so far elsewhere he had just lain there and wondered. After, she'd asked him where he'd been, and he had said, 'Some good place,' like a man in love. Hell, he wasn't in love.

Twelve

Hattie was frantic. 'I tried to stop her, but she wouldn't hear it. She ain't here. She took her bag and started walking about half an hour ago. She said she was done, and she was heading home. I tried to stop her. I did.'

And Colm bent down, pulled his jean bottoms out of his boots, and took the afternoon trawling the riverbed north while Martha was south with Aubie.

Aubie'd found her on the I-285 hiking south and slowed down past her and turned the truck around. 'Where to?' he'd said after he'd let the window down.

Martha saw it in his face right off, a softening glowing under the skin; she struggled against this. 'Aubie,' she said, 'I thought through the night about it. I was wrong to come.' She struggled to find the right word amid all the words chattering through her body. She felt heavy; her body was heavy. 'I was presumptuous,' she finally said. 'I did not need to know. And now, knowing this little bit I do know, I feel satisfied. I don't need to know more. I should have trusted. I'm going home. It would be better if I went home.' She was headed the wrong way.

'But what about —' Aubie looked down the road. He could see down it until it disappeared miles and miles south; there wasn't anything until Roswell and then miles of nothing to Artesia. He was going to say what about Hollis but pulled back from that line of questioning. Instead, he said, 'You going this way?' and pointed down the road. 'I can drive you a ways if you like.' Before she saw, he pushed his phone and his gun off the passenger seat, caught them with his other hand, and put them in the glove compartment.

'If you're sure you don't mind.'

'I don't mind.' And Martha got in. It was a solid half-hour before he told her they were heading south, and it sank in to him that she had already known this. He felt caught.

'Shit. Why'd you do that?'

'I didn't mean to. I headed first north and then crossed the road. I felt scared and crossed the road. I crossed a few times back and forth. I thought if I came down to Artesia and found you I could at least talk to someone. I don't know what to do.' She had played at fishing him. That had been a normal way in for her, but then there had been more; she had felt her body. Not exaltation. Not the frisson of God's hand reaching out, but Aubie's hand. She was scared; she had lost some game she'd never known she was playing. She was all by herself, she had suddenly thought. And she did not know what to do with that thought. It wasn't something easily explained to an outside person, and she didn't know if she could talk to Aubie about it, or if she should.

So she was quiet. They listened to the radio reporting rain. The air was thick with it; Martha felt it portentous. 'It's bad.' Martha fiddled with the radio dial and came up with Lion's radio, the announcement of an upcoming rodeo, *Coast Guards get two dollars off admission* and then the tail end of a report about a NATO peacekeeper losing his life in Afghanistan when a rocket-propelled grenade hit his convoy.

'Peacekeeper,' said Aubie. 'That's the new code word for soldier.'

Martha kept seeking and found a tune that she recognized from the 1960s, though she could not tell the name of the song or the musician. It was familiar. She didn't want to think about what Aubie meant about peacekeepers and soldiers, did not want to think about the general state of things, did not like this sort of small talk. She wanted familiarity, but there wasn't any of that around, so she settled for Aubie and this song. 'Where are we going, anyway?'

'I don't know. I could take you on an oilfield tour, take you to work. You want that?'

'Sure,' she said, though she had hoped he was taking her to his house. She could not imagine how he lived. 'How are you? I mean —'

'I feel good,' he said, smiling over at her. She had meant whether he felt sanctified, but could not dare put this in words to him. She had caught him, fished him from the depths of unbelieving, saved him, she hoped: God ought to be moving through him.

Aubie started to say something, but she interrupted, laughing. 'Oilfield?' She would pray to God in the oilfield; she would wander out into the field and let loose a wild prayer such that God could not ignore. 'I was just thinking that Curtis was maybe not the only one brought up on crude.'

'The hell.' Aubie wasn't sure how he'd been brought up except without much help; he was sure of one thing though, and that was that he must pleasure-seek to forget the rest. He wasn't debauched; he just turned to the sun. He had pulled Martha off his ma's kitchen bench and brought her half stumbling to the bedroom. It wasn't much of a lovemaking, he knew. Well, he was slow enough taking off her clothes. He wanted to see every part of her in case it was the last time he ever did, but then it was fast with his own jeans, and he was looming over her body lying there on the spare room bed. All Martha had to do was smile and he was in her, a train ride that ended too soon. He pulled out and lay next to her, smelling of salt, looking up at the crack in the ceiling that was beetling across the corner, and said, 'You like that?'

'Well, it was efficient.'

Then he tried to touch her so she wouldn't think he was nothing at all. And then, up close, he had seen the thin white striations on her skin, down her breasts, a thicker scar knotted on her nipple, and it had shocked, but he had pulled back, said nothing. Thin white scars, like bars down her skin, and he pulled back from commenting.

He recalled then about the tail end of his prison time and how they'd let him do work release, roaming the highways in leg irons along with a busload of other good-behaviours, picking up the garbage good people tossed out just to rid themselves of it, to get themselves pure real fast, and how he'd fantasized some hot-blooded woman in a race car rescuing him. He'd fucking yearned for this, watching all those cars swoop past him. Aubie jarred when Martha spoke, turned to her like he'd found something. 'And where do you live?' she asked, staring at him, into him, which frankly unnerved.

'Live? Oh, yonder.' He pointed with a swayed finger to nowhere in particular, direction home. Freedom. Freedom is what he had been yearning for, in the shape of a woman, a car moving fast.

'You just said yonder.' She talked so slow, to herself. 'I can't believe I had sex with a man who says yonder.'

Aubie eyed the road, flicked a plastic filter holder of his cigarillo between his teeth, around and around. He was thinking, Sex? Is that what that was? Was there ever going to be freedom? He thought of his trailer, and the carpets, and whether he really was ever going to be free. Martha put her hand on his thigh. Maybe yonder is funny, he thought after a time. 'Maybe, you are right there.' And then he said kindly, 'What's this game?' He was looking down at her hand on his leg. 'What is this about?' He was thinking about that pamphlet she'd slipped him, what crazy things people got to thinking in this wide world.

'I just want to help you.' She moved her hand and pulled back to the passenger side. Martha drew a line down the window with her finger, then she breathed warm on the cooled pane and drew another line down the condensation. He smoked as she ran her finger absentmindedly over the lines she made. Martha leaned down then and pulled a wallet out of her satchel, and out of the wallet she pulled an old school photograph and handed it to Aubie. 'You know who this is?'

'I wish I didn't.' It was a school picture taken when Curtis was about ten — all impish in front of the fake-sky backdrop. Aubie even remembered what the photographer looked like. Curtis was freckles and teeth and future. Aubie handed it back and watched Martha looking at it.

'If I started to hate him,' she said, '— and I did sometimes — I'd only have to look at that school photograph and I'd be back loving him. Somehow, what he was always seemed to start with that picture.'

'You shouldn't of kept the picture, I guess. Love and pity. There ain't that much between them.'

'Are you saying you pity me?'

'No. And this sure as hell ain't love neither, honey,' Aubie said. His shoulder twitched. 'I wasn't talking about us. I was — forget it.' Like that, Aubie was hard edge and fury.

'But you were once fond of Curtis. He told me.'

Aubie heard but said nothing. He pulled the cigarillo out of his mouth, tore the still burning ash off, chucked it out the window. Then he turned the cigarillo around, sank it into his mouth, and again, to moisten it. The leaf tasted stale, and a piece of tobacco had strayed just behind a lower canine. He worked his tongue along his gums and tried to pry it out. He would spit it out if he managed this. Curtis. He'd been mostly successful in not thinking about Curtis too much for all this time. Why did he need to waste his time thinking about that little mouse shit? Well, he did, he knew.

'What was he like back then?' Martha had turned her body and was watching him.

'Curtis? Well, he was a bit of a weasel, as I recall.' He lit the cigarillo up again.

Martha leaned over, fussed with her leather bag, getting something out and then securing the bag good. There was a pull string and then a latch, and she tied the one in a double knot and latched the other and shoved the bag under the seat. Aubie got to thinking what else besides memories might be in that bag but decided to save that thought.

'No,' she said. 'He's not like a weasel.'

Aubie shook his head. 'Oh, yes, he is. I recall him running this one time. Running, mind, like no one had ever imagined to see such a lazy boy run. He had a girl, that's Clarissa married now to that Wilson boy, and Curtis and her had been making a name for themselves running around town together.' Aubie was slowly moving his hand up and down his breastbone, disrupting his shirt. He was staring into space, the white line painted on the road, and there wasn't a car in sight on all that long highway, him catching sight of her body sideways in snatches. 'Curtis used to fly out of Clarie's house when her parents came home. This one time, though, he was running yet faster; he looked like a colt that's seen fire. It was this little friend they had, Timmy, who used to look up to Curtis, and who he used to give advice to, mostly about how to avoid his drunken dad. Hell, Curtis knew all about that. It was Timmy.'

'I have heard this piece of the story from Curtis.' It was in a gathering speech he made, and she had heard him mumble the name anxiously in his sleep, and she had petted him to calm.

'The boy hung himself. Took an old jump rope and strung it over the porch rafters. That shitty little shack was more porch than house. He took a plastic pail and turned it upside down and stood on it to get the height, and then just kicked it away when he got the set-up right. Father like that boy had, he was better off dead. That was the general opinion.'

'No one should think like that.'

Aubie had liked Curtis back then, had liked him a good deal, but he couldn't and didn't any more; it was helpful to focus all the bits of his lousy life on that one person, and keep the sights steady. He looked Martha dead in the eye but saw only thin white lines dead straight down her abdomen, like she'd been combed with knives. 'Where was Curtis running? He tell you that?'

'Yes. There had been a phone call to Clarie's house. Curtis got a call from Hollis or one of his brothers. There was a message from Timmy asking him to come over right away. That Timmy had never called before made Curtis worried, so he ran.'

'Good. Sure.' Aubie was talking to his cigarillo.

'What, "good?" What do you mean by that?'

'I watched with my own eyes, Martha. I saw. Curtis never ran to Timmy. Curtis was running away, sweetheart. Away. In the opposite direction. He was running home to Hollis.'

Martha's eyes twitched and her face crumpled into some kind of sorrow, confusion, upset. 'That's a horrible thing you just said. I have a hard time believing it.'

Aubie grappled his tongue along his bottom teeth and stuck the tip out. A small brown fragment of tobacco was perched there, and he pinched it with his fingers and flicked it toward the back seat. 'That was around the time the interstate went in, when Hollis converted him to armed robbery, converted me too, for that matter.'

Aubie was keeping at bay the nagging fact that in Curtis's shoes, he would have run to Hollis too. It was jail that had broke Hollis's hold on him. No, wait, it was Edgar that had. Then he wasn't too scared of nothing any more. It's like he had seen the smoke and mirrors. It's like he told himself he had anyway — truth was, mention of Hollis still made him jumpy.

'Why would Curtis run home? You think he had a hand in what happened to Timmy, don't you?'

'Hell, we all had a hand in what happened to Timmy. Death by silence. Did Curtis help Timmy kill himself? I doubt that.'

'Then what are you saying?'

'He was scared. He ran because he was weak. You asked me what Curtis was like. He was like what he is still: a scared little kid, obeying orders and taking cues from whoever was stronger. He ain't no different now; people don't change. God's higher orders or Hollis's. Well, it don't make no difference in the end, I figure.' Aubie hauled in the smoke. 'Mmm,' he said. 'So, how long you think it'll take?'

'Take?'

'For Curtis to get here?'

'Curtis hasn't a clue where I am.'

'Curtis knows where you are every second of every day.' Aubie closed his eyes, wished himself away from this thought line: What if Curtis was here, would he kill him? Sure he would, and let the buzzards at him.

'You all right?' She asked like it was normal she read Aubie's thoughts, and he answered that way too. His mother sometimes talked about Hollis this way, like he could read her and she him, like they were parts of a puzzle. Aubie didn't want to fit with anyone.

'I'm good.'

'Do you miss him?'

'If he was here right now, I don't know what I'd do to him.'

Martha turned away. 'I shouldn't have slept with you.' She wrapped her arms around her waist. Something brewed in his eyes, something bad, and she was smiling at him to calm that. 'He's not the same person, you know.' She was bracing herself in her huddle. 'People do change. I know they do.' She herself was changing. This sudden thought unsettled her; she felt heavy with it, as if the clay of this place was filling her legs and making her grounded and earthbound. Martha did not like to feel solid.

She was fucking beautiful, Aubie thought. The light was edging the skin on her neck, making her look holy, but Aubie knew she was not holy and wasn't even convinced she was all that good. She was good trying her hand at bad, maybe, or the other way around. No, maybe she shouldn't have slept with him. 'Tell me, Martha, why did you sleep with me? And while you're at it, tell me: that bastard cut you, didn't he? Why shouldn't I hate him?'

She was fully turned away from him as she shook her head. She had deserved the punishment. It was an atonement; it was clearly that. Curtis was not weak. He was pure and by his purity could help her. She pulled the purse up onto her lap; the gun he'd kept to remind himself of what he had once been. 'Let me off here,' she said.

'I won't. Tell me —'

'When I asked whether you missed him, I didn't mean Curtis. I meant Edgar. Let me off.'

'Tell me —'

She reeled on him. She didn't want to answer his question. The gun was in her purse. She wished the bullets were in the gun, but they were not. She'd taken his body and brought him into her thoughts. It was what they did; it was perfecting, a striving toward that. God ought to be moving within him. So she said, 'It's just what we do.'

'We? Who are we?' And when she didn't answer and only looked at him, struggling against answering, he said, 'You think you can shed light on my darkness. You think you can save me. That's nice, lady. But I am not a good man.' He didn't intend ever to be one. Aubie pulled in to a gas station north of Roswell, slowed, said quietly, 'I miss him.' When he stopped at pump number two, he left the truck to pay ahead, as much as daring her to run. He came loping back with a few bottles of iced water and some potato chips, which he tossed on the seat, smiling — she had not run.

Martha glanced up at the side-view mirror, at Aubie's butt shifting side to side while he waited for the tank to fill, then she pulled a sandwich bag of weed out of her purse and leaned down to sniff it; there wasn't anything yet that could replace the good smell of clean weed, except maybe man stink, except maybe a combination of the two. The purse fell hard to the truck floor, shocked her. She looked down at her fingers gathering the grass into a line on the rolling paper she had in her palm. She hoped Aubie didn't mind her smoking in the truck, because she would, no matter what. It was the last of her weed. She pushed her hand between the buttons on her shirt and ran her fingers along the ridges of scar. She had earned these. They rose as she touched them.

He got in the truck and said, 'What the hell is that now?' The pot, he meant the pot.

She held up the joint and smiled. 'If I share?'

'Okay, open the glove compartment, will you? I've got to show you something.'

She pulled the latch open. There was a gun lying there, a Browning replica, same sleek wooden handle, same engraved silver steel barrel, same catch-in-the-heart beauty. Twins, she thought, gun twins, and felt like her heart stopped. 'Where'd you get this?' she said.

'Not that.' He had forgotten it was there. 'Damn. You watch; that's loaded there, careful there.' His head spasmed once, twice. He was irritated. 'It's... Look under that.' She cradled the gun and pulled it out and onto her lap. A joint and a gun sitting on her lap. Under where the gun had been was a pint of tequila. She could see the larval worm spiralling when she picked the bottle up and handed it to him.

'I smoke yours. You drink mine. Put that gun back, will you?' He rolled his forearm around and around cajoling her to put the gun back, and she did. He smiled. 'Gun sure looks good on you, darling.'

Darling. This word brought her back to Curtis. She prayed quick that he wasn't coming, felt this scuttling, this rattle, thought, No, please. She did not want him to find her. She wanted to return on her own. She'd press the thin needles in and then pull, leaving fine red lines that turned white over time, a manifested reconfiguring. A reminder of penance. Proof. She could return, and this would be better than being retrieved. Aubie pulled away from the pump and was already heading south, first a town and then nothing but fence and water holes, arroyos, thirsty plants.

Martha cracked the window, lit up, and passed the joint over to Aubie. Aubie had touched her along her body; it had been a fast episode, and it was meant for him, to bring him closer, but no, he'd run his hands along the flesh between her legs, her thigh, her cunt, his dirty black hands, and she had not exalted, not cum, not exalted. But she had felt real. Was this the devil? She said, 'If I go back on my own, it will be better.'

Aubie took a long toke, and she watched him suck his cheeks in and hold the smoke. 'Shit,' he said. 'What does that bastard do to you?'

There was a little room in the great-house kept aside for meditation, when a member had trouble keeping on task, or when, at daily Meeting, criticism had led to suggestions of mild punishment. It was a light comb, and the member used it on him- or herself, as a reminder to the body. It was some method they'd uncovered in the early days, and they had tried it and it had seemed to work. Martha looked out the windshield. 'He doesn't insist on anything. It is up to the individual.' Talking about it to an outside person felt disrespectful; the truth seemed to shift around. She pulled her purse close to her again and said, 'Aubie, I've seen a gun just like that before.'

'Yeah.' He kept quiet for a bit, handed back the joint, put the bottle in at his crotch, and used the leverage there to spin the cap open. 'There are six of them guns in the family. Or at least there were six given out. It was the gift each boy could count on getting from Hollis should he turn eighteen, that and the truth about him being the great, all-powerful patriarch. Well, he didn't figure on the truth shifting depending on who was receiving it. I guess some of my brothers and half-brothers have sold or tossed theirs. Edgar, he never lived to see his. Mine was delivered to me after I got out of jail. Got it in the fucking mail.' He took a slow drink from the bottle as Martha watched. 'So Curtis still has his, then?' he said.

'Yes,' she lied.

'Rebel beekeeper,' Aubie said. 'He killed my brother with that damn thing.' Yes, he erased him pretty good, Aubie thought. The joint had gone out, so Martha relit it, and they were quiet for a time passing it back and forth, just looking out the window, at the ranch cattle grates, at the fences, at the beasts chewing cud, still and unknowing, along the fence edge.

'Everyone lies,' Martha now said, wishing her mind wouldn't draw her back. Why could a person outlive the good but not the bad things they did in their lives? She said, 'He never said he'd killed a man. We understood him to be peaceful.'

Aubie snorted. 'Curtis must think he has it made.' He looked in his rear-view and side mirrors moving only his eyes, keeping his head straight on the road. 'Tell me about this shit with Curtis; I want to be prepared for the second coming.'

Martha reached over and took the tequila and poured the bittersweet drink, a gulp, into her mouth. It burned so, and then she took a series of short tokes. 'Don't make jokes. I won't even talk about it then.' The radio programming went over to a local preacher man saying, 'Don't run from a crisis; face the crisis. Ask, "What is it this crisis wants to teach me?"' And then he went on to Joshua 1:3 and '*every place that the sole of your foot shall tread, I have given to you,*' and something about '*walking with faith.*'

They drove for a time, ten miles or more, and still the ranch fence and the cattle grates of triple V showed up, and she thought they might be driving in circles. 'This is a big ranch,' she said, and he was quiet again, chewing the inside of his cheek. After a while, he reached and turned off the radio. It was all stillness in the cab then, only the sound of the engine for a good space. He broke silence coming into Roswell, taking the bag of chips and opening it using his teeth. He made a hard left onto a red dirt road and handed her the bag. He smiled. 'Come on, lady. Tell me about your cult.'

Martha pursed her lips and turned away from him, looked out the back window at a roiling storm cloud she saw in the very far distance: northeast. The farm, the gate-house, the barn, and the outlying buildings came to mind. Aubie had his hand on the seat between them. Work hands, she thought. She said, 'It isn't a cult.' She wanted the ecstasy, fast, she thought, she wanted the familiar, as it was easy; it was not a cult, she thought, it was a utopian community. 'No,' she said, 'it was the way.' He would stop the truck in this wilderness and she would have him there in the desert; if she could do that she could believe again. A wild prayer. She nodded. 'It was the way.'

He did not want to laugh. 'I didn't mean it bad,' he said.

'No, I know.'

Aubie turned off this road and onto that — dusty caliche roads, a web of them. She didn't know where she was inside ten minutes and what with the pot and the drink, she didn't much care. 'Aubie, I've been following him most of my life. Curtis is a good man. Blessed.' She was having trouble feeling this the way she had before, but saying it helped it come back a bit. 'We want to enter this,' and she gestured out to nature. They would burn thick oil in the offering pit, and the undiluted earthiness of it was a testament to the infinite. They chanted and let the self dissipate. They culled from so many sources, and built this true thing. Curtis was a good man. She suddenly felt she was replicating something, the original of which had lost its beauty. Truth was farther away than she liked. She took Aubie's hand and pressed it deep between her legs. And then there they were, stopped in front of countless jacks pumping oil, like huge sewing machines slowly sinking into and rising out of the earth. 'Holy,' she said.

'You got that right — the articulating Holy Cross of the United States of America. Don't it just speak to you.' It was ugly and all she could do was shake her head. She was undone by it.

⚙

Aubie left the engine going to keep the AC circulating. It was damp hot and he had said, quiet, to himself more than to her, 'That storm's brewing east over the Tucumcari hills,' pointing east and swinging his arm north. Then he said, 'Well, Curtis was my best friend, or something close, before he shot my little brother; no one would have thought he could do that without factoring in Hollis. Curtis was a big disappointment. I had thought he was stronger against Hollis than that — I wished he was. You say he's blessed? Well, that'd be a strange God doing the blessing.'

'You don't know him like I do.'

'No, and thank you.'

She turned away, looked out; Curtis had kept the gun to remind himself of something, and she felt she knew suddenly: his own fall from Grace. The gun was a talisman, ironically, of peace. 'Those are all pulling oil out, all day, all night?'

'Yup. That oilfield's the Abo, been pumping going on sixty years now. I wanted to show you because I've been working there lately and because these pumps are what eventually made the old man rich. After his father died the family ranch went to him, and even though he lost a lot when the station got sidetracked, this come to him, and now he's flush. I hate to say it, but his money holds us all in orbit some.'

'He owns these?' she asked, and thought how by that he owned them all. The jacks slowly sank their pipes into the ground and rose, sucking at muck. She would meet Hollis, and he would give her money to take back to Curtis. An offering from Hollis, who loved him, and it would soften her return. There was a smell to the air, acrid, and she made a face.

'That'd be hydrogen sulphide,' Aubie said. 'You get used to it and don't smell it any more. It can kill you, the not smelling it. That's what those wind socks are for, not for the wind, but to warn you of the poison. And no. Hollis don't own these. He owns the ranchland and some of the deep mineral rights, so he gets a cut on every barrel got off here.'

Martha said, 'I'd like to meet him, your father.'

'No, you don't.'

'Yes, I do. I really do. It would be interesting.'

'Like a car wreck. Biggest fucking pile-up ever.'

'How much money do you think he has?'

And as he responded with 'Why do you ask?' it slowly dawned on him, and that dawning brought a wry joy alongside it, that she was human enough to be after the money too. He whooped, honking the horn to punctuate. 'You're going to ask Hollis Woolf for money? I want to be there when you do. He's likely to devour you whole. That man hoards the treasure. He don't share nothing, never.'

The weed was rattling around in her, her teeth tasted of metal. She leaned down to her bag and tightened the leather drawstring; the sack had been gaping open, and she could see the barrel of the gun.

'You have any idea what part Hollis plays in this?'

'No,' she said. She wasn't sure she could bear this news. 'Why don't you tell me?'

'That bastard had Curtis on a string back then. I hope he don't still. Hollis said "Jump!" and Curtis didn't wait to ask "How high?" Hollis said, "Go down to the river and shoot Edgar McCann, save me from a jail sentence," and off he went.' Aubie watched Martha look away and added, 'You think Curtis has integrity? You can't prop up truth with lies.'

'Maybe Hollis owes him something,' she said. Aubie gave her such a cold glance she shifted in her seat away from him.

Aubie engaged, reversed rough and quick to turn the truck around. 'Hell, we all feel owed.' She wished she knew what he felt owed by, and at the same time was relieved not to know. But then Aubie was sucking in breath and she looked over to where he was looking. He said, 'Looky here,' and she did. A shiny new white pickup was cutting across the pastureland like it had a purpose.

'Are you about to get in trouble?'

'Could be.' He drew the gearshift to neutral and idled. The man in the white truck pulled up along Aubie's side of the truck, pulled his black cowboy hat off, replaced it with a white construction helmet, and pressed a button to let the window slide down.

'Howdy, Aub.'

'Richards.'

'I heard some honking, thought I'd check it out. What brings you out this way?'

'I was just showing a new girlfriend what I do for a living.'

'Is that so?'

'Yes, that is.'

'H. W. know you're out here?'

'He don't know much of anything, these days.'

'I'm sorry to hear that. Well,' he said, 'keep yourself out of trouble, I guess.' The man brought the window up, changed his helmet for his hat, nodded, and drove away. Martha and Aubie sat quietly watching the dust billow behind him and then settle.

'What was that about?'

'That was a modern-day feud. We ain't got energy nowadays for the real thing. You see, that man is the son of the man who most hated my father in his life, and also the man who owns most of these suckers out here. Old man Richards. He died not long ago from a stroke. Ninety-five years old. He was a good friend to me and my brothers and our ma when we needed friends, so, you see, it's complicated.'

Martha just stared at him. She had meant what was that about calling her his girlfriend. She was not a possession. No one owned anyone else at the farm. Such talk was forbidden. She stared until she could see he was uncomfortable and whispered, 'Don't call me your girlfriend again.'

'Shit,' he said. 'I won't. Scout's honour.' He started to laugh, then stopped and turned the key in the ignition. 'Where to?'

'Hollis.' And when she saw his face tighten, she said, 'No, wait. Your place. I want to see where Auberon McCann lives.'

'Like hell —'

'Please,' she said. 'I really do.'

Martha lost herself in the lefts and rights Aubie made and the recurring theme of mesquite, greasewood, and young prickly pear lying there defeated in the red clay. She found she had a nice buzz going, and that the confusion of caliche roads only added to its grace. Martha just wanted to sleep with him, let light into all this, try again, once they got to wherever he called home. She missed Curtis, his vulnerability, his assured belief. What did people do who did not believe? She suddenly missed taking care of Curtis, missed the expectation that she would take care of him. Yet she was headed the wrong way home.

'Aubie?' she said. 'I'm scared. I'm always scared, either I'm with him or not with him. We're bonded, and I can't seem to cut him away no matter how I try. It's like I'm a piece of him. Early on at the farm, I began to have dreams of Curtis. We'd be on a train, and he would look over at me. Or he would be rowing a boat on a still lake, and there would be a feeling of safety in that dream like I have never known. He made the bees seem like a prayer, everything offered up to God, and we were all going to be safe in that. He was always praying for us.'

Curtis's voice always caught in the space there behind his tongue, and his body kept a rhythm, a backward and forward motion, while his whole torso swayed. She did not know from where such a prayer could come. He prayed, moving in and out of euphoria. Then one day, he shouted for her. 'Martha!' Curtis was tending the hives, had pulled the smallest corner off a honeycomb and set it in his mouth. Martha ran nervous from the mill-house to the apiary. She heard him call from the garden; she must attend.

'Martha!'

She was moved that it had been her he had first called. He waited until she came right up to him; the shuffling of cloth against skin seemed to unsettle him a little. It was the nervousness of her, he said later. He'd been stung. He hadn't seen the small bee, ass backwards in the comb cell, and so was surprised when he felt the numbing heat of its stinger enter his tongue. It did not register as pain in his mind. He reached in and drew the struggling insect out with his finger and thumb and watched it die there on the palm of his hand. 'The poor thing,' he said.

'Curtis.' He seemed to Martha to be in shock.

'I have been stung. A honeybee, one of my own, has stung me inside my mouth.' He allowed her to look inside his mouth and examine the tongue; it was swelling over his larynx. He kept the prayer going under his breath, she could hear it like a roiling storm, building far off.

Martha said, 'I think we need to get you to the clinic.'

'I won't die from this.' Later, he told her that by this prayer he suddenly knew the sting would come close to suffocating him but that it wouldn't. That his breath would resume if he could only maintain the prayer.

She had seen and heard a change. She stepped slightly back from him and held his face, not lovingly, but with revulsion, or maybe fear. Yes, it was fear. 'The clinic is open another two hours today, Curtis, and your tongue looks pretty thick.'

He was fainting. He muttered, 'A thousand guns and bombs

and the weapons of the world all around me. I'm dying in the space of that.'

'Curtis?'

'Oh, God.' His eyes were rolling back in his head, and he had already begun to slump into her arms, dead weight. It was a thinning, as if the whole world was somehow inexplicably moving away from him. She felt it, too; the air was less dense, and she considered he might really be dying even though he told her he wasn't going to.

Martha was now examining the lifeline along the palm of her right hand. 'You know,' she said, 'I was not the only one.'

'The only one what?'

'We all dreamed of him. We dreamed him.'

Aubie stared straight out the windshield; he hadn't dreamed in twenty years. But this wasn't strictly speaking true; he'd had that dream with Martha in it. He had also woken twice this past month with strange turbaned men poking at him, dreams he put down to watching too much CNN, so he had unplugged the TV.

Martha looked over the fields at the jacks pumping as they passed them by, the green-grey industrialness of them. The corroded edges running their length appeared beautiful to her, and even up the curved cast-iron hinge. There were mingling cattle, their brands widely scarifying the fur on their flanks. Where the desert lacked shade trees, they congregated in the shortening shadows of the jacks.

She said, 'A sickness built up inside him, built up and built up until the only way his body could cope was to piss and sweat it out. The first summer of our living there at Soltane, Curtis was thin, but with the fever, he wasted up. There wasn't anything but faith holding him together by the time the sickness passed. There was no one else on the farm that caught that cold. The fever left him just like that. He went from delirious to coherent, or some proximity to coherent. I saw the miasma of sick pull away from his eyes.'

'Which means?'

'Like a rebirth.'

'You believe in that shit?'

She did. Curtis had taken her hand — the one that was about to change his compress — in both his own hands and the thing, his electricity, went right up and into her. She didn't know what to call it, but he would say energy, a kind of energy that did not shock but rather comforted. She had thanked him.

Martha stared at Aubie with such conviction as she said, 'Once Curtis said to me, "It's so difficult; there are so many." He really helps people. He's been bestowed with qualities. He cures people.'

'Oh.'

Farm people, and then, over time, the people from the city, too, began to pay him homage, to seek solace in his presence, solace in his sad nodding responses to their questions, with his infinite and eternal community. Well, there had been a lot of people through the farm over the years. They came, he touched them, they left money, and he gave them small jars of honeycomb, Jesus candles, and hope to take away with them. Some petitioned to stay, were screened for suitability, and signed contracts; these were the selected ones, the ones committed to perfection.

'And can he?' Aubie had been slow to ask this, and though he tried to sound simple and easy with it, Martha heard something self-interested, as if he had some damage he wanted repaired. 'Can he heal people?'

Well, she thought, those people who came believed he did. She looked down at her purse, then out the window and said, 'Who can say what truth is?'

'Hollis always thought him special,' Aubie admitted, 'in between beatings.'

Martha had seen the change around Curtis's eyes mostly; they were serene, as if they were not held so tightly as before. She saw when his fever broke, had noticed also that he spoke with a deeper drawl, spoke in riddles. He clothed himself in white cotton and linen. He became a sun they all turned to. She smiled at Aubie, recalling this, smiled too at the afternoon light braising his skin. The pot had found its rhythm in her. They were on a highway again. She looked ahead and then back. There wasn't another car or truck in sight. A happiness crept up inside her, but then she thought how she really did miss Curtis, and she tried to shake this sentiment as far away from her as possible. This missing interfered. 'Where is Artesia exactly?'

'It's where nothing ever really happens. Podunk oil and gas capital.'

Thirteen

Michael Dama felt the question rising in his gut and experienced it rippling through his scar tissue. Some of the old wounds had scarred into his body, and he could feel the pull of the web along his back ribs, like the damn things were gripping his skeleton. He had been shot a few times since that first time, and he had been aimed at so many times he had lost count. He heard the phone going like the whirr of a rattlesnake; in his dreams that night he'd been back home walking in Bottomless Lakes, daring his brother to go deeper off the trail. They'd been dropped off for the day by an oilman who had business out of Roswell, a pump that wasn't pumping good, as Michael recalled. They were going fishing, though they had no rods, nothing.

In his dream Michael'd jerked his legs away from that phantom snake so hard, it woke him up, and he was panting, reaching for a weapon, the dream waking into nightmare. Where was the damn rattlesnake? And where was he, he wondered as the infernal buzzing shifted slowly to its rightful place, the telephone, his hotel telephone. Then how to stop it making that noise. He fumbled around and finally picked up the receiver. The digital clock read 3:17 a.m.

'Two gentlemen to see you, sir.'

His eyes were already beginning to adjust to the filtered light; the bathroom switch had been left on, and a bar of light landed on the box. Early, he remembered thinking, they are early. 'Send them up the slow elevator.'

'As you wish, sir.'

After a few minutes, Michael looked through the peephole and saw Omar with another man, a young man. They were fishbowled by the convex peep, making them look jowly and serious. He ought to have thought this strange, this Omar and a friend at his hotel room door, and he did, but not strange enough to hesitate in opening the door. He had his weapon, after all, and had let them into the room, the three of them standing crowded with the steel MANPAD case sitting there behind him.

'I wasn't expecting you, Omar.'

'No, brother, you weren't, but I have come just the same.' It was then he considered that Omar looked wrecked, that his eyes had an unnatural wetness. 'This is Khaleed. He is my cousin.'

'Nice to meet you.' The word *brother* triggered something.

'The pleasure is mine.' The man did not look at him; his eyes were downcast, sullen.

'My cousin wishes to make your acquaintance. I told him about you and he wanted to meet you immediately. He has something to sell. Show him, Khaleed.' Khaleed kept his eyes down, bent slightly, and tugged at the hem of his long beige kameez.

Michael believed that this would be it; he expected the boy to be strapped with explosives and that this fast death would likely go unreported in the media. The shirt was fine linen, either new or expertly ironed. Michael reached out his hand and pressed down on the boy's arm. 'I am not buying anything, now. You should go home, sleep, think about what you are doing.'

But the boy was persistent and brushed his hand away and continued to pull his shirt up. Michael wondered if his face showed fear. He was not really afraid. There was a point at which he felt relieved and another where he felt like laughing — dying seemed to be a kind of joke. There were only two civilians who knew who he was and where he was, and only from the postmarks they deciphered stamped on packages he sent back to them. Iran, Sudan, Afghanistan, Pakistan, wherever the fuck they sent him, wherever the fuck there was trouble, wherever they needed someone there and also not there.

It was the guns that told his contacts where he was — the guns knotted in intricate and sometimes garish threads on all those carpets he had rolled up and sent back home to Aubie McCann. The instructions: *Do not wash, do not sell.* Or else: *Wash. Sell for two hundred. Buy your mother something nice.* But it was almost fifteen years before they heard from him at all. And thirty years, all told, of Michael learning how to live inside a secret, how to be a secret. Fifteen years. Thirty years. It slips by like a quiet river when you don't care about nothing any more. There had been one war, and then another. There had been false friendships, aliases, dumb code names — Otter, Romeo — and trading of information.

It had all been a game, Michael manipulating pieces on a board that he cared about only superficially, as if humankind were truly made up of little plastic markers. People — individual people with families — were dying horrific deaths every day. That kind of witnessing might have tweaked him had he had any stake in death, but he did not.

Michael tried to convince himself of the ineptitude of his team, for this particular stance helped him in moments of moral questioning. Moments that had lessened the longer the game endured. War had shattered something in him.

The wars were a kind of shield, just large enough that maybe no one would notice him at all. And then there was a lull, right after the Russians and right before the Taliban, and he'd been given a task, and then he'd lost touch.

He'd been hired, contracted, to quietly retrieve man-portables: ballistic guns called Stingers, which the United States had handed out to the Muj in its successful bid to defeat the Red Army. When his 'Fellas, them guns was only loaners' failed to work, he'd had to steal, trade, or pay for whatever he found. He was up against Iran and North Korea and the democracy of fair market trade; the United States wasn't the only country interested in having the Stingers, and $150,000 was starting to look like a deal from the point of view of some of the 'owner-operators.'

Hell, it started to look like a deal to Michael too. There were perks to being invisible: some of the guns got lost in transit, Michael's bank accounts reflected net gains. Shit, in his darkest moments he had thought: did it matter which asshole killed which other asshole so long as he didn't die, so long as he got richer? And now, here he was, about to die.

Michael's hand hovered in space and then moved toward his weapon, another joke that would not help him if what he suspected was right. He wondered why Omar was smiling.

'You might be interested, Michael. Who knows?' Omar did a half-turn and bolted the door shut behind him. 'Privacy,' he said.

Michael looked at Omar and realized he hadn't really seen him before. He'd spent the day with him and yet hadn't taken much notice of him. Omar was handsome, and had features that would be described as dignified, aristocratic almost. He looked like he could be a diplomat, almost French-looking in his angularity. He had deep-set eyes and a pleased alertness to him. His nose ran thin and parallel in its slope to the plane of his face. He had beard stubble on his chin and a soft line of hair above his lip.

No, Omar was better described as beautiful. He was smiling. And Michael smiled back. He found he could not look at

Khaleed; it would be better to die quickly without seeing the device the man would use. He did not need that information in the final analysis. He smiled too widely, he expected, and tried to curtail his smile by saying, 'What's he got to sell to me right now, Omar, and why?'

'He is poor and needs the money. Look. Please.' And Omar's beautiful long fingers waved in front of his eyes and he followed their sweep, to Khaleed's belly. No belt, no explosives. Instead: a tattoo. It was fresh, he could see little droplet scabs. Urdu. It read right to left, *I am not a terrorist*. And Michael looked up and saw that the boys were laughing at him. Omar was hitting Khaleed playfully and both boys were clearly pleased with the joke they had had on him. He was off-guard.

He shrugged his shoulders and pulled his hand away from his waist, from his gun, and that is when things went wrong. 'Put them in the air, your hands,' Omar whispered; he already had a knife along Michael's neck. How did he move so quickly, this middle-class student? But he had, and so Michael realized that death, when it came, would be slower, and likely symbolic — not an idea he treasured. He put his hands above his head, moving them slowly alongside the knife tip and the body of Omar as it pressed into him. It was Khaleed who came around and pulled his arms behind him, pushed him to the ground, and bound them tightly with plastic handcuffs.

'I might yell,' he said.

'You won't.' And Omar pushed a scrap of cloth into his mouth, saying, 'We just wish to speak with you. That is all we desire. We are not bad people, you have to accept this, and everything will work out fine.'

Khaleed crouched down in front of him, very close. Michael wished he could age the boy twenty or thirty years and make him look back on his own foolishness, but then he saw how very old the boy was around the eyes. Khaleed was speaking to him.

'What is it you import and export?' He said this very clearly in the softest Urdu Michael had ever heard. It was like a child had spoken. Then Khaleed leaned over and pulled the cloth delicately out of his mouth.

Michael said, 'Carpets,' and nodded toward the gun rugs in the corner.

'Yes, and what else?'

'Nothing. I'm a simple merchant.'

That is when Omar had said what he did about Michael being a misery importer-exporter. Khaleed shushed him. 'It doesn't matter.' And Michael asked them what they wanted. It was Omar who put the piece of cloth back into his mouth and who did most of the talking. Khaleed paced, grunted approval, and slapped his left hand into his right hand every so often saying, 'Yes.'

A lifetime ago, yesterday, last week; what did it matter? Michael wondered at fate. What had Omar said? That there was but one God and that was Allah, that therefore it didn't matter what god you prayed to, you were praying to Allah, therefore there was no such thing as a religious infidel. That all praying men prayed to one god, and that god was Allah, and that Allah was patient and would wait. Michael chuckled at that logic and Khaleed muttered in Urdu, 'What is he laughing about? We have solved the biggest problem in the world at the moment and this man laughs at us.' They pulled the cloth from his mouth to let him speak.

'This is what you guys came up with?'

'What is so amusing?' asked Omar, and then he gently added, 'Who is feeding you? Who cools you down in the heat?' and tucked the cloth carefully back into his mouth.

Michael shrugged.

'Be grateful. That is all there is.'

There followed a sweaty hour of listening to the two boys argue and counter-argue. Khaleed waved the hotel Quran at Omar, and Omar made calming motions with his arm. Michael's clothing was musty with his stink. He tuned in and out of what they were saying. They were talking about the Stinger, a conversation Michael wished wasn't happening. They seemed to be justifying its theft, and he found himself shaking his head, thinking, No, Christ, no way.

'We will take this bad thing and we will destroy it. It will be broken in hundreds of pieces when we are finished. Don't worry. We will shatter it.' Michael shook his head violently at them, made his eyes as imploring, as kind-hearted, as he could, but they did not seem to understand.

It was frustrating being bound up, and a few times he tried to reason with the boys to undo his arms. In the end Omar rigged up a dull kitchen knife, taped it to two books from Michael's side table — hell, it had been a Gideons and that Quran — and set this device behind him in such a way that he could slowly saw his bindings open. And then they left, salaam alaikum-ing and nodding with respect to him before they grabbed the Stinger in its case and shuffled out the door.

'You are generous in Allah's eyes,' Khaleed said. 'Be grateful!'

He heard their footsteps running down the corridor, heard the elevator door clunk once, twice, and all the while he rocked back and forth over this cutting tool that Omar made, and was grateful, grateful for the knife, grateful he could concentrate on maintaining his breath so he, too, could run.

Then, finally, he was free.

Then the phone ringing, the phone ringing again, Christ almighty, and the dread at having to decide the best route — picking it up or letting it ring. Sure, the damn concierge knew he was still in. 'Send them up the slow elevator,' he said.

'As you wish, sir.'

And he had taken the stairs down, had left the runner carpet, after shoving the other fragment into his bag. There had been no packing, just his emergency bag, the one that was always packed: plastic, gun, passports. He left the door to his room open so they wouldn't have to break it in, and he just disappeared again. Another day had already begun. A beggar beyond the front door approached him as he hustled past, nudging at him, and there, suddenly, three children appeared — the beggar's children, he wondered — and salaamed and stretched their hands out, asking for rupees, candy. There were sores on their mouths and hands, but this was normal, and he hurried past and into the morning crowd.

Fourteen

Colm thrashed around in the Pecos looking for traces of Martha until Hattie came down and found him. 'I got a call from the care centre,' she said. 'Hollis is in a rough spot. They say he keeps seeing someone in his room, and he won't let them clean him up. I said I'd go calm him, but they said I better let him be. I don't know.' Hattie had had two calls though. Aubie had let her know he had Martha, so she added, 'And if you want that woman, it turns out she's Artesia way with you-know-who. You might as well sleep here tonight.'

'Ma,' Colm said, and it had the weight of everything in it, of spending the day in the dry bed, of the heat, of the low pressure eating his head, of Hollis dying so slow it hurt them more than his living, of his ma, and of how Aubie had that woman with him and he didn't. 'I won't stay for breakfast tomorrow, I don't guess. I said I'd bring her to Hollis and I better stick to that plan, kill two birds with one stone; I'll head down and get her first thing.' Hattie knew jealousy, said nothing.

Colm left before the sun cracked the dark, taking the I-85 to the 285, speeding, sharply watching for police, and praying to his angel who looked over him. He didn't want to catch them in bed or nothing. The image was there before he could stop it. He drove fast to dispel it.

Aubie didn't much like the idea of having Martha at his place. He felt it was a mess, even though he kept it tidy. Well, as tidy as he could under the circumstances. He had been unwrapping carpets, the garbage was waiting a trip to the dump. The brown papers were folded and tied neatly, that wasn't it. The mini kitchen was clean because he hadn't eaten there in days. His clothes were stacked because they always were; he couldn't even stand them sitting in a clothes hamper and had a habit of pulling them out of his stackable, folding them, and putting them away still warm so the creases lined the shirts like seams, dead straight. It was that the tidiness was itself revealing and he didn't like guests much. 'There's a nice inn I'm bringing you to tonight.'

'No.'

'Why no?'

'Please, no. I need to.'

He had relented, but not before driving her back and forth and through the small streets nobody'd ever bothered paving until even he figured she might suspect he didn't want her to find her way back here. His place was not pretty, but he didn't want to bring attention to himself.

There was no yard, just ramshackle living space set into the desert on the outskirts of town. Middle-class folks and poor intermingled; it didn't matter much where people lived when everyone drove and nobody ever walked. He didn't know his neighbours: the richer ones had high adobe walls around their places, and he kept to himself.

The metal door scraped the threshold, like it always did when he pulled it open, and that naphthalene-and-foreign-dust smell plumed out the opening into his nose. Carpet stink and mothballs. 'I hope you're not allergic or anything,' Aubie said.

Martha pulled back against the smell but caught herself, nodded, blinking as he flicked the lights on. From a distance, the carpets glowed, a dull, cacophonous rainbow of earth hues, and he suddenly considered what effect the wall covering might have on her. He was so used to it himself, didn't much think about it. Today, it glowed out at them, and he smiled.

'The inside and the outside are so different,' she whispered. 'It's like a medieval castle in here. Where did these all come from?'

'I collect them.' He looked up, and saw the extent of it as if for the first time. It was a terrible accumulation of carpets and rug fragments. Had she seen the guns yet? he wondered. His eyes roamed the walls. There wasn't a piece of the wall — except around the light switches and fixtures — that wasn't covered in red or brown or ochre pile, some with a variant abrash in the silk or wool, some so old, or so hard-lived, they were more hole than cloth. Martha was up close to the all-over fighter jet Baluch he'd got over a year ago. The note had said *Sell*, but Aubie hadn't been able to part with it, not the note or the carpet.

It wasn't that he loved the rug, it was something else, something he found unspeakable: he hadn't been able to sell anything the man who called himself Michael Dama sent back for a great long time. Michael Dama was an enigma, as well as an alias. He had stopped thinking of the man as Edgar, because keeping the distance of Corporal Michael Dama, or simply Dama, afforded some respite from his own feelings on the matter. Still, he could not sell the carpets. It would feel disloyal, as if he was severing some hope he had that his brother might still contact him. The carpet was coarsely woven with a beige-and-blue background, and while the jets lacked any animation, were simply in battle array, they made up for this in number.

The piece was bordered with a repeater of tanks, Kalashnikovs, and scattered arrows, which Aubie had taken to mean directional firings.

'What are —' She had seen. 'Oh, God.'

'War rugs,' he said. 'The Afghan people weave them.'

'Oh, my God. Why?' Her eyes were so wide, he felt suddenly sorry for her.

'I haven't a clue.' But he had. He had spent long evenings puzzling it out, searching out articles on the Internet, talking to dealers in Santa Fe and New York City, and just wondering. They didn't sell particularly well, this he knew, and so there wasn't much of a market value to them. It was that they were powerful, that the weavers couldn't read and write but they could draw, and the drawing, the long process of knotting a rug, say three or four months, was a slow articulation of their anger and frustration. 'You like this one?'

'They look like the women, the jets do. You know, those long cloaks, those veils they wear.'

'Burqas?' He hadn't seen this before, but she was right: the wings looked like arms opened in welcome or supplication, the jet exhaust pipes were tiny feet peeking out from under the gowns. And as he took this in, the carpet changed, gave off a sorrow he hadn't before considered. He wished he was better at decoding and wished he knew for certain whether the weavers were even trying to convey a message.

'Oh,' Martha said, looking around the room. 'They are covered in weapons, every carpet you have.' She wrapped her arms around herself and shivered, though the air in the place was stagnantly warm. 'You're stockpiling.'

'They're just carpets.' He hadn't heard from Dama in a long while. The letters had stopped, and he had not had a rug shipment in more than a year. Aubie had been wondering for months why he hadn't heard from him. He'd begun unrolling the carpets from old shipments looking for clues. But the rolls had become mixed up, so he couldn't be sure which were the most recent, and the tags, *Made in Pakistan*, offered no help. He had no idea where Dama was, which he considered may have been intentional on Dama's part. *Do you miss him?* From time to time, he had thought. Oh, God.

'But why? Why collect these rugs?' she was saying.

He thought there was beauty in the struggle, that the work made the thing beautiful. He also believed Dama had an unhealthy or maybe under the circumstances healthy obsession with armaments. Inherent in the carpets was also a history of Michael Dama's whereabouts. If he looked very carefully at them, at the particular nomadic tribe responsible for tightly knotting each tuft of carpet on any particular rug, he might gain insight into the dilemma that was his brother, and where the hell he was. He could no longer separate the individual pieces that Dama mailed or — as it was and had been for one long torturous year — had *not* mailed, from the trajectory his brother's life may have been taking.

The carpets had become the man — insofar as that was the only information Aubie was receiving. Lately, he had begun cataloguing everything he could glean from them: type of weapon, frequency of the weapon's use in the histories of the various wars, progeny of weapon, monies and history of monies used to purchase weapon, how the weapon may have been witnessed by the individual weaver and how his brother might have found the thing, and then, more esoterically, why Dama might have been drawn to that particular carpet over other ones.

One thing he noticed was that a number — a substantial number — of the rugs depicted man-portables, Stingers, the ground-to-air missiles that had won the Cold War. These were details he did not want to express to Martha right now, or ever. 'It's a kind of archive. My guess is they may be worth money one day, so it's an investment.' Not for Dama, not if Dama is dead, is what his mind quietly told him, but he shook this off as he had shaken it off time and time again. He pointed up at one asymmetrical piece, said really softly, 'That gun in the corner is an Enfield; the big one in the middle is a Stinger, strong enough to shoot down an armoured helicopter. That's a clue, I think.' And he right away wished he hadn't said that out loud.

'A clue?'

'I mean a piece of the story.' No. Shit. 'An important part of the weaver's communication. They can't read or write, these people.' Martha looked entirely broken; the weed and the drink had shed her, sending her into a dark mood. Aubie felt again that it had not been a good idea to bring her here, that whatever reason she might have had for wanting to see his place, and he could only imagine what her motivation had been, she herself clearly no longer saw her task as possible. He had failed to supply her with a locale for her particular cowboy conversion fantasy, and he was suddenly disappointed in himself and for himself. 'It isn't what you expected.'

'No. I don't know what I expected.' She was fingering the goat-hair fringe edge of a Taimani prayer rug. He thought she might be about to cry and then saw she was crying already. 'I expected something nice, homespun,' she said.

'I'm sorry.'

'Yes, I know.'

'Martha,' he said. He wanted to tell her about the courage of this one weaver, about the note Dama had sent with it. It was stapled roughly to the back of the piece: *The weaver, from the southwest, risks death from the Taliban for this rug. I mean, it's a fucking prayer rug. Is this not perseverance?* It was scrawled in pencil and — Aubie was certain — in his brother's hand. He had received this one in 2002. He thought to tell her about the camps where the refugees lived, huge desert tent cities, but he just watched her wipe her face.

She said, 'Say that again.'

'What?'

'My name. Say it again.'

'That inn,' he said. 'I could take you there, Martha.'

'Thank you and no. I'm fine. It's just so sad, all of it.' But she was over crying.

'I think it depends on how you look at it.' This was what he had said to the few other people he'd let in, when they'd been shocked to see the war motifs, but it wasn't something he believed. It was damn sad. Terrible sad, but having the rugs over everything, nailed to the rafters, layers in some places three thick on the floor and coiled against the walls, lent credence to that sorrow, didn't it? Yes, it damn well did. She was looking at him, now, not at the rugs, and at the same time rummaging in her leather bag.

The purse was one of those ones he'd seen years ago at the craft shows that had popped up across the state. He hadn't ever hung with hippies, but, for a time, you couldn't swing a dead cat without hitting some long-haired peacenik. It was a purse with that earnest, rough-sewn God-feeling to it, and he watched her watching him, as she hunted around for whatever it was she was hunting for. 'It's possible the women weave these war icons as a therapy,' he said. 'Or as talismans.'

'No. I don't mean that.' Martha sat down, falling vertically into a cross-legged position in a huddle of coiled and unwrapped carpets; there was a broad, obvious, chemical-red Kalashnikov carpet that lay in such a way it appeared to be strapped to her back. 'Does Hattie know you collect these ugly things?'

'What the fuck is that supposed to mean? Does my mother know —'

'It's so clearly messed up. All this collecting. The guns, you know. It's all so violent, so hateful.' She had such pain scrawled over her face, and then it was like she couldn't look at him and she looked down, poured out some of the contents of her purse. He had said talismans, and she thought, Talismans for whom, what was he protecting? What was Curtis protecting? She would not be able to live amidst all this hatefulness.

'Ma doesn't know I collect these things. She doesn't know nothing.' They'd made a pact they wouldn't tell Ma about Edgar. First it was to protect Edgar, since Ma was so loyal to Hollis, then it was to protect Edgar when he went secret, then it was habit and not wanting her to know they'd lied all those years. Hattie didn't want to know, anyway. She liked to live in her own world; it would have been better if Colm hadn't known either, but that couldn't be helped.

Aubie stared at Martha, at the window, at the night streaming past her, at her face lining up what little she knew. He saw a small stretch of skin over her left cheek twitch and it all culminated in him, and he snorted. She said, 'Oh, poor Curtis.'

Poor? he thought, and then he realized what Martha was saying, that Curtis actually believed he had killed Edgar. Who the fuck would think a man could be so fucking stupid? Aubie's torso clenched up. Oh, that was good. Thirty years of turmoil, or was it thirty years of redemption? It amounted to the same, anyway. Curtis thinking himself mighty. Thinking himself worth thirty years' atonement, thinking himself into the middle of the story. While all the time he was just a piece of shit. Aubie was shaking his head, thinking this was better than any punishment he could have ever dreamed up on his own for Curtis; it was like a barroom joke. He couldn't wait to tell Colm so they could clink bottles and shake their heads and laugh some more. Well, the meek shall inherit the earth, so he supposed Curtis would do okay. Aubie scanned the carpets, then turned around, serious and dark, his wild eye roving her body, and said, 'You asked earlier if I miss my brother Edgar.'

'Yes, I did.'

'Well, I do miss him.' The way his brother had resurrected himself out of the dirt, out of that pool of blood and ripped flesh, that whole history was as fresh as if it had happened yesterday. He could still see the flies dropping down to drink off the wounds.

'I'm sorry.' Her pity was so genuine, then. No sign of Dama, he thought. And Martha herself suddenly seemed like the tail end of an omen, as if she'd come down with a message even she didn't know she was transmitting. He was ready to think Corporal Dama was dead, she made his absence seem that urgent.

On the floor now in front of Martha were Kleenex, lipstick, a notebook wrapped in suede, pens and pencils, and a wallet stamped with Billy the Kid that Aubie figured she'd bought recently, maybe at Fort Sumner, maybe Clines Corners. 'Oh, there it is,' she said, reaching into the bag again. The Browning.

'Curtis's gun,' she said.

Martha held the gun in the flat of her palm, like an apple she was going to give a horse. Aubie thought for a half-second that she had somehow Houdini-ed it out of the glove compartment, so close a mate was it to his own. But darker, he noticed, the wood was darker, as if it had been handled more. Curtis's gun. Aubie felt the blood rage pounding behind his eyes when he thought of that boy, felt the rage and felt like soon he would even that score. He could near taste Curtis on his way. Martha shifted the weight of the thing forward and clasped it, cocked it up to his face, and smiled. 'You recognize this thing? It's Curtis's going-away present, that's what he told me when I found it.' She was pointing the damn thing straight at his head.

Keep level-headed, Aubie thought. He swayed out of the way, saying, 'You couldn't hit a barn with that thing, you know that? And Curtis never got that as a going-away present. He got that months before he left, from the old man, when he turned eighteen. That's the gun that got me in jail, the one that fat bastard store clerk would recall so good, the one Curtis had been worrying him with. Nine hundred dollars, and five years in jail. That same fucking gun. He shot my brother with that stupid thing.' Aubie tightened his chest, as if by stressing it out to the maximum it would become a kind of flesh shield; he suspected that she didn't have the nerve to shoot at him, but he also knew she had a gun pointed in his general direction, and belief was fighting the known world across the nerves in his body. 'You ain't going to shoot me, are you?'

'With this thing?' she said, lowering it into her lap and cradling it there. 'Why would I shoot you, Mr. Auberon? Besides, the gun doesn't have any ammunition in it. It's empty.' And he saw she just wanted to test out her power, like he'd thought. She said, 'I saw you were afraid, just a little.' She waved the weapon up and behind her. 'These rugs — they must occupy a great deal of your time.'

'Like any importer.'

'So, you sell these, I suppose.'

'Well, that's the idea. That is the general idea.'

'They don't do well? Outside people don't like this sort of thing?'

'No, they do. There's a fellow in Santa Fe and another in Long Island who will buy everything you see here. But I can't sell them. I can't seem to part with them.'

She had the gun again in her crotch and had pulled her feet up over her knees, yoga-style. Aubie figured it must hurt some. She grabbed her feet and pulled them higher up her legs and looked up at him, steel eyes. *Clues*, Aubie had said. 'Where do you get these?'

An image of the flies came to his mind, the bees and flies waiting for death to come, but it had not. It wasn't difficult to die where Dama was now, it was the easiest thing in the world. And Aubie knew he wouldn't ever find out about it when it did happen. 'I have a military contact. It's not really important.'

'Why do you collect these things?' The question was plaintive. And he struggled to answer it. He struggled against the lie, thinking maybe he should just tell her. That maybe she deserved to know the truth. It had been so long he'd held this secret, though, that it sat like a contract between him and Dama. He told, Dama died; he honoured, Dama lived.

'The closer I get to completing the collection, the better I feel,' he offered. 'Like it's an accomplishment of sorts, I guess. Plus,' he added, 'it keeps me busy.' And he saw she didn't have a clue what he was talking about. 'This is my life,' he said. 'This is all I have.' Aubie swept his hand around at the walls and ceiling, indicating the carpets, and wondering why this damn woman dug at him so. Other girls had eaten at him, sure, crawled under his skin, but not like this woman. Martha seemed to give a shit, he guessed she might only give a shit insofar as she cared about Curtis's stake in all this, and by proxy her own, but still it was more than most, and he suddenly felt indebted to her, a feeling he didn't like to hold on to.

'Let me find you something now.' He went over to the tiny kitchen he'd separated off the main container, which held his bed, his computer, his phone, his unplugged television. He knew exactly where the letters were, shoved in a paper serviette holder, in back of the toaster he never used. Still, he checked in several places because he knew she was watching and he didn't want to appear obvious. He picked up a few bullets from a box in the cutlery drawer and stood in the quarter-ply doorway he'd made, even though there had never been an actual door, and to himself he read this: *Dear Aubie, I won't be writing much and wouldn't even be writing this if I wasn't so damn stupid and sentimental. It's your birthday today and I guess you might probably be thinking about me. That doesn't matter. I just want you to know that one day, I'm going to come home and we can laugh about all this shit. I'll bring the drink and you bring the girls.'* Aubie folded it along its original creases and tucked it back in the envelope. He felt really dumb; he wished he had some respite from missing his brother, some freedom, pretty sure as he was that his brother wasn't thinking too much about his health and welfare.

He leaned over her, took the gun. 'I might as well load this up for you.'

'No.' Then she said, 'Why?'

'That's the whole point of a gun, ain't it?'

'No.'

She said how she'd bought bullets for it herself and then got too scared to put them in, and Aubie laughed softly at that. He asked why she'd brought the gun, if it scared her so.

'I found it on the farm, in his room,' she said. 'I took it to figure out what it meant. I took it to show him I wasn't afraid of what it meant. But I never thought it could mean he'd killed someone. I never thought it would lead here.' She looked down at the gun cradled in her lap. She looked up again. 'I miscarried. I was carrying his child and I lost it.'

The only thing he could think of to say was 'That's terrible.' He could see that's what she wanted him to say, and he knew loss well enough to know that any sort was terrible.

'If I stayed in the farm, they would have relegated me away from the community. We consider it imperfect to be barren, and a sin to spread imperfection; the idea is a lifelong atonement

— meditation, reflection, good works in His name. I felt I had no choice but to leave.'

He slept with her, that night, on his bed in his office. She had hauled a couple of the more violent rugs out of the room, asking first if he minded. He was over minding anything much when it came to her, and he thought back to his dream. He watched her body, the way she seemed to offer it up. He watched her hands opening up and reaching for him, and it curled back at him what she might be up to. 'I love you,' he said.

Martha smiled and thought, Are we not one? The line from a speech Curtis was fond of giving, likening the body to a conduit, driven by God, direct to Him. But her thoughts were not dissipating into that truth; they were wanting. She reached up to Aubie, closed her eyes against her own feelings. 'It's a love instinct; Curtis would say the bees had that, the workers, how they saved up their sexual impulse and never used it, and so were better, more pure, honeykeepers.'

'But it ain't like that.' He'd slid between her legs.

'No,' she admitted.

'I don't feel no God here.'

'No.' She started to cry, then, and he stopped, held her until she stopped, before he started up again. That she would not go back to Soltane was a relief and a pain; she did not know which possibility was more frightening to her at that moment.

Fifteen

In the morning, Colm had been waiting in his car outside, and he would take her to see Hollis. It was Tuesday, and Aubie'd stayed up with Martha too late, cost him a coffee at Hastings. He didn't like coffee, the way it ran through him and tried to own him. The day would be shit on the oilfield. And Colm was thinking he'd better make haste. Colm could just about see Curtis on the road heading toward them, straight to Aubie's gun if he wasn't careful or smart or some combination of these two things. The sooner this woman had a clue what she'd got herself into by rustling up old stories the better. At least he would never blame himself that she wasn't aware. It's just there were so many ways you could look in on a story, and even though there was only one truth, it wasn't until you saw the thing from every angle that you began to see it. He had three-quarters figured out himself, and once they were settled in and were bumping out of the laneway, he hoped she would provide the rest.

'What's Curtis been up to, anyway?' He looked down at Martha's ring. 'Besides marrying pretty girls.' It surprised him when Martha began to laugh a slow, deep laugh, devilish. It put the fear of God into him.

'What's Curtis been up to?' Martha said. All the Family members wore matching silver rings, silver for humility, rings for their covenant. She looked out the window, noting street signs and geographic markers; she'd had enough of being lost. 'He's a kind of preacher.' Curtis wasn't really, but it was the easiest way to explain the community to outside people. She looked at him to see what his reaction might be. He knew already, so he didn't shift.

'Ordained in what religion?'

'We never named it.'

'He's a crackpot.'

'If you agree that Jesus was a crackpot, and Mohammed, and Buddha.'

'Lady.'

'Time will tell. Aubie calls it playing at God, playing at playing at God. Time will out —'

'You're pissed.'

'I am and I'm not.' Martha pulled her bag from the floor, pulled some rolling paper and some tobacco out of it. She carefully licked and stuck sheaves of paper together. She had run out of pot, and on the way out of town, she'd asked Colm to kindly pull in to a gas station for leaf. 'You don't mind, do you?'

'It dulls the senses.'

'I'm in the habit of it.'

Maybe this woman would outdo the old fucker. He regretted instantly thinking of Hollis as a fucker. Besides, Hollis wasn't a man you could hate and not also love. Colm didn't like to stand in judgment of his father; he stood in awe. He looked up at the Holy Virgin Mary air freshener hanging from the radio dial and thought a hard sorry, and then quickly atoned for the swear by way of a string of inner Hail Mary Full of Graces. Then he went back to thinking that probably that old man, his father, would just eat her whole before she got a word out.

When Martha turned her head and exhaled what little smoke she made out the window, Colm noted for the first time something — fear, desperation, loneliness — ghost her face. And what he thought, and then discarded as fast as he could, was that she was family, that Curtis, and now Aubie, made her family, and that they were all pretty much ruined.

'Well,' he said. 'I don't guess the old folks' home is expecting visitors so early in the morning, so I'm going to take you over to Ma's place for a piece.'

The little house looked withered that morning, tired and sinking. Years ago, his ma had planted a mesquitilla, and it was now blossoming despite the drought. The pink fairy-duster flowers gave hope, so long as he kept his head up out of the dust and looked at them. Colm walked past the shrub and into the house, right along the fishing lures, asking Martha if she had looked at them. 'This one here,' he said, 'I recall this was one of ours. Edgar used to whittle them, and we'd test them out in the Pecos.' He had unhooked a thin, long, wooden fish that looked like a minnow to Martha, but she did not know about proper fishing. She only nodded, and handed it back almost as soon as he'd handed it to her. It startled her to touch something Edgar had touched, and Colm seemed to take satisfaction from that.

Hattie said, 'I have to get out to my rain barrel; there's water on its way, don't you think, Colm? I almost forgot what that felt like, water coming.' Hattie was watching Martha that whole time. 'I heard on the radio that water is falling in West Texas and that it's on its way. *Prepare for flash flooding*, is what the radio said. Sounds Biblical, don't it?'

Colm had pulled up a broken wicker chair from the corner of Hattie's bedroom to the kitchen table and was sunk into it. He looked young, peering over the edge of the table. He was running his fingernail down and down a fault in the denim of his blue jeans, not daring to look at Martha in between looking at her hard now and again, like an assault. He'd driven with her a couple of hours, let her smoke in his car, let her sit there quiet and still, and now he was going to be bringing her to old dying Hollis, and the inconvenience of it was getting at him.

She had surely slept with Aubie, and this got to him most of all. He said, 'No one's sure what in heaven's name you're doing here.' He looked at Hattie's lenticular lying on the table and nodded in a sanctimonious way. Martha recognized this. Hattie looked up at Colm and then got up and went to the door. Colm said, 'What are you doing here?'

Martha looked at her hands for some time before answering, and even then, she stayed looking down at her hands. 'I'm sorry I have bothered you both.' She was thinking why couldn't she, even when she ran, run away.

'Aubie, he drove himself pretty much wild talking about you the other day, asked me to bring you around to Hollis, keep an eye on you. He thinks you'll bait Curtis. I'm sure wondering what brings you our way.'

Keep an eye on her. 'Aubie said what?' Martha drew her fingernail against the ribbed plastic card, liked the sound, and did it again. She was hankering for a smoke, some reprieve. She looked over to Hattie but found no solace there; Hattie was staring out the window, seemed in her own thoughts, far off. Martha looked up at Colm and said, 'My life is a mess, you could say.' Hattie turned and stared at her then.

Colm looked like he couldn't say anything for sure. Looked like most women freaked him out, and she more than most even. 'So you figure your life is bad, I suppose,' he said. 'You figuring you've walked away from a car wreck? Truth is, you've walked right into another one.'

'That's what Aubie said too, word for word.'

'He's right.'

'Well, at least I'm gone from that last one.' She could feel the constriction in her chest loosen briefly and then tighten even more. That devil tickling at her; she oughtn't talk like that about Soltane, about Curtis. She slowly opened and shut her fingers, made a mental note to take some anxiety tincture. Ida used to rib her that she should just keep a flask of it, forget the little eyedropper. Curtis had laughed, said privately that he'd always been fond of her anxiety, and she had not known how to respond.

Colm made his eyes small and smiled over at Hattie. 'Big, slow train wreck.'

Hattie clicked her tongue. 'Colm?'

'Yes'm.'

'Why are you trying to scare her?'

'Someone's got to ask a few questions here.' His voice had gone shrill. 'It sure as heck won't be you.'

Martha made to get up, but Colm held her in her chair with his eyes, and then a faint gesture with his hand, like a priest blessing something, and she felt bad. Felt it all pressing down on her, flattening her into a sheet, on which anyone could write his own true history of her. Colm looked at Martha and said, 'In this house, if she stays too long, she'll be family before we even know her middle name.' Colm was staring at the place where Martha's hair met her forehead. It had the slightest widow's peak. Her hair was pulled back and held with a headband and the roots were greying to a line that started up black where she'd dyed it.

Martha felt his hunger, and she wondered about Aubie and what had already transpired between these two. Whether it meant anything to her, and how she ought to behave. Maybe he didn't like it that Aubie had done what he'd done and he couldn't entirely pin his reasons to why he felt this way. He was envious, sure, but he couldn't ever charm her like that — she could see that all flickering across his face, in the uncertainty that looked like sorrow in his eyes. She felt sorry for him. But it was something else as well. It had something to do with what was moral and right, and not that this wasn't exactly but, no, she couldn't pin his feelings. It just wasn't right even if it was. He was conflicted about what was right. He said to Hattie, 'She'll be formally adopted before too long, knowing you.'

'Knowing me?' Hattie came over to him, picked hard at some lint that may or may not have been on Colm's sleeve. She wanted the visit over so she could carry on, let this woman be here or not, let the world carry on, let it be calm, static again. She had chores to get done. 'Who says you even know me one little bit, Colm McCann?'

'I guess I don't.' Colm watched Hattie pick at his shirt. Martha wondered what she had seen there. Colm glanced down, his face unnerved, and Martha followed his eyes to the thin silver band on her finger again. Her stomach leapt around. She knew you couldn't fish a man if your heart wasn't true to it. And hers wasn't.

'You ever hear about the old man from Curtis? I wonder what he might have told you,' Colm was saying. 'I hear you might want to meet him.' Hattie made a face, Colm saw and he shook his head and whined, 'It ain't done to invite strangers into your house to live, Ma. No one does that; that's just crazy in these times. Don't you listen to the news?'

'I've got sense,' she said, warning him. 'I'm an old woman; I've lived some.'

'You ain't got no sense, Ma, and Aubie ain't got no boundaries, and so I have to have both.' He gestured at Martha, wailed, 'Why the heck don't this woman know she's overstepping?' And he said again, peering at her: 'You sure you want to meet the old man? You have any idea what he did —?'

'I have to go get something,' Martha said. 'I have to go get something in the bedroom.' She straightened; the line of her shoulders broadened out and her small chest opened up, like she was finally, after a long time, breathing. 'Then we can go,' she said, and she picked up her purse and kept excusing herself, saying how sorry she was.

'That awful man.' Colm made his eyes large.

'Don't you call him that, Colm.' Hattie leaned over, clung to his wrist, and squeezed it hard. 'Don't you dare call anyone that.'

'That man's as nasty as any ever lived, I'd say.' Colm's gaze shifted back toward Martha leaving the room, until she was gone. 'I'm talking about old man Hollis Woolf,' he called after her. 'My father.'

Hattie pressed into his wrist harder. Colm's knuckles were frozen white, but he kept still, letting Hattie clench so that she cut off circulation, he did not move to stop her. Could a person die this way? It was ugly that his mother did this now to him. 'Let me go, will you?'

'You never would listen, you boys,' Hattie said, then she let go.

'I have as much right as anyone to have an opinion.'

'Don't you stand in judgment. No one talks about him like that in my hearing.'

'I don't judge.' Colm's corneas were like tunnels. 'God will judge. I won't.'

'Everyone thinks they know,' Hattie said. She had to hold both arms of the chair and press herself out. She willed her fat body to stand as straight as it would, took a plastic grocery bag from under the sink, and did not turn around as she went out the front door. Colm's eyes, how they were about to suck Hattie down somewhere she didn't want to go. The pressure in the air was so thick it almost had a flavour, and Hattie went over to the side of the house.

Martha came back out of the bedroom to the table, and ran her finger back and forth over the wood grain on it, slicing her nail up and down the plastic ridges of the Jesus lenticular, trying to trance out as best she could. She was pretty good at it after all these years. She did not know what to make of things. She'd seen Hattie's face switch from determined to scared as she looked into Colm's eyes, but didn't want to consider this. Nor did she wish to look at the man who had elicited this change in so kind a woman as Hattie.

'You don't dare look at me,' he said. 'Did I scare you?'

She couldn't bear that he'd read her thoughts, and so she did look at him. His eyes were caked in sadness, she thought. He looked like the saddest thing, like grief, like she wanted to wrap him in her arms. He was like Curtis, like Aubie, like every man.

'I dare,' she said. 'I do dare.' Her chest felt like shit, like a huge hand was holding it and clamping at it slow and steady and cruel. This was all Curtis, she thought, this pain; and so much began to be clear. There was no running away, only running to, and she had run headlong. Colm's teeth were crooked, and he had a bland face. He looked like a fucked-up little kid. And he read her reading him so fast it was like an animal lashing out.

'And what do you see that my ma wouldn't see?'

'You're like Curtis. You and Aubie both.'

Colm's head twitched to the side. 'Hell.' And his face scrunched up with some regret she could not entirely place, and so she tried to put it away.

'I mean to say, you are sad. Or there is a sadness to you.'

'Oh.' Colm considered what she meant. He leaned over the table and pulled the lenticular toward him, running his palm along its ridges as if smoothing it out. He rose from the table and tacked the artifact back above the sink and spent some time making sure it was straight. 'I never did bother with grief much,' he said.

Martha thought it had certainly bothered with him, but she didn't want to say so. Instead she reached over and held his forearm briefly until it was clear this made him uneasy, and then she began to wonder herself why she had reached over and touched him, made him uneasy. 'Sorry.'

'Never mind.'

'That wasn't nice of me.'

'Never mind.'

Martha and Colm sat there for some long time not talking. It wasn't a silence that comforted; it was the charged quietude of strangers flailing around trying to think up something of easy interest. Colm was back running his square nail along the denim ridges on his pant leg. 'What's it like, north?'

'It's the same more or less,' though they both knew it wasn't, couldn't be. Martha watched his hand run back and forth along his leg until he noticed her watching and stopped.

When she had got up and gone to the bedroom with her purse, she'd sat on the bed. It had not been that hard to press the bullets into their slots. Curtis had kept the gun to remind himself of who he was, and now it was loaded.

Martha said to Colm, 'I would be honoured to meet Hollis Woolf.'

'Honoured?' Colm was shaking his head. 'He eats little girls, you know. Pretty much whole, he eats them. I've seen him devour a set of twins once. Just like spit, they went down.'

'Where does he live?'

'They've housed him in a grey-blue unit in a facility for demented old folk. The joke is, he isn't demented. Or if he is, he always was.'

'You'll take me?'

'I'm sure you won't like it, but I'll take you just the same.'

Sixteen

From Illinois, Curtis went west to Missouri, skirting Kansas City because he knew one of his brothers lived there, and there wasn't any sense in disturbing things further. He drove through the night to Tucumcari, listening to a church radio station: *All you got to do, folks, is call in and sow the seed of God's love. I know fifty-eight dollars a month is a heck of a lot of money, but think of it like this: it's a small price to pay come harvest time.* To the left and right was suburban development where once, Curtis supposed, were farmers' fields. It made perfect sense that the term *harvest* had been co-opted by the preachers, for it was nostalgic, and people loved nostalgia, as if the past was somehow cleaner than the present.

Curtis knew he wasn't going to be the one duped out of fifty-eight dollars a month for any harvest, but he knew this other thing for sure too. He knew that this country — this United States of America — was sacred soil. Hell, you'd have to be a clown not to feel it right down in your bones. And looking out through the rain at the flick of light from farmhouses and big buildings and streetlights, and the whip of car lights as they advanced and passed him on the highways, and the windshield wipers repeating their function, he knew God was present.

It was the country's dogged belief in itself maybe, the stars and stripes bunting and mailboxes — that belief was what brought God to mind. He'd lost that for a time, when he fled north. Yes, that's what he'd lost — his true belief. But he'd gained it back, hadn't he? He'd gained it back in spades. The farm had helped him, nature having a singular way of healing. It sounded lame, but he couldn't help that. It was he who'd moved them all to the farm, and they were grateful. It was his tenacious desire to get back to the land that had brought them all there. He, who hadn't ever even gardened. He'd spent days and days driving around looking for the right spot for them, looking for a place to form into their own paradise, a place where he hoped to attract like-minded people and get along outside society. They would pool their resources.

When he told Martha, the grin edging right off his face, he saw she knew it was right. 'You will come?' he said. They were in the city, in the yellow kitchen. A stream of chlorinated water ran into a scratched pink aluminum tumbler, the odour of thin bleach rising up. The floor was made up of black-and-white squares of linoleum. A mop emanating a mildewy stink was propped up against the basement door frame; it was a sculpture of dried, cotton wick in flight, and the everything of the kitchen had caught in Curtis's mind and held there. He wouldn't forget that moment so long as he lived. 'Damn,' is what he finally said, though what he was thinking was that he would follow that girl to the end of the earth if he had to. But the land was the right thing. It was pure and true. They'd have the space to be themselves, the way he imagined it would be.

'Yes.' Martha was beaming at him; maybe he'd never seen her so joyous since. They had been so happy.

The land was northeast of the city. It was a spectacular, undulating property with a small, mature hardwood forest and a planted coniferous acreage. There was a wide meandering creek along the property line. The land was truly a paradise that rose from a gravel road onto a picturesque rise from where, if you happened to be so inclined, you could look down on the land below as if onto civilization itself and feel you really owned something, that you were master over something. There were weatherworn buildings in unexpected places too, hidden by cedar copses — pig sheds and chicken coops — but the two houses and the mansard barn, with its red paint preserved in patches on the sheltered south walls, were exposed in a way Curtis thought was 'Perfect. They are perfect.' He had wanted to be a part of something in his life, and his good fortune was palpable to him; it was like a vessel, this fortune, and though it did not ease into gratitude, he did feel in a state of grace himself.

They went from one building to the next, Curtis pointing out beams that were already special to him for their fine joinery. He caressed the lids of ancient grain boxes as if they held treasure. 'The light!' he said. 'Look.' Shafts were piercing the fir planking in the hayloft. Martha looked as if she'd actually witnessed the second coming, like she wanted to lie down and bask in it, she was that happy. And Curtis recognized this, thought, I can live here. He had never seen so much green.

Martha nodded. 'It's beautiful, Curtis.'

The farm was the opposite of city, of every moment of their lives — for Martha and Benjamin and the others, that is, not for Curtis. Curtis never spoke of his thoughts, and why would he? Hide, he thought most often, build a life. Recompense. He rarely talked of the past even to Martha, but it sat in him, heavy and dormant. And now, in the white noise of highway driving, driving south as the fates ordained, Curtis wondered if it had sat heavy enough, if any of it was recompense, or if he had just called it that, all this, if he had just given it the veneer of atonement, when really it was a buffer from reality, a carefully built wall to protect from the past. He pushed these thoughts back. They did not matter. Here he was, and he toasted the windshield with his empty hand. 'To radiance,' he said. 'To Truth!'

All these years they had been off the edge of the world, giving the earth respect, and it had reciprocated. People of all kinds were drawn to the community. And together, over the years, they had codified it, given it integrity and therefore meaning. Years that he was completing, that's how it felt — as if briefly, in fleeting moments that as they occurred seemed infinite, he was becoming whole, of a piece. That by this perfecting he achieved a Divine Erasure, a joining of himself to everything. He did not have words to speak about this and so he did not. He must push through it all, now, push through Edgar, gunshot, blood, Hollis. But meanwhile it tried to press in on him.

Curtis didn't like where his mind was heading, flipped the station around to a Johnny Cash tune he recalled from way back — that one where Cash tells June Carter what a big mouth she has — trying to keep the refrain from letting his mind go back off toward Hollis. It was spitting rain, but he kept his eyes on the road, reaching over every hour or so to grab the jar on the passenger seat and take a sip of honey. You could sustain on honey, he knew, if it was a honey with integrity, which this sure was.

Breathe, he told himself. All those years on the farm had been good. Even the hard shit had been real, and that counted. He tried breathing in the hard and the bad, imagined his breath to be some machine, forcing air down his lungs and converting bad to good. It's what he would have told the Family any day of the week, and he would have had faith he was telling the truth. The body could act as a purifier, he was dead certain of that. It had been clear through the night, thank God, but now he had to switch on the wipers as the spattering rain built up and began to fall, thin tracks down the glass impeding his view. Behind him, the sky was a sickly green.

It would be only six a.m. by the time he reached Tucumcari, and nothing would be open, Curtis reasoned. He'd go to Fort Sumner, pay his respects at Billy the Kid's gravesite, and hopefully by that time someone would be up and he could get a bed somewhere and sleep to dream, get in a dry place before the sky opened up. Fuck, he was tired. His hands were itchy from holding the steering wheel. Well, from nerves is really what they were itchy from. He took a look at one of his palms and discovered a welted rash, like a hole that'd closed over, like that rash his pa always had. Calm, he thought. Stay calm. But he couldn't much do that. The rash bent along his palm, recalling the shape of his gun. It wouldn't be long now he'd have it back, could draw his finger along the etched silver. He could as well smell her, she was that close: Martha.

The rain would not let up, the cloud was surely gaining on him. Curtis slowed the Volvo to a near crawl and limped into Fort Sumner. He was daydreaming as he parked the car beside a tractor trailer outside Fred's Restaurant. He saw himself walking like a robot along the Pecos, finding Edgar, and saw the bullet splash him open, and this sight gave him such unmitigated pain he closed it down, shifted his mind to safer ground: it was not Edgar whose body rose in Curtis's mind, alive and full, but Curtis's own, being drawn up again by himself — an arrogant redemption, to be sure, but familiar. And then came a corpulent man's body, the neck and chest disfigured with scaly blemishes; it was Hollis who walked across Curtis's mind, turned to face out, and grew, as if walking toward him but then fully in him, until his father was no longer a dream but incorporation. The flesh of his flesh. He knew this.

It had been years and years that he had lived through this metamorphosis; Curtis had grown used to it. The ever-presence of Hollis under his skin. He thought at first that he'd die from the proximity, but it just changed him. That's how he felt about it now. He didn't even like to think any more about how he had thought it would make him sick and kill him. It had sullied everything afterwards. But him not wanting it to happen, that didn't bear weight any more. A man couldn't avoid becoming himself, and he was now thankful he hadn't tried to. A man added up to what came before, he was as sure of this as anything Hollis had ever said. The begats. But not entirely like Hollis meant it, the ancestors, the blood culminating into some potion of this or that.

No, for Curtis it was more, even if it was that, too. He owed something to all the events of his life; these things had formed him. It seemed inevitable that his trials, his brief moments of completing to wholeness, should come to this end. It had happened naturally. Hollis entered him, saying as he did, 'People who believe in you.' Curtis had been beholden, had scraped Hollis's rash, had taken the gun and done that man's bidding; by this he had learnt, by this he had recompensed his whole life. And people had believed in him, and he had not once been able to believe in himself without their believing.

Curtis shivered, though it was damned hot out, hot and humid as hell with the rain, hot just like he'd missed it being. Hot enough to melt the thoughts out of a man's busy mind. There would be no Billy the Kid today, the rain was that thick. He ate at Fred's, chips, salsa, and blue corn burritos such as he hadn't tasted in a long time, and the guacamole was reminding him how good it could be done. Guacamole for the gods, was that all right to think that? He watched the picture window, the rain more like waves, and worried about Hollis.

Curtis would see him again, his father, and there would be

a reckoning. He did not know how or why, but he knew Hollis. There would be a reckoning, and he would be weak. He saw himself, witnessed his own weakness, himself standing before this man, exposed; Hollis could see through all things. He stared at the rain sheeting into the dry earth. He thought, No. He would go to Hollis, and he would ask politely for his due. It would be substantial, he knew, what was willed to him. He would ask politely and he would not mention the past. It was the only way the farm would be saved from foreclosure. He would forgive Martha and they would go back and save the farm; he would reconvene the Family around Martha and help her forget whatever it was she might have learned down here.

The rain. At first the dust had seemed to repel it, and he'd seen the rain bounce away, but now it joined and thickened into red mud runnelling down the roads. It was like the damn weather had followed him to clean up this mess. He wished that it could. He was so close now, less than an hour from home if the rain would let up. He pushed around in his memory for something light, something joyful, and recalled his first sexual intercourse, with Clarie.

He wondered what she was doing now, wondered about her marriage to Robert and those kids he half wished were his, wondered what things might have looked like if everything had been different than it was. There was so much light back then he didn't even know he was broken, or even that he could break. Curtis wasn't fourteen years old. Clarissa was only fifteen. Her folks were out working and they'd been talking in her bungalow bedroom. She dared and he double dared. 'You ever do it?' she had asked.

She and Curtis took turns taking off one bit of clothing. His shirt, her sock, his tennis shoe, her earring.

'That don't count,' he'd said, referring to the earring.

'Like hell.'

'I never seen a naked girl.'

They were sitting straight, looking on each other, Curtis in a wicker chair Clarie's mother had painted pink to match the wallpaper and everything else in that room, and Clarie, with her legs as wide as you please, on the dusty-rose bedspread. Curtis was motoring about in his mind about what the hell was she sitting like that for, it troubled him. Was he seeing right? And how did you drive one of them things? He had recently learned how to drive his father's Mustang beater. Where's the ignition? is what his mind was asking him.

'It's nice if you look in a girl's eyes, Curtis. It is customary and all.'

Looking her in the eyes would be even worse. But he did. He shifted and stared right into her eyes and saw, but was not able to explain, that she was manipulating him, and he knew, but did not know how he knew, that he didn't care. She could manipulate him forever if she wanted, though he doubted forever, doubted it even though he was that young. He had a hard-on so hard, felt like his cock was bigger than he was. And then there hadn't really been much to it. It was two kids fitting A to B in the crudest way they had heard tell of, and how that could feel so damn fine; the orgasm was like a road out.

Curtis slumped now in his chair and stared at his plate. This memory of Clarissa had suddenly pushed up against another. Timmy. He motioned the waitress and asked her for sopapillos, something he saw on the menu and realized straight away he'd been missing. He hadn't thought about this food in thirty years, not Timmy or Clarie much neither. When the plate of deep-fried pastries arrived, little squares of puffed dough, he split one open, squeezed the liquid honey that came with it into its cavity, bit in. It paled, this honey. It was a shadow flavour of what he'd grown used to; he pushed his chair out, scraping along the linoleum floor, said, 'Be right back' to the waitress.

'Watch your step out there.'

The Volvo was parked between two eighteen-wheelers coming out of Texas. He got his key ready under the eaves of the building and ran; there wasn't any point trying to be quick, as he was soaked to the bone right off. He flipped the trunk, tucking his head inside to keep the water from his eyes. He needed to show the waitress this, let her taste it on the sopapillos, let her know that kind of perfection.

The rain was crashing against the trunk lid and reverberating inside the hold. The hive had spread outward, between the jars and the box edges, all of it an undulating mass of sweet-smelling wax. The bees were quiet. Curtis looked out at the road and was surprised to see the rain elevated into a shallow creek running west. He grabbed a jar, pulled his head out of the trunk, slammed the door shut, and broke to the restaurant. The wet was soaking into his running shoes, cooling him.

'I made it,' he said, gesturing with the honey jar. People looked up and then back down quick. 'Come,' he said. 'Come.' He felt really strong, beckoning the waitress over. She was a chubby Mexican girl. He scooped some out and into the pastry, handed it to the girl. 'There.' And then he said a silent blessing. The waitress thanked him for letting her taste the honey and excused herself quickly to the kitchen.

So few people could be counted on to understand, he thought. Clarie had understood him, he thought. And Timmy. Poor Timmy hanging off his own front porch, twirling there, dead, and Hollis overbearing. The phone call had been Hollis: 'Timmy has called you to him, and I am calling you to get yourself home. Right now, boy.' And he had.

Flesh beneath the flesh, he had run home. One of his brothers had shook his head and not uttered one word as he'd run into the yard, and Curtis only stopped briefly before passing his mother in the diner. There weren't any customers and she was washing dishes in the deep sink. 'Pa called me home,' Curtis blurted, and she had only nodded.

The room had been dark, darker even than usual, and Hollis was sitting with his back to the door.

'Son,' he said.

'Yes, Pa.'

As Hollis told it, Timmy's porch had been strewn with things: a hollow plastic doll, foraged firewood, a dented galvanized pail pushed over. There were Timmy's tennis shoes hovering mid-air, and his body looking longer than it had in life, the skin on the boy's face was white going to blue going to black. Timmy was dangling dead, and he had called, and Curtis had not been there.

Curtis said, 'I might have been able to stop him,' and Hollis turned to him and glared so deep into his eyes, he thought he would burn. He had then cut him, a thin line of beading blood beside the first line. It said, Don't question. It said, You mind your own business, and Curtis had done just that, knowing that three scars on his forearm would be it for Hollis, that their relationship would end there and that he would be cut off. Curtis had heard Hollis mutter more than once: three strikes, you're out, and he didn't ever want to be out, did not know what out would even be like, and feared that unknown. And then that thing with Edgar along the river, and he was out.

Curtis looked down at his arm lying on the Formica table, pulled the linen jacket up, and rubbed his finger over the three-line brand his father had given him. A brand — he hadn't thought of it like that until just now. That his father disowned him by his ownership, and that Hollis held tight the more he let go. Curtis figured he could learn from that.

He would go soon, and find Martha and he would entreat her to come back to the farm, though even now he knew this was fruitless, that this was not why he had come all this way.

He had made this journey to let her go, because letting her go was on his path. He was coming into something truly important here. He spooned the farm honey onto the last of the sopapillos, and tasted that healing. Good.

Curtis took a room across the road and slept through the day. The rain hushed his dreams, and he slept into the dusk.

Seventeen

Guadalupe County Long-Term Care Facility. Colm pushed the wheelchair entrance button and waited for the doors to open. He liked the effortlessness of the technology, the tiny power it afforded him — time. He thought about what Martha had said about Curtis and him being alike in sadness. He'd never really put much stock in sorrow. It was a quick path to action, a kind of catalyst to getting most anything accomplished. You went fishing when you were down, you got your gun and went hunting, you sank into work and made overtime, you went to church Sunday and prayed and sang it away. Sorrow never stayed sorrow, far as he was concerned. He wished she hadn't touched him; he didn't like being touched much, made him jumpy. He wondered, was he sad?

Also, he had never considered that Curtis might be sad. That Curtis would have a conscience at all had not been factored into any estimation Colm had ever made of him. And knowing it now did factor in, unpleasantly, in a way that interfered with his blind hatred of the man. Sympathy and compassion might have been the expected results of this factoring, but instead Colm felt exhausted and angry. Exhausted because he did not like changing his mind about things. It showed a certain weakness of spirit and lack of foresight. And angry because of the exhaustion and its corollaries. He simply felt weakened by this new information.

Colm decided to do what he could to alleviate this feeling, and so he sat Martha down in an annexed waiting lounge that had been designed to look like a mid-Victorian sitting room, set her down between the mahogany false fireplace mantel and the ceramic elephant leg umbrella holder. She was tired, he saw, she seemed reduced. 'I'll wait here,' she said when it was apparent he was leaving her there. She slumped slightly into a deep crease of the sofa. She had on a skirt, a pretty one.

Colm made his way to the men's room, a two-stall affair with three open urinals. He walked into the pasty-yellow room and into the first stall. He did not like the imagery of rest-room prayer, but at least it afforded him privacy. Colm kept his pants up, sat down on the toilet seat, clasped his hands together, and flailed around in his mind until he had located God. 'Forgive me for I have sinned. I come seeking strength that I know only You, Lord, can offer. I am sunk low and need Your help pretty bad.'

It was a lame prayer, he knew, but finding God required concentration and hard work, and he had to start somewhere. There was graffiti: *Marion sucks cock*. Who would put that on the bathroom wall of a care facility? The hollow, painted-metal door of the stall was pocked and dented, and rust had started to form along the bottom edges. Colm began to feel dismay at how rundown the can was, the way the rust revealed something about the place, about the way the facility viewed itself.

The *truth* is what it revealed — decay, disrespect for the body and its natural functions, and that Marion sucked cock. What was this place but a waiting room for death? Who was this Marion? He knew he had to push all these thoughts out of his head. He knew he couldn't be standing in judgment of the facility, of bathrooms, of this particular public restroom, of Marion, or even that there might be anything remotely crazy about this talking to God on the toilet, if he wanted to — and he did very badly want to — enter the simple rapture of prayer.

Besides, what did God care about the setting? Colm shifted and thought as hard as he could, thought and found himself swaying backward and forward until he knew he had God's line, until he could feel the euphoria begin to power him up. If his eyes stopped at the industrial roll of toilet paper and the way the spool had been left to unroll and had wadded in an admixture of condensation and urine on the fake terrazzo floor, and the way this putridity was wicking up the paper sheeting, and if his nose twitched against the false, strawberry-scented cleaning soap residue coupled with the wet and stench of previous guests, he was careful to bring it into prayer, to let it enter the sanctity of his communion, not to waste even the banal against God's good grace. And so it came to pass that Colm experienced a good ten-minute prayer, and when he was done, he headed back to find Martha wide-eyed and birdlike, perched on the edge of the green chintz sofa.

'Are there any vending machines in this place? I have a craving for salt.' She would have eaten dirt, if she could have some mineral from it. 'Potato chips or something.'

Colm jerked his head and she rose and followed him. The lighting shifted as they passed the waiting room threshold, from a subdued and peaceful dimness to an over-lit flare of what one automatically associated with hospitals — the over-litness of fear. They had to press themselves along the wall to let two gurneys slide by each other heading in opposite directions: the one ghostly, empty, the other rattling with bags of matter going in, coming out, last breaths, hope, hopelessness. The snack machine was just around the corner. Colm stood beside Martha and tried to ignore her sighing until he could no longer. 'What?'

'It's all so narrowed down like this.'

'Less choice, you mean.'

'No. It feels like an analogy.' And seeing he didn't understand the term, she added, 'I just don't feel myself.'

'What do you want?' he said.

Martha glanced at him, smiled the tiniest bit, pressed her choice, and they made their way up to Hollis. He was sitting alone in a metal and upholstered chair in his room. He was settled in under the halo of orange-yellow light coming from a gooseneck desk lamp that Hattie had once brought and placed on the wooden side table for him. Hollis did not read but instead warmed himself by the hundred-watt bulb he'd screwed into the lamp for that purpose. He believed the light positively affected his skin condition. He had been sitting still, letting the light spread over him for more than an hour since the nurse had wheeled him back upstairs from lunch, such as it was.

'Goddamn brown bread,' he muttered. 'What is the good of eating healthy food now I'm pretty near dead anyways?' Colm knew his old man's routine: Hollis had drunk four cups of coffee during lunch, had got himself wheeled back to his room, and then nipped into a mickey of gin he kept. His room wasn't much. Grey walls, grey carpet. If he kept the overhead pot lights out and the blind pulled, Hollis could cope with it, as long as he had the ring of heat. It spread out over his arms and lit up his chest, the silver-white hairs there, and the fat up his chin and jowls.

'I smelled youse as soon as the elevator doors opened. The pong of lime. No. The pong of the chemical notion of what that smells like. Come on in.' Colm had barely knocked; his knuckle had only just scuffed the surface of the door. Martha spilled some potato chip crumbs, and when Colm glared at her, she folded the bag shut. Colm recalled the whine of the vending machine as she made her selection, its liveliness in satisfying her desire, the dull thud of the chip bag falling to the machine floor, and the visceral response she'd had when she tore open the purchase. She had moaned.

'You've brought me a wombat.'

'This is a friend of Curtis's visiting from Canada, Pa. I thought you might like a visit with her.'

'Oh? I heard about her. Where's my boy? Where is he now?'

Hollis was addressing her, Martha suddenly realized. She was standing pressed into the door, the bag of chips and her purse clutched up against her chest. She appeared tiny, until you watched the eyes roving all over Hollis, taking in the scurf, the flake of him, the way his skin was so bad it blurred his edges so you couldn't hardly find him, and then she did. His eyes were large and widely set and handsome, there was a piece of his youthful beauty still there — no, not beauty, power — and Martha was looking there now, and Colm could see her relax slightly, gain her strength back. It was ugly and it was funny. Colm was put in mind of cock fights, like he'd seen when he was a kid, and that moment before the birds started in, when they were strutting and assessing, their beady eyes stupid with anticipation. How was God just now answering his prayer?

'You got chips there, lady? I could use some of those.'

Colm tugged them out of her hand, walked over to his father, waiting for him to shift and reach, and handed them over to him.

'Thank you.' When she didn't respond, he said, 'What d'you have in that purse, lady?'

Martha squinted. 'Hmm?'

'I said thank you. For politeness' sake.' He wheezed a kind of laugh, and when she looked over Colm was smiling, the smile of satisfaction, of proof, of I told you so.

'I will sit down, if that's okay?' Martha said.

A fuss was made then. Hollis shifted again to let Colm through to the room's only other chair and let him pass with it.

Martha made faces that it should be set down close to the door where she yet stood, one hand holding the other holding her leather purse, her clutched hands pressed into her genitals so that her cotton skirt creased up there. She was holding on to herself for dear life. In the purse? She thought how Curtis'd kept it to remind himself of who he was. She watched as the chair, by Hollis's explicit orders, was placed at the edge of the light cast by the gooseneck lamp, so that when she sat down, her knees and fingertips were warmed by it.

'It aids my eczema, so I don't know what to do without it.'

'I'm sorry to hear that.'

They sat for a long while, and nothing seemed to happen. Time sprawled out, and it was Hollis's breath only, and the light, and the wanting of salt. Then Hollis said real quiet, 'You sit as still as a wombat if ever I saw one.'

'I'm sorry.'

'You are sorry a lot.' He leaned back and smiled. Martha tried to slide her knees to the side as if to avoid the community of the heat from the lamp, its intimacy, and so it was she bumped up against Hollis's leg.

'Excuse me.'

Hollis slammed his palms on the table then. His fingers were squared off, like Colm's own, but weighty, where Colm's were all skin and knuckle. Hollis's hands lifted and slammed again onto the table and he was looking directly at Martha, into her. Hollis's chest was massive, framed by the light, the edges of his striped pyjama bottoms at his waist.

Colm recalled him arriving unexpected back home, this man who presented as a fatherly figure and gave them something like male affection where they otherwise had none. He recalled the giant of the man rising up after a dinner meal, recalled thinking how lucky were the real sons of this man, and how it was hateful not to have a proper father. He recalled his own jealousy, was inside it, felt it crawl over him, so that he wished he had prayed longer in the toilet for the inner fortitude to stay with him.

He'd discovered that Hollis was his father at fourteen, and he'd felt so deceived, he had run off by himself and drunk so much that he'd lost track of time; for weeks he had only drunk and drunk. Now church and prayer and regular work helped, and that Aubie and Edgar were such messes helped too — they edged his role, giving him room to be good, with all their badness.

'I don't even really know what a wombat is,' she said.

Colm could see Hollis'd been drinking; he looked vacant, right back at Martha, like he used to look when his drink rampage was easing out of him, when he stumbled in at Hattie's place seeking whatever solace Ma offered, some kindness in the shit world, he would say. Hollis'd be almost weeping with drink and rage and what Colm now recognized as self-loathing. Hollis had that look to him now, that look that, for Colm, only Scripture could assuage.

Hollis said, 'It will become just as I have said it,' and Martha looked queerly back at him, as if she'd heard it before. She shuddered, seemed to file some connection, maybe to Curtis. Hollis tugged the bottom ridge of the chip bag and let the contents slide along the table, twenty or so little curled hosts.

'Help yourself,' he said and ran his palm vertically through the pile and swiped a portion into his other hand, now cupped ready for it at the table's edge. He tilted his head back, and before he tipped the chips in, he said, 'Tell me. Where's that boy? Where's Curtis got to?'

'I don't know. He doesn't know I'm here, and I expect he is in Canada.'

'Where is he?' Hollis shut his eyes up tight and let his fat head loll back against the chair. 'Where is he, Colm? I need him by me.'

'We haven't seen him, Pa. Aubie and me are waiting on him. We guess he's on his way.'

'You don't know that for sure, do you?'

'No, I don't. I just figure it.'

Hollis's eyes snapped open and he looked at Martha for a long while, like she was a specimen. He looked carefully at her face and then for a long time at her hands. Colm saw they were thin hands that had worked, had blue lines running along them and gnarled knuckles, long fingers. She took care of her nails just enough and not more.

Hollis lifted his hand and for too many seconds held it over the table near where her hands were resting but not near enough a person wouldn't wonder he just wanted another handful of chips. Without looking up, he said, 'You pray lately, Colm?'

Colm grunted yes. Hollis was mocking him, and it worried him Hollis might ask the circumstances of his prayer. He wanted to make certain Hollis did not pursue the line of questioning. But you never could get away with anything if Hollis had anything to do with it.

'You grunt like you're a pig. Answer proper, son.'

'I prayed not half an hour back.'

'Half an hour, you were in the elevator.'

'No, I was in the men's room.'

Hollis laughed then so it reached his feet, so you could sense every organ in his body tingling with the kind of joy Colm expected Satan enjoyed. 'The Lord sees everything,' Hollis said finally, 'but it don't mean you got to bring attention to it.' And then for good measure, 'Shit.' His huge hand came down softly on Martha's left hand, and Colm watched her wonder just briefly whether she could still move it away. 'What do you want from me, lady?'

She did not try to move but sat there with her eyes locked onto his. Hers were wet with such a fear, but then she seemed to soften into his hand holding her, and it was not so very awful. Hollis's eyes were as dry as desert bone and smiling. Just seconds is all it lasted. Hollis looked down at his hand as if he hadn't meant anything at all and watched his hand as it slid along hers, his broad fingers slowly making their way along the veins that creased like arroyos along her skin.

Hollis was reminded of someone. 'You're very like someone I used to know,' he said. Hollis kept his eyes on Martha's hand. His index finger was the only lingering digit and it held her, that one finger, held her, everything except her eyes, which skittered every which way, absolutely still. 'Curtis never told you?'

She shifted her head to the right in an aborted shake, no. Her eyes showed her confusion and again she was mortally scared. She did not know where this was heading. Finally, she asked, 'Told me what?'

Hollis broke contact, leaned back in his chair, and looked over at Colm. 'You tell her, son.'

Colm crossed his one leg over the other. 'You remind him of Curtis's mother, Maeve Woolf, who died some twenty years ago.'

'Twenty-three.'

'Some twenty-three years ago.'

Martha took her hands off the table, out of the circle the light made, and even though she craved another chip, she put her hands in her lap, clasped together in a way that reminded her immediately of the faith she had at Soltane, all the fervent prayers being answered, even in light of the fact it never altogether was. That Curtis and Hollis were so alike they chose the same kind of woman sank to a bad place, and she sank there with it. She was filling with clay and salt crystal, droughting down to some reality she never knew could be.

'No,' she whispered. 'No, he never said.' She corkscrewed her body to the left and lifted out of the chair and began to move toward the door. She did recall though that Curtis had known of Maeve's death, had wanted to go home for the funeral but couldn't; he'd been afraid of crossing the border. The memory unsettled her further. He was weak, he was afraid. She had not really known this, or had not allowed herself to know it. 'Thank you for the visit, Mr. Woolf. It has certainly been interesting.'

Then she saw there was a problem. Colm was no longer standing in the shadows by the window; he was in front of the door. 'Shall we go?' she asked him, though she already knew his answer.

Colm's legs were spread, framed by the rubber baseboard casing they'd used as a door frame. 'Pa?'

Martha told herself she would not cry in front of these men, whatever they might now do to her. Her mind went to the gun in her purse. She was finding it troublesome to breathe. She grappled with her purse without any clear intention and said, 'What do I want from you? I just only ever wanted to solve Curtis, and maybe I just did.' She felt she must look like an animal, that old wombat Hollis was on about. She touched her hair reflexively, thinking she must comb it. She wanted to ask him for money. She knew how to beg, but she didn't dare.

'Curtis?' Hollis wasn't even looking at her, and then he was, square at her, his eyes sleepy and holding hers. 'My boy don't need solving.'

'I think I want to leave, Colm.'

'Okay, Martha. Okay,' Colm said, but he didn't move, he just looked over at Hollis, his face distorted: how he wanted to help Martha and how he couldn't bypass his old man.

'Curtis was solved at birth, that boy.' Hollis's eyes seemed to have woken up, and there was a need to them that softened her reaction. 'I'd like a private word with you, Martha.' There was a kind of wheezy longing to him. 'Colm, you step outside, find your way down to the foyer, and I'll get her to you.' And Colm nodded and then nodded to Martha, and though her eyes were beseeching him, he left, a pain rippling along his mouth that she could not read.

Martha heard him padding down the hall, heard the elevator door shush. Her heart sank, balled up. She sorely regretted being there, wondered, too, if there was any other language that would speak to this father of the man she'd tried to honour, tried to assuage her entire adult life. The gun would bridge the communication gap, she knew.

'Come back and sit you down,' he said.

And she did.

'I think he's here,' Hollis whispered, leaning in to her. His voice was shrill now, and fiercer, meaner. Martha watched the lit circle of him, where the chest dugs met the armpits, the white scales burning, and beneath them, a fiery, painful-looking red, and then she looked up into the most vacant eyes she had ever encountered. Hollis Woolf was looking at her. No. He was learning her by heart. No. She had no words for what he was doing. *Possessing her* was close.

'Who?' But even as she spoke, she knew. Curtis would be on his way, like Aubie had said, sniffing her trail, following her to save himself, to maintain Soltane, keep it all intact, as he would have convinced himself was necessary. Hollis smiled, nodding at her in a way that suggested illness and pity and malice all wrapped up together. She could suddenly feel Curtis hurtling south, and the feeling brought with it a vapid hunger for freedom, for some passionate flavour resembling freedom, and she reached over the table, and her hand hovered and then snatched a chip that had curled into itself.

'A wish chip,' she said and right away felt dumb for saying it; it was a leftover from her childhood she'd forgotten. The light was so energetically painting Hollis, dark and brooding, that Martha found herself nodding too, a weird echo. The two of them and the chip and the light. Her instinct said run and don't look back, but Martha did not. The meeting had overrun her. She pressed her tongue against the limed and salty chip, and held it there until it dissipated into her palate. She wished she had stayed at the farm, a wish she knew she was too late for. Should have wished for world peace, and wasted the chip better, she thought, and then suppressed the thought when it, too, went into a place of despair.

'I saw him sitting right in the window ledge, or I saw a vision of him come to me. It was a powerful sight, I tell you,' Hollis was saying. 'He's in our midst.'

'He's coming for me,' she said, half yearning for that, half proud of it, held still by him. 'If he's coming, he's coming for me.'

'He's coming for us all, lady. But I thank you for bringing him here.'

So, she was a sort of decoy for this man. Martha held her purse close to her then, pressed the leather into her belly. There were second-hand images coming to her, delusional pictures of Curtis and Hollis bent over talking, the quiet insanity of two. She saw Curtis with Aubie, clear as day, masked and armed with rifles — she had not much idea what a sawed-off shotgun looked like — flicking their heads toward five bewildered cashiers, and money being transferred, shaky hands putting bills in an old potato sack. It was a nightmare rendering of something Aubie had told her. How easy it was to rob a store, like pecan-picking in November, he had said, and, memory being stronger than will, the elation had haunted his face. She saw a man crumble and roll away into the river Pecos.

She mourned for what Hollis'd done to Curtis, for the specific ways in which he had hurt Curtis and for how this had played out all over his life and into hers. She had cowed to that, she had placated that prayerful ruin, she now saw; she had cut space in her heart to accommodate that wreckage that was all this: the spectre of Edgar, the long-held, distorted memories of Hollis, Maeve, Hattie, Aubie, Colm, and it was how this manifested Curtis's guilt, and how that guilt manifested God, the Family, Soltane, and Martha's own strange self. Was there really such a thing as redemption? She gripped her purse yet tighter, and seethed, 'You have caused so much misery.'

'What's in that purse, lady?'

'It isn't your business,' she said. It came out so solid, even though she knew it was his business.

Hollis put his palms up in the air, and she smelled his drink. He said, 'I have only ever demanded strength.'

'And you *dare* —' and she stopped because she did not dare. His hands supplicating like that; what would he bring on?

'I dare what?' he said.

She tried hating him with unmitigated wrath, but she was not good at hatred; her whole life had been love. She watched the line where the lamplight blurred at the edges and became shadow and his body only hulked and did not elicit any sympathy. She would not allow herself to see the flake and scurf of him, only the dark form sitting awkwardly. His breathing rattled and she could smell the stale booze sweating from him. He was old, and old in a dying way. You dare to be so diminished, she thought, so ineffectual, so pitiable, realizing that instead of hatred, it was pity she felt, and anger at feeling this pity.

'I dare what?' Hollis grinned at her and she saw Curtis's charm, his aging face exuding that same tired charisma. The chaotic rebirth, what is born of bad thought and misplaced will. Hollis said, 'You were expecting a real dragon? Hell, I see you were hoping for one.'

Martha had not thought about it in these terms before, but now he said it, she knew that, yes, she had come expecting something grander, something monstrous to press up against all the rest she knew, and instead she had found this lumpish, diseased *man*, nothing more. She was eating lime chips with an old, dying man.

'You came to say something, lady? Or you came — wait. You came to threaten me and chastise me for something. You came to come clean? Out with it. Crap. Out with it, I said!'

Martha was holding her purse so close she'd formed sweat on her shirt. She'd held on to the Browning for so long, and it was still there in her purse, a weapon, with a weapon's power. She was mortal; she said, 'I came to aim the gun that killed Edgar McCann at you. I came armed with the Browning; it's here — in my purse, loaded. I don't know how to shoot a gun, and I don't believe in violence —' She hadn't known she wanted to kill him, and now that she said it, it sounded ignoble, but ignoble in a way that if she didn't go through with it, she would further diminish everything. Hollis would die, and it would be her fault.

Hollis's face was bent into his neck and he was laughing mean again. 'I always like to hear that. How a person don't believe in violence. You ever turn on the news or read a newspaper? You don't have to believe in violence, it ain't a religion, and it don't depend on anybody believing. Hell, no.'

'I don't believe in personally enacting violence, and I don't believe in violence as a solution. I want to pay you out. I know Curtis never will, and I feel it should be done. There has been so much pain. Do you have any idea how much pain you are responsible for? I have the gun right here in my purse.' She was shivering with nerves; it was occurring to Martha that it would be easy enough for Hollis to have a gun too, that he might reveal one at any moment.

Hollis was scraping at a little patch of scurf on his forearm, and he looked over at her. 'I gave Curtis that gun. I would very much like to see it.' He reached over to the purse, while she pulled it back out of his reach.

'No.'

'You ain't got no gun. You couldn't cross the border with it, now, could you?'

'But I did.' Martha stood and backed toward the window. She wanted to see if Colm was waiting for her in the parking lot, and she looked down to the Camaro. The sun shimmered off the hood, and off to the right she could see dark clouds and the green-grey of rain. Something flicked just outside her glance, the chrome of a bicycle handle perhaps, or a watchband. There was bush along the Pecos River — what to her was barely a creek — and there it was again, movement, someone. But not Colm. He would be sitting with his arms crossed waiting for her, like he'd been told. 'Storm,' she said, thinking, Curtis might already be here, and how she did need him.

'Ranchers'll be happy.'

Martha felt defeated. The day had worn through her, and she was rattled, and protein hungry. Maybe Curtis was there. She watched Hollis ease up from the little table and hobble back to bed, watched him and watched him, for it took him some time to execute his plan. Each movement was calculated and painful-looking, he was that close to dying, and she would shoot him. She waited until he had manoeuvred his legs up and nestled himself into the bedclothes.

'I was going to pull the gun out,' she said, and she did so then.

Martha held it up, and squared it, aiming toward him. She aimed at Hollis's chest; she did not know where else to aim, and his chest was formidable. She continued, 'I wanted to say how awful you were, how you had wrecked so many lives, how you were irresponsible, how you were self-serving, and inconsistent in your affection, how you cared only for money, how you used love to inflict the utmost hatefulness on your family, how you lied, how you continue lying, how you hoarded and tricked and how all this had brought only ruin upon you, and upon your sons, and possibly countless others who had come into contact with your lineage. I would point the gun at your heart. I would say how I was pacifistic, earth-loving, God-loving, faithful, and that I was sorry, and I would look menacing. You would be scared, and when I was sure you were sufficiently afraid, when your face crumpled and you begged me in your fear, I would tell you —'

'Ain't it hot in here.' Hollis leaned over to the nightstand by his bed and pulled a mickey from the drawer and nursed sips from it while he watched her like she was a TV. His fat face was haloed with the white velveteen coverlet, which was wrapped entirely around him, like a veil. Something about him lying there so vulnerable now reminded her of the gun shop, with its metal grating and armoured windows, its chintzy signage, *sale, sale, sale*, and everything about it was so foreign to her, and so not her, that she thought she would never be brave enough to enter the door.

'Who told you all these lies about me?'

'Curtis. Aubie. You only have to look at Colm to see —'

'Mind your own concerns, lady.'

She was too afraid to go into a gun shop, too scared to purchase ammunition, even to pull the thing out of her bag. Guns would always be a mystery to her, and her ignorance would sway in two directions: righteousness and weakness. And yet she had gone in, and purchased, and loaded, and was now aiming. She now felt both righteous and weak in the face of Hollis's nonchalance. He glared at her. 'What did you see out there, lady?'

She couldn't stop herself in time; her face shifted back down to the bushes along the Pecos. Curtis, she thought.

'He's here, ain't he?'

'It's nothing, a tin can, beer, a candy wrapper catching the sun, something lost. I thought I saw something, but there's nothing there.'

Hollis shook his head. 'He's coming.' He said it like it was a prophetic announcement, like the son of God was about to make an appearance. Curtis would like that — he had bet the farm, so to speak, on that sort of acknowledgement.

'I imagine it would upset him that I left the farm,' Martha said, 'and that I took his gun with me. But he isn't what you think. He's not the same.' Hollis looked to be sleeping and Martha wondered if he'd heard anything she had just said. She moved a bit toward Hollis and held the gun like she meant it.

'Put that thing down,' he said, swigged some more gin.

'No.'

'I made you.'

This deflated her further. Made her? Her face twisted; she did not understand.

'There wouldn't be no you, without there was Hollis Woolf.' He shut his eyes. 'You're this pure thing, and I as good as made you.' Then he shouted, 'Look at yourself; where did you come from? Shit, lady, there ain't no you without me.' He laughed quietly, in a way that looked like pure joy, the way it can look like crying too. Then he called out, 'Colm!' sudden, loud, a blast of sound into the quiet. 'Come and get her, Colm.'

She was being dismissed.

Martha leaned back in her chair and squeezed the trigger of the gun; it made sense, then, this gun. There was a loud noise, and a kickback that ran down her body, reverberated like an awakening, but Hollis did not flinch. She watched the light beside her shatter, and then it was near dark in the room. She put the gun down on the table, ran her finger along the barrel where it was warm now, and waited on Colm. There had been such a noise, surely someone would come.

No one came, though she waited, and Hollis was still, so she picked up the gun and moved toward the door, rotated the doorknob slowly as she let herself out. She would go on her own. She had slayed nothing, she knew. The door was closing when she heard Hollis, and she held it open for one last glimpse of him. He was painful to see, all red and scabbed over across the cheeks, with the white coverlet framing him. He was falling into sleep, a stinking drink sleep, peeling, dying, all of it hateful and real, and there wasn't anything she could do to make it any less of either.

'Curtis was always the special one,' he was muttering. 'I knew that the day he was born he would save us all. I knew that. I never stopped believing in him. I never did for a minute stop. He ain't changed. Not that boy,' and then the door sighed and snapped shut and she felt her inadequacy as a great burden, how she had been made by him, and ran from it down the hall, taking the stairs instead of the elevator.

'I'm going to walk back,' she said to Colm. They were exiting the building, the shush of electric doors closing behind them. 'I need to breathe.'

'No one walks in America,' Colm said. He was joking, but all the same, she thought about the glimmer of light refracting, off what? The movement in the bushes. Who was watching her? She could see the steeple of Santa Librada off to the right. Colm looked at her, and asked, 'Did you stand up to him?' And she saw he hoped for this.

'Not really,' she said. She shook her head, wished she'd done it better.

He was nodding and nodding. She thought he might want to say something more, only that he didn't know how to go about it. He looked at her so strangely. 'You're free, I guess,' he said quietly.

No, she was not free. She felt so heavy; there was no lightness to her. But perhaps this was freedom, heavy and hurtful and lonely until you got used to it. 'Colm?' she said. 'I think I saw someone hiding by the river.'

He looked out the windshield toward the Pecos, but he couldn't see nothing from that vantage point. But as they pulled out of the parking lot, a dead end, and onto the defunct 66, they saw Hattie moving along the side of the road. Colm's window slid down, and as he was saying 'Ma, there's a storm on the way' and 'What are you doing out here by yourself?' Martha was out of the car. 'Well, I can drive you both.'

The women just stood there, said no.

Eighteen

Hattie walked with Martha along the Pecos homeward. It was wet down there in some of the meanders, but they mostly stayed along the edge where the river had dried out in scars, and where it was thick with scrub: sagebrush, Mormon tea, willow. Hattie moved ahead doggedly, pushing grass and young cholla cacti aside as she went, bending if anything caught her eye. Rain was coming on slow. And there was the broken tail of a minnow lure; Hattie found that faster than it took Martha to catch up.

The silver paint was creased into the oak grain, and there wasn't but one of the forked hooks left on it; Hattie wrapped it in Kleenex and pocketed it, figuring to put it up on the wall with the others. She liked the damaged ones just as well as the not, and besides, she knew this lure. One of the boys had made this lure, maybe Edgar, and knowing this felt right. Martha was struggling to keep up, and the find gave Hattie time.

'He's something,' Martha said.

'Most people don't know how anyone could love a man like that. I don't know either, but I do. He still makes me crazy when I see him. Much as I hate it, he does. Much as the boys hate it. You can't please everyone, of course.' Hattie thought she heard thunder off to the east.

'Hollis didn't think much of me.'

'He call you a wombat?'

'How did you know that?' Martha was looking carefully at the ground where she walked, panting, wheezy. She had just pulled a trigger.

'He's more predictable than you'd imagine. Especially nowadays; he just goes around and around all the old things, mixing everything up, and making it more crazy where it was less, and less crazy where it was more.' Hattie could feel the rain edging up against the day, that storm over Fort Sumner way. Water. 'It'll rain soon.' The radio news had given flood advisories for the last days — Colm had mentioned this too — but the news was often wrong. Some days the lightning flashed around and nothing, not a drop, fell. She looked over at Martha and realized the woman was scared.

'Are there rattlesnakes around here, you think?' Martha asked.

So that was it. Snake fear. 'Sure,' Hattie said. 'But I've never had a problem. They like quiet and I stay quiet. No problems between us so far.' Hattie could see the oak up ahead and she went off into the past. How old had she been? Eighteen by then, maybe. The trench left over from the river was good and steep, and where Hattie stood, a quarter-mile from home, there was no easy way of exiting.

There was the tree, all gnarled with age and wind pushing it this way and that. It was familiar to her; it was one of Hollis's meeting places. He'd say, 'By the wrecked scrub oak,' and she'd wait there after dark. She always heard him before she saw him; her skin prickled. And then the moonlight glanced off him and she thought she might bust open. Didn't matter he was getting married, then it didn't matter he was married. 'Pick me up and hold me in the air, Hollis.' She wanted to feel what it felt like to be Maeve at their wedding hoisted up like Hollis loved her all the way to heaven.

His eyes shone and he smiled at her. 'Why?'

'Just do it.'

'Why do you want that, Hattie?'

She just stomped at the ground. 'Just do it.'

'Aw, shoot,' he said. 'Women.' He put his hands under her little breasts, his thumbs pressed together and into her ribs where the flesh met her skeleton and she could feel the skin at her nipples tighten. He drew a deep breath, kind of steeling himself for it, and lifted Hattie and held her up in the air. She waited for the good feeling to wash over her the way she had dreamed it would if only he would do this thing to her that he had done to Maeve. She waited for a long time.

It did not come.

The night wind brushed against the hair on her arms, his thumbs pinched at her and slid up until they held her breasts like tiny cups. Hollis fumbled his face into her crotch. 'Okay,' she said.

'What?'

'You can let me down now.'

He dropped Hattie down so fast the hurt went up her shins and into her knees and belly. She let loose and swung at him then, her fist connecting with some soft piece of him and sinking. 'Christ,' he cried out. 'Now, why did you do that?' But she was already running, the grass and wet sage at the edge of the river whipping her legs, and she could hear him trailing her, laughing. 'Hattie, I was. Only. Joking. Don't you got no sense of humour? Hattie?'

'No. No, I don't.' She let him catch her so he could say how sorry he was, say she clipped him in the balls, and he wasn't going to be able to make any babies. 'That's okay with me,' she said. Hattie poked at a slimy piece of grass on her calf. Hell. Nothing she did ever stopped him having babies. Maeve popped one out every year or two, but it was a while before Hattie's body started stretching out, becoming hard in some places, soft in others. She was working in Montoya for Richards, who was kind enough to let her move to the backroom of the grocery so no one would have to see her in that state. Townsfolk thought the baby would go for adoption and the whispers would die.

'I did love Hollis.'

Martha was looking at Hattie, but Hattie didn't care. She could stare right at her and think her thoughts. Richards's store. There was gold and silver and other minerals coming through that store — itinerant miners, oilhands, and such — and she got a glimpse of that treasure. She showed Hollis once, and regretted that, the mere sight of gold sending him off for weeks on a jealous rage. He couldn't stand anything shiny that didn't belong to him.

Richards was an oil prospector type from up north who Hollis didn't believe had a real stake in the land, just come in to steal and likely he'd be out when the last crude got sucked out of the earth. He was about to go deeper than anyone thought normal. Down to the middle of the earth, it was said. Speculating. Hollis always said, 'Thief.' He ought to know, is what Richards always said right back. Hollis said, 'That man comes out of the ground and stinks like sulphur. I don't understand your affection for him, Hattie.'

'Well, he takes care of me, Hollis.'

The working men came into the store for a soda pop at the end of the day, the mud still sticking to them. They sang all gravelled over, songs found down there too, in the depths. Men in battered felt hats, rough cotton shirts, clothes so ill-fitting, you never see that any more. They were rough men, had hands they couldn't keep to themselves, but Hattie didn't care. No one'd touch her; being Hollis's girl, no one dared. She had a belly on her, oh. Could have stopped a truck.

'What's that girl got under her dress? She hiding a ranch heifer?'

'Fool's gold and Pecos diamonds, nothing worth a damn.' That's what Richards always told them. Hollis had the only profitable gas pump around, and even though Richards lost money on his gas pump, he wouldn't lower himself to shut it down and fill up his machinery at 666. Richards sucked up the loss with scornful laughter. He could afford to. No, there was no love lost whatsoever between Hollis and him.

'Let me feel that lumpa gold you got there, girlie.' New derrickman with his hands black with crude, fingers spread out to grab at her.

'You don't want to touch that, sir.'

'No?'

'I guess not. She's pinned to Hollis Woolf.'

The man pulled his hands back fast then. 'That must weigh,' he said, glancing at her belly. The men chuckled, drank down their colas.

'What's it like?' Hattie said, once, making conversation. 'What's it like in the field?'

Mister with the hands glared at her. 'She talks!' His face was greasy and flecked with hair because he didn't get a shave too often, his ears flapped out by his head. He was one of the ugliest people she'd ever encountered, ugly from inside, ugly from years of neglect and not knowing how to be pretty. But his eyes were blue pools, deep, salt cenotes, and Hattie was locked there.

'What's it like?' he said. 'Well, I'll tell you. It's waiting and then the rumble of fire as the earth gives up her booty. The crude comes up like brimstone, and the money flows along with it. But if there weren't no money in it, they'd call it Hell. Uh-huh. Hell itself can't be uglier than that. What's nicer is the mines, though, and I been down there too.' The man wasn't looking so much at her as in her now. But she knew he wasn't speaking to her, he was speaking to himself in a way that made her want to look away.

'Done everything you can name in my short life. The mines are black and rough and leaking water and sulphur stink and men's piss. One minute you are breathing fine spring air, then you slip down and for a time you cannot see a thing. Another world. Your flare blinds you until you figure out to hold it off to the side and then, and then, you see them. The gold and turquoise and silver veins.' He said veins like they were human, and caressed the air.

Hattie looked away. The man had moved closer to her, moved very close, and she could smell his mouth rot, his man sweat, and the metallic reek of clay coming off his skin. He jerked his face around trying to maintain an eye lock, so she shut her eyelids, tight. 'Like being born.' She opened her eyes, not trusting him. His eyes had wandered to her belly. A flood of merciless laughter poured out of him then, and the other men joined in, relieved. 'Or reborn.'

'Jay-sus.'

'And look at her. Rightly inside out she'll be in no time at all.'

She would too. She could feel the beginnings of labour washing over her every now and again already, only eight months past, the freezing hand of God clutching at her and the cold cramp of it sliding along her abdomen and down between her legs, into her thigh muscles. She'd stop and catch breath, half of her anxious from this possession of her very skin, half of her proud to bear all the pain in the world for the bit of Hollis she'd be able to claim her own forever.

That was baby Edgar. He popped out exactly the same as he ever was, serious and upright and no mistake. A whorl of hair at his crown that only dried up and got thicker. He looked like Hollis, square-jawed and gaze you down. People got the idea he was smarter than they were, even though he hardly said a thing. And could that child suck. Hollis would come by and look on in wonderment. 'That child won't leave an ounce of you over for me.'

'And between the both of you —'

No, Hollis couldn't keep his hands off Hattie. By that time he was already getting fatter and fatter. And things weren't great at home. There were already six children in that bitty trailer. Hollis'd built on a room at the back. Over the years, that house became a long corridor of rooms so that you had to go through the children's rooms to get at the TV. And Maeve wasn't well, hadn't clotted too good after the third baby, and she was pale and scared around the eyes.

After Edgar came along and Hattie moved down Pecos way, she'd see Maeve at church; found she couldn't hate her. She just watched the priest place the host on her tongue, and after a while, she started praying it'd take. Maybe that's all that kept her going. After mass, Maeve's children would hang from her arms; Hattie could just see the pain and tolerance mixing in her eyes. 'Maeve.' Hattie always gave greetings no matter how sad and hypocritical she felt. After all, a person was a person and deserved that. There was no sense in wasting hate. Maeve seemed to feel the same way.

'Hattie. Good morning.'

'Pretty dress you got on.'

'That's kind.'

Hollis never showed himself in church. The gas pumps needed manning, and he stood one arm on each, pinned to the pumps like he was an electrical line, in union with that energy; Hollis kept up the looks of that place like it was sacred. Those pumps were Hollis's own altar, make no mistake, and when he prayed for more — as blasphemous as it seemed — it worked. For years and years, his prayers were answered. The washed-out stream of travellers kept coming. They didn't have money for much except gasoline, and the motion of their cars on the road energized them with hope and sustained them on their journey toward that hope. People asked Hattie privately, 'Why don't Hollis give you work over at 666?'

'That devil's pump? No, thank you. I'll stay on with Richards.'

The fact is she liked the static charge of Hollis's jealousy toward Richards. It kept everything alive. And there was no way Maeve was likely to stand for Hollis having Hattie around the pump as a sort of trophy, trailing her halfling around — no matter how civil she was come church-day. Richards would sometimes drive her home from mass. They'd pass Hollis and his pumps and Richards would say, 'Wave, Hattie, and smile pretty.' Used to get Hollis all hot and bothered.

'You don't own me, Hollis.' Hattie wasn't never cowed.

'Hell I don't.' And the time went on and on, like it does. There were three boys from Hollis running around Hattie's life; Maeve had nine children — the four boys and the girls then.

Hattie found a spot she liked near the old scrub oak and lowered herself down for a rest. She said, 'I got a pistol in the event of rattlesnake anyhow. Aubie got that for me; he doesn't like it much neither that I walk down here, but I ain't about to stop it.'

'You carry a gun?' Martha's eyes went to her purse, then back up to Hattie.

'Yup.' Hattie sat down and reached in through the buttons at the front of her dress and pulled a small gun out of a holster. It was grey plastic and chrome. Martha took a minute to smile. And then she sat beside Hattie and looked down at the Pecos. It ran a trickle here, you could hear it plashing against small rocks and the eroding edge of the river wall. Hattie watched the water, let that calm into the question she wanted answered since she'd met Martha. 'So, how'd you end up with a fellow like Curtis anyway?'

'Curtis? I thought he was honest.' And Martha told Hattie

about the draft dodge and how Canadian youth had felt about Vietnam and how Curtis had come across so wild and alive. She told Hattie about the evening they spent together and about how important it was to her those days to be politically active. 'I was young,' she said.

'And then?'

'And then it was too late for thinking.'

'He never woulda made the army anyway, that boy. Something wrong with his heart, I heard.'

'Murmurs? Sweet God, I never made that connection.' Martha stared off briefly before continuing, 'And then he opened to God, and started bringing people to him. Before long, we had the farm.'

'I guess you fell for that.'

'I guess I fell. Yes. I fell badly.'

Martha and Hattie sat there for some time. Hattie thought about how she knew about falling for someone who wasn't good, but seemed to be right, for you. She knew about long-term bad decisions and how they became the only way that seemed safe, or the only way a person could feel worthy. She thought about Edgar and how his death might be Hollis's doing, and even though the instinct was there to hate the man, she couldn't; she couldn't ever leave off the habit of him long enough to get the nerve.

'I wish you'd have never come this way,' Hattie said.

'Me too,' said Martha, and then grew silent like there was so much to say, she couldn't begin.

Hattie thought there were things neither one of them wanted to say, they couldn't or didn't dare; it was fear of reality wedged in between them. Hattie pulled the broken lure out of her pocket, rubbed it, said, 'I had just about begun to forget all the reasons for my misery.'

Martha felt like crap; she should have left when there was

still an opening for leaving. She missed the safety of home, how she knew what was expected of her. Martha missed Curtis, that's what it was too. She was sitting on the edge of a foreign river — some river that was reminding her of home — with the mother of a man her man had shot, and she missed him. They had been sitting for a long time and Martha's ass felt sore, bruised. Hattie was staring out over the scrub toward the nothing water. Martha was watching her, noticing the woman's almost rubbery skin; she took in too much dairy, is what Martha was thinking, and then that that wasn't a kind line of thinking, and there it was she suddenly knew that Hattie was sad.

'It happened right around here, I guess,' Martha said. It came out of her mouth before she had time to assess the damage it might cause.

'So they say.'

Martha weighed apologizing on Curtis's behalf, but knew it was too late, time had slipped away. Martha wished she could quell her own loneliness, wished herself back at the farm doing chores and having routines. There would be a baby now, she thought, and that would bring a busy time, a joyous one for the Family. She heard a rustling in the green, said, 'What?' as she pulled her legs up.

'Cricket.' They laughed together a little.

'We had some hippies around here for a bit. They tried, I guess.' Hattie's voice was tired. 'Did Curtis try?'

'He tried. He's still trying, more than most, anyway.' Martha said this and instantly wondered whether what Curtis was doing could really be called trying. He'd gone over from trying into something else. The air felt thick and Martha wanted to get inside somewhere, away from this new set of rules, this new set of wild creatures, this air. 'We should head back, shouldn't we?' Hattie looked at her skeptically, but got herself up slowly and they began to walk back along the path they had come.

They tried. Martha hated to think the Family had just tried. Looking back, she could see small fissures and cracks in the whole set-up, but that was reality pressing in on God, truth on Truth. It was nearing spring when she had misgivings, but she had already lived there for years and years. There had been nothing at first, and then, more alarming, a late miscarriage. Blood loss. Fingerpads — she had seen its potential. And she had looked back on it all: just Curtis and her and the others, and there was only routine to what they had in the end, sameness — shifting moods and erupting anger, then lulls, the thin air of disappointment hanging just so against the bright joy. Soltane was a dream that was lively enough that it would not let her wake.

The bees, she thought. She did not know why her mind took that direction. Curtis's beehives. He'd seen a strange handmade apiary on his way north. A decoy Confederate soldier standing on the edge of a forsaken cornfield. He had been astounded by it. So when he got up to Canada, and built up Soltane, he decided to make a battalion of them, recalling, he said, the Book of Mormon: Ether, and Deseret, the beehive the Jaredites migrated with, and wondering whether if he built them, the bees would come. He believed they would. He prayed, but the hives sat empty.

Some time later Curtis'd found a book on bees in the farm library and read it through in one day, first book he'd read in years, since school had obliged him to. Curtis went over to the library and held the book up to Martha. 'I don't understand more than one sentence in three, but it feels right. You have anything more by this man?' He told her then how he'd read about bee sting, that it could cure some skin conditions.

'I'd like to hire a van and take a hive down to my scurfy pa and cover him in nectar and lock him in there with them. Watch the old man whip and scream. You wouldn't see him for the bees. Heal him up, I guess.' He was joking in a way that made her feel sorry for it; it wasn't nice.

Hattie tapped with her cane along the pavement beside her. Martha said, 'We did try. I guess part of that trying was selfish. We wanted to live this particular way, and we believed it was our purpose to do so; we just didn't realize how hard it would get.' They'd been eating groats and rice through that first winter and into the spring. The apiary was still standing dormant. The bee book had fallen apart, the glue having lost its integrity to the heat of the gate-house. Curtis wrapped it in a criss-cross of elastic banding and handed it to Benjamin, saying how the farm would sustain itself with a little industry. He sent away for the bees in early spring, and it only took three weeks until he had them.

It was a cardboard box, insulated with Styrofoam, but even still he said he could feel them pulsing inside, feel the aliveness of the box. Curtis would not open that box until she and Benjamin had held the sides of it, felt that life. He passed the box around, watching the face of each community member as the vibration rolled up his or her arm. The apiaries' guards were rebels, of course; they were bearded where he scrubbed off the whitewash; he had got one saluting, one working the action on his wooden bayonet; and Curtis built another — a crouching, wounded soul, said he'd seen it in a movie, that pose. They were guarding a larger, traditional apiary behind them, fifty wooden bee crates, and then all the bees. Curtis didn't have much on this earth that he felt proud of, but he had the bees.

And then that one stung him. It was really the beginning of Soltane.

'Maybe we just need men.' Martha said this out loud, and Hattie stopped, gaped at her; the cane was skewed out to the side, and she was leaning into it.

'Or maybe they need us,' is what Hattie finally said. Martha didn't know where to put this, so she got walking again.

'I don't know how to define what it was we tried at, what it was we thought we were achieving back then. And then it changed. It changed so fast, I can only think what I was before was like a dream, where you wake up and you think that wasn't me or that was just a dream and it's got nothing to do with me. We emptied out, or at least I did; I emptied out.'

Martha recalled sending Benjamin away and bathing Curtis. Even as it happened, she knew this had something to do with Curtis's past, what he would never talk about, it was this dreadful thing manifesting itself outwardly, it was this evil sweating out of him. Things caught up. They had to catch up eventually. There were scratches on Curtis's legs and he rocked his head. He'd been tripping for days and had wandered off into the woods. There wasn't a square inch on him clear of mosquito welts. 'You'll want that, Martha.'

They were all concerned. You help a man when he's helpless. And there was no energy to Curtis, unless you counted the energy of loss, of depletion. Curtis, up to then, was nothing but a compilation of little anecdotes he'd told her. That's all. She wished then and still wished now he had told her more, wished she could piece together the pieces he had given her, but it was impossible. So she made the rest up in ways that justified him. This allowed her to continue caring for him, and maintained her too, in so much as any couple formed itself. Even then, she figured this is what a person did, what all people strived toward: fixing reality into something, anything. But what she perceived was inconsequential. Curtis was just an unspeakable, unknowable gathering of ephemera.

'Things change,' said Hattie.

'Yes, they do. Things change.'

In her dream of him, all those years back, Curtis had been drawing Lazarus up. She told him that as he lay there: 'I dreamed that you saved Lazarus; you held him aloft.' Curtis only groaned. 'In my dream you are full of love.' Curtis appeared to be asleep, the thin short breaths only occasionally jumped and popped. 'In my dream you have people who believe in you.' Curtis's eyes did not open, and Martha did not know then, but he was listening.

Hattie and Martha had crossed the old 66 and the I-40. Hattie kept moving, wanting to get home, to rest, to eat. She looked ahead. 'Hollis has a special place in his heart for Curtis. He can't see any wrong in that boy.'

'I wonder if there is wrong in any man.'

Hattie stopped then and held Martha's arm tightly. 'You can't compensate my boy being gone, no matter what you think. Curtis can't compensate this.' A drop of rain, and then another fell onto them.

'It's starting,' Martha said. She looked up and witnessed a darkness like a wall hurtling toward them, blacker than night, which itself was coming on. They moved as quickly as Hattie's pace allowed, Hattie saying, 'Come on, come on,' and this to the rain itself, and laughing too. They were wet through when they arrived home.

Nineteen

Aubie knew, sure as shit, as soon as he opened the door. No. He knew even as his boot touched earth out of his truck. He'd seen a Ford Focus that he'd never seen on the street before. He wasn't scared; hell, he had the Browning, and he wasn't often scared; he'd made peace with that shadow a long time ago. The building was dark, but when he opened the door he could see a thin light coming from the back office where his bed, his hotplate, his microwave oven, his computer, and his telephone were set up. He could see there was a man sitting with his back to him. 'Who the hell are you?'

'You don't recognize me?'

And then he did. 'Oh, Jesus,' he said and clipped across the cement floor, over a carpet that looked like it had Cherokee Indians knotted into it.

'Watch the rug, man. It's a —' Edgar was caught up in a clinch before he was finished his sentence, breathless. 'It's a damn masterpiece, that carpet. Worth tens of thousands of dollars. It shouldn't even be on the floor.'

Aubie was thinking shut up, shut up, and holding on to his brother like he might slip away if he let go. 'Edgar. Holy fuck. Holy fuckin' fuck. You're here.'

'Yes, I am.'

'I been missing you, and worrying. Shit.' Aubie pulled back

but still held Edgar's arms. 'I was beginning to think you were dead over there,' he said, beaming.

'Well, I guess I was almost, a few times.'

'Shit.' Aubie's smile was about breaking his cheeks. 'Corporal Michael Dama. I'm so — I'm so fuckin' happy to see you, brother.' Edgar was huge, bigger than he remembered him. He was a good two inches taller than Aubie, and cut. It was like Aubie had to search in all that muscle to find the brother from before. Edgar sat down in the swivel chair and there seemed not to be any room left over; Edgar was distant happy, he saw, careful happy. Behind him hung a Baluchi runner, a favourite of Aubie's. The weaver had worked four grenades into an otherwise traditional medallion pattern, lots of blue and red. He had no idea what they signified, but he liked the mystery. The power it held was explosive.

Edgar swivelled around, looking at the pieces hanging and draped over the bed, the tens of carpets rolled up and stacked along the walls. 'I like what you've done with the place,' he said.

Aubie had never seen his brother so unkempt. His hair was clipped pretty short, but he'd grown a beard that hadn't been trimmed in some time. His black eyes receded with all the hair edging them. It was a face that didn't seem to recall how to smile. He wore camo fatigues, no shirt, and army boots; he was a sight.

Edgar said, 'I always wondered what they looked like over here, wondered if they'd travel well. You've done good; it looks just like a cheap Pakistani carpet shop.'

'I couldn't keep them all rolled up. Shit, I've been trying to trace your whereabouts with them. I haven't heard from you in a year or more, dude. Where the hell you been?'

'If I tell you —'

'Yeah, if you tell me, you have to shoot me after. Seriously. Where you been?'

Edgar frowned and glanced up. His brother. How whole and strong Aubie looked to him right now. 'I missed you,' he said. 'I've seen Ma and Colm, seen they are all right.'

'Did Ma see —'

'No.' Edgar couldn't believe he was sitting in the same room with Aubie. He'd been country-hopping for weeks now, shifting sideways out of that bad situation, Peshawar, Lahore, Cologne, Brussels, then Montreal, Albuquerque. He'd used three passports and never once blinked. It was like he had a magic presence around security; he was not there. Fuck. Then he'd surveyed Hollis; Hollis was real old now. His breathing sounded like what Edgar imagined the worst kind of slow dying would sound like, raspy and hiccupping and embarrassing as shit. And he'd watched his ma, his little brother, Colmie, and kept his eye on that woman, trying to figure out who she might be. He looked down at his hands, said to Aubie, 'I've been offering janitorial services. There was debris after the commies pulled out of Afghanistan.'

'You're shitting me.'

'No. They gave me a mop and a budget and told me to get to work. I've been very busy,' he said, then asked pointedly, 'Who's the woman?' Aubie knew he meant Martha.

'We've got a bit of trouble, lately.'

'Yeah?'

'She's a woman of Curtis's. Or was.'

'I haven't seen him,' said Edgar. He'd watched Hattie and that woman cross the 66 back to Hattie's place, and didn't much like the idea of Curtis and his ma in the same room together. Why should she have to deal with that?

'Curtis'll be here inside twelve hours, I figure.'

'You best bring that woman here.'

Aubie wondered whether this was the best tactic, and how that would go. Martha'd be thrilled Edgar was alive, he knew, thrilled that poor Curtis was not a murderer after all. Maybe she would go back north to her Family. He could deal with that, he imagined, even if he knew already how he could get used to her staying. 'Where you been, Edgar?' He imagined clandestine assassinations, tidy deaths, and money changing hands.

'Pakistan is where I've mostly been at. I've been holed up in a grand hotel in Peshawar, Pakistan. Like I said, cleaning up messes. I ain't proud.'

Aubie did not laugh. He stared at his brother in the hope it would shame him into giving up more information, and when that failed to work, he stared out of disappointment, hoping that might cajole him. Nothing. So he tried another tactic. 'How many times have you been shot at, brother, and failed to die?' The man spent his whole frigging life trying to get killed a second time, he thought, like he was some kind of freak perfectionist.

'I'm not proud,' Edgar repeated and looked up to see Aubie over by the only window. It was raining, spattering a bit against the glass. And he got up, went to the window, and stood there beside his brother.

Aubie said, 'It's been years since we had a proper rain. Look at that.'

Edgar watched a huge prickly pear cactus bend and arch to cracking, and then the rain began in earnest. The wind was hurling garbage across the yard, a takeout carton tumbled, a beer can jangled past, swirling, and then fell off into a tussock of grass. The sky was black; Edgar felt himself to be inside the rain and could not really hear anything but the rain pummelling the corrugated tin roof. He felt all jangled and fucked up from the last week, and he hadn't felt much of anything in so long that feeling was a terrible exertion.

He watched Aubie make a sudden move toward him and went tense. But it was only the phone his brother was picking up, either to call or because it had rung. Edgar had not heard it ring, but then he couldn't hear anything but the rain hitting the container boxes. Aubie looked concerned, and Edgar could read his lips, repeating, 'Yeah, yeah, yeah,' and then he put the receiver down and leaned in to him.

'Hollis's gone. The care facility called Colm. The old man apparently ran off.'

The wind picked up again and Edgar watched the prickly pear branch scuttle across the asphalt. He was recalling how he'd run, run from the hotel, and past a group of children, then fast around a walled compound into an alley. He hadn't seen the foot thrust out until he was falling, hadn't even got much of a look at who then kicked him and hit him with something metal, a tire iron, or rebar, it must have been.

He had woken up with the rain, found himself in an alleyway on a pile of rubble in downtown Peshawar, half covered with rags and filth and left for dead. Nobody got away with any-thing in this godforsaken country, he remembered thinking, as his brain scrambled to align. Whoever wanted him gone had thought him dead. They had run away fast, maybe being chased themselves, and he was grateful, then, as he felt his bag under him.

'I best go,' Aubie said, and when he got no reply, he said, 'Did you hear what I said?'

Edgar hadn't.

'I'd best go find him.'

He was looking outside, maybe measuring how big a hassle driving in the storm would be. Or maybe, Edgar thought, Aubie was measuring how long it had been since he'd been with that pretty woman. Edgar'd been watching these long days, finding an opportunity to talk to Aubie in private, slip in, slip out. He hadn't figured on this woman being something of Curtis's, and he didn't like the memories it poked at. Now, he just wanted to meet this lady, know better what Curtis had done for himself, hold on to her and wait. He would like to have a word with Curtis. He thought he'd whispered, 'Bring her back with you,' but realized he'd only said this in his mind.

Aubie was saying it would be better if Edgar stayed behind while he went and found Hollis back. It was a no-brainer as far as Edgar was concerned; he had already seen the old man and wasn't keen on seeing him again. No. He would stay put, where he belonged, right here, in this room. He would stay here and he would mull over what he was going to do next. He would wait for Aubie to leave, look around at the trailer walls, and then wait for him to return.

The rugs didn't press in on him so much as envelop him. He felt — well, he knew it wasn't right or necessarily good — he felt kind of warm and homey with those bright images. And even though they were guns, bombs, tanks, shells, helicopters, you-name-it, he had an edgy, regretful consideration he wouldn't feel half so good amid a battery of tree of life and paisley flame prayer rugs. It just wasn't who he was. He stared as Aubie opened the door and turned to him.

'You okay, Edgar?'

'I'm good,' he said. He nodded and found his head still bouncing a bit long after Aubie was gone. He wasn't okay, he guessed. His head ached. There must be beer somewhere, and when he'd found one, he'd sit back down to drink it.

It seemed about right, anyhow, sitting there with all those rugs, brooding over his escape, or whatever it had been. He still didn't know who had tried to kick his head in, because frankly he didn't know who he'd been selling the damn gun to: the United States, North Korea, Iran, or maybe some Podunk rogue state that'd cobbled together some cash.

Yes, he did know who he was supposed to be buying it back for, but somewhere along the way, he'd lost sight of the fine line. His mother used to call him The Judge, and that unmitigated sense of fairness had predestined him. What had those two Pakis said? *Haraam*. What is forbidden by God. And *Halal*. What is permitted. Had he not once been ruled by just such a simple ideology? Goddamn.

He was back in that hotel room, fucking Pearl fucking Continental, recalling Khaleed pacing, but it wasn't a nervous back and forth; it was a thinking man's pace, like Khaleed was a university professor, or like he was mocking one, Edgar wasn't certain now, and he sure hadn't known at the time. Khaleed was speaking in this flourished Urdu, using one hand to slice against the palm of the other by way of emphasizing his points. 'A gun is a weapon of God,' he said.

Omar was perched on the edge of the bed, and the gun case was open in front of him. The tubes and electronics of the machine were in separate bits, pressed into cut-outs in a durable foam holder. Omar seemed sleepy, seemed to be mostly ignoring Khaleed as he went over and over the various points that seemed for him to be so important. Omar was twisting an edge of the bedspread, fidgeting it looked like. But every so often, suggesting that he was, in fact, paying the utmost attention, he would stop what he was doing and make a face.

'No,' Omar said. 'Haraam. The gun is no weapon of God. No weapon is a weapon of God.'

'You were listening,' said Khaleed. 'Good. Yes. The gun is haraam. We are in agreement.' He continued pacing, starting from the threshold of the bathroom, which Edgar wished he could use, to the outer edge of the television, which was on with the sound down low — a Bollywood soap opera with a sari-clad old lady singing a dirge of some sort. Perfect. 'But this man drinks,' said Khaleed, gesturing to where Edgar sat on the wall-to-wall. 'Alcohol is haraam. We need to act upon this heresy to God.'

'Okay, let us act then, inshallah.'

'Omar. We must be sure this is the right thing to do.'

'Khaleed, my friend, we have gone over this for hours. Inshallah. Inshallah. If God does not will it, it will not happen.'

They were kids, for Christ's sake, so young their beards wouldn't sprout thick for years yet. Edgar would have liked to ask them how old they were, but his mouth was stuffed with cloth, and besides, he kept thinking, did it matter? Maybe everyone's life hinged upon the bullshit he enacted or had enacted upon him between the ages of sixteen and eighteen. He felt a bristling all up and down his scar web when he thought that. Fuck, he wished he were home, greeting his mother and letting the past slide away. Nothing mattered. He wished he could convey that to these boys, this joyous news that had just now sunk into him so deep and true he knew it must be so, that it did not matter. Only he knew for certain that they had a stake in it mattering, and that the news wouldn't go over too good.

'Stealing is haraam.' The hand cut against the palm and Khaleed looked skyward, to the hotel room ceiling.

'Point,' mumbled Omar.

'Stealing a haraam object is haraam.'

'Point two.' Omar nodded. Now they were getting somewhere.

It was a game.

'Stealing a haraam object with the purpose of destroying it, though? Haraam or halal?'

Omar gave him a broad smile and slapped the bed on both sides of his body. 'Easy,' he said.

'Halal.' Godly.

'Point.'

Khaleed bent over and flipped the lid of the gun case closed, and Omar pulled all the brace locks shut. 'We are finally ready.' Omar was the bigger of the two. He lugged the case, moving backward out of the room, genuflecting, saying, 'Salaam alaikum. Salaam alaikum' in the most courteous manner. Edgar began moaning loudly. He did not want to be left here for the next people — the fucking *buyers*, he was thinking — to find him. He rocked against the bed and got enough momentum to fall lengthwise onto the carpet. The cotton in his mouth shifted, and with his tongue, he forced it out.

'You fucking cut me loose or I'll scream so loud, your fucking Allah will hear it all the way in paradise.'

Khaleed's eyes got big. 'What shall I do?'

'Save him,' said Omar. 'He is a guest. It is not the martyrdom that counts' — he was almost giggling as he said this — 'but the story of the martyrdom. Let there be no story to find here!'

Then what had the kid said while he was rigging that knife? He had said the Arabic word for justice. No. He had said struggle. To struggle is to live, or to be alive, or to be enlivened, something. Edgar couldn't remember now.

He rubbed his hand over his chin, through the beard hair there, wondered if Aubie had a razor and a mirror anyplace around, and thought briefly about whether he had ever really been just, or true to himself, or even careful. There had been a general belief he was, but he wasn't sure if that belief made him just, or if that belief was simply wrong. If he could shave off this beard he'd been cultivating in Pakistan, he might find himself.

The bedroom was a mess. Aubie'd left an old Browning on the table beside the bed. He knew that gun. It was a beautiful tool with all that etching. Useless but beautiful. Edgar picked it up and admired the heft to it. He opened it up and saw it was loaded, tucked it in his belt. A black bra lay beside him on one of the pillows, and the bed wasn't yet made.

He sucked back his beer, got up to get another, tucked the bra under the pillow, thinking it must belong to Curtis's woman, the girl Aubie was sleeping with, and then he pulled the sheets, the blanket up, and squared the corners hospital-style. He wasn't fussed, just liked a thing to look neat, is all. He found a jug of bleach under the sink after that. There was a razor and a bar of utility soap down there too. It was a kitchen sink, but Edgar couldn't find a bathroom sink, or even a bathroom for that matter, so he settled on this, figuring that this is where everything happened. Thought he better clean it up too. He rinsed out the sink good, chlorine catching his nose hairs, and began to lather up. Bitch of a soap stung on his skin, but it was better than nothing.

Propped on the window ledge was a four-inch by six-inch mirror that Edgar peered into as he shaved. He could see the splashes of colour behind him, through the mirror, and when he shifted, a knotted bomb here, a Kalashnikov there. Aubie had even tacked a few rugs to the ceiling.

One indicated a helicopter, which from that perspective had an interesting kamikaze effect. It was an ugly carpet but large enough. Might have taken the knotter three or four months of effort. Hell, it felt good to clean up. Edgar moved closer to the mirror, scraped a line of hair higher than he thought he had any, and where he'd missed, catching a pimple along the way. A line of thin red trickled along his cheek. 'Shit,' he said and dabbed at it with a piece of toilet paper. He tore a square and twisted it onto the wound to staunch the flow.

He was thinking, dancing around thoughts the whole time, about those two Pakistani kids and how they hadn't deserved what life had served them up. How their bodies, crumpled and beaten, had been found, how their mothers had keened. It had been written up in the local news the day he left. How justice had not prevailed.

Well, it nearly never did, as far as he had witnessed in all his time. He'd pretty near given up on justice, which grieved him. He thought just then how grieved he was to be so dirty cynical. For he sure had forsaken the whole damn God thing somewhere back there in the desert; he'd gone from justice to righteous to just plain fucked. He wanted to claim it back, his youth, his beliefs, but it was likely too late. He felt suddenly bad for those poor kids who had believed so strong. That they'd died for that.

How to die, he thought, and how not to die. Flies had gathered fast. They landed, drank, and flew in drunken spirals above the wound. Edgar had felt a thin pulsing and a wetness, and he had felt a tug under him as the fishing rod slid out from there. He thought this was death, that the sliding was him being carried away, that the conduit to heaven was a sort of sliding mechanism, like a conveyor belt, and death was just about finding the right fit onto this mechanism. He did not feel pain, not until much later. He slept for a time, and when he woke, he was still along the riverbank. He was just about eighteen years old.

He was looking now at Curtis holding a gun at him; he had thought then about how he didn't understand, and how he might have done something to draw out this strange thing. But what? And he thought Curtis should have stood closer if he wanted a fair shot of him. He'd said, 'Let me stand at least.' Then Curtis said 'Brother,' and shot him, and in his delirium, he wondered whether they really were brothers or whether Curtis had begun to use the revolutionary hippie jargon of the day, a language Edgar himself did not trust.

He believed that Aubie would know the answer, and that since Aubie was not far away — was only some four hundred yards through the brush at their home — he would rise and go to him and directly ask. He would make sure their mother was occupied in order to save her any grief she might have in their knowing this information and also in her possibly seeing him thus compromised.

He clenched his abdominal wall in order to facilitate lifting his body and felt a warm gush. He had upset the wound. 'Oh, Christ almighty.' Another man might have been cussing here, but Edgar had a strange faith in God back then; he meant the words as a reminder of a sovereign pact he felt he had with the Good Lord. How he had strayed these long years, he now thought. Edgar had bundled leaves and held them over the hole in his chest, tried not to notice the feel of soft tissue beneath the makeshift poultice. With his hand holding his body together, he tucked his legs under him as well as he could and heaved up.

He fell directly to the ground; there would be no up for him. He then tucked his legs under again and pressed them along the ground. He heard a girlish shriek as the pain hit him. It was his shriek, a fact that unnerved him more than being shot. But he had moved. And so he made his way, inching forward: progress, pain, progress, pain. And it became connected like that in his mind forevermore: progress, pain. He found, after some yards of movement, that he could manage the shrieks until they were entirely sublimated, and he shrieked only internally. But the flies continued to follow him. There were some bees too.

The insects gathered and persisted, and he had to constantly wave them away. He imagined himself in a war, and this helped him to sustain hope and integrity. He had been ambushed and mortally wounded; he had no weapon. And he vowed he would never have no weapon again — that had been his first mistake. The second was not paying attention. The third was naivety, the not knowing that Hollis would do this, and it could only be Hollis behind this. It was also the not knowing that this could happen to him. The hubris.

His ma was out when he was found half in the front door, bluebottles buzzing about, swooping down; the insects were pissed he would not stop fighting and die so they could get at dinner. Aubie and Colm did not stop to gasp, Aubie especially. He was holding his breath, he told later, trying to locate understanding and that did not take long. 'Fucking shopkeeper,' he said, scrambling to pull Edgar into the house. 'Fucking stupid shopkeeper without sense to procure himself a goddamn safe and all that money... goddamn bastard stared at me, and at that fancy fucking gun Curtis had; fucker was memorizing.'

Looking up at the increasing blur of his brother, Edgar mused that sixteen years of petty adventures and messing around hadn't left a trace on Aubie. Was he dying? Aubie was dark-skinned and dark-haired, the eyes held only self-confidence, humour, and a distinct recall of playing tag. And he had not a pimple on his face. There were girls, and women too, lining up, and all his brother Aubie could see was that bastard, that old, nothing-left bastard shopkeeper stealing that away. Edgar had been watching Aubie a year and a half, standing by as he gave lies and falsehoods to their mother as to where he was out to and where did the money come from, and why was he so cocky? Aubie would confess to him later that nine hundred dollars shrank in value when he considered the exchange rate. Aubie just gawked at the blood pumping out of his brother's chest.

Edgar was trying to say something.

'What the fuck, Ed?'

'Is Curtis family?' It was more a gurgle, how it came out. Colm and Aubie were wide-eyed as they took in the question. And without them speaking, Edgar saw, and laughed once real quick. 'My own brother shot me to die.' He started laughing again, which looked more like convulsions or some kind of seizure, and they tried to settle him, wrapped a blanket from their ma's bed around him and then another one as the laughter went over into shakes. Everybody there knew that Curtis prowling could only mean one thing — that Hollis was after a weak link in the fence and had found it. Colm was solemn.

'It's always the good ones.'

'Hell.'

'Here. We're going to lie him flat and get him over to help.'

'Aubie,' Colm said, 'you best get out of town, find a shack somewhere, and give me warning where you are in a couple of months or so. Lay low.'

They made arguments and counter-arguments on the way down the US-285 to Richards, to the man they knew they could trust to keep pretty much anything from Hollis Woolf, even if they couldn't quite trust their own mother to do the same.

Colm was thinking what they were all thinking, that Richards was the man their mother should have married if she wasn't so true to her heart, or whatever it was led women to make bad choices. They weren't thinking it long. Edgar was gasping little wet breaths, and his skin was cold to the touch. The blankets were seeping blood. 'Shit.'

'I ain't running away,' muttered Aubie. 'If I run, anyway, Hollis'll know he ain't dead. That is if he don't die, I guess, I mean.'

'There is no dying here.' But already Edgar was shaking again. 'Oh, shit.'

Richards saw what needed to be done, got Edgar in the back door of the clinic, Colm beside him, whispering, 'Don't be a chicken shit. Fight this. You got a life ahead of you.' Richards's doctor didn't flinch when he saw Edgar's wound and seldom spoke, simply nodded to a nurse, who wheeled him into a backroom, a makeshift surgery. Twenty hours, Colm whispering at his ear and Aubie pacing the length of the gurney and back. By the end of it, Edgar had a web of stitching, a criss-cross roadmap etched on his back, and a lumpy hollow just under his heart. A couple of less important organs had been nicked but had survived.

Richards's grocery was his keep, a spare room behind the kitchen. Colm and Aubie came to visit daily and brought him food and news. The walls were bare save an old calendar with a naked lady, her butt looming at him over on the pullout couch. He cursed his birthright — birthwrong, he thought — and he cursed Aubie's stupidity. Edgar lay on his side and sometimes almost on his belly, the pain from his back, growing skin and scar mass under the surface, added discomfort to the pain, like it was crawling bugs. Looking down he could see an old, foot-worn Persian rug, with big octagonal stamps running down it and a wave of leaves around the border. Edgar traced the brown-red line over and over and thought about how he would proceed, but he did not answer his brothers' queries about what he would do and where he would go.

He lay still for many months, scenes playing over in his mind: Aubie swinging his leg into Curtis's truck, Aubie target shooting, Aubie laying money on the kitchen table like it was a meal he'd just hunted down. That damned highway construction, cranes like church steeples on all them trucks, it wasn't justified, he knew, and Hollis was hurting, and so were they all. And now this shit.

The whole thing was tumbling down, and when it had completely fallen, he would look to Richards again. Edgar's finger must have rolled along that knotted wave a hundred thousand times. He was seventeen years old. He was a dead man. The certificate the doctor had kindly written out proved this, and regular reviewing of this fact gave Edgar a strange personal tenor; he was practising being not there. There must be a place on this good earth for a dead man not dead, he thought.

The kind doctor had handed him a birth certificate. 'It was a stillborn baby, but they had to give him a birth certificate before they could give him a death one. Nobody ever did file that one. You take care now.' Michael Dama was his new name. Edgar found out years later that it was the doctor's own son, who'd died twenty years before, and that he hadn't stopped looking for a use for the death. The doctor stood and nodded as he watched Edgar make his way past the front desk, held upright by his brothers. 'You come back if you can't cope, right?'

'I'm good.'

Then Edgar faded away. Not dead, but not there. It had been Richards who first directed Michael to the Marines, where both men felt Michael could get suitably lost. They called him back some weeks later. 'What happened to you, son?' It was a sergeant recruiter named Dicks, peering at him over the application form.

Michael was relocated to Virginia, where he took free courses in Urdu and Arabic, as well as, over time, communications and weapons; the Marines had a special purpose for him that no one was outlining. It did not matter. If he told you what he knew, he'd have to kill you, that was a joke he often made. The Marines consumed him, got him strong. Michael learned more than one man ought to know about guns, he learned how to fall out of the sky, how to hide so no one could see him, and how to contain himself in such a way that even fear had no adrenal effect upon him.

He was huge. The web of scars stretched across his back; they would tear him open if he got any bigger. And even with his bulk, he found he was still invisible, that he had erased what little charisma he ever had, that he was not there in a way that made him very effectively present.

And now he was home. He looked at his raw, clean-shaven face in the mirror and felt happy to be here, away from that mess. And then a deep pain began in his body. His whole body ached, and he wanted to cry. He didn't really know how to cry any more. Instead he looked up at the bombs and the helicopters — there was a particular carpet on which he counted seventeen hand grenades exploding, all in ochre and khaki — and he prayed out an apology, half an apology, because he did not know how to be fully contrite any more either, about how he was sorry to have participated, and sorry for who he had become.

He lay rigid on the floor to try to unwind from the pain, to release himself from its grip. He knew somehow it stemmed from an emotional fount, but he had no idea how to unlock it, and so he lay there in the slicing pain and looked around him. He spent hours doing this, trying to relax. And he must have succeeded eventually, because he found himself waking up from sleep, and the pain had subsided. He stood up and shook his limbs. He wondered at what the pain might have been, and put it down in the end to stress, how stress had a way of eating the body. It was dark outside. He opened two beers and put them side by side so he would not have to open the fridge again. The storm was wild, and he sat still, smoking and drinking in the dark, the ember from the cigarette moving back and forth from the ashtray toward his face.

Twenty

Hollis had woken in the early evening. Where had the girl gone to? He must follow her to Curtis. He'd had another strange visitation, a shadow guest in the deep part of the night, and he knew in the sanctum of his heart that finally, after all these years, Curtis had returned: Oh joyous joy! And in the white heat of this realization he got up out of his bed and took his walker out of the closet where it had been since the day the nurse had brought it to him. He had managed never to walk with this contraption before.

There were but two cars in the parking lot. This shit facility was already in decline though it wasn't longer than five years open. He hadn't thought much of it when his own children stuck him here, but on the other hand, it was familiar, not more than two hundred paces from where he'd run his pumps, where he'd raised them all up. Where now all that history sat rusting and hanging on in the dry heat. His pumps. That's it. That's it, he thought. He'd go there. He hadn't known he wanted to so badly, but now it occurred to him: it was the right thing to do.

It wasn't far, and he now already desperately wanted to go there; he felt sure that at the pumps he would find Curtis, his long-lost son, the prodigal, the blessed. Things went well at first. He swallowed a couple of codeine pills down with the gin he had stashed under his mattress. He filled his pockets with change — just in case — from the table beside his bed, took his mickey, his fancy flint lighter, and a pack of smokes along; hell, he might as well smoke while he was outside. These items weighed and jangled in his pocket in a way that pleased him.

He balanced himself against the walker and made his way down the hall to the elevator. He was euphoric as he hobbled past the empty front desk, as the doors to the facility shut behind him, and the humidity settled on the sleeves of his pyjamas. Hollis saw it had rained hard — the ground past the parking lot was muck — and was surprised he could have slept through it. He heard thunder coming from the east; there would be more rain coming this way. He must move fast. It was dark, but there was a purpose now where there hadn't been one in so long. He thanked that damn Canadian woman for bringing Curtis back; he would thank her in person when he next saw her.

'Maeve,' he whispered. 'Maeve.' He'd remembered her again in that woman; he liked it that Curtis had sent a messenger, a woman like that. 'I knew you wouldn't never fail old Hollis, Maeve. There's a reason for everything, and I see now how rightly you've forgiven me. I always will hold you in my heart.' He heard a rumble off Tucumcari way and broiling up from Artesia, and he looked east, then south. Yup. More storm brewing. 'Did I not treat you well?' This last he felt he'd said a bit overdramatically; there was desperation in his voice, so he tempered it with a quick 'Hell.'

He was already planning to light a flick. Tear a piece off his shirt and, well, he didn't expect much twirling with that dumb walker but, looky, the moon was edging toward full, and god-damn it was beautiful outside. God's country. And he felt it: his boy was on the way. Jesus Christ. If a man could be happier, he didn't quite know how. Hollis was almost across the parking lot. He'd had to skirt the two staff vehicles — a monstrous Chevy pickup that made him downright jealous and something so beat-up old, the whole roof was rusted through the paint — and it didn't matter anyway, as the car was a Jap make, and if he wasn't already busy he would have spent some time figuring out who-the-hell administrator drove the damn thing and given that person what for. Foreign cars. Hell, but that Chevy was a beautiful monster, he thought; he could practically picture himself in it.

Hollis could see it wasn't going to be easy out on the road. This was a piece of Route 66 nobody cared much about any more; there was grass and some other vegetation Hollis didn't know to name bursting up through the baked asphalt. And even that plant life was dried to brittle brown, born of thirst and raised on thirst. Well, plant, he thought, you just tasted your first water. And it's going to rain more. He could feel it building in the air, his inner ear was pressing in on him from the pressure. There were distant rumblings; he fumbled with the walker, thinking about what was coming up for him. He must hurry and beat the downfall.

The walker's wheels jammed into the broken asphalt here and there and he almost lost his balance. He wished he'd once in a while practised with the damn thing. It was an hour or so he'd been outside, he figured. He stopped, knowing exactly where he was — well, a man didn't spend his formative life in a place for it not to seep in. He could almost smell the fume from them pumps. Hollis bent his knees and straightened them, inhaling sharp. It was due north from here, he knew. He crossed the road and pushed the walker into what had once been a tar road, but it sure wasn't any longer. There was a tangle of barbed wire crossing the way, and beyond, as far he could see into the night, a makeshift dirt road. Never mind.

He swung the walker over his head, concentrating hard on holding his centre of gravity low, and dropped it over the fence; it didn't weigh much, but it was unhandy, and he almost fell into the fencing. There had been contact, a scratch along his hand and down his forearm — that metallic whiff of blood told him so — but never mind that neither. A fence never stopped Hollis Woolf before and it sure wasn't about to now. His ears had truly begun to ache. 'Glory be!' he said.

The sound was ridiculous, almost rude, thinning out on the empty field. But even still, he couldn't help saying, 'He's a-coming!' though this time more quietly; he felt a bit shameful to be speaking out loud, felt that it wasn't proper, that whoever might hear would hear his silent thoughts anyway.

The wire fence was tight up and down, too high to straddle safely and, well, it wasn't no mean feat for an old-timer like Hollis to bend over double and slip under the thing. In the end, he jammed his walker down onto it and easily bowed the metal, thinking how they didn't even make barbed wire like they used to, the whole world was so lean and pinched it was a wonder God ever much bothered any more.

But He did, Hollis knew that now. He was bringing His one true son back to him, hadn't the woman said as much? A kind of prophet, he understood from Colm. And hadn't he made him so, anointing him all those years ago? And wasn't all this preparing the way for his arrival? Yes, the earth was damn-straight ready for a good soaking, and Hollis was going to bring it on in style. His skin itched; he could feel it crawling up and down his legs. When he got back to his room, he would ask the nurse for a new light bulb, see if he could repair that light.

He was astride the wire now, leaning heavily on his walker. There was a *No Trespassing* sign, but that was bullshit; it was his own damn land, and he hadn't put up any sign. Hollis slit his eyes and peered out into the field. He recalled it as side-by-each gas stations and sprung-up motels. His had been the first, and his had been the best, with that set of pumps and that diner. Then Samson had died and left the worthless ranch to him, and then he'd had the foresight to buy as many dead ranches from poor old debtors as a man could carry. In them tough times, before the oil came in, he'd held the bankers back with a string of profitable robberies. It had been right and fair. The deep rights on that land still paid him dividends, and he didn't do diddly. His will gave all this — his legacy — to his only son, the only one that counted; and now he would see him, his fleshly son, and give him, personally, his due. He squinted into the night.

Well, there wasn't a thing to see out in the distance now but a couple of lonely pumps and a crumbling adobe hut. He shifted his weight and pulled his second leg over the wire. The barb caught hold of his pants and below, into his skin. He didn't feel a thing at first, in part because his arm was paining him, but mostly, he figured, it was just too far away from his brain.

He didn't know what had snagged, but he thought it might be his balls; there was wetness wicking down his pants, hot and gluey. It wasn't going to be nice fixing that up later, but still he pressed on, certain he must get to the pumps, enact the idea that had already built in his mind. If only he didn't feel so tired. And so damned ear-achy. He stopped and took a swig of gin, well, two.

He turned the walker around and sat down on the pull-down seat. From this vantage point he could see the over-bright lights from the care facility. It looked like a modern-day gas station, he thought, one of those convenience store gas stops that are so full of mistrust they make you pay ahead. He shook his head thinking how times had changed and then recalled being ripped off once or twice. He reconsidered the situation and left off regretting he hadn't thought of prepayment himself.

He wasn't far from the spot where the children had played on their bicycles, spinning on the packed dust, keeping the side-winder population down. Hollis lit a cigarette and dragged deeply on it; he felt the languishing crimp of his lung as the smoke hit it, and savoured that. He thought how he did not miss his other children, though he did feel bitterness at their abandonment of him. 'I never did nothing but good for them lot.'

His arm hurt to raise it up to smoke, and his balls pulsed in a strange new way. There was nothing really unpleasant about pain, Hollis thought, it was just another loud feeling to add to the rest. He took one long drag on his cigarette and crushed it under his boot, waiting until the few sparks extinguished. There was an urgent line of light on the horizon. His head lolled. He tried to get up but found he was spent, and let the gravity pull his head down into his chest. He slept for some time, the night air lulling him, rain splattering and stopping on and off, but he did not notice.

And when he woke, the day was breaching the night. He saw a line of dim storm light along the horizon eastward. The way was onerous. Dirt made it difficult for the small walker wheels. He tried to press the thing forward and ended up pressing it deeper into a wet rut. He must leave the walker, he realized. He did not know if he could manage without it, but the knowing of such a detail, or the not knowing of such a detail, seemed beside the point.

He must leave the walker. Hollis let that realization sink in to him and resolutely tried to fling the thing away. It didn't much respond except to totter briefly and then right itself much where it had been, where he was standing. This bothered him. What had he done to deserve this? What had he cared about in his life? Only one thing: family. Protecting his own family. And his own damn family had flouted him. And now this walker would flout him, even in his resolution. It wasn't fair.

'This a test of some sort or another?' he muttered. 'I guess it must be. Where are you, son? I know you are coming.' He tottered toward the pumps, his pyjamas ripped down the crotch, strips of cloth, and pockets flapping and damp. He could feel air on his privates, but he didn't mind the nakedness. He thought he was just a man, and a just man. The pumps were not more than ten paces ahead of him. 'Look at this. It's as if I never left.'

This was not strictly true. The pumps were mostly rusted, and kids had spray-painted expletives onto them. The adobe building that had been his shop had sunk down into the earth on one side. 'Lord, have mercy.' It hurt to move, but he used this as motivation to propel forward, finally landing on the western pump and grasping it as if it were a kind of saviour; well, hell, it did save him — he was about to fall. He caressed the glass number gauge, marking where time and vandals had cracked it. It read $4.50.

It looked like a bullet had bounced off the eastern pump and frayed the paint around the impact point. 'Rust ain't death,' he said, gaining stability and leaning over to pull the nozzle off the handle. He squeezed the trigger and said, 'I'll be damned.' Hollis had expected a thin drizzle or nothing at all from the pump, but a steady stream of sweet old gasoline splashed out of the end, down his pyjama shirt and onto his boots. 'How-dy.'

He set himself down on the ground, using the pump station against his back for support, and propped the nozzle between his legs. 'That'll do fine.' It had been years, and yet he suddenly remembered everything about it: the thrill of ignition, the beauty of the fire, the way the sparks flew off into nothing and left a shadow glow behind his eyes. He looked down and saw blood and some other wetness trickling from his balls, said, 'Crap,' and wiped at it with his sleeve. He would deal with it later, get the nurse to fix it. He couldn't feel a damn thing he was that excited. Damn. He was wild.

He reached along his pyjama leg and yanked at the fabric. It wanted to rip, and the cloth just came away in these perfect strips. He wound and knotted it carefully. He pulled a strip off his pyjama top, ignoring the high-pitched whine down his inner ear. He thought, God will take care of that. Hollis had four knotted wicks lined up between his legs when he noticed the light. He must hurry.

It had been years ago that he'd fire danced, and now he would dance not just the rain home, and the day, but also his chosen son. Hollis felt noble as all hell. He pulled himself up onto the pump, his cock exposed beneath his plush belly, the remnants of his pyjamas comical against his scurfy fatness.

He reeled the nozzle up, rigging it in such a way that it was triggered against the holder, leaving him hands-free. A freshet of gas streamed onto the clay; he felt his boots dampen and he breathed in the good smell of fossil fuel. He held the wicks one at a time under the gush, let the gas seep into his hands, felt it sting the wire cut he'd earlier received. 'This will do,' he said when he was finished soaking them.

He laughed then because it hadn't occurred to him at first to leave the gas pump spilling. 'It will be glorious,' he whispered. He knew it was what he must do. He was already imagining the magnitude of this fire dance, as if it had already transpired, the joyous bloom of heat. Hollis walked away, two wicks in each hand. He must be careful but he must be quick, else dawn would take the glory out of it, else he would have wasted everything; his son would not see how loved he was.

Hollis was twenty paces from the pump. He was light-headed and happy. He set the wicks down and fished the lighter from his pyjama pants pocket. He had always liked the scratch of ignition of this lighter and he liked it now. He leaned down to bring the flame to the wicks.

The flame scurried along his skin and caught on his pyjama top. He kept bending, though, almost dumbly, automatically, to catch flame to the wicks and grab them and dance. He would not be daunted. The flame flicked down and up his clothing. He began to spin. 'Mercy!' he called out, again and again, not noticing the extent of the flame. He was as happy as he had ever been.

Clumsy, twirling, crazy, he saw, in stop-action, the flame jump from him and hop across the desert floor. Heard it before he saw it: the pump whooshing aflame. He could feel, too late, his skin blister along his back, but it did not hurt; he felt a relief, and called out to the wondrous leaping flames ahead of him: 'He is coming, I know.'

The rain began to spatter, but it was not enough. The metal pumps shifted on their foundation and melted; it was a terrible beauty. Hollis had fallen to the ground. He leaned forward and stretched his hands out toward the pumps, touching the ground before he rose. 'Praise be to God!' he screamed. It just came out of him. He wasn't sure he believed it. And he did not know where he had heard this conflation before — from the TV, maybe, or the radio — but he liked the rhythm of it. 'Praise,' he repeated more slowly, 'be to the one God.'

Hollis felt a tremor of energy along his knees then. He saw a burble of liquid where the pumps had been, and then saw the flame expand, a great paisley-shaped candle flame. The fuel would trickle toward him, immolate him in a lozenge of prayer, and he would burn, and then the rain would come and come and come, but for now he watched the fire, transfixed. Behind it he saw a dark shadow. It must be Curtis. Yes. His son had arrived; he could feel his son's love coursing over him.

✦

But it was Aubie standing there. He had driven straight to the care facility and listened to the male attendant on night duty try to cover his sorry ass, saying he had been at the front desk all night and into the morning, and that he couldn't begin to imagine what had happened to Hollis. It had just started to rain when Aubie heard the whoosh and bang not far north. All he had to do then was look out the window to know where Hollis was. 'Excuse me,' he said, sidestepping the attendant out the door, toward the fire. He felt his waist for the Browning, but it wasn't there. He'd left it by the bed back home. He thought how he hadn't been without that thing for years and years. He stood there, watching Hollis.

An onlooker might have argued that he was there just in time, but there was no onlooker, and Aubie let time buy him this justice. The fire ran all up and down Hollis, and Aubie let it. There wasn't nothing he could do any more there. The rain came in hard down on Aubie's hat, licking off the rim and running in a stream down his back. He waited until he saw no more movement. Then he heard a siren deep in the distance, which alarmed him, and he walked back to the parking lot and drove his truck into town. He was hungry, so he stopped and ate at Joseph's, thinking only of Martha, and her skin on his, how good that made him feel. Well, it made him *feel*. He would go and get her and take her to Edgar. He felt he owed her the satisfaction of knowing the truth. He suddenly wished to heaven for Curtis never to arrive, wished he could drive out of the scene with Martha, start a new life somewhere by some new rules, but he knew full well there wasn't no God listening.

Twenty-one

The rain was local, moving west. Curtis could see storm heads in three separate directions; it could rain here or not, depended on the wind, and God's good will. He drove on the interstate past the Santa Rita, day dropping now to night, and up the small incline to the bridge over the Pecos, where he parked and got out in order to look over at the current. Cars sped past him, but he did not mind.

It was dry here, no rain yet, and there wasn't any current. It was incredible to Curtis how low the poor river was, and he stood there for some time, high above it for a quarter-hour, maybe half. He couldn't reconcile whether the river had always dwindled to this state or whether the world was sucked dry or whether the Pecos had diminished in his own mind based on the northern rivers he'd now seen. It didn't even seem like a creek.

It was just a red, sludgy trickle, a spittle of a river.

He went to the back of the Volvo, opened the trunk, and pulled out two jars of healing honey. The beehive was now sprawling across the box the jars were in, alive, thick, and sweet-smelling, over a coat he'd left in there when he packed; there was a throbbing pulse as the bees gathered honey from the open jar and moved it to the hive. They did not sting him but seemed to respect his hand in this. He took two jars without any reaction from the bees, then he gently closed the trunk and turned around. He would heal the river.

The rain began to catch up to him again, even as he approached the rail. He tried to empty out to God, to offer himself up. 'Hallelujah,' he said quietly, and he pulled the lid off first one and then the other honey jar and poured the contents down the side of the bridge in a thin golden line into the river, the same river, he suddenly considered, where he had killed a man. This recollection was not pretty, and it forced him toward remorse. He witnessed himself shudder and made it part of the prayer that was him. Hollis, he thought, just Hollis, and his pa's face and his pa's back, and his pa's own hurt that had become his own. Make it prayer, he thought, make it all prayer. Please. And by the time the last of the honey had spilled to join the Pecos, the rain was edging at him like a wall of grace.

'Yes,' he said, and then louder, 'Yes!' as if to convince himself. And then it got so he couldn't stand there any longer, with the wet and the storm, so he got in the car, chucked the jars under the seat, and wound through the back streets of town, navigating to Hattie's place up on the other side of the highway. After all these years, he still knew where it was, like it was a lost limb.

He stopped driving when he saw Martha swaying along the dirt road north with an old old woman, who he already knew to be Hattie. He wanted to call out to Martha, for her lively sway reminded him of how he loved her, but he couldn't. The old woman beside her burdened him with thoughts he could not name, so muddled were they: fear, anxiety, guilt, joy to see Martha again. He had killed a man, and Martha now knew it too.

Martha and Hattie had begun to run against the rain coming at them, and he watched the old woman shuffle, her skirt rising behind her round knees, showing creased skin where her socks stopped. Martha was laughing. He could not recall her laughing so freely in some time. He watched them turn in to the drive of Hattie's place, turned the engine off, and sat there on the side of the road letting these feelings he had run through him. He knew he must go and knock on the door, and he was waiting for calm so that he could do this. He found prayer only compounded his upset.

It must have been past midnight when he knocked on the door. There didn't seem to be any lights on, and for a minute he was afraid no one would answer, and then he was afraid someone would. He went back and forth between these two states of fear until the door opened and it was Martha standing there in jeans and a T-shirt. They stood there in the doorway studying each other. He reached out to touch her and she moved away.

'Martha.'

He could see that she had not been sleeping, and that she was more awake than he recalled seeing her, alert awake, and there was no trance to her, as he had become used to, as he had preferred too. She was looking him up and down, and then he heard her say, through his own thoughts, 'I miss you.'

It was a kind of opening. 'I've come to get you,' he said. 'To take you home.'

Any softness disappeared then, and her body braced itself, and it looked to Curtis like a hive when it's opened and the air is cool and the bees all move in close, as one body, for warmth and security. Her body was doing that. Something bad was hurtling toward him. 'I can't go back,' she said.

'I'm going to take you home.' Curtis tipped his head toward the Volvo. It had the honey and the hive in it, there for her, all of it. 'Do you have a bag or two you need to pack?' She had been gone long enough, he reasoned, long enough to have spread her belongings out. There was another thought dawning on him too, that she might not feel this way about coming home, that she might not sense the wondrous thing happening in the trunk of the Volvo, that she might not comply, and here is where he did a very stupid thing.

'Come,' he said, and he grabbed her arm, frantically, in a way that projected all his just-now fears, all his stresses, all his insecurities. What would Jesus do, he thought, what would Joseph Smith do, what would any normal Holy person do in this situation, when it was imperative that His will be done, and worrisome that it might not be? Oh, God, he thought. Oh dear God, help.

She shook him off. This surprised him, that it was even possible to shake him off with such ease. She said, 'No, I'm not going home.' She was so awake.

'Well,' he said. 'Please.' And he made his eyes as imploring as he had ever made them. 'I loved you,' he said.

Martha was laughing, her eyes were laughing at him. 'Loved?' she said.

But no, he hadn't meant it that way. He had meant that his eternal love for her was infinite. The past tense was as solid as the present viewed through this lens. 'No,' he said. 'Always.' He grabbed her again then, all his sense lost to this grand want of his. He pinned both her arms against the jamb. This was important, and why didn't she know, just know, that however large her will was, his was larger, because his was Divine and hers was only a conduit for his. It was him, Him! 'Please, darling. Let's just go. Just go.' She squirmed and pushed at him, told him he was a damned asshole. He tightened his fingers around Martha's biceps until his hands began to hurt, but she didn't show pain, only glared at him, right at and right through him until he began to believe she meant it.

Martha prayed the old lady would not wake up, and these prayers were answered. Hattie slept through that long night. 'Let me go.'

'I need you,' Curtis said. He softened his hold on Martha, said, 'Ida needs you. The baby.' She looked hard at him, hard to cover the yearning, he saw, and he began a thin, murmuring inner prayer.

'Just tell me why you shot Edgar,' she was saying. 'Just tell me how you could do that and then run off. Tell me why you left him to die, and when you get around to it, explain to me how you think it is okay, the pain you left behind when you ran off?'

'I paid —'

'You never paid Aubie or Colm or Hattie.'

'I retributed to the Almighty.'

'Crap on the Almighty,' Martha said. She stood back, and there were tears streaming down her face; she seemed real, and outside of him. There was something fearful in this, but he could not name it, and did not want to name it, or respond to it. He did not want the responsibility of that recognition.

'Help,' he said. Martha shook her head. So he said it again, to the wilderness, 'Help.' There was a quietude, and a thickening pressure on his heart; he was pinned to the door jamb with it.

'Give me the car keys,' Martha said. She said it so quiet, but so maternal, there was no going against it. 'Give me the car keys.' And he did.

They were halfway to somewhere, heading south, the Volvo rocking, and him trying to think out how to tell her about the bees in such a way she would see the miracle of it.

'Where are you taking me?'

'Aubie McCann.'

He did not know exactly where they were headed. He figured Roswell or Artesia. It might be Carlsbad, but he didn't know where Aubie might be living these days. He had not thought about Aubie much in all these years, except as a thought to push away, suppress. He had killed Aubie's brother and now Martha would make him face it — he did not want to face Aubie. Couldn't she see how he'd already paid?

He had killed a man, he had asked God's forgiveness, and God had given him this gracious agency to heal, to lead a people, to follow his linear, God-given path; forgiveness had damn well been granted. He'd watched the spray of blood, time slowing down, the crumbling, had felt death move in, Edgar's head growing heavy on his own chest, his complicity in this awful thing, and the sweet remorse, the aching sweet culpability and how it had defined everything about his life up north. He had created a new family out of it, a new Family that would allow this sorrow to take its rightful sacred position. There had been an awakening in him, of himself, of the self he had hardly known, and a realization of his pa, and what Hollis was and what he was not.

Where was his damn gun? Curtis watched her warped reflection in the windshield. She was beautiful, and maybe if he touched her nice, she would turn around and head back home, and they could pretend nothing had happened until the pretending felt real. He ran the back of his fingers along her cheek. 'Come home,' he pleaded. But he knew his pleading wouldn't make a difference in the end. Things would unfold in the way they were meant to, as they always did.

Thirty years of sacrifice. Thirty. He just kept on saying it to himself; God was watching, surely. He was paid up. He said, 'The farm is waiting for you, honey; Ida is expecting you. The bees, the hives, the Family. We all want you back.'

'I don't believe in it, Curtis. It's gone out of me. The farm is broken for me. You can't pay for what you did. Not like that.'

The blood down his shirt, over his hands, and the way it had trickled out of the pump water and into the soil behind the gas station, pink and lively. Martha had gone mad these last days, he saw; perhaps this was inevitable outside Soltane. He pulled at his linen jacket and did and undid the one button still left hanging. 'I don't need fixing.' He was still thinking how no one needed to know anything about this back home.

He would talk her into returning. He needed a bit of time for it. He would get his gun, bubblewrap it, and express post it back home. He could head north as soon as that was accomplished. The Family would be there, they would adore him, and he would be safe again. I'm good, he thought. He could feel the energy coming from them already; they were there with him, supporting him, almost holding him up, like psychic buttresses. They all needed one another.

'Where is it?' he said. It was a reactive question. He almost despised himself asking it. 'Where is my gun?'

She shook her head and said, 'It's safe.'

He thought then of the bees in the trunk, of the passage in the Book of Ether: *and they did carry with them swarms of bees; and they did carry with them Deseret, which, by interpretation, is the honey bee.* And then he pondered Judges, and dear Samson: *and behold there was a swarm of bees and honey on the carcass of the lion he had slain.* And the lion was God. Curtis felt clean; he had done the right thing. It was good. The bees — he would show her the bees. 'I have a surprise for you, Martha. I have something to show you,' he said. And then he added, 'I love you, Martha.'

'I know.' She was staring straight ahead, and she meant it, he knew. He knew.

Edgar must have heard the car pull in to the short lane, though he would not be able to recall later whether he had just sensed it or whether it had startled him to look over. It didn't matter. His eye gave way to the outside. The sky was still black with rain and night, but Edgar could see a car pulled up, a rusted, baby-blue Volvo sedan. 'Who the hell is that?' he muttered, and then he knew. He heard Aubie's voice in the back of his mind: *Twelve hours.*

That woman was getting out, the rain soaking into her clothing, her hair. Skinny, forty- maybe fifty-something but intact, like she knew a thing or two: tits and ass to break a strong man's heart. And there he was. Edgar had daydreamed about this moment, and the daydream had taken on various forms, but here it was. He looked out the container window, and he could only muster surprise and an anxious 'Shit.'

His hand went reflexively up to his face and pressed on the toilet paper lodged there. 'Shit. Shit. Shit.' Curtis could have been five hundred years old, and still he would know him. Edgar regretted he didn't have his own gun on him, but that was fine; he had the Browning. He swung the door open even before they'd knocked and said, 'Howdy. Come in out of the weather, why don't you?'

'Aubie here?' The woman was looking at him, brow furrowed, recognizing something but not knowing what it was she recognized. 'We came to see Aubie.' She looked at Curtis, at this old man with a long beard, with filthy linen clothes, who seemed to be muttering to himself as he walked past him into the container.

'Aubie went out to help,' Edgar said. It was true enough, though it made him smile to imagine anyone going to help Hollis Woolf. They smiled too, or at least she did, and Curtis said how obliged they were, and if they should wait in the car. 'No,' Edgar said. 'His father ran off.' He stared openly at the man who was his half-brother, that grown-up now man-child who had tried to shoot him through the heart.

Martha said, 'Hollis ran away?'

'That's what I was told.' Edgar stared still, bored already at how long this was taking. He wasn't the savouring type. He said, 'You don't know who I am, do you?'

There was a slow dawning then, and Curtis's face went scared and then pulled away from scared. His eyes lit up and he glanced at the woman. 'I am so grateful to God,' Curtis said nervously, offering his hand to have it shaken. It hung there until Edgar decided to put him out of his misery. He placed his thick hand into it and squeezed. 'Martha, this is Edgar,' Curtis said, all eager and forthright. Her eyes, though — like she was seeing a ghost.

Edgar had seen her twice with his ma, and had watched his ma walk alone once across the parking lot and up toward Blue Hole, and he had followed without her seeing him. He could become a shrub if he wanted to, or a FedEx box, didn't matter; it was about becoming the thing more than it was about hiding. Like acting, only more so. He had imagined always that he would want to call out to his ma, if ever he should see her again, and run and hug her, tell her that he had tried to be good. But watching her, his desires changed. He had not been good, and he could not bear having her see him, and having all the memories distort, and fall away when she spoke, moved, reacted to him. He was too used to being not there to know how to cope with being there.

He had seen his ma arrive at the care facility and had waited the half-hour or so it took her to see Hollis. Nothing had changed in all the time he'd been gone. He saw how his mother was still captivated by Hollis, held in a maintenance pattern by what? Habit, laziness, love. He did not know much about any of these things and reasoned they amounted to the same thing. It was good to see her though, and to close that part off. He would need to start fresh, disappear somewhere where no one would find him again. He just needed to close a few things down first, that's why he had come home, even though there were any number of smarter choices he might have made.

'It has been a long time,' said Curtis. The smile on his face reminded Edgar of a blissed-out, post-sermon, Bible-thumping minister. Curtis pumped his hand up and down now and smiled too big. Edgar thought how he would overcome all this, but he was having trouble knowing how.

Edgar wished Aubie was back then; he didn't know quite how to behave. 'Well, thirty years,' he said.

'I prayed for this, you know that?' Curtis was smiling with his mouth, his eyes, his whole damn body. He was about dancing with joy. And the woman was sunk into herself, holding her body kind of caved in, like she didn't know how beautiful she was, or like she was ashamed of it, or ashamed of Curtis, or just pure ashamed — that could be it.

'When's Aubie coming back?' Martha asked him.

'I don't know.' And they looked at each other too long then, and he could see she knew how this would go.

'We'll come back.' She did not like the part she had played in bringing Curtis here.

Curtis was saying, 'I prayed and prayed. God is my witness. I'm sorry —'

'Don't.' Edgar had eased his hand out of Curtis's grip, and had moved it behind his back. He did not want to know Curtis too well. Did not want an apology. Did not want anything like that.

Edgar looked at the woman, Curtis's woman. Her eyes were pleading. He had seen that many times before, and he knew to wall it in. They were standing in the middle of the container, and she pointed up, turning. It seemed to be dawning on her that these were his rugs, and that him being alive wasn't necessarily a good thing.

But Curtis had not looked up. He was looking directly at Edgar, pointing. 'My gun. That's my gun,' he was saying.

Edgar pulled the door closed, thought how happy he was he'd tucked the Browning into his belt, thought how impossibly perfect it would be if this *was* Curtis's gun. He held it good and straight, smiling over it at Curtis's heart. He said, 'You're joking.' And then he looked over at Martha. 'This ain't your gun; this is Aubie's piece of shit.' He was in no hurry.

There were gun rugs everywhere around them. There was a haphazard pile of Baluchi war-on-terror rugs right beside the man. Edgar could see a drab olive map rug with *Tora Bora* inscribed on it, and in Farsi: *The Russian army is leaving Afghanistan.* There was a knotted RPG pointed roughly at Curtis's head, and everywhere Edgar looked — the walls, the ceiling — the man was completely covered. And then Curtis saw this too. 'Oh, Lord,' he said. 'So many guns.'

Edgar thought how well they would insulate sound. 'I've dreamt of this moment,' he said, nodding.

'I have too.' But Curtis did not break his gaze from the carpets. He stared. 'I'm sorry,' he said.

'We should go,' said Martha. 'Come, Curtis.'

But Curtis seemed not to hear. And Edgar wasn't listening to anything but his droning inner monologue. It said: This gun is impossible to aim. So he held it as steady as he could and pulled back the trigger, and again and again. Martha screamed and then held her hand over her mouth to stop the screams, and let her purse drop. Edgar would have to deal with her somehow too, though he was already confused about how he would do this. He might have to wait for Aubie; there would be a time lapse and this would be unpleasant, he expected, and complicated.

Curtis fell backward, his eyes so soft, like there was love in them. 'I knew,' Curtis said jubilantly. 'I wanted you to see them.' And now he was smiling. 'The bees,' he whispered. 'The bees.'

And Martha said, 'No, Curtis,' and Curtis said, 'Perfect. This is —'

Then it did not matter, because the life seemed to scurry out of Curtis, and his face relaxed as he slumped sideways, slumped against Martha and then slowly to the ground. Martha looked down into Curtis's dead face with what looked to Edgar like pity, and grief, and maybe even a bit of resignation.

He would have to leave her there to cry and keen, whatever she might have to do until he got back. The rain was a solid cover. He would not wait for Aubie; he would grapple this dead thing into the Volvo — he would not have to dirty the rental — and he would head over to Bottomless Lakes and make it disappear, and then he would disappear too.

Edgar looked down at the dead man and thought Curtis was lovely in his death, that he looked innocent and vulnerable, how Edgar remembered him to look as a child when they had fished together along the Pecos, those freckles and that broad, easy smile. He eased his arms under the slump of Curtis's body and was beginning to lift it when he heard Aubie's truck on the grit. He let Curtis drop, then, and thought to wait, thankful he'd have some help.

The woman just sat there with her head in her palms when Aubie walked in. Aubie said, 'Shit,' and sat down and stared at the mess in his house. 'Oh, Martha —' Aubie looked from the body to Edgar to Martha, shaking his head, saying, 'Shit. Shit. Jesus, Ed—'

'I better deal with this.' Edgar looked down at the blood that now smeared his chest. Curtis was one less evil in the world, he knew. It came to Edgar then what the Paki kid had said, how it was not the martyrdom that counted but the story of the martyrdom. He'd best keep moving. No one was awake, he thought, no one would hear a thing, even if they heard something.

The dawn rain had quit again, and the sun was wet hot. Edgar went out to the Volvo and popped the trunk. It was a pulsing blackness, like a cloud, like fear, erupting out of the trunk. Bees rose into the day and descended on him, onto his camouflage pants and along his bare, bloodied chest. Edgar took some steps back. There had been flies, and later bees, and he would die by the Pecos, on a conveyor belt to heaven, only he hadn't. He'd lived. He watched the honeybees alight in clusters over his chest. He brushed at them, trying to push them away, but they only kept coming, faster, and more of them, so that after a time he could not be seen for the bees. There was no end to them.

Acknowledgements

I am indebted to my family for putting up with me for the last eight years while I dreamed this all up.

Former US senator Brooks Douglass and Michael Beattie were instrumental in some of the earliest research. They both spoke to me at length about war, covert activities, personal scars, and global issues. Thank you to them and to energy and climate change lawyer Elisabeth DeMarco for introducing me to them, and for her energetic support.

Darrell Atkins toured me through the Yates Petroleum fields, and LuAnn Beardemphl of the Yates Petroleum Corporation supplied me with not only this opportunity, but also a written history of Artesia's oilpatch, and some great swag. Warrugs.com carpet guru Kevin Sudeith took time out of his busy market day in Brooklyn to speak to me about war rugs, and the Mormons of Nauvoo, Illinois, were nice to me even after I told them about my project. I am thankful for the kindness of all these strangers.

Thanks to Mary Anne Causyn for sharing with me some of her memories of the '60s and '70s in rural Ontario. Jihan Hassan helped contextualize Islam in innumerable ways for me. Thank you to Sarah and Alex Godoy for exposing me to Pakistan. All of these encounters helped form *Perfecting*, and for this I am eternally grateful. Any errors of fact are my own.

Thanks to various writers and friends for their generosity: Marianne Apostolides, Heather Birrell, Catherine Bush, Ailsa

Craig, Christine Fischer-Guy, Lee Gowan, Ann Ireland, Marc Kuitenbrouwer, Dawne McFarlane, George Murray, Brian Panhuyzen, Jordan Peterson. A special thanks to my impossibly astute editor, Bethany Gibson, and copy-edit Queen Heather Sangster, and to Goose Lane Editions, the Ontario Arts Council, and the Canada Council for the Arts for supporting this work. Thank you to Hilary McMahon of Westwood Creative Artists for representing me so wholeheartedly.

So much of creation hinges on belief.

Permission to use the quote from *Manual for Draft-Age Immigrants to Canada* by Mark Satin is given by House of Anansi Press. The manual was a much-photocopied document for American Vietnam War Resisters during the call-up. It went into a fifth edition by 1970, and was purchased mail order by upward of sixty-five thousand people.

The duet 'In a Town This Size,' sung by John Prine and Dolores Keane, was released in 1999 on the album *In Spite of Ourselves* (Oh Boy Records). An excerpt from the lyric is reprinted by permission of the songwriter, Kieren Kane.